RED STICKS

RED STICKS

Jad Davis

Ordering Information:

For orders and inquiries, please contact:
1-888-404-1388
www.goldtouchpress.com
book.orders@goldtouchpress.com

Printed in the United States of America

Dedicated to:
George Walker

Chapter One

The District of Columbia's thermometers had flirted with a hundred degrees for nearly a week. Black billows of clouds backdropped with ferocious electrical shows, served as nothing more than a torturous tease for those living near the Potomac River. There was no rain in sight.

At 10:00 on Sunday morning, Paul Doggins stopped his buggy a few feet in front of 'Mansion House Farm's' iron gate. Paul hopped out of his single horse drawn buggy and placed a bouquet of flowers in between a couple of the gate's metal bars. He then got back into his fancy racing coach and rode east from there.

Negro George knocked on his master's door. By the length of time it took the general to answer comingled with an assortment of high pitched giggles, the former president's head slave knew his boss was not alone.

"Top of the morning to you, George. What's the matter?" slurred George Washington through his closed bedroom door.

"General, Mister Doggins put another bunch of flowers on the gate! Do you want me to fetch them for you, Sir?" asked George.

"Thank you, Sir, that would be most appreciated. Also, while you're doing that, kindly ask Joseph and Harry to escort Ms. Hastings back to the academy.

She dropped by last evening and I'm afraid the poor thing isn't use to my whiskey. Please hurry; she'll be late for vespers as it is!" instructed George Washington.

Paul Doggins was a Culper and a very good one at that. Something very important had happened; otherwise, he wouldn't have so conspicuously delivered his message in broad daylight. The last time he had done such a thing was when the British put a price on his head.

Thirty three white roses had been tied very tightly in the day before's VIRGINIA GAZETTE. Washington's Culper gang number was, "711"; it was printed in the top right-hand corner of the 'Obituary Column'.

George poured himself a goblet full of his masterfully distilled bourbon and went searching for his spectacles. They were on his nightstand.

With the use of Franklin's "other key", President Washington was able to decipher the message pulled from an article regarding the bankruptcy of the "Indian King Tavern" in Baltimore.

Thomas DeWitt had written in July of that year, a laborious accounting of the reasons for the Inn's eventual closing. In actuality however, the decoded message 'told' General Washington, America was about to be invaded by the Illuminati!

Another knock on the door jolted Washington back into a semiconscious state. It was his wife; Martha's knuckle wrap was loud and rapid.

"Good morning, Husband! I hope Dorothy managed to find her way back to the school. I'm not sure if that woman's sights aren't set on you, my dear!

It is certainly evident she adores every dance she steals with you as well as a liquored up kiss, I'd guess!

What time did she leave, George?" bluntly asked the former First Lady.

"Darling, I'm not quite sure when Ms. Hastings left but I do remember asking George to have Harry and Joseph escort her back to the academy.

As far as her flirtations are concerned, I lavish each and every one of them! I am not the 'red-headed wonder' from yesteryear, you know!" smoothly said Washington.

"Where are you going? It looks like you're packing for a week!" asked Martha.

"I'm afraid it's a "Blue Dawn" issue. I have to go to Fredricktown." Said George.

"Is that why Paul Doggins dropped off those flowers this morning around ten o'clock? I believe that my reading club's number one tale-spinner, "Dorothy Hastings", managed to leave shortly after your bouquet's arrival. I thought that might assist you with your sequencing issue!" struck Martha.

"You are so atrociously beautiful when the green monster latches on to you! I love you with all of my heart, my precious one!

I'll be back by Wednesday." Whispered George.

George Washington blew his wife a sugary kiss and then left for the stables. He planned to ride "El Diablo" because he was the only horse he owned that was tough enough to run a hundred and thirty eight miles.

"Partidge Hill Inn" had been rented for five days. Except for the Inn's staff, Washington and his host were to be the only guests.

"G.W. Snyder" was sitting on the front porch when Washington rode up. It was dusk.

"Tis a lovely evening for a refreshing drink I'd say there, Mister Snyder! Said General Washington.

"Indeed it is! Are you Doggins' architect?" asked Snyder.

"I'm his land surveyor." Answered Washington.

"Are you hungry, Mister President?"

"A little but mostly, I need a drink!" responded George.

The two men sitting on the front porch got down to business. Both G.W. Snyder and George Washington poured through the writing of John Robison's, "Proofs of a Conspiracy Against All the Religions and Governments of Europe, Carried On in the Secret Meetings of Freemasons, Illuminati, and Reading Societies".

Snyder's concern after the night's reading was that some of the Masonic lodges in America "might have caught the infection of the Illuminati's plan to overturn all Government and all Religion!". He then asked a favor.

"General, please find it within your power to prevent their horrid plan from corrupting the brethren of the lodges over which you preside!"

Washington at that point quite drunk, replied to Mr. G.W. Snyder.

"The fact is, I preside over zero lodges; but, it is my firm belief, none of the lodges in America would go along with the principles ascribed to the Society of the Illuminati!

However, there is no doubt these same lodges you speak of, G.W., are aware of the Illuminati's ideologies; but, I do not believe the "Lodges of Free Mason" in this country, would propagate their diabolical tenets!" adamantly said Washington.

It was apparent to George, G.W. Snyder was far more concerned with where the former president stood on the Illuminati matter rather than the effect the organization's slither onto American soil might actually have on its people!

George chose to get to the bottom of his confusion with force. He withdrew a pistol from behind his back, cocked it, placed the barrel between Mr. Snyder's eyes and then spoke.

"I shall give you exactly thirty seconds to explain why I was summonsed here and the person's name who told you to do it! You now have twenty five seconds to live!"

""Adam Weishaupt" sent me to make you aware of something! You, Sir, have been chosen by your peers…throughout the world…to be our King!"

"Who set this meeting up? Fifteen seconds!" seethed Washington.

"Thomas Jefferson, Sir!" snapped Snyder.

"Ten seconds to go, G.W.!"

"Stop! Stop!" Snyder dropped to his knees and then slid down into a prostrated position at the tips of Washington's boots. With deep-chested sobs, he told America's hero-like former first president, the truth!

As soon as G.W. Snyder completed his admission, George Washington sent a lead ball through his brain.

*　*　*　*　*

From the crest of Wilkes Street as it merges with Wolfe Lane, Washington was able to glass the east side of the academy without being seen by Alexandria's nosey community members. Gossip was the ticket used for hierarchical height adjustments within the Washington square.

Having rock-solid knowledge of the former president's affair with the academy's principal, would hoist up that kind of citizen to somewhere close to "Saint" status. That's why he and Ms. Hastings had always been careful.

"The Alexandria Academy" was a three-story brick structure serving on the first floor as the "Alexandria Lodge of Freemasons" and an "English School" teaching grammar, writing, arithmetic, and physical sciences to paying students.

Its second floor held the "Learned Language School" where the classical languages were taught. The academy's third floor provided a safehouse for "special individuals".

After six evenly spaced taps, Robert Adam, the Lodge's Superintendent, unbolted the metal door leading from the academy's stable to the basement headquarters known to the Culpers as, "Blue Dawn".

It was there and much to Washington's surprise, his lover Dorothy Hastings and Johann Adam Weishaupt were sitting behind a table. They had an offer to propose to him. Weishaupt was the proposer.

"My plan, George, is to grasp your nobly heralded baton and to lift it from your mortal grip to the hearth of our utopian home! "Estarcion", America's new name, is to become the hub for a society who bases their decisions on "Reason", allied with the spirit of the "Golden Rule" of not doing to others what one would not wish to have done to oneself!

Therefore, I shall take your revered mantle and in return, I will promise to carry forward your good wishes of virtue, philanthropy, social justice and morality!" Johann Weishaupt then neatly sliced Washington's larynx wide open.

Due to the precision in which Weishaupt flicked his scalpel beneath the chin and at the same time avoiding the messy arteries, Dorothy was able to make a perfect mold of George's face. Adam was now safely hidden.

After gassing his accomplices, America's first president, Ms. Hastings, and Robert Adam were burned in the incinerator Benjamin Franklin had engineered for the Alexandria Academy two years before. Adam Weishaupt then mounted George Washington's horse, "El Diablo" and rode it toward Mount Vernon.

"Sall Twine" was curled up under the horse troughs. She had taken a tablespoon of turpentine and the same dose of quinine so the convulsions had started panging again.

If "Mary Ball Washington" ever caught wind of her son having "intercourse" with the "darkies" she would bust up Sall's family and scatter them throughout "Hell and half of Georgia". Sall thought.

That was why she didn't say anything about the odd way the "General" rode into the plantation nor the fact that he didn't drop off the money he had promised George (Sall's husband). It was the gratuity for sneaking the Academy's principal off the plantation grounds.

* * * * *

Adam had meticulously studied every inch of Washington's plantation on the map his intelligence officers had provided to him. 'It would be the small things, the private idiosyncrasies, the noticeable habits that would get him caught', Weishaupt considered.

On the Monday following George Washington's murder, four men walked down the "Dragon Fly's" gangplank. They were to meet at Partidge Hill at 2200hrs..

"Baron Adolph Freiherr von Knigge, Duke Ferdinand of Brunswick, William Spence and Johann Wolfgang von Goethe" piled into a carriage rented under the name of "George Washington". The men did not interact with one another.

Duke Ferdinand of Brunswick handed the dock constable a Spanish doubloon. Another coin was promised for a week's worth of forgetfulness.

Partidge Hill Inn had certain odd features which set it aside from most other inns of its type. There were no noticeable doors to enter the abundant square footage within. Even the front porch provided no seeable way into the living quarters.

Puzzled, the men sat in the constable's police wagon. No one said anything; they just watched and waited.

It was 10:00 o'clock when a rock wall rolled open. They took the rented two horse rig underground.

Von Knigge then stood up in the police wagon. He turned his body so as to better speak with the others seated near him. His jaw proudly jutted out as he spoke.

"Gentlemen, soon you will be introduced to the great sorcerer! No man actually knows who he is or even what he physically looks like but as we shall see, he is quite authentic!

Subtly, a greenish fog filled the underground space surrounding the occupied Baltimore police wagon. Within the swirls of their imaginations, the passengers as if embalmed, sat upright on the wagon's benches. An image formed above them.

"Baphomet", the pagan goat-headed deity, spoke. He held the "Distorted Cross" high above his long-horned head.

"I believe you already know who I am! Our responsibility is to overthrow the Catholic Church, destroy democratic republicanism, and then replace it with a "natavistic" philosophy held within the bounds of adjudged logistics and common sense.

All groups, religious or otherwise, will be prevented from their evolutionary climb. "Man" no longer will be shuffled around like overfed cattle but will soon be able to choose his own fate!" preached the well hiding Weishaupt through a megaphone.

Torches appearing to be stuck in drilled pockets into the cave's sides, burst into flames. Scalding fire licks surrounded the newly inaugurated Illuminati Priests.

Like awakening from a dream, the four 'priests' found themselves returning the police wagon. The jolly constable waved goodbye as each (on foot) passenger left in separate directions. There were no 'well wishes' exchanged.

Weishaupt knew he would never be able to fool those close to George Washington. Therefore, he ordered Martha, George, Harry and Joseph, along with the rest of the house help, to go to Mary Balls place known by all as, "Dogue Run Farm".

Johann Adam Weishaupt wearing her husband's rubber face, explained to Martha he had been exposed to a child who had contracted the measles. For the safety of his loved ones, he felt he must quarantine himself for two weeks, he said.

Adam let a couple of days pass before gathering together Mount Vernon's field workers. He wore George's finest hunting jacket and was riding El Diablo.

The well-nourished slaves looked up at the "General" with big smiles on their faces. Not only had they been given a bag of silver coins, they also got "temporary deeds" to the Mansion House Farm. It was divided up into thirty seven family parcels.

Since none of them could read, Adam Weishaupt simply drew a map of the house and property and sectioned it out so each head of household could make their mark on his or her family's apportionment.

The plantation house and outbuildings would belong to everyone. The only catch was, they had to turn the Mansion House Farm into an impenetrable fortress within five days; otherwise, the deal was off!

By four o'clock on Thursday afternoon, Johann Adam Weishaupt had the broad backed breeders in white priest's robes. Each woolen garment had an upside down red cross sewn onto the front of it. A helmet and a cape went along with the uniform.

A steer was butchered, whiskey was served, daggers and pistols were formally presented. The negro "crusaders" were then drugged and sent out into the darkness to slaughter every living soul at the Dogue Run Farm.

Two nights later, the same band of silver helmeted marauders repeated their actions on "Mason Island". It would soon become the Illuminati's headquarters.

* * * * *

The very next night at precisely 0200hrs., a fiery object appeared over the village of Hull, England.

It hovered only a few feet over the Humber River.

An immense moon-like globe with a black bar across the center of its face illuminated the port town in blue light. A green gas fell over Hull.

Sculcoates Asylum's population slept through the whole event except for a few inmates who were expecting an explosion. The wall surrounding the asylum disintegrated.

Following a terrific flash, those in on the "bust out" were beamed up into a cigar-shaped craft and flown to America.

* * * * *

Two fishermen while setting their nets, saw a "sunny disc" rise to the surface of the Potomac River. The sheriff wrote in his report the following:

"The fishermen stated, 'a woman came from this previously submerged vehicle and walked across the placid water toward us. She spoke a language we had never heard before but for some reason she set us at ease.

At that point, the floating ship imploded and seven comet looking spheres disappeared into the morning sky. We both wanted to move but we couldn't; however, neither of us were scared because the lady on the water told us we were safe.'"

* * * *

Benjamin Hawkins had been up since three. He had questioned the fishermen until he was quite positive there was nothing more to extract from the two. As outlandish as the men's tales were, the detective believed them.

He had been on wild-goose-chases before but this case was different. The fishermen's faces were "sunburned". Small bubbles just under their exposed skin told the story. Boils had erupted all over their bodies telling those medical examiners who looked at them, the boatmen had been exposed to an enormous blast of heat.

Singed eyebrows supported the physicians' theories. The most confounding thing about the matter was, after the flying objects had passed over the heads of the fishermen, they were stripped of their memories. "Fugue" was what the doctors called it.

Hawkins had just taken his boots off, eaten a big breakfast and was planning on getting some sleep when he realized there was someone sitting in the corner of his bedroom. Had the visitor not illuminated his face while lighting a pipe, Ben more than likely would have shot him.

"Hello, "Number Sixty One". You've been a busy boy." Softly stated the President of the United States.

"Yes, and I'm afraid the news I have is not good. I believe they're here!" exclaimed the federal agent.

"I knew it this morning! People were claiming they saw fiery objects shoot through the sky! Some are saying the "reckoning" is underway!

One of our local street vendors swore he saw "Jesus" riding a camel down the Federal Road less than six hours ago! At least their imaginations leave them vulnerable to logical answers. That may buy us some time!" chortled Thomas Jefferson.

"Have we heard anything from "Seekaboo"?" asked Hawkins.

"Yes I have. We've learned that "Karl Theodor", the Duke of Bavaria outlawed all secret societies in the Illuminati's home base of Bavaria. His task force known as the "Hermetics", were quite successful and as I understand, have pretty much cleaned his empire out of the devil worshiping bunch.

Unfortunately, Adam Weishaupt's luck allowed him to barely escape his capture. The wicked bastard then went underground!

The Hermetics picked up his trail and traced his whereabouts to the "Sculcoates Asylum" in Hull, England. As you know, Seekaboo has tried to keep us informed but the cult's diversionary tactics and its irregular disappearances have made his valuable contact with us a rarity." Said Jefferson.

"So, you believe Weishaupt is now in Virginia?" Asked Hawkins.

"I, of course, don't know where Johann Weishaupt is; although, I'd bet the farm, he's within a stones throw of Mount Vernon.

I'm afraid our mighty "General" has mellowed in his old age. Tragically, ole George has fallen in with bad company, Detective Hawkins.

Two days ago, William Spence and three other of his travel buddies walked down the "Dragon Fly's" gangplank into oblivion. We don't know where they went!

What makes me believe Weishaupt has chummed up with my old friend, George Washington is because William Spence was recently employed by the Washington families to landscape their properties." exclaimed Jefferson.

"Mister President, what action should I take if I run into Weishaupt and his band of merry men?" asked Hawkins in a wicked tone.

"Shovel quickly and whistle even louder, Ben!" laughingly stated Jefferson.

* * * * *

Thursday was the day in which Christ was supposedly crucified or so the sailors' superstition goes. Consequently, Hawkins knew it was bad luck to leave out on Thursdays and therefore was aware he had time to ride by his house to pick up a few things he was going to need.

Sometimes an investigation took three or four days so he had to make preparations for that. His yearning for rest had been replaced by electrifying adrenalin rushes. 'This was his chance', Ben hoped.

The "Dragon Fly" was docked at Fells Point and had been for the previous seventy two hours. It had not left its moorings since.

As far as the ship's description, it was a normal transport craft primarily used for bringing dry goods and more expensive things to the American merchants who in turn, would sell the imports to the increasing numbers of European aristocrats' making their new homes in the coastal cities. Big money started coming into the United States.

The "Dragon Fly" had captured the reputation as being the most luxurious transatlantic cruise ship in the world. 'Not a common way to get here for a gardener', mused Detective Hawkins.

Although there was an echo bouncing back from the wheelhouse, nothing gave Ben the impression anyone was on the ship. Right off, he smelled stale whiskey. 'Of course people drank on cruise ships!' Ben, whispered to himself.

'Okay, so people would have to mix and mingle over a month-long cruise together. Folks would want to scribble down the names and addresses of fellow passengers if for no other reason but for a souvenir. People are like that.

But, where could they have gone from here?', Ben pondered.

Twelve staterooms. None used.

Very little food had been taken from the galley. What had been stored in the dry bins looked old. There was fingerprint less dust on the jars.

The ship's coal stoves were below room temperature. Hawkins carefully made his way down the steps into its hold. A good lantern and sturdy rails made it practically effortless to get to the transport compartments.

Some old furniture and a stack of cracked mirrors were all there was to see. Ben heard footsteps above him.

"She's a mighty good ship, she is. This baby and I have traveled all over the world together, we have.

It may sound silly to you, young fellow, but we've grown close over the years, she and I have. Yep, we've been through a lot, the ole "Dragon Fly" and me.

Mister, excuse my bluntness but what do you want? It's against the law to trespass on a man's docked ship, you know!" said the dark face from the upper deck.

"I am Detective Benjamin Hawkins of the United States Government. I am looking for a "Captain Jeremiah Yellott", the owner of the "Dragon Fly". Would you know where I might be able to get in touch with him?" asked the detective.

"Well, that's me but let me tell you right up front, I do not cotton to anyone including government men, snooping around my property!

State your business, climb out of there and then get the hell off my ship!" yelled Captain Yellott.

When they had walked back down to where the official carriage was parked, Benjamin in a brotherly way, pulled the jittery sea captain close to him as if he were hugging the man farewell but then, whispered in the man's ear.

"I am here to help you. Let me do so!

More than likely we are being watched. Invite me to your home, it's right up the street, I believe." Pleaded Detective Hawkins.

Yellott declined Benjamin's offer and then sheepishly asked him to leave. With a slight smile on his face, he thanked the detective and shook his hand while swiftly shoving a gold statuette into the government man's breast pocket.

The ancient sea captain turned and ran up "Old Joppa Road". A minute later, he was out of Hawkins's sight. It was noon.

Ben examined the tiny statue Jeremiah had dropped into his uniform's pocket. 'It was a Shaman holding a couple of ceremonial shakers', he thought.

Based on his lack of clues, his first shot at a real federal investigation would end with a dismal climax. Hawkins knew, if he couldn't "catch ahold" of at least a hint of some criminal wrongdoing, Jefferson would bring someone else in. All he had so far, was a golden Shaman and a hunch.

"Spurrier's Tavern" was no more than an hour's ride from Fells Point. If a man wanted to find out something about someone's past or needed some information about an individual, there was only one place to go on that part of the eastern seaboard, "Spurrier's Tavern".

Before the detective reported back to Jefferson, he had to have something substantial to speak with him about. A ghost ship wasn't a bad start but he needed one hell of a lot more evidence than that!

It was two o'clock in the afternoon when Detective Hawkins ordered a bottle of scotch to the tavern's library. Several older gentlemen were helping him to matchup his gold Shaman with drawings thought to depict other African jewelry pieces by their shapes and molding techniques. They came up with nothing.

Hawkins's luck changed while he was paying off his tab. A "Johann Wolfgang von Goethe" offered Ben a limp handshake.

Both men were Masons as identified by their flicking middle fingers tickling the other's palm. That signification has been with them since the Middle Ages. It was a way in which "good" men could recognize others of their ilk.

Hawkins gleaned as much as he could from their interlude. He noticed things like the smell of opium on von Goethe's once expensive coat and that his shoes were spattered with red dust. More was sniffed out after Johann Wolfgang spoke.

"Forgive me, Brother, but I overheard the responses given to you by those dilatants scamming you for more of the fine whiskey they ladled down their throats at your expense!

For the two bottles of scotch you wasted on them, I'd of told you the whole story as to how a "Captain Jeremiah Yellott" came into possession of the golden Shaman you once had in your breast pocket of which, is now in mine!" teasingly said Johann von Goethe.

The utterly exasperated detective felt his breast pocket. Sure enough, he no longer had it!

In an almost knee-jerk reaction, Hawkins reached for his four-barreled pistol tucked within his shoulder holster. His firearm was also, gone! "Wolfgang" began laughing.

"This 'gold Shaman' your tavern anthropologists found such a conundrum, in actuality is…." Wolfgang removed the three inch high statue from his own breast pocket and handed it back to it's last handler and continued speaking…"something once belonging to a friend of mine."

"What is it? Pushed Hawkins.

"My fellow Mason, it is a gift from 'the old man of the mountain'!"

"What is the purpose of this 'gift'?"

"Brother, it is everything!" Whispered Wolfgang.

"Mister von Goethe, I do not mean to be rude to you but to be very frank, I have little time to spend discussing these mysterious wonders!

I'm afraid I need to get back to my office so, if I may, I'd like my pistol back."

"Of course, how thoughtless of me!" Said Wolfgang as Ben's pistol rose into the air paused for about three seconds, and then slid beneath the detective's arm and back into his shoulder holster!

Wolfgang then dissipated into thin air. Much to Benjamin's surprise, the man left no lingering smells. It was as if he had never been there or like it had been a dream.

Jefferson's inauguration was underway. The possibility of getting a personal appointment with him was nil; but, Detective Hawkins needed permission to expand his investigation.

After a good night's sleep in a forgotten number of days, Benjamin Hawkins met with Thomas Jefferson again. Their discussion was brief but poignant.

"The United States is in big trouble. It is thought, the Niburians have broken their three way agreement with the Mason's and the Cerians. If that is the case then America's center of government is now under assault!" Said the President.

* * * * *

When Mount Vernon came into view just over the mountain where the estate's property boundary leaped into the sky, Ben Hawkins was taken back by the vastness of Washington's family's holdings.

Field upon field all spectacularly producing fruits and vegetables of assorted types were backdropped by a panorama of splendid geography. Red winged blackbirds jealously protecting their territories alongside fertile streams, set the standard for a gorgeous plantation.

Waterfalls and meticulously manicured riding trails with paralleling wheat fields, seemed to lengthen the distance to the big house. Ben rode down the freshly raked driveway toward the place where he saw a moving human being.

"Good morning, might I trouble you for a drink of water for this poor beast? She's getting sort of old and I have to rest her more often these days.

She's like a family member to me; I hate what time always seems to do to the things we love! Say, would you happen to know a "Mister William Spence"?" Queried Hawkins.

"Sall", negro George's wife, kept hoeing a garden size plot of ground. She never looked up at Ben, the twenty-some year old slave pretended to be deaf, or at least that's what Detective Hawkins thought at the time.

He got off of his horse and then approached the ambivalent girl. Her eyes looked like black marbles, Sall's complexion was ashen.

She was for sure, a 'mind-dead' woman just hoeing a useless spot of earth. Ben saw some smoke. It was about a half mile away.

What had once been a rock barn was now a deep hole. Hawkins guessed it was a crater. Piles of ashes still smoking, emitted a reddish dust which smelled like pine tar.

There were no people nor skittering chickens visible. The wind's sound was the only abbreviating agent of silence.

Ben kicked his horse in the ribs, he pointed her toward the Dogue Run Farm.

When he and "gypsy" arrived at Mary Ball's plantation, they found the exact same scenario…nothing! Just a big smoking pit. 'Inauguration ball or not, he had to speak with the president!'

It was eight o'clock by the time the federal agent made it to the Capitol Building's front gate. Two guards required him to dismount.

They frisked him thoroughly and then one of the door goons took gypsy away. The other soldier escorted Hawkins toward the ballroom's entranceway.

A butler opened the door. Music filled the street outside but only for a second or two.

The ballroom's vaulted ceilings made the couples dancing appear to be metal 'people' belonging in a toy box. Their movements although well practiced, somehow made Ben think of "Nero" and his fiddle.

Such foolish yet dangerous men and women all spinning around and keeping the beat with the others. They were so preposterously fake. He saw the President.

"Sir, may I have a word with you?" Fretfully requested the dressed down gumshoe.

By twice flicking his left wrist, Thomas Jefferson's personal security guards dragged Benjamin out of the ballroom feet first. They took him down two flights of stairs and shoved the battered sleuth into the basement's coal bin.

There was very little light. As Hawkins put his ear against the ballroom's chimney, he heard Jefferson delivering his second inaugural address of the day. The newly elected president was finishing up.

"From the guidance given to us through revolution and reformation, the wisdom of our sages and blood of our heroes all for the devotion to "HIM", we hope we shall never wander far from our creed even during moments of error or alarm.

We have our texts of civil instructions. We know what we were destined to do! Let us retrace our steps! Let us gain even a higher road than before, a freeway to peace, liberty, and safety and do it without the sword but with the peaceable instrument of rational. Let them be who they wish to be!

We will provide all they need…..they give us their brawn. Estarcion then, will continue to be the lucrative mineral producer as it has been for so many thousands of years….Our responsibility is to keep it under control, to squelch adversarial movements against us, to stamp out all organizations requiring uniformity of actions; such as, and mostly, churches and especially the Catholic ones!

Universities who discourage scientific investigation rather than the acceptance of the doctrines, they must go. Governments, large or local, those substituting common sense for tradition will be the only societal conglomerates allowed further existence." Voraciously screamed Jefferson.

The music started up again. Ben could hear them dancing and wondered if they were going to kill him.

About midnight, the third president of the United States came down the coal bin's rickety stairs. On one knee, he apologized profusely for the "goat-rope" that had occurred upstairs.

Even his guardsmen shook the senior detective's hand and offered their scripted apologies. Ben had "not just fallen off of a cabbage wagon" as the saying goes, he of all people who should have known better, had fallen into a den of vipers.

Hawkins made every attempt possible to neutralize the toxic situation. He jubilantly greeted his boss.

"Tom, I congratulate you! Your predecessor almost got himself killed a few of times because of his loose concerns." Said Hawkins.

"Yes, ole 'Quincy' would of bought the farm if it hadn't been for some wet powder in an assassin's rifle. And, if I'm remembering correctly, I believe that was why his inaugural address was cancelled!" responded the person pretending to be the President.

Sir, could we speak in private, I've got one hell of a lot to tell you?" baited Benjamin.

The detective and the "President" sat alone in the coal bin. Ben told him everything; he left nothing out except for two things. Hawkins never mentioned the golden Shaman nor the interaction with Wolfgang.

"Do you have that golden statuette on you?" Pointedly asked Jefferson. He was not smiling.

""No" to your question, Sir. Captain Yellott ran away with it!

My question, now, is, Mister President, 'Where do you want me to start'?

"The "Dragon Fly" is where it seems to have begun; but, the 'why there' and the 'what for' questions lead me to hypothesize that the end of this mystery-ball will roll out on Mount Vernon!" Stated the imitation Thomas Jefferson.

"Sir, may I be brutally honest? Asked the special agent intentionally breaking the conversation's candor.

"Of course, Ben, we've been friends for years. Speak your mind." Softly answered "Jefferson".

"Very well. I strongly suspect our founding father, George Washington is somehow mixed up with this anticipated Illuminati invasion; but, I don't see the group as an invader at all, Thomas!

In my professional opinion, Sir, I believe the Illuminati were forced out of Europe. Washington in his mellowing years, assumed they were nothing more than an ancient offshoot of those like the Masons, also in constant search of the "Holy Grail".

More than likely, he offered to make a home for the 'refugees' and they took him up on it. The poor fellow in my opinion, is as innocent as a lamb but unfortunately, quite dead, I'm afraid." Darkly stated the federal agent.

As Benjamin Hawkins was walking up the steps leading toward the ballroom's floor, he stopped in his tracks and turned toward the gang of men looking up at him. With 'molasses' oozing from every vowel, he boldly spoke to his boss.

"President Jefferson, I intend to protect you and your office with my life! If Washington is mixed up with this, T.J., should I whistle?"

Jefferson nodded.

Feeling as if he had gotten a last minute reprieve from the gallows, Hawkins turned gypsy toward the northeast. Spurrier's Tavern felt like the safest place to go.

* * * * *

It was two o'clock when Hawkins got to the tavern. Mr. Spurrier was still up shining glasses from behind the bar. He spoke first.

"Well, don't we have a night owl up and about! Come on in! Could I pour you a drink or fix you a little something to eat?

My oven has gone out but I have all kinds of sandwich makings. Pickled herring is the favorite around here! Do you need a room?" asked the tavern's manager.

"'Yes', to all of your questions, Mister Spurrier, but before I lug my things upstairs…." as Benjamin was saying before he was interrupted.

"You are Detective Benjamin Hawkins aren't you?"

Spurrier's question alarmed Ben. In response, the detective ignored the innkeeper's query and continued with his original requests.

"I would like a bottle of scotch, biscuits with the herring you mentioned, the key to my room, and an apology for not minding your own business!" curtly snapped Ben Hawkins.

"My mistake, Sir, I misspoke! Flappingly said Mister Spurrier.

"Look, Sir, forgive my boorishness. I've had a terrible day; anyway, I was going to ask you, if you remember a man who goes by the name of "Wolfgang" or something like that?

He was here just day before yesterday, around midday, I believe. A tall, striking man, he was!" Formally inquired the Culper.

"As I "rudely" interrupted you to say, "Johann Wolfgang von Goethe", the Spurrier's Tavern's new owner, expected your return today!

You have the bottom floor suite at the rear of the building. I am sure you will find it an accommodation fit for a king!" boasted the tavern's seller.

Hawkins was stunned. In a hangdog fashion, he turned toward Spurrier's Inn's former owner, shook his hand, apologized for the second time and then asked where Wolfgang might be.

The answer he got made Hawkins almost choke on his pickled herring biscuit.

"He's waiting for you in your quarters, Sir. Room #101."

The agent removed his pistol from its holster as soon as he entered the hallway ending at his room. It was already ajar so his key wasn't necessary.

Johann von Goethe had taken a chill off the room's temperature by lighting a mound of coal in the suite's fireplace. Two glasses were setting on the breakfast table.

Wolfgang was seated by the hissing blue fire. He had taken his boots off and was drying their insides out.

Hawkins noticed a chalky red clay caked on von Goethe's boots' heels. He felt for his pistol tucked behind his back. It was still there. Ben spoke first.

"I was hoping to find you here. I believe I am going to need your help!"

"I thought you might. I'm sorry President Jefferson disappointed you!" Sincerely stated Wolfgang.

He then stood, filled both glasses to the brim with scotch, offered a toast to the rising young detective and then sat down. Johann opened a notebook on the table and handed Hawkins a freshly sharpened pencil.

"Detective, are you aware of the consequences which will most certainly occur should your unraveling come up with the 'truth'? What will happen to you when you discover that all you have ever learned, even as a youth, was a lie?

Mister Hawkins, can you imagine a world in which there are no wrongdoings, a place with worries of war simply being part of a fable, a country you live in that provides 'only for it's own', the necessary comforts of life…all at no cost of labor or coin?

As 'people', our responsibilities revolve around doing research for mans' betterment and to pay homage to "HIM" (the old man of the mountain) three times per day. We as his citizens, are encouraged to 'turn in' our work's results to the "State" in order for all to benefit from our labor.

What is found, discovered, manufactured, reported, cased and transported determines a person's societal strata. Your home, your rations, travel permits, basically all that is given to an individual is determined by that person's contribution to HIM!

It is a wonderful way of life we live, Benjamin. In my mind, joining us is a perfect fit for you. Just think of it, higher rewards for less effort!

There would be no more long hours of dangerous work nor having to deal with the whims of narcissistic politicians. With you as head of "Estarcion's Secret Police Force", your only responsibility would be enforcing the "old man's" commandments!" Zealously screamed Wolfgang.

The scotch had temporarily eased the effects of sleeplessness. Adrenalin was all that was left to keep Hawkins ambulatory. He kept dropping his head. A green vapor rose from the floor.

Ben Hawkins with all of the strength left in his body, jumped through the suite's open window and got onto gypsy's bare back and rode her all the way back to the capitol. President Jefferson needed to weigh-in on this!

The black suited Capitol soldiers made quick work of taking Hawkins to the ground. They caught him trying to enter the 'servants' door' dressed as a tall hatted chef. The sun was a knuckle high in the sky.

After handcuffing him and bagging him in a canvas tarp, the security men dragged the cursing lump into Jefferson's study. Benjamin could smell bacon cooking. He laid very still.

"Benny-boy, you're becoming quite a pain in my ass! All I asked you to do was check out what the "lights in the sky" reports were all about!

Twice now, you have barged into my "private" business asking for further orders and 'four times' you have been told the same thing, 'Go see the "Madam" in Alexandria, she has information about the fisherman who saw the "Blue Dawn" dock!'

If you are unfit to accomplish my simple requests, maybe it's time for you to get on back to the Carolinas. It's an easier life there, provided the "Mohawks" don't scalp you before your days are done enjoying it!

Don't come back here until you are absolutely sure, America is safe from an Illuminati invasion! Until then, be gone with you!" Snarled Jefferson's voice.

By the sounds of shuffling feet, Hawkins knew there were others in the room with the president, 'people whom Thomas didn't want him to see or maybe, it was the other way around', Ben thought.

Ben Hawkins was sure of one thing, Jefferson had clearly set up a meeting with him at 0400hrs. in the basement of the Alexandria Academy. The Culper headquarters was there.

With his head covered by a hemp sack, two men drove the detective in the back of a wagon to a grove of trees just ten miles from the capitol building. He was released and told where gypsy had been tied up in a nearby clump of woods.

As Hawkins walked to where gypsy had been put, he couldn't help but think about the mess the country's President was in. It was conceivable Ben thought, 'those people calling themselves the Illuminati might already have captured the Capitol'.

* * * * *

A carriage with a single driver, sat quietly in front of Alexandria Academy's gated driveway. Detective Hawkins could see no movement nor lights except for a man in the carriage puffing on his pipe.

The courthouse bell rang four muffled clangs. Hawkins approached the lone man's carriage from the rear. Both hammers of his pistol were cocked.

It was seventy five degrees outside; nevertheless, Jefferson had a top hat on, heavy boots, a lined overcoat and a double-barreled shotgun propped up against his seat. He was quite nervous because he kept looking out his carriage's back window.

Men's voices came from three blocks away. Jefferson whispered.

"Get in the goddamned wagon! They'll be looking for me if I'm not back in thirty minutes. Benjamin, there is no person in this city you can trust!

Half the senators have been preparing for this for over three years. 'Who's who' is a dangerous game to play these days.

The capitol's gardens are now full of corpses. All of my staff are gone, the cook, everybody, all zapped!" Lowly spoke the President..

"'Zapped', Sir?"

"They point a black wedge at their target, a strong light shoots out of it, there is no report and whoever the thing is aimed at becomes motionless until they die. It's the most frightening weapon I have ever seen, Ben!" Panted Jefferson.

Horses' nays and men's yells came within earshot. Benjamin Hawkins turned toward Jefferson and spoke.

"We have little time left! What can be done, Thomas?"

What sounded like a housefly whizzing by but with an ugly thump when it stopped, brought to surface the enormous tragedy which had befallen the nation's governmental center. Hawkins leaped from the carriage.

As Jefferson was zigzagging toward the protection of a cluster of elm trees, he yelled out "Andrew Jackson's" name! He said, "Jackson was trustworthy and knew about Indians".

The men on horseback then closed in on their quarry. They took the U.S. President and his carriage away. No one followed Ben.

*　*　*　*　*

Although Jackson was in Tennessee, he was still the hottest topic in the District of Columbia. The gossip about him had to do with his living in "sin" with an adulterous woman.

That shot Andrew Jackson to the number one spot on the "Bad Christian" chart. That 'hotness' however, made it difficult for Detective Hawkins to ask questions about the whereabouts of Jackson without advertising the fact that the man was being investigated.

"Lt. Col. William Burrow" was a war buddy of Andrew Jackson's. Burrow was the Commandant of the Marine base which manned the warships protecting the Baltimore shipyards.

It was said, he was a hardnosed bastard to work with; therefore, he had been nicknamed, "Barnacle Bill" by those unfortunate enough to have served under his command.

He was a "lifer" in every sense of that word. But men such as Colonel Burrow after becoming 'long-toothed', had a tendency to blindly follow whomever was perceived to be the highest ranking man in the house!

To further complexify the matter, there was the possibility that Barnacle Bill had also been 'affected' by the Illuminati infiltrators.

'If either of those two paranoid ideas were a reality, he'd never get out alive', Ben surmised.

The Culper carefully climbed down the aspen tree where from near its top and for two hours, had glassed the heavily fortified marine base. Hawkins was scoping the going ins and outs of freight deliveries.

Items such as coal, fish, produce and empty garbage disposal wagons came in and were lightly looked over by the sentinels. Upon exiting, the guards allowed those same wagons to pass, unchecked, back through its forty foot walls.

Outgoing security reflected the height of ambivalence. More than likely, the gate guards wouldn't have noticed an ape leaving the premises.

It was their "Achilles' heel", the detective thought. He needed to enter the port's military complex and meet with the Commandant.

"The Horse", a wharf saloon, was the kind of establishment where there were two kinds of patrons, those wishing to make money and those wanting to spend it; but, the end-game for both 'species', was pleasure. In Hawkins's case, he just needed to get in front of Burrow.

Drinking joints located on rivers or places where ships come and go, are not easy places to start conversations. The patrons have already seen every flimflam artists' tricks imaginable in dives like, "The Horse."

Cards, chances, numbers, potions, sooner or later you'll see them come through if you sit long enough but Benjamin Hawkins knew that. He had a different approach in mind.

There is one thing which will most likely 'break the ice' with 'squirrelly folks' and that is with a 'demonstration', a free one, and one offering to the "yay's" booze and succulent finger foods afterwards!

The detective thought the Commandant might be interested in seeing the 'golden Shaman'. Ben took the statuette out of the leather bag he had buttoned into his breast pocket.

Hawkins 'lifted' a monocle from the head of the guy passed out on the closest barstool next to him. For the first time, Benjamin was able to examine the precise details the artist had put into the Shaman's facial expression. The golden "medical man" was crying.

Before Benjamin had time to spin his well plotted story of the pirates from whom he had stolen the ingot, Lt. Col. William Burrow had the detective hanging by his boot heels from the low hanging branch of a live oak tree. Ben discovered immediately that Colonel Burrow was a man of swift action and few words!

One sergeant and one corporal began building a miniature fire about eighteen inches below Hawkins's hatless head. Little balls of singeing hair raced toward Ben's scalp.

He began swinging at the end of a hemp rope. Burrow asked for more wood to be put on the fledgling fire before speaking.

"Let's just skip right to it, shall we? Who are you?"

"I am Detective Benjamin Hawkins!" screamed Ben as he jerked above the stinging licks of flame.

"What brings you to Baltimore, Mister Hawkins?" unhurriedly questioned the Commandant.

"President Jefferson has been sequestered within the capitol building by the Illuminati! I came here to get your help!

Jefferson requested that I contact you in order to reach Andrew Jackson! Now, goddamn it, get me down from here!"

"Why didn't you just come directly to the fort and ask for me like normal people do?" sarcastically toyed Colonel Burrow.

"Because they have infiltrated our entire government, you idiot!"

"Cut this man down! Bring him to my office within the hour!" said the Commandant before he stormed away. The fire crackled in Burrow's draft.

Ben chuckled to himself as he pretended to be agitated by being carried into the fort by six thick backed soldiers. He had pulled it off! He had gotten his meeting with Colonel Burrow.

The lieutenant colonel and the detective spoke in private for nearly three hours. By the time their conference was done, Ben had won William Burrow's trust.

Together, they had constructed a theory. It was hoped their construct in application, would hold the invaders at bay until America could make it a fair fight.

That night, Colonel Burrow sent four messengers after Jackson. Each man left traveling individually in a different direction and at a separate departure time.

At dawn, Benjamin Hawkins left the marine base with the intent of "interviewing" Jeremiah Yellott, the captain of the "Dragon Fly". He was the man who gave the statuette to Hawkins.

Ben needed more clarification as well as a tighter focus on the anomalies the fishermen reported. Plus, the government sleuth wanted to know more about the gold Shaman.

* * * *

"Old Philadelphia Road" was already packed with carts and wagons. Mostly fish but also vegetables had to be rushed to the street venders, hotels, and taverns in time before the shoppers arrived. Pungent odors bubbling from ditch water proved that business was sometimes slow.

The "Dragon Fly" was still moored at exactly the same place it was four days before. There was still no sign of life onboard.

Benjamin reconstructed in his mind, the direction in which the frightened captain had run that first meeting. He knew it was uphill and to the northwest.

Things had moved rapidly that night; however, "Market Street" was the closest fit into an illusively dim memory slot, within his mind. He headed toward it.

Following a twenty minute climb up a fairly steep incline, Ben saw a cluster of dilapidated buildings. Some had trees growing through their busted out windows while others had been overtaken by climbing vegetation.

An old sign claimed the detective was at the "Spring Grove Retreat". Hawkins thought the institute was defunct until he noticed a pair of human eyes looking down upon him. Someone was in the old chapel's bell tower.

Ben looked up, smiled, and then offered a friendly wave to the timorous individual. They waved back.

Benjamin took off his jacket. He wanted to appear less official looking.

'Just a good ole guy asking a few questions for the well-being of all mankind!', Ben pinched himself for his sarcastic thought.

He waved again at the person in the tower but this time, Hawkins had the neck of a bottle of whiskey clinched in his left fist.

What looked like a young woman disappeared from the bell tower's louvered window; Ben expected her to come down to meet him. He was right.

"Aah, we've been waiting for you, Captain! Wharf gossip has it, it's your birthday!

You know, dear sir, it was not necessary for you to bring such a fine bottle of scotch with you, we already have plenty; but, the more the merrier!

Wait until you see the spread the ship's cooks have prepared for you. All of your favorites, Captain, in celebration of the planet's greatest seafarer, "Captain Adam Weishaupt"!

Come, come, everyone will be so happy to see you!" said a seventy five pound scraggly young woman as she pulled Ben into the chapel by his free hand.

They walked into a fire gutted sanctuary. 'The pews had been chopped apart for firewood', Ben assumed.

There was a table but nothing was on it, no one sitting around it, just dust! Hawkins turned toward his hostess and spoke.

"Darling, I believe the orchestra is playing our song! Would you care to do the light fandango?" gallantly asked Benjamin Hawkins.

Blushingly, she accepted. So they danced and they chatted the day away. By night fall, Benjamin Hawkins had learned a lot.

"Carolyne Jacobs" was the detective's dance partner's name. As a gift from her father, she and her new husband, "Myron", were treated to a cruise.

Once out to sea, about two hours from their port of "Hull", Carolyne said that the "Dragon Fly" was lifted into the sky, spun as if captured by a whirligig, consumed by a floating disk, and found herself where she was. Only her dreams, she said, filled in the blank spaces.

Carolyne Jacobs admitted that her nightmares played out like very real people were in them. "Indians flying in the air, probing tools, gas, abnormal faces, darkness", were a few descriptive words the Jacobs girl used before she drifted off to sleep.

Hawkins thought about doing the merciful thing; but, he couldn't bring himself to it. Carolyne threw Benjamin a kiss as he bid her a 'good night'.

Ben immediately left for the base. He and Burrows had to talk again.

This Illuminati invasion was far greater in scope than either of them could have imagined. It was true, America's nerve center had been commandeered by the Illuminati.

Hawkins remembered something Jefferson had said the other night, "go see the 'Madam' in Alexandria"! Detective Hawkins changed his direction.

The federal man needed more facts. 'Maybe some clues could be picked up where integrity was measured in ounces?' Ben said to himself.

Ben quizzed himself, 'who was the most renown madam in Washington?'. He was sure he had heard such a person's name but he couldn't remember the details.

It was a sweltering summer night so Ben elected to tie up gypsy in front of the "Black Rooster's Gulch". He'd toss a few down, ask some questions and then go home; it'd been a long day.

There was an open stool at the centrally stationed bar. Annis "Boudinot" Stockton, the saloon's owner, a buxom redhead, extremely outspoken and considered to be the most powerful woman on the east coast, was bartending that night. She knew who the detective was as soon as he was seated; or so, that's what Ben gathered by the look in Boudinot's eyes.

"Good evening, Sir! Scotch and a splash of branch, right?"

Detective Hawkins nodded while demonstrating a surprised smile. 'A couple of months ago was the last time he had been there'.

'Either this old girl had an incredible memory or she was expecting me' was exactly what Ben thought to himself. He then spoke.

"Wow! What an amazing recall you have, "Mrs. Stockton"!" said the gumshoe in an antagonistic way.

"It's 'Miss', you silly ass! How are you, Franklin, longtime no see!" Boudinot loudly exclaimed but then leaned into Benjamin's face and whispered, "kiss me".

In the midst of their publicly displayed intimacy, Miss Stockton via a curled tongue, transferred a message to Hawkins. After which, he sat back down on his stool and slid the waxed roll of paper into his pocket. He finished his scotch and water and left.

As Ben Hawkins approached his Georgetown cottage, he was overwhelmed with melancholy. Perhaps it was the alcohol or being just plain bushed, but Ben found himself very sad. He put gypsy in her stall.

It wasn't so much the disavowed marriage his father had seen to, hell, his old man had a point, 'Son, a man of your stock has no business rutting with the red-tails even if they are Creeks!', kept playing over and over in his mind.

It was pure loneliness, Ben told himself.

Someone knocked on his front door. It was "Boudinot", Jefferson's 'mystery madam'.

"I followed you here. Have you had time to read my message?" asked Washington's lover (something which had just dawned on Hawkins).

"Please come in, Miss Stockton. Obviously, you're not out for a morning ride; I assume there is something on your mind. May I pour you some 'cheap' scotch?" said Ben in an attempt at levity.

"Honey, you're going to need that scotch for yourself but thank you just the same! Jefferson sent you to me, didn't he?" questioned Lavinia.

"In a coded way, yes! He recommended that I 'speak with the 'madam"; that's the only description of you he made. Why do you ask?" queried Hawkins.

"Did you mention this to anyone?" slashed Lavinia.

"No, the "Black Rooster" was on my way home."

"Benjamin Hawkins: Mason, Carolina Assemblyman, language specialist, a Jersey scholar,…Culper. All of which spells, 'bullshit'!"

Boudinot pulled a hairpin from out of the rear of her flaming red bouffant and swiftly placed its point a quarter of an inch into Benjamin's left nostril. She whispered.

"Take your shirt off, Ben, and turn around!"

He did as she asked. A second later, she apologized.

"I had to make sure, "number sixty one"; I am sorry for doubting you but you know what they say about, "assumptions"!

Is George alright? No one has heard from him in more than a week now!"

The two of them tried their best to put together some kind of theory, some explanation as to the 'why's' and 'who's' of this invisible invader's purpose.

They made a pact. In two days, they would meet back at the Black Rooster's Gulch to share their findings. He would checkout Mount Vernon while she got into the britches of some of her Capitol House 'regulars'. It was 0345hrs..

Sundays are big deals for large churches. First, because it gives each institution a chance to strut their stuff on piety's playing field and secondly, it's pay day!

The Christ Church's front left pew was bought by Mary Ball Washington nearly a half century before. If a 'Washington' wasn't in attendance at some service for some reason or another, no one was to sit in that particular pew if they weren't at least, a relative!

Benjamin Hawkins sat one row behind the Washington's empty pew for the entire service. Afterwards, he rode back out to Dogue Run Farm.

He dared not ride gypsy too close to the hill top overlooking Mary Ball's plantation. It was a stormy afternoon so anyone there would be checking the horizon looking for thunderclouds.

Agent Hawkins found a clump of rhododendron to glass the farm from. What he saw made his heart drop into his stomach.

A fully armed fortress sprawled out over the Washington plantations. The surrounding hills had been turned into bunkers, spiked fences protected whomever were in them.

Not seeing one single sign of a human being made the hair standup on the back of Ben's neck. 'The tunnels, walls, turrets, all had to be constructed by a whole lot of people very quickly. Impossible, and yet it was there.' Thought Hawkins.

Ben pulled his oilcloth over his head. Rain was turning into ice pellets, the clouds seemed furious.

Luckily, he and gypsy had found a slanted rock to get up under. The storm roared overhead but passed quickly. Hawkins's pocket watch had stopped.

Night was coming on. Halfway home, Benjamin pulled gypsy to a halt. The dirt was dry!

The Culper spun his horse around and rode her back to the slanted rock where he had tied her to a cedar tree. He returned to the same vantage spot he thought he had seen the blinking purple lights.

Five flaming balls swept some twenty feet above his head and zipped into a hole that opened up on the side of the opposing mountain. Again, Benjamin saw purple lights as the tunnel closed.

As he was ready to hop on gypsy's back, the detective realized there were close to a dozen camouflaged marines pointing their crossbows at him. Colonel Burrow, on foot, approached gypsy, grabbed her reins and then looked at Ben. He placed his finger over his lips and gave the sign for his squad to become very still.

Ten seconds later, a miniscule glowing ball whizzed way above their heads. The colonel motioned for Hawkins to follow them.

Burrow's unit remounted their horses which had been kept by two other soldiers, and rode back to the base at an enormously rapid pace. After that, it was into the interrogation room.

There were three big chairs setting side-by-side. In front of the three judges' seats was a stool.

Stripped of his clothing and chained to the "accused's" metal stool, was Ben Hawkins. In the Judges' chairs, from left to right respectfully sat, "George Washington, Thomas Jefferson and William Burrow".

Their rubbery faces showed no expression. Colonel Burrow spoke first.

"Detective Benjamin Hawkins! Is that your correct name, Sir?"

"Of course, Colonel!" said Ben as Burrow quickly stood. He seemed angrier than a hornet.

"What the hell do you mean, "of course", you belligerent asshole! Yelled the pan faced marine commander.

Ben had experienced this schismatic behavior with Jefferson just a day or two ago. 'They had been gotten to!', was what went through the detective's mind.

"Sir, I received a directive from your office to report to your base at 1100 hrs.. In your orders, you referred to me as, 'Detective Benjamin Hawkins'. I therefore, made the erroneous assumption you had only summonsed one Detective Hawkins to your base, Sir. Pardon my error!"

"You watch your tongue, Mister Hawkins, that is, unless you wish to have it ripped from your mouth! Do you understand me, Benjamin?" snarled Thomas Jefferson.

"Clearly, Sir." Answered Hawkins. He then 'rolled the dice' with a humongous lie.

"Your first sergeant, Franklin, I believe, asked me to ride through the country and report any irregularities to him when I arrived at your fort, Sir. That's what I was doing when your men brought me here, Colonel." Explained Hawkins.

"And where did my first sergeant make contact with you, Mister Hawkins?" prodded Colonel Burrow's imposter.

"At my home."

"Why in the world, would anyone deliver a 'verbal' message and an official one at that, to a detective at his home?" pecked the Colonel.

"Because, Sir, I am the "Senior Investigative Officer to the President". There are numerous ways in which messages are transmitted to me; I assumed your sergeant's visit this morning was some sort of obtuse communique', that's why, Sir." Lied the detective.

Hawkins noticed Lieutenant Colonel Burrow's head turn toward Jefferson. The man was looking for a "lifeline" because he was clueless as to what to say next. 'Washington' then jumped in.

"How'd my place look, Detective Hawkins?"

"Mister President, it was a little dark by the time I was passing by Mary Ball's place; however, I did notice the fishing lake had been filled in!

If you'll remember, Sir, my little girl, 'Lavinia' caught her first trout right there off your mother's pier! She'll never forget that, Mister President!

I did see that you were terracing the hill edging up to your boundary line; it is possible, Sir, someone cut into a gas pocket up there because I saw some blue lights flickering.

Gentlemen, have I done something wrong?" further rolled Ben.

Thomas Jefferson stood and pronounced Hawkins's sentence.

"Death by hanging."

The penalty was to be carried out, immediately.

Chapter Two

Benjamin Hawkins sat on the only piece of furniture in his cell. What he could see through the log wall's junctures was enough for him to determine whether it was day or night.

There was little to no sound and not much hope. A key rattled in the stockade's metal enforced door. It was Colonel Burrows, four of his armed marines, and Lavinia Stockton. Barnacle Bill spoke.

"Greetings, before your sentence is carried out, you are entitled to an hour of 'reflection' with either a priest or a loved one. By your own selection, you chose your wife to share that precious time with you. May your soul rest in peace!"

No sooner had the lock been turned in Ben's cell door when Lavinia ripped the floppy hat off of her head and tacked it over the cell's peephole.

Some guards pay 'high dollar' for the shift including a conjugal visit; however, this time, they got gypped.

What was actually taking place in that stockade room had nothing to do with conjugality at all; Lavinia was preparing Hawkins for his escape. There were four Culpers dressed as marines, waiting in a metal plated wagon south of the fort.

They had planted explosives around Ben Hawkins's cell. The fuses were lit.

Answering the most plaguing question on Ben's mind, Lavinia pulled a folded piece of canvas out from beneath her hoop dress. She then speedily unfolded a rubbery material out into what, after being exposed to air, looked similar to a giant child's ball. The Culper motioned for Ben to join her within that canvas sphere.

The first bundle of dynamite blew the stockade's roof completely off. The second, planted beneath the cell's floor, propelled the ball containing Lavinia and Detective Hawkins some fifty feet into the air and down a hill. It rolled for a long way.

The third and the fourth explosives used were designed for crowd control. When detonated, they delivered no shrapnel nor caused casualties; they left their watchers with no sight. Flash bombs do that to the unwary.

Amidst the pandemonium, the troops, the priest and the hangman all looked at the other for guidance. The conglomerate were frozen in shock.

Once the operation was done and without so much as a whisper of a 'goodbye', the Culper team split up. They left in different directions.

Lavinia did look back at Benjamin but for only a second; nevertheless, it was a very powerful moment for both of them.

* * * * *

'Only a fool would return home', Ben thought. There were a few mementos he would miss but staying alive was his only priority. Where to safely hide became the object of Hawkins's focus.

Roads, docks, trails, and even rivers would look like an ant hill covered with soldiers soon to show up. It would be practically impossible to slip through their lookout posts. But then, Hawkins had an idea.

If he returned to the "Dragon Fly", no one, even those in the know, would likely look there. They, probably, would think he and the rest of his jail busting crew had burrowed themselves back into their familiar hiding spaces.

The Culpers had provided him a horse, some clothes, a shotgun and enough money to flee on. The two things he did not have and missed the most, were his pistol and gypsy.

His confiscated statuesque was still in the hands of Lieutenant Colonel William Burrow 'whatever good that would do him', Ben thought. They had done a number on him and from the looks of his condition during the sentencing, that golden Shaman would serve him best as a pablum spoon.

As for the "first and third presidents", the jury was still out on those two; Ben couldn't tell whether their actions were real or performed. For his own survival's sake, he would err on the side of cowardice; until, they were either dead or under lock and key.

"Trust" at this time, was nothing more than a relic; it was no longer available. Benjamin Hawkins was afraid of these invaders. They seemed unstoppable, deadly and unmerciful.

He saw the masts of the "Dragon Fly" as he topped the hill leading to Fells Point. A lantern was burning in the ship's wheelhouse. With no telescope, he would have to get closer.

Hawkins didn't want to board the ship for fear of alerting whomever was on it. He crept along the side of the ship until he could clearly see if someone were in the "Dragon Fly's" wheelhouse. There was.

The federal man cocked back both of his shotgun's hammers. With a hardy head start, he raced up the ship's gangplank at full speed, it broke and of course, gravity did its job. The detective fell into the Potomac's brackish water.

Captain Jeremiah Yellott lowered a ladder for Benjamin's convenience. The captain handed the detective a towel.

In a fatherly manner, Jeremiah placed his hand on Ben's shoulder. He asked him to sit down and listen.

"I knew bloody well you would return! All the rest, were being paid to find out the answers to the 'whereabouts' of my ship's passengers; but, your passionate interest makes me think you're on a mission of some sort. Do I have that about right, Detective Hawkins?"

"Right on the nose, Captain!" muttered Ben.

"Have they taken the Capitol Palace?" asked Yellott.

"I believe they have, Sir! I, in past, have worked with all three of the presidents, I know them well! But now, it's as if, they see me as an outsider!

Captain Yellott, just four hours ago, I was on death row! But thanks to some acquaintances of mine, I was able to escape the noose!

I returned to the "Dragon Fly" because I figured, "they", the "Illuminati", I think, wouldn't expect me to return here.

Probably, their initial forces have seeped into our ruling government and I don't think they're here to better us! More truthfully, it is my firm belief, America's governing mechanism has already been overpowered by them!

The Illuminati's intentions I suggest, are to replicate what they have done here in Washington! They should be expected to do the same to other population clusters!

There have been no reports of troops of any nationality, being launched in our direction. We'd know it if they had; therefore, one must assume then, their attack force imbeds themselves just long enough to recruit others into their cult!

That, Sir, is why I think these Illuminati chaps are planning to rile the Indians up and maybe the slaves as well! Where else could they get them from?" stormed the Culper.

"Listen to me, Mr. Hawkins! I realize you are excited and scared too! But, son, your enemy isn't the Illuminati! It is one man! His name is, "Adam Weishaupt".

"Captain Yellott, I realize I am interrupting you, Sir, but can you explain to me, the difference in the neurotic "Captain Yellott" I met the other day and the rather eloquently speaking gentleman standing before me at this moment?

You must admit, Captain, there is little similarity?"

"I was getting to that!" scolded Jeremiah.

"Sorry, Sir." responded Ben.

"Without doubt, Mrs. Jacobs mentioned "Weishaupt's" name and thank you by the way, for the kindness you showed her. The poor thing is as crazy as a loon but it's because she was exposed to the 'green gas' for too long. That too, might surreptitiously explain my behavior.

You see, Ben, Johann A. Weishaupt's intentions are not motivated by greed nor want for 'world power'; not at all, he simply want's to stop "mans'" evolutionary climb.

Weishaupt believes that "human beings" were a mistake! His job, as directed by 'Satan', is to correct that error!

He intends on turning America into a cesspool of cannibals, one snapping at the life of the other, and then another and another! War against all others, even ourselves, is to become the norm!

The object of Weishaupt's "societal putsch" is to bend mans' evolution back around on itself. To turn the homo sapiens' progression around so instead of our planet's people "reaching for the stars", or finding cures for illnesses of the mind and body, or mastering the 'laws' of the universe (example: learning how to fly), Adam's aim, is to witness mans' return to his natavistic roots; e.g., human beings ridding themselves of their, so far gained, technological advances.

In Adam's "new world", the 'illuminated' inhabitants will go about their lives void of 'machine assisted' developments. The gun will be replaced by the spear, the wagon by shoe leather, metal for stone, and so on…!

Bottom line, Detective Hawkins, if Johann Weishaupt's scheme comes to fruition and there is little doubt that it won't, America will become an underground fortress. It will evolve into the world's darkest mystery!

This continent will become a forbidden place to visit and for those who do, there will be no return. The foolishly curious, will be swallowed up in macabre obscurity. That's what is happening, Mister Hawkins!"

"Stop! How do you know of such extraordinary things, Mister Yellott? Where are you getting these outlandish theories from and who agrees with you?" wildly asked Benjamin.

"Adam Weishaupt is my godson. His father died when he was five years old; he was under my care up until six years ago. My real name, Detective, is, "Johann Adam Freiherr von Ickstatt"!

Embarrassingly, I must admit, I failed, clearly, at raising that boy. His father and I shared a post at the "University of Ingolstadt" as professors of law, when Johann (the father) died.

I, for political reasons, opened my big mouth and stepped into the responsibilities of seeing to it that, "Adam" took the proper paths afforded to a fatherless young man of unlimited wealth.

Even at age twelve, young Weishaupt was known to be the fourth wealthiest person in Bavaria. By the time the boy was fifteen, he was lecturing the passerby's of Ingolstadt's busy streets on "Kant's dictum"!

I lost touch with the lad just after his twentieth birthday. People said, he and a few of his "disciples" had set out to 'discover' the secrets of the "underworld".

Supposedly, they left for the Far East where they were to be taught the powers of "Black Magic". Until this week and only now did I realize that Weishaupt was still alive.

I thought I had hidden myself well; but, I was wrong!"

The humidity was causing the windows in the "Dragon Fly's" wheelhouse to fog up. Both men had to take a leak so they moved to the waterside of the ship's mooring and did it off the starboard side. Ben then asked Captain Yellott a series of questions.

"Captain, here we are, a war weary country, a bastion, a safety net for thousands of people wishing to escape the kings and churches of Europe and now we have some wealthy sociopath who by himself, has managed to topple this American dream; how can that be?

Jeremiah, if all of this we hear is true and I believe it is, then how can we stop this man from doing what you say, "he is determined to do"?

We have a damn good military, you know!

I hope you do not believe for a fraction of a second, our generals are going to sit by idly while men with bows and arrows attack them, do you?

Isn't this whole thing illogical, Captain?"

"Illogical? Indeed, but as you can see with your naked eyes, he has already done it!" humbly stated Yellott.

"But, how?" marveled Ben.

"Magic and gas, Detective, 'magic and gas'!"

Ben was no longer having fun. To demonstrate his dissatisfaction with Yellott's obtuse answers, he kicked the side of the ship.

He turned toward the captain with a mixed look; the detective's face exposed both fear and anger. He cried out loud and then fell to the floor in a prostrated lump; Hawkins was sobbing while he spoke.

"Oh my God, man, we have to stop this! I don't need cliffhanging riddles such as "magic and gas", when I ask you a serious question!" mockingly spat Hawkins.

"Forgive me, Mister Hawkins, you are completely correct! This is most definitely not a laughing matter so let's get down to your deserved answers, shall we?" lightly stated Jeremiah.

Captain Yellott moved a couple of heavy chairs and a bookshelf away from the center of the wheelhouse's floor. Even the rug was moved so all that remained was a naked wooden space. He asked Ben a question.

"What do you see, Benjamin, within this emptied area?" queried the captain.

"Only a floor."

The shriveled up professor then put three peanut shells on the dusty surface. They were side by side and spaced an inch apart. With the speed of a cat's paw, Jeremiah reached into his pocket and withdrew a capsule. He held it between his thumb and forefinger in an innocent manner.

He asked Ben another question.

"Do you see three striking rattlesnakes, Sir?" He broke the capsule.

Immediately following the green gas's strands being sucked through Hawkins's nostrils, the detective athletically vaulted himself to the top of the captain's table. He began throwing books and such at the three docile peanut shells.

Just as the detective was about to set his 'imaginary' serpents on fire with the remaining fluid in the captain's desk lantern, Captain Yellott snapped a Sulphur capsule flat.

The detective came back to his senses; however, Ben did crush the three peanut shells with the heels of his boots just for safekeeping, one would assume.

"'Magic and Gas!', Detective Hawkins, mighty affective stuff wouldn't you say? That's how he does it!" gleefully yelled Jeremiah Yellott.

"How does he spread the gas out like the fishermen told me about? I can see where they got the maiden traipsing across the water part from; but, I'm curious as to how Weishaupt so surgically places his gas on the targets he chooses?" asked Hawkins a little less histrionic that time.

"He 'salts' the air above his victims. His "suggestions" (like striking snakes), are transmitted by music. He sets the mood so to speak!" morosely said Jeremiah.

"Flying, music, salting the air? Kindly explain!"

"Detective Hawkins, the "University of Ingolstadt" is the same to the "Hermetics" as your "West Point" is to the "Culpers"! It is the research center, the intelligence headquarters and the training site for special agents.

Their job, like the Culpers', is to maintain harmony on this planet and to honor our promises to the Cerians.

These heavily tongued words, "world order", actually apply here; we, the educated people of this earth, have a responsibility to continue our two thousand year old bond with them. They protect us, after all, Mister Hawkins!"

"That's where the flying comes in, right? Those scientists, the smartest in Bavaria, friends no doubt with our friend, Adam, who fell under his 'spell'.

I'll bet those were the boys who were whisked off into an institution nestled somewhere in the mountains of Tibet! Is that what I'm hearing from you, Captain?" spouted Hawkins.

"You are correct, Detective." flatly qualified Yellott.

"That's what I was afraid you'd say. Now what, Captain?"

"Well, based on what you've told me and added to what I know, I'd say there's no need to do anything around here. Weishaupt more than likely has his 'death mask' on every marginally important person in Washington by now.

For as long as he can keep them 'chemically entranced', they are worthless to us. Our best option is to figure out where he plans to put on his next show and beat him to it!" said Jeremiah Yellott.

"'Indians' came up in several of the conversations I had this past week, Jeremiah. In Jefferson's and my parting words, he referenced the 'Mohawks' as being in the Carolinas.

In the same breath, he also told me to 'get' "Andrew Jackson"! What do you think he meant by that?" asked Hawkins.

"Obviously, a whole lot! The new president must not have been 'gassed' at that point; although, he might have been by now!

Are you sure it was 'the real' Jefferson, you met with?" probed the "Dragon Fly's" captain.

"Jesus! I never thought of that! But, 'yes', now that I think about it, it was the authentic "Jefferson". He scheduled our meeting at "Blue Dawn". We met and then he was overtaken by the palace guards. Why do you ask?" pressed the detective.

"At what point did you see Jefferson with a 'death mask' attached to his face?" intrepidly asked Yellott.

Ben's jaws felt as if they were welded shut. He mulled over the question and then recalled it's accurate answer: 'it was when he sentenced me to hang!'.

"Good!" "That means his recommendations came from a lucid man!" exclaimed the arm flapping old salt.

"Jackson is definitely your man. He's not in Washington, is he?"

"He's a judge in Tennessee." dourly stated Ben Hawkins.

"Detective Hawkins, I am ninety three years old; that's too many "moons" for me to be of much help to you in Indian country! But, I can still be of great assistance with your escapades!

As I am sure you are aware, the Hermetics and the Culpers have close ties. Lavinia Stockton to coin a phrase, 'a double-agent', is a case in point.

You must inform her of your need to contact Jackson. She, in turn, will locate the whereabouts of "Seekaboo" who is currently embedded with Weishaupt's "disciples". She will alert him of any changes in the schedule.

Colonel Jackson will more than likely do exactly what the Duke of Bavaria did. He will use an army to annihilate every member, relative, acquaintance or passerby of an Illuminati follower and pound them into extinction!" emphatically yelled Jeremiah.

"And do you think Colonel Jackson will ultimately be waging war against our own troops? I saw what happened at the marine base; they were "all-in" with their mask wearing commandant!" argued Hawkins.

"At this point, "no". I would guess Adam's little force of zealots will choose a course of lesser resistance; it's my guess, he'll hide his band within a certain tribe, gas them, mesmerize them with his magic, and then use their tribal nation to disrupt our own!

Adam Weishaupt's belief is, he is this millennium's 'Satan'. In his mind, it is his duty to dissolve man's attempts at distancing himself from the humans' original ways.

'Yes', Adam will use the Indians and then kill them off when he's done with them!

It won't necessarily happen if we can somehow find out where Weishaupt is….and kill him. However, if I were making an educated guess, I'd say he's already stationed himself where he's planning to infiltrate next.

Detective Hawkins, I'd go back to the Black Rooster's Gulch, find Lavinia and get in touch with Seekaboo; figure out where Weishaupt's clan is and then inform Jackson of your findings!

Before you go, Mister Hawkins, let me advise you of this, although Weishaupt is of this planet and not clad with real 'super powers', he is a deadly character.

He is brilliant, clever and above all, void of a conscience and one other thing, he is a master magician!" closed Yellott.

With that, Jeremiah and Ben Hawkins parted. Captain Yellott walked up "Old Joppa Road". Hawkins watched him for as long as he could and then kicked his government horse in the ribs and headed north.

The Black Rooster was cram packed with it's regulars along with a slew of travelers, a mixed bag of them actually. There seemed to be no congruency among them which made Hawkins feel more at ease. He did not see Lavinia.

Another woman was behind the bar. She had manlike body odor and bad teeth but nonetheless, she had a wonderful disposition.

"Howdy, you tall drink of water, welcome to the Black Rooster's Gulch! What can I get for you, handsome?"

"Some descent scotch and a squirt of water, please." answered the sleuth.

"I've got ice. Do you want it?" asked the gushing bartender.

"Sure. I'll deduct the surcharge from your tip!" Said Benjamin in an attempt at flirtation.

"Here you go, sweetie! The man sitting at the end of the bar to your right, paid for your drink. Let me know if you want another. Just whisper my name and I'll be right there. Okay?"

"I can't whisper it if I don't know it, Mam!" said Ben as the barmaid leaned over the bar's ledge in a suggestive manner and whispered something to him.

"After you casually finish your drink go to the stables. You will see a covered carriage; hide in the back of it and don't budge an inch. Lavinia will come get you when the time is right. Now, kiss me like you love me!"

Hawkins did as she had instructed him to do. Beneath the carriage's cover, there was just enough light to see that a family of field mice probably several generations of them, had made their permanent home in the driver's seat's padding.

Under the trickle of the tavern's lights laid a dried out blacksnake's skin all four feet of it. 'Miserable', was the word that popped into Hawkins's mind.

He guessed it was around 1300hrs. when the Culper felt the movements of the carriage being attached to a horse. He heard no voices.

Following five or six agonizing minutes, the wagon's forward thrust pressed the detective against the carriage's blanket box. Ben peeked his head out from under the flapping tarp and found himself staring directly at Lavinia's bulbous backside.

Her shrill voice rang out warning him that a telescope could catch his movement. She told him to stay still. He did; but, it was a brutal experience.

After twenty or so minutes of teeth cracking bounces, Benjamin elected to free himself from his bludgeoning chamber by climbing over the passenger's side of the bench. His nose was bleeding and he had a busted mouth but he smiled at Lavinia anyway. She grinned back.

"Your hair in the moonlight makes it appear as if I am being kidnapped by a fiery goddess! Might I ask where thou might be so rapidly taking this failing prince?" theatrically asked the bloody faced detective.

""Mount Weather!" Jackson is meeting us there. Burrow was gassed after he sent his messengers!" said Lavinia in a low toned voice.

"Where in the hell is, Mount Weather; I've never heard of it?"

"Neither had I, until the man who paid for your drink gave me a map to it along with an explanation of what it is…" as Madam Stockton was saying when it became evident the road ahead was blocked by four men with shotguns.

Each wore a badge. The tallest of the four approached the driver.

"Mam, it's three o'clock in the morning! And what might a liquored up painted lady like yourself be up and running so "late" in the night for?" asked the abrasive lawman.

His men felt the tension build. They walked to the rear of the carriage.

Giving Ben Hawkins not one second to prepare, Lavinia stood up on the carriage's seat while pulling out from beneath her hoop dress, one double barreled mares leg with which, she capped all four of the men with it!

Burying them took an hour.

A grey tinge overlapping objects before unseen, caused Ben to realize dawn had arrived. They had only thirty minutes before being swallowed up in "Winchester's" early morning traffic.

Unless they wanted to stand out like a sore thumb, they would have to downgrade their aura. They threw dirt on their carriage and then loaded the backend with sticks and road debris. Madam Stockton lit a cigar.

Benjamin Hawkins and Lavinia were trying to pass themselves off as junk hucksters. The wheels' reaction to the cobblestone street caused their worthless payload to shift. Some of it fell off onto the roadway but only the horses paid attention to it.

People were walking in all directions. Some hurriedly crossed the street while others ambled wherever they pleased.

From two blocks away, despite the noise of the city, Benjamin could hear the wails of a doom-tongued evangelist. There was going to be a hanging.

"Man, what a blessing! I mean, I'm sorry for the poor sap but I'm damn glad it happened today! We'll just breeze right through this old town!" said agent Stockton.

An hour out of Winchester, Lavinia pulled off of "Plank Road". She motioned for Hawkins to help her release the sweat-slick animal into the wild. Both helped burn the wagon.

A signal light flickered some quarter of a mile from the northwest. Neither of them had any luggage or anything else so their trek in that direction was reasonably easy.

Three camouflaged soldiers met them at the mouth of a cavern. They made hand gestures but spoke not one word to either themselves or to their newly arrived guests.

Two of the ghillie suited commandos stayed back while the federal detective and Lavinia were escorted into the cavern. Ben looked back but by then, he could see only tangled undergrowth.

The doors to a trolley car were opened. The stringy hatted escort removed his headcover; it was Andrew Jackson.

Amidst the noise created by the tracked carriage's wheels, Jackson so eloquently spoke.

"Rarely, has our country seen such brave responders that with imminent danger ahead….." Jackson was saying when the madam very abruptly interrupted him!

"Andy! Knock the bullshit off! Honey, I've screwed you three times, twice, you paid for it; so, let's just get right down to the brass tacks , shall we?

Colonel, the governmental palace has been taken over by what are assumed to be the, 'Illuminati'!" glibly said Lavinia.

With a big ole grin on his face, Jackson stood while the electric trolley car was rocking back and forth and then attempted to speak in a normal way.

"We will be moving directly into the debriefing room when we stop. We'll all have a chance to throw our two cents into the ring at that time.

I'm sure, Lavinia, you'll be interested to know, your Hermetic agents informed us over a year ago of Adam Weishaupt's plot. At this point, we feel we are well prepared to counter his attack!" calmly explained Jackson.

The trolley slowed to a hissing stop. The doors opened into a surprising scene. Seated behind one large table was the great Shawnee chief, "Tecumseh".

On both sides of their spiritual leader were six Shawnee councilmen, six Kickapoo chiefs and six Winnebago Shaman. Unbelievably, they stood when the three arrivals entered the debriefing quarters. Tecumseh was the first to say something.

"Please forgive the abrupt manner in which I had you evacuated from the Black Rooster's Gulch. Unfortunately, you were about ready to be pounced upon by a couple of Washington's carnivores. Kindly, allow me to explain."

The very tall Shawnee chief then walked around the conference table and sat down on it so he could be face to face with Ben and Lavinia.

"Here's what's happening, a very rich but crazy man was chased out of Bavaria. "Johann Adam Weishaupt" is the bloody bastard's name!

He slipped into Philadelphia by pretending to be the governor of one of the Bavarian islands. It's name was never noted.

In less than six months, through his fantastic magic shows and stellar showmanship, Weishaupt stole the hearts and won the trust of Washington's 'upper-crust'. That's when the Culpers got into the spin of it all.

The Hermetics' most valuable agent, "Lavinia Stockton" was gracious enough to give us the needed information to nail this guy. He got away because of an inside tip, no doubt!

Johann Weishaupt slipped away close to a year ago; but, we now know where he is!

I'll ask Colonel Jackson to explain the rest."

Tecumseh continued to sit on the table until Jackson stepped up beside him. The great chief went back to his chair.

"Detective Hawkins , all jesting aside, your country needs you now more than ever!

I, speaking as the interim "Commander and Chief", am appointing you as "America's Southeastern Indian Agent". That puts you up to my 'paygrade', if that'll make you feel better! You and Lavinia, are to report to the "Dragon Fly" in twenty-four hours. You'll need a good night's sleep and some provisions packed. You're going into Alabama so get familiar with the map of the coastline laid out in your room.

Your destination is what Weishaupt calls, the "Holy Ground". "Seekaboo's" last transmitted message stated that is where their headquarters had been moved to.

We're not sure of it's exact location; however, all indications point toward the place where the "Cousa and Tallapoosa Rivers" join to become the "Alabama". That is where his "Red Sticks" intend on turning our country upside down!

Sadly, we have run out of time. It is expected that Weishaupt's "magical henchmen" will start their attacks on the white settlements within the month!

With the Presidential Palace already under their control, we expect Weishaupt to think he has free rein in the Indian Territories. Your jobs will be to capture or kill this man as well as his followers." Said Colonel Jackson.

The nineteen Indians then quietly stood and left the debriefing room leaving only Andrew Jackson, Lavinia, and Ben Hawkins. No one said anything for a good long while until Madam Stockton broke the silence.

"Andy, what the hell is going on? Who in god's name are these Indians and why in Christ's name did Weishaupt choose them as his minions? This whole thing seems so preposterous to me!" said Lavinia in a fit of frustration. Hawkins then asked a question. "Colonel, how are you planning to squelch these 'Illuminati' led 'savages' without tipping off the "already gassed" powers that be?" queried Hawkins. "Well, Ben and Lavinia, that's where you come into play! In eight days, Captain Yellott will take the "Dragon Fly" to the port of Mobile.

"Judge Harry Toulmin" will meet you at the landing. He will unfold for you the next part of your mission. I wish I could be more specific but I can't.

While you are in route to the Gulf of Mexico, Tecumseh along with his multitribal councilmen, will begin at the mouth of the Wabash and visit with the people of whom they call, "the five civilized nations" (Creeks, Cherokees, Chickasaws, Choctaws, Seminoles).

Tecumseh's message is twofold, first, he intends to warn his people of the invading "Red Sticks" but secondly, he will announce the long overdue settlement of a dispute between the red and white men over this place called, "America".

Finally, it will be decreed that all lands west of the Mississippi and running into the Pacific ocean, would forever, belong to the native Americans.

Future transcontinental travel will take place on designated routes with both governments promising safe travel for those wishing to do trade with the other. Land sales will be forbidden!

The United States can deal with the French and Spanish anyway they want to but the Spaniards are going to have to leave Florida! It's a solid agreement and I believe, it's beneficial to all concerned. Weishaupt's use of the Indians is to simply create chaos. He wants to see this country along with its technological advances return to the ways of the Neanderthal.

Adam Weishaupt's vision of "Estarcion" from the perspective of a future explorer, is to advertise a land void of lights, no good ports, no waving prostitutes, no cities to visit, just nothing but a pretty land to be buried in!

What that 'white devil' really wants is to be surrounded by bowing natives who will shudder beneath his lionlike roars; while in actuality, he is isolating himself from the people who recognize him for exactly what he is, a fraud!

My guess is, he'll be an easy kill. What needs to be done at present is to find him and bring him to justice!

Get some sleep; we'll pull out in ten hours!" said Andy.

He then showed Hawkins and Lavinia to their room.

They were too tired to embrace or to talk. Through an unspoken agreement, the odd couple just smiled at one another and fell asleep. Both, still had their boots on.

* * * * *

Promptly at 1500 hrs., Jackson had several Seminoles and a wagon full of explosives, the American Indian agent (Hawkins) and Madam Stockton on their way to the Baltimore docks.

Captain Yellott was to take the "Dragon Fly" south to Tangier Island. They were scheduled to switch off to a much faster craft later on.

The ship's launch went flawlessly. Jeremiah Yellott had made a pleasant suite for Lavinia and Ben. It was the first opportunity for the three of them to talk.

Strong northeastern winds had pushed the "Dragon Fly" southward at an amazing clip. During that time, about three hours, Yellott told "Mr. and Mrs. Hawkins" every detail he could remember about Adam Weishaupt's life.

What they learned, was how Weishaupt accomplished what he did by using a type of nerve gas, one that caused a mild paralysis, provided a hallucinogenic affect and at the same time, gave the recipients the euphoric sense of wellbeing.

"Captain, what kind of gas does that?" questioned the Indian agent.

Tangier Island was in sight which gave Yellott enough time to explain some technical details in order to answer Hawkins's question regarding Weishaupt's extraordinarily powerful aerosol. He explained.

"It comes from the "Tatzelwurm" (a highland reptile which only lives in cold and dark caverns) dung or at least from the spores that grow out of it.

Adam learned about them during his "magical tour" of the Far East.

Supposedly, the young Johann Weishaupt fraudulently purchased the 'secret' of the tiny dragons' scatological byproduct from an elderly monk in exchange for the 'indisputable' ownership of "Zugspitze Mountain".

Weishaupt claimed Bavaria's highest peak was an unwanted inheritance from his father.

The Tibetan monks have protected their mountaintop villages for years by the use of the Tatzelwurm's excretion. I'm told, the monks add yeast which causes minuscule mushrooms to bloom. After that, 'they' capture an emitted green gas in metal containers.

How they put it into transportable cannisters, I do not know; but, I am sure the gas can be compressed into walnut sized bombs. From what I have researched, after one of those gas grenades is tossed into a crowded area, the victims become more gullible than schoolchildren!"

"What about an antidote?" curtly asked Lavinia. "Time and fresh air will do it although that takes at least a half day. Sulfur gas however, has an almost instantaneous effect because it allows a person to regain his senses long enough to escape their confinement.

Avoidance is the best salve, Lavinia." Yellott said with a comforting smile on his pinched face.

"Tangier Island" was just a dot on the map. It was a fishing village which boasted a whapping seventy three human beings living on it.

With "Fort Albion's" presence on the island, the total population shot up to five hundred if a boatload of colonial marines happened to arrive before another bunch had not yet left on furlough!

It was a sleepy little town and home to America's most secret intelligence agency. It was an island where new technologies were tried out.

The "Dragon Fly" was forbidden to get within two miles of the fort. American warships saw to that. A sloop was on its way to pick up the agents.

A tall man speaking from behind a woolen mask, introduced himself as Judge Toulmin. Other than pointing out where Lavinia and Ben were to sit, he nor the four masked rowers, said another word. Hoods were gently pulled over Ben's and Lavinia's heads.

From Hawkins's perspective, everything occurring after the sloop landed on Tangier's beach was done beneath the ground. Sharp echoes ricocheting off of sandstone walls suggested that.

"Good Evening!" a voice said through a speaker mounted on the wall.

"Please remain focused on my instructions. They are important!" continued the voice coming from the wall box.

"What do you think this is, Ben?" asked Lavinia in a panicky way.

"I'm not sure; but, I believe we're underwater. Do you feel pressure in your ears?" responded the Indian agent with an added question.

"Yes, but I feel it in my sinus cavities even more." Answered the madam.

"I shall now ask that you sit back in your chairs. When you awaken, you will find yourselves basking in the sands of the Gulf of Mexico!" and then a sweet smell permeated the cockpit's air.

* * * * *

The "Dragon Fly" travelled up the "Tombigbee River" for most of the morning. Around a quarter till twelve, the ship docked.

When the gangplank was slid into place, 'the nation's first pro-Indian agent' and his "wife" were welcomed to "Tookabatcha" by five thousand whooping Creeks.

Tecumseh had told the Creeks of his purpose for inviting "whites" to their annual council. Those in attendance had come painted for war.

Terrifying red and black faces cheered as the highly promoted Indian agent and his "blushing bride" stepped foot on Alabama soil. Tecumseh walked forward to greet the arriving Culpers.

"We have brought you here for judgement! Big Warrior the Creek Counselman insisted that he look into your eyes before he would listen to you. He puts little trust in the Europeans' words.

I have told him of the "ironclad" offer made by the United States of America. I explained that all lands west of the Mississippi River would be off limits to whomever the tribes did not wish to be there.

Additionally, I emphasized to the Creeks this agreement will be codified into American law; i.e., it will be deemed "an illegal trespassing" if an American citizen is found in violation by entering the Indian Territory!

"Tustunnuggee" (Big Warrior) is convinced the white man's interests are bent on land acquisition and it's extrapolation of gold and other resources and since he has witnessed already the "blue eyes'" treatment of the earth, it is his vote, that the European invaders be removed from the North American continent!" Whispered Tecumseh before he nodded to Big Warrior of his turn to speak.

The Creek Counselman stepped out of the rowdy multitude behind him. Six buckskin clad warriors surrounded their chief . Their faces were frighteningly painted and each was well armed.

"Frankly, I believe Tecumseh was a little rough on me. I'm not quite the 'Attila' he makes me out as. Actually, I find the idea of "everlasting peace" quite intriguing.

American Indian Agent, Mister Benjamin Hawkins, I happen to know of a quintessential hut where we can hoist a few and chat a bit. After that, we'll decide on which side of the table you'll be served dinner on!" said Tustunnuggee with an alum mouthed grin on his face.

They were seen no more until dark. When the two fairly drunk men emerged from the cabin and danced the northern war dance together, five thousand Indians followed suit. War hatchets were raised high over their heads into the late evening's buttermilk sky.

Big Warrior raised both of his arms toward the heavens. The noise ceased and the Indians listened.

"These whites come with good hearts. They are not our enemies per say, but they do bring alarming news of what is to come!

Their proposal was not authored by a white man! Quite the contrary, their offer came from the "Great Spirit" and I know this to be true!

So....I shall call for a "pole vote". Tribal representatives report to the square immediately!"

Slightly under one hundred loin cloth wearing Creek warriors each with a tobacco pouch suspended beneath their left arms, swarmed onto either side of the square. Hawkins, Lavinia, Tecumseh and Big Warrior walked toward the center of the village's square where a single pole towered above their heads.

Opposing views, inflammatory remarks, insulting one-liners could be heard coming from both sides of the voting 'box'. Most of the venal comments were aimed at the Indian agent.

And...those tribal representatives were never so shocked as they were when their new Federal Indian Agent defended himself and then verbally thrashed them in their own language (Muskogee). The opposing sides quieted down. Vigilance returned.

For six or maybe seven hours, each representative of their Creek tribe had a say and when all had spoken, the meeting was adjourned. As every tribal leader was leaving the square, individually, they would approach the pole, walk around it three times and then drop an unshelled peanut on either the left side (peace to the west) or the right side (war to the east) of the pole.

As everyone could see, Tecumseh's divine proposal was the undisputed champion of the debate. Showing humility, he let out a horrendous war whoop and then presented to Big Warrior a wampum belt of five different strands and a Shawnee pipe decorated with two eagle feathers, four porcupine quills and a slew of beads sewn onto it.

Once the crowd of Indians had gone back to their tepees, Lavinia could smell cooking fires coming from everywhere. The surrounding hills were speckled with signs of wonderful living things.

Big Warrior passed her the peace pipe again.

For the first time, Lavinia and Benjamin made love. They did it on the bank of the Tombigbee River under a three quarter full Alabama moon.

An hour before the sun came up, Lavinia was awakened by a tiny pebble bouncing off of her forehead. Realizing the angle from which it had been thrown was not from up above as first thought, she concluded it had come from the river!

Upon closer scrutiny, Lavinia awakened Ben; they then slipped out from under the lean-to. The newly 'christened' couple crawled toward the Tombigbee's edge. Someone was calling Hawkins's name.

A man's head rose above the waterline. He spoke English.

"I am, "Seekaboo"!

The man for whom you are searching, "Adam Weishaupt", lives within the Creek nation but further north from here!

There, Weishaupt's name is, "Hilis Hadjo". He is addressed as the "Prophet".

The Prophet's followers known as the 'Red Sticks', have segregated themselves from Tecumseh's control by living in caves and unexplored wildernesses.

Find 'Little Warrior'. He will show you where Hadjo's village is located." whispered Seekaboo before he disappeared beneath the river's surface.

Locating an Indian in the midst of hundreds of them packing up and leaving the sacred town of "Tookabatcha", was like finding that proverbial 'needle' in a haystack.

Lavinia had a 'brainstorm'. She then spoke of the 'epiphany' with her most recent lover.

"How old would you guess this "Little Warrior" is, Ben?" playfully queried Lavinia.

"I'd guess, since his father, "Big Warrior" is in his late forties, his son would be around sixteen, I'd say. Why do you ask? queried Hawkins.

"…And what does every full-of-sap sixteen year old 'brave' want more than anything else in the whole wide world…other than "pussy"?" The madam asked with a laugh.

Hawkins pensively stared out at the rumpled up mountains' skyline before returning his roughly thought through answer.

"Fame!" responded Ben.

"Bravo! Now, what would a "Federal" title do for the boy's ego would you suppose, Detective Hawkins? Especially when you figure Big Warrior is an egotistical bully!

I'd bet that young lad would crawl ten miles in the snow for a chance to exercise some authority over his overbearing father. If you were to put the word out of him being chosen by "George Washington" to fill a newly opened position, odds will get you ten, he'll come to you like a hungry dog!" Arrogantly stated the Hermetic agent.

Ben Hawkins stood up; people all around were just beginning to stir.

"Folks, before you leave, please do not forget to place your votes on behalf of Little Warrior's "nomination" to the "Creek's Congressional Committee"!

General George Washington asked, 'Of the Creeks' braves, which one would they prefer as their "Congressional Representative"?'.

Simply cast your ballot in the usual way!

Place your peanut on the "left" if you want "Dark Horse" to represent your people; or, our local boy, "Little Warrior" on the 'right' side, who will go to Washington and do some good for us!

Your selectee will go to Washington to represent the Creek people!" Announced the Federal Indian Agent.

"Who is "Dark Horse"?" questioned Lavinia in a whisper.

"He's 'Someone's' son." Answered Benjamin.

"I've never heard of him!" bristled Lavinia.

"No one else has either, darling!"

Apparently, Ben's predawn announcement spread all the way up to the mouth of the "Tensaw River"; because, by noon, Little Warrior and his cronies had set up a liquor still near the voting square and were handing out moonshine shots and bags of hot kettle corn to their fellow Creeks before they spun around the pole three times and placed the "right" peanut in the cup. It was a landslide victory.

Ten men, six canoes, one woman and a bloodhound named 'Bean', were paddling up the "Mobile River" at sunset.

All had been "deputized" and given their 'certification medallions' which in actuality, were gold coins with King George's picture stamped on them.

With what Lavinia described as "haughty behavior", Little Warrior filled the bill.

Sharp orders coupled with snide remarks eventually caused four canoes full of Creeks to drag Little Warrior out of his birch boat. After the beating of his ass with fresh cut saplings, he was civil from there on out!

"Fort Mimms" on the "Tombigbee River" and "Fort Stoddard" on the east side of the "Alabama River" were within cannon distance of the other. Both were American installations; nevertheless, they hated the other with a passion and it wasn't in good spirit either!

* * * * *

It was suspected the "Red Sticks" had burrowed into the surrounding hills ironically named, "Mount Vernon" where the "Saint Francis of Assisi" wannabe, "Hillis Hadjo" (Adam Weishaupt) was known to live.

Although Hadjo was rarely seen, the farming residents of Mount Vernon called him the "Prophet". His soldiers, those carrying 'red' painted clubs, did not make themselves strangers to the community's three taverns; however, other than with the prostitutes, they never entwined with the locals.

"Thatch's Inn" held the most promise because it had the greatest number of horses tied up in front of it. Lavinia almost shut the place down when she sauntered into the 'house' with her red dress on!

A man who swore to his neighbors he was Blackbeard's grandson, speedily approached the 'limelighter'.

"Mam, now hold it right there! Women ain't allowed in here!" loudly exclaimed Mister Thatch.

"Well, Edward, you didn't expect these men to keep passing around your slop-bottomed wenches forever did you? I think it's time for them to have a shot at a real woman!

I'll tell you what, Mister Edward Thatch, I'll perform and then we'll split the house's nighttime drawer. If you are offended by my offer, I'll gladly prance my fine 'behind' over to your competitor across the street, with that same offer!" Coaxed Lavinia as she began removing her clothes.

"What do you say fellas? What should ole Eddie do? Do you boys want to hear Mama sing or should we go and play at the "Black Spot"?" Rebel roused the half-naked Bavarian double agent.

With his hands waving in the air, Edward Thatch surrendered to his customers' pleas. He rolled out a piano and let the 'bombshell' loose.

By sunrise, Eddie's money was gone, all the liquor had been drunk, his girls had vanished. Lavinia along with Ben and the Creeks were paddling back to their camp. The Bavarian agent had a very rare map tucked in her brassiere.

Little Warrior's mouth dropped wide open with surprise when he saw what the woman had scrounged from her mission. Rings, watches, promissory notes and money were the first things to come out of her bag. The most awestriking snitched item however, was a map of the "Holy Grounds". It was a schematic of the "target's" lair.

After hours of cautious planning, Hawkins, Little Warrior and Lavinia considered planting explosives at the mouths of every opening into the two mile stretch of Mount Vernon's foothills. The only problem with that was, Seekaboo would be killed along with the Red Sticks.

Finally, 'infiltration' won the decisive battle of strategic models. Little Warrior along with his braves, would declare themselves "expatriates" of the Creek nation and ask for asylum within the Holy Grounds.

Benjamin and Lavinia would set up an ambush site of which, somehow, their "sanction" (Weishaupt) would be lured into and killed. They along with Little Warrior, would then make their way back to Washington. That was the plan.

At sunset, five canoes stealthily made their way back up the Tookabatcha River toward Mount Vernon. From a distance, they looked like paddling bushes.

After an explosion followed by an amazingly dense bank of green fog, the passenger less boats floated aimlessly back down the river. By the time Ben and Lavinia saw what had happened, it was too late.

Hadjo's artillerymen were laying down a blanket of fire. The Culpers had no choice but to dive into the river.

With fictitious animal sounds exchanged for only a few minutes, the two agents were able to locate one another. Their well laid plan had been foiled. To both, it felt like they had been expected, but how?

'There wasn't enough time for Little Warrior's men to betray them; so, how in the devil's name did they get found out?' This was Ben's question. Lavinia's was, 'how was she going to cut Hillis Hadjo's dick off?'.

By the time the Culpers docked their canoe, it was dark. Tookabatcha had been leveled to the ground. Not a building, a voting pole nor statue, stood upright.

Parts of people not yet carried off by the animals, littered the side ditches. Deep pock marks dotted the roads the Creeks had been attacked on.

Lavinia and a cattail stalk, forensically determined that the victims' bodies had been penetrated by tiny iron balls. The ball shaped shrapnel had entered, in some cases, the person's skull and gone straight through their body and imbedded into the ground beneath their feet. Death had come to them from above, Madam Stockton concluded.

"Good Sunday morning to you both! It's going to be a scorcher today so I thought I'd drop by to see how you kids are getting along!" yelled Jeremiah Yellott down from his hot air balloon.

Like two domesticated turkeys, Ben and Lavinia frantically searched the sky for Yellott's voice source. They could not find it!

A rope then dropped from above. It dangled in front of their eyes. A request was then made from a treetop height.

"Hey, Ben! Grab that rope and secure it to that rock over there! Ya'll move aside, I'm gonna land this thing!" Yelled Yellott.

Although the balloon was quite visible from an upward looking direction, it was nearly impossible to see from any kind of far distance at all. Sheets of a ferrotype material covered the persnickety giant which made what was beneath the wrap, appear to be the same as what was surrounding it. The thing was "ninety five percent" invisible!

"Hurry, jump in! We've got to get the hell out of here! They're a couple of hundred Red Sticks coming toward us, so let's not tarry!

Untie the anchor rope, Mister Hawkins, and quickly do so!" Spoke Jeremiah in a nervous fashion.

The craft rose into the sky. Because of the Red Sticks' affective three-pronged attack, Benjamin figured he and his lover would have been killed had it not been for the amazing Captain Yellott's drop-down from the heavens.

From all the way across the river as well as from beneath the reflective sphere, the rebel Creeks launched wave after wave of metal tipped arrows. They bounced off of the balloon's mirrored skin although one slipped through Lavinia's body. She'd never made a sound while dying.

The old captain threw his arm around Benjamin. He handed the Indian agent an unopened jug of corn whiskey. The federal man then drank most of it while he watched the sun go down.

* * * * *

At 0430hrs., the silver balloon touched down on an empty field three quarters of a mile east of Fort Mims. The soil was sandy so Lavinia Stockton's body could be deeply buried in it. Jeremiah said some nice words; but, Hawkins couldn't say anything. No marker was left.

With the basket and deflated balloon safely hidden away in a miniature forest of cottonwoods, Yellott and Hawkins made their way toward the fort. Yellott won the toss so therefore, the detective had to do the talking.

A wagon with two screaming passengers interrupted their semi-collaborated story.

It was a one-horse rig with leather harnessing strips bouncing beneath the Clydesdale's hooves. 'Someone ran out of time and had to flee!' thought Yellott.

Two black men, one about twenty, the other in his early teens, were yelling at the top of their lungs. Flaming balls of green fire flew harmlessly over their heads but landed a couple of hundred feet in front of their galloping beast causing it to twist it's half ton body enough to flip the carriage upside down!

Both negroes were thrown high and far through the air but miraculously recovered and continued their panicked race toward Fort Mims. When those green fireballs hit dirt they skipped and then exploded into impressive clouds of vapor.

The wind took the fumy stuff in a direction which blocked Jeremiah's and Hawkins's view of the wooden fort. Staccato vibrations began shaking the ground beneath their hiding spot. Both men dove for cover!

An ancient root ball which for many years provided for bear cubs their first look at an Alabama swamp, was now for their unabated use. Horses and many of them as hypothesized, were the tremor agents. Black faced Red Sticks were on their horses' painted bodies.

On several occasions, the denned up men could see horse legs whip by their root ball hole. None of the Creeks stopped to look inside of it.

Strangely, there was no gunfire, no bugles, not much of anything could be smelled or heard. The vibrations returned.

This time, the retreating Indians left the fort at a snail's pace compared to the way they rode in. Many could be heard joking back and forth as they ambled by the old bears' den.

Ben thought he heard one of them use the word, "Tookabatcha" but, he wasn't sure so he didn't say anything to Captain Yellott about it. The two of them remained laying quite still.

Each knew the Creeks used clean-up crews (ghost dancers) after successful raids. Their jobs were to count the dead and to collect precious artifacts for their battle tales to come.

It was late August. The outside temperature was a sticky eighty seven degrees. Inside the bear den coupled with two stinking men stuffed in it, the degree count hit three digits. A moccasin boot darkened the den's entrance.

A pair of ghost dancers were searching for bodies. As picked up from their northern Muskogee accents, Hawkins understood their were no survivors at the fort. Two hundred and sixty five of them all accounted for; "their scalps were in the bag", one of them said.

The two white-faced dancers moved on. They pulled a child's wagon behind them. What was in that wagon will never be known for sure but whatever it was, didn't rattle much.

Weighing the value of that first breath of fresh air can only be accurately measured by someone who has been deprived of it for a considerable period of time. Jeremiah and Benjamin fell to their knees and prayed and sucked that beautiful humid Alabama air into their lungs. It was 1900hrs..

Probably, the longest minutes a man can endure during his lifetime is getting a hot air balloon launched in the night without alerting the surrounding Indians of your doing so.

"It's the goddamned light, not the noise, that lets them know what we're doing", was Jeremiah's sage remark. And, he was right.

He told Hawkins, "From the second we ignite the hydrogen gas, it will take twenty minutes to launch this baby! That's about ten minutes after we get within range of their arrows". A distraction was needed.

It was already dark so there was no need to peruse the area for a lone horse or anything like that. But, Hawkins did need to move a ten pound bomb from the balloon's basket to the other side of Fort Mims. Close to a three mile haul, all toll.

Having equipped himself for what he hoped would be an hour turnaround run, and packing the ball with an hour's worth of fuse stuck into its powder hole, Jeremiah lit the fuse a split second before Benjamin Hawkins took off running through the most visibly open field he could find.

He was sprinting toward the fort and he wanted the Red Sticks to be curious, to come after him, to be drawn to the mysterious spew, and to be blown to smithereens!

Yellott in the meantime, would be filling up the balloon while Ben circled back around in time to go skyward.

Hawkins pushed himself but kept his pace to a sustainable speed. He was halfway to the fort when the first flare exploded in the sky.

That was a bad thing because it ruined his charade but on the other hand, the flares were a great distraction from Jeremiah's fiery preparation. Hawkins's carefully put the 'sparkling' bomb on the ground.

Seeing that the balloon was lurching and its anchor rope was uprooting the sapling holding it down, it became clear to Hawkins, he wasn't going to make it. The bomb exploded behind him. Indians on horses began their pursuit of the running man.

Arrows whizzed past the detective's body as the balloon carrying Captain Yellott passed over his head. A looped rope offered one chance.

As Benjamin Hawkins reached for the bowlined anchor rope, a spear was released from an atlatl. It's velocity was so great that the spear's entire shaft passed completely through his right shoulder.

That same arm did hook into the oncoming loop but sadly Benjamin couldn't hold on and dropped onto the top of a pine tree. The Red Sticks circled around it. Two of them started to climb up the tree; they had knives clinched in their teeth.

Ben was losing a lot of blood. He could hear the climbing braves cursing him because of it dropping into their eyes. Just as the Indian agent slipped into unconsciousness, he thought of Lavinia and their making love on the banks of the Tombigbee River.

Captain Yellott began dropping hot ten-pounders on the massive mob of Red Sticks below. They threw spears and shot arrows back at him.

The first explosion alone and there were six more afterwards, killed twenty of them right off the bat! When the other bombs went off, pandemonium broke out among their war party.

Over a hundred men and eleven horses had been smitten beneath the pine tree Hawkins's was hanging on to. Yellott was attempting to land the balloon in the midst of the mayhem when Tecumseh and a thousand or more Creeks, stormed out from the swamp and chased the Red Sticks away.

Four strong warriors winched Benjamin Hawkins down from the top of the tree. He wasn't dead but close to it.

Hawkins had sustained massive puncture wounds from the atlatl launched spear, one broken-off arrow protruding from his femur and not much blood left to bleed.

A "Shaman" had Hawkins transported to a tent which had been erected on his behalf. The medicine man gave his prognosis. It was not a good one.

The Red Stick not fortunate enough to have died from one of Jeremiah's bombs, was hooked up to a modified water pump. The "witch doctor" sucked the blood out of the prisoner's femoral artery giving Ben a transfusion. It was a sloppy operation but it did the trick.

Tecumseh had a wagon pulled up from the decimated fort. He hooked up the only two cavalry horses his warriors could find on the battlefield and prepared a cot for Hawkins to lay in. The medicine men then hoisted him up and into the wagon's bed. Captain Yellott was the driver.

The ambulance of sorts, was to deliver Benjamin Hawkins to Mount Vernon. There, a "Metisse" (half Creek-half Anglo) physician named, "Dixon Bailey" who cared for the Creeks during their times of sickness, was to get the Indian agent back on his feet. The Red Sticks had been attacking both white and tribal settlements all over southern Alabama and the Creeks needed warriors!

Mount Vernon was a river town but not a big one. It was a unique place in that it's population including its government as well as the town's professionals (prostitutes-physicians), were either full-blooded Creeks or "Metis".

It symbolized were America had to go with the white mans hunger for land ownership. The Indians felt the earth was for providing food for their people.

By fencing it, the animals, the crops and the fish, were denied access into the world after death.

Besides the fact that Mount Vernon was a fully amalgamated township, it also kept a very big secret. Beneath the city was America's largest arsenal.

It was where the country's "most delicate documents" were stored along with seventy six tons of platinum bricks protecting them. Generals, presidents, military strategists, scientists and many others came to Mount Vernon for the sole purpose of making war plans.

New explosives, enhanced bullet tips, rockets and experimental weapons were all products developed under Mount Vernon's streets. On any foggy day, smells of cordite and Sulphur would remind it's natives of the goings-on below.

The Tombigbee, Alabama, Tensaw and Mobile Rivers were stuffed full of military vessels. Interestingly, some of the invasion crafts moved beneath the water's surface. At other times, muffled sounds roared through the earth's weak spots.

Even from Ben's supine perspective, he could see that Mount Vernon was a dangerous place to be. It was easy to realize, with that much firepower the United States was protecting "something" of tremendous value.

As if he could read Hawkins's mind, Captain Yellott turned around in the army wagon's seat and juxtaposed into Ben's personal hypothesis's.

"Every six weeks, the Masons and the authorized American officials, load on to those underwater things you see swimming around out there, hundreds of tons of gold.

"Here", is the main exchange point for the Cerians and Masons to consummate their millenniums long installments. Bottomline, the aliens get the gold and the Americans receive their military surplus.

Actually, that's what this whole Creek civil war is all about. The Creeks from the north, those led by the likes of "Red Eagle" and "Tustunnuggee", are convinced the white man is bent on diluting their culture into oblivion. While the southern Creeks, Tecumseh's people, who can read the tealeaves, have latched on to the white man's way of life and thusly, have greatly profited from it.

The fighting itself, is not over an ideological philosophy, it's about the bloody gold. That's why our mutually known mystery man, "Adam Weishaupt", with all of his pyrotechnic antics, is here!

He, the Red Sticks, and his cronies along with the assistance of the Spanish, the British, and French have every intention of sweeping across this country and ridding it of the "trespassing" Anglo-Saxons. But before Hadjo (Weishaupt) can make his invasion, he'll need a lot of cash and firepower.

Even a nearly dead Indian agent, can put the rest of those pieces together. Within the next four days, according to Seekaboo's latest transmission, the Red Sticks will stage an all-out assault against the southern Creeks.

Their real mission will be to rob the Cerians of their promised gold payment but our objective will be to lure the Red Sticks into a trap and then bury all of them, at sea!" said Captain Yellott.

The rest of Benjamin Hawkins's day was spent recovering from Doctor Bailey's "shade tree" surgery. Dixon's drugs were superb; so, the pain was manageable.

Twenty hours later, Hawkins was able to walk and keep his food down. That was fortunate because at seven o'clock on Thursday morning, "William Weatherford's" Red Sticks (est. 3,000 men) attacked the town's northern perimeter. "Peter McQueen" along with his warriors (est. 1,500 men), stormed the banks of the Alabama and attacked from the south.

As the Red Sticks came into view, the awaiting townsfolk and the bivouacked fort's soldiers, distinctly heard "spooky" and "ghostlike" sounds coming from the Red Sticks' fronts. But then, a most spectacular incident occurred, Hadjo rose into the sky.

The glint of the morning sun advertised the infamous "Creek Prophet's" supernatural powers. The "nerve racking" sounds continued as the "holy man" flew above the heads of his ready-to-pounce fighters.

His warriors below, began squealing like stuck pigs when their "savior" darted over the tops of Mount Vernon's church steeples. That was intimidating no doubt, but don't forget who were beneath the quaint village's streets.

Talk about whacking a beehive, about the time the Creek prophet was making his third pass over the town, somebody, Cerians or U.S. troops, no one knew, sent out precisely aimed barrages of rocket fire.

Once the smoke had cleared, Yellott claimed he saw one tiny gunboat submerge itself into the Mobile River.

Hundreds of wild-eyed Red Sticks fled in all directions. Some even ran through town black faced and butt naked.

Most were shot by Metis snipers from their home's upstairs' balconies; but, one was not. Seekaboo had finally escaped.

Having only one arrow wound in the buttocks which pretty much sums up what happened, Seekaboo on his own recognizance, walked into Doctor Dixon Bailey's office looking for some needlework and Benjamin Hawkins.

"We haven't much time. Doctor Bailey, would you kindly remove the piece of metal I have lodged in my pelvic bone. And while you're busy with your trade, Detective Hawkins and I will be doing ours!

Ben, this incredulous character portraying himself as, "Hildis Hadjo" is one dangerous man. While he charms his young followers to trace his footsteps, Adam Weishaupt and his henchmen slip into the homes of their most promising boys, kill them, dispose of their bodies, gas the witnesses, switch their places with one of Weishaupt's buddies and make it appear that things are copasetic.

William Weatherford and Peter McQueen, two cases to make my point, were and are, only figments in the Red Sticks' imaginations. Actually, those two are Masonic expatriates who also were an integral part in the attempted Cerian gold heist.

"Baron Adolph Freiherr von Knigge's" profile states, he is a Metis named, "Weatherford". "Johann Wolfgang von Goethe's" handle is that of another half breed called, "Peter McQueen". Those and hundreds more like them are scheduled to follow suit.

Detective Hawkins, it is thought that Adam Weishaupt and his projected thirty thousand Indian followers, three navies from three of America's enemies, slaves and young white men from throughout the country wishing to taste the nectar of glorious warfare, are preparing to wipe North America clean of its prosperous white people!

Andrew Jackson has summonsed you and me to Pensacola. Doctor Yellott, you are to return to your patients at Spring Grove.

I reckon we'll be moseying down to the waterfront in a bit. From here, I guess, we'll catch up with the rest of them at sea, follow our orders and I expect, go to heaven!" Said Seekaboo with a lower Muskogee drawl.

Chapter Three

The closer Seekaboo and Hawkins got to the concrete wharf the more "military" the workers started to look. Pressed indigo blue trousers, subdued buttons sewn onto white dress jackets, spit shined boots and a firearm strapped onto their thighs.

They wore a utility belt with all sorts of combat tools attached to it which squashed out any doubt in Ben's mind, as to who they were.

Last hypothesizes were expunged when the doors to a rather large craft opened up in the exact place where the two men were waiting. It was that same material, the mirrored stuff, covering Yellott's hydrogen balloon which made the vessel so difficult to see.

As soon as Seekaboo and Hawkins were seated onboard, the door squealed shut and the ship's captain came back into the passengers' area to greet them. It became crystal-clear to the Culpers they were in the middle of something far more complex than doing a hitjob on a flamboyant Bavarian.

Benjamin Hawkins's bravery was shaken when the Cerian submarine suddenly slowed to a stop. The oxygen within the ship was growing stale. The cabin's lights sputtered and then dimmed.

When the doors again opened, two masked commandos entered the passenger quarters. The soldiers came to attention and slammed their right fists onto their left breasts with the Culper salute.

Ships of all descriptions were moored within the domed port. Chinese junks, French warships, blockade-runners, you name it, they were setting tightly tied. Each seacraft was numbered.

Friendly voices interrupted their private odysseys with an invitation to join "some old friends" on the upper deck. The commandos showed them the way to the elevator doors.

When the doors opened, standing in front of the Culper agents was a delegation comprised of the most powerful Indians living on the northern hemisphere. Promptly, Seekaboo and Ben Hawkins were shown to their seats.

The welcoming smiles quickly faded from the war room's attendees' faces. Things got serious, real fast.

Tecumseh rose from his cushioned seat and stood before his eminent listeners. He was nervous as his hands slightly shook when he sipped his water glass.

"My Brothers, Hear me well, for the second time. We the Shawnees, Winnebago's, the Creeks, and the Miami's have all had our lands taken away from us. But, we have reconciled this!

Right here and among "this" group just one year ago, our people's agreed upon an amenable segregation with the decisive "Mississippi River" acting as the judge and jury. The Americans are trying to honor their end of the bargain while some of us have broken away from our tribes and joined in with the "Red Sticks"!

As we remember the death of one of our great Creek leaders, "Captain Isaacs", and more painfully recall the circumstances surrounding his murder, let us never forget how that happened. We let our guards down!

You and I, folks, 'rested on our laurels' as we laid in the shade of complacency. And while we were resting, "Paddy Welch" a man we all knew and trusted, turned. He joined the Red Sticks.

Normally, that wouldn't be a matter of much concern; however, in Paddy Welch's case, he happens to be a Niburian 'Mamba' (assassin)!

When he didn't return from one of his balloon excursions of which he did often, it was discovered the goddamned Nib had stolen a trunkful of Cerian blueprints. We now know the gravity of that!

Of course, any fool can see, "Adam Weishaupt", who holds himself out to be a prophet and a stalwart flagbearer for the "neo-Neanderthals", is identically the same "devil" attempting to turn North America into a desert.

And now with he and his new "high priest" (Paddy Welch), they just might pull it off!

Gentlemen, we shall soon be joined by another agent. His name is "John Ross". The three of you will be attached to Jackson's troops.

Our first insertion will proceed by landing craft down the "Big Escambia Creek". Seventy balloon craft will bomb the Red Sticks' headquarters with bunker busting payloads.

We expect Weishaupt's forces to flee in hopes of reaching the Floridian border and thusly securing sanction within the Spanish forts. Adam's surviving men will have no choice but to escape in a southeasterly direction.

With their destroyed Mount Vernon base and Jackson's men pushing the Red Sticks toward the southeast, the assumption is, most of Weishaupt's men will panic and run east toward the Big Escambia. Our marines will be waiting for their arrival.

Simply put, our intentions are to trap the Red Sticks within the Alabama border. We want them to believe they are safely inside the Spanish held fort at "Flomaton".

I have dispersed our intelligence agents to "Fort Atmore". They will be switching about the road signage, removing various markers and redesigning Fort Atmore so it appears to the escaping Red Sticks that they crossed over the Spanish border and made it to the fort." Concluded Tecumseh.

Ben Hawkins and Seekaboo were escorted to a landing pad where the Cherokee Chief, John Ross was waiting for them. Without any formal introduction and only a few nods of certification, the three Culpers lifted into the sky beneath an invisible hydrogen filled balloon.

Ross's orders were to land his craft two miles west of "Fort Mims" on a natural peninsula formed by the Alabama River and nicknamed, "Horseshoe Bend". There, the attachment would merge with Jackson's assault.

At two o'clock in the morning, a fleet of heavily loaded balloons attacked Hadjo's "Holy Ground". The bombs fell like sleet onto the sandy soil beneath the lethal balloons.

The bunker-busters which had been dropped from a thousand feet above Hadjo's fortress, penetrated the ceilings of the Red Stick's headquarters. Disquieting belches rumbled beneath the earth's surface. Flares confirmed that no one had escaped the underground hell.

Hundreds of Tecumseh's commandos lined the existing escape routes. The Red Sticks who were not in the headquarters at the time, were ambushed as they attempted to cross into Spanish Territory. For those escapees who tried to swim to safety, the Creek snipers stopped.

Three hundred or more, Red Sticks sprinted into the fake Spanish fort at "Atmore". All were killed.

Peter McQueen, Hadjo and hundreds of their warriors did make it to the 'real' Spanish fort in Flomaton. Judge Toulmin and others under Andrew Jackson's command, had literally chased the rebels into Fort Flomaton's gates.

Toulmin's tenacious efforts cost him eleven men. They were shot by the Spanish fort's soldiers.

"Don Mateo Gonzalez Manrique", Fort Flomaton's commander, found himself in quite a 'pickle'. A standoff ensued.

Outside of his fort's flimsy wooden walls were hundreds of Jackson's Indian fighters. A thousand or more of Tecumseh's warriors were hidden in every place an Indian could be in, and seventy bomb dropping hot air balloons were suspended above. A note from Colonel Andrew Jackson dropped from the sky; it outlined two alternatives.

"Governor Manrique, realizing that our countries are now under a peace treaty, I shall approach this situation with thoughtful alacrity; therefore, you have three hours to turn your latest "arrivals" over to the United States. After which, this encounter "never happened".

Or, if you choose to make this an international issue and stand recalcitrant on the matter, you, your fort, Hildis Hadjo and his Red Sticks followers will end-up as if their lives "never mattered". All will disappear!"

After reading Jackson's message no less than ten times, Governor Don Mateo Gonzalez Manrique looked toward the heavens and then from his office chair, he stared out at the black abyss surrounding Fort Flomaton. He called for his staff and Hildis Hadjo.

"Gentlemen, I believe we are surrounded! I have the unfortunate responsibility to tell you men, we have been given an ultimatum.

If we do not turn over to the Americans our most recent quests, "they" claim they will wipe all of us completely off the map!

Personally, I feel their threats are real; therefore, I am ordering you, Mister Hadjo, to gather together every last one of the men you brought into this goddamned fort, and leave immediately!

All we can afford to give you and your men are a thousand pounds of powder, some lead, and a promise of future support." Said the Spanish governor.

The Creek prophet then angrily stood. He turned toward the fort's staff, popped a canister of green gas open by throwing it against the log wall, shot the Spanish governor in the side of his head, waited a few moments until the gas discombobulated the officers, and ordered the fort's troops to fire on the Americans.

With the speed of a rattlesnake's strike, the Red Sticks leader and his three hundred or so warriors stripped the fort of its valuables, loaded pack mules with whiskey, munitions and food, ordered the fort's cannoneers to open fire and then slipped through the blockhouse's escape tunnel.

At the end of the mile long passageway, the rebels came out at "Burnt Corn Creek" and disappeared into the surrounding swamp.

After Jackson's men explored the smoking pit which had recently been the site of "Manrique's fort", it was discovered what the Red Sticks had so craftily done. Colonel Jackson dispatched a thirty man "tracker" unit to go after them.

"Colonel James Caller" and his bloodthirsty crew wasted no time in pursuing the runaways. As a matter of record, Colonel Caller was in such a hurry to wipeout the remaining Red Sticks, he ignored caution.

As a result, Caller and his men walked into a trap Peter McQueen had setup at the edge of a cane field. There was an artificially covered dried up pond hole, then green gas, and finally a scalping party who sent Caller's remaining three trackers screaming back to Alabama.

In essence, the Americans lost that one and the Red Sticks escaped.

By the time Ross, Hawkins and Seekaboo had regrouped and joined back up with Tecumseh and Jackson, half of the Creek fighters had deserted on account of being frightened of Hadjo's magical powers.

For a long time, the Creeks had been warned about crossing the "prophet". They had done that and now were subject to his ire.

* * * * *

Tecumseh did his dead level best to stop the panicked Creeks from believing the propaganda but superstition prevailed. About a third of the Creek nation withdrew their support for the peaceful "settlement" with the Americans and chose to back up the Red Sticks instead.

At that point, many of the tribe's young men left their villages and joined up with the renegades in Florida.

"William Weatherford", a Creek leader, and a few hundred of his skilled warriors, met up with the Red Sticks in Pensacola. Following a solid month of resupplying, recuperating and logistical planning, plus gaining a dozen Spanish cannons, the Red Sticks launched what they called, "the fall offensive". Their first onslaughts were aimed at the U.S. forts contiguously situated near the Spanish boundaries across Florida.

The week before the Red Sticks mounted their attack, Peter McQueen and William Weatherford approached Hadjo (Adam Weishaupt) with a philosophical conundrum. Their issue had to do with the survival of their mutual "clan of the wind"(the Red Sticks' nickname).

"Nativism" (sticking with the primitive old ways) was the subject of the argument. The "obvious" question was first posed by McQueen.

"We are the ones who have whacked the hornets' nest!

Our enemies include not only the white man but also those in our tribes who wish to give the Americans our land east of the Mississippi. Those I speak of have guns and greatly outnumber us.

We have fewer warriors but our "great prophet" insists we fight them with bows and arrows! I beg of you, Lord Hadjo, let us use the white man's weapons against them!"

William Weatherford humbly stood. Peter McQueen then handed him the 'talking stick'.

"Great Prophet, due to your prayers to our creator, Paddy Welch was sent to us! Should we not appreciate our god's timely gift?

We have in our hands the schematics of the 'star people's' weapons. Should we cast those away as well?

Have we not seen their underwater boats, their bomb dropping balloons and have we not felt the ground's reverberations caused by their cannons?

Of what value to us, is the stubborn idea of fighting with sticks attached to a piece of flint against an enemy who destroys us before we can get within range to launch a single arrow?

To me, it likens a rabbit tangling with an alligator; therefore, we should utilize every advantage we can in order to slay our foes!

If we return to our "natural" ways after the white giants' blood has drained from their bodies, that's well and good but for 'now', we must destroy them first!"

With a nod of approval and without speaking a single word, Hadjo left the tepee. Soon afterwards, maybe five minutes later, Paddy Welch entered the council tent. He brought his 'blueprints' with him.

For three days they planned their attacks. The Red Sticks would simultaneously attack the American forts; after that, they intended on destroying entire populations.

Their timetable covered only one year. Conventional weapons would be used before the snows came. After that, weapons would no longer be necessary.

Welch and his "smallpox" bombs would have "ole whitey" in his grave by Christmas morning.

* * * * *

It had been two months since any word of Indian attacks were reported to Tecumseh. This concerned him very much.

As any military analyst would say, 'one unseen enemy is more dangerous than a regiment of bayonet-affixed soldiers'. This was most certainly the Shawnee Chief's biggest worry.

He had to find out where the Red Sticks were and what they were planning. The answers to those questions could only be gotten in one way; they needed some prisoners. Tecumseh called for Seekaboo, John Ross and Benjamin Hawkins.

Fifteen hours later, all four of those Culpers were sitting in the basement of "Fort Morgan's" magazine room.

It was September. The temperatures were still in the 'muggy' eighties which made it difficult for them to write anything on paper. Sweat drops would blotch it; consequently, they were forced to plan their strategy by using whispers.

Their thoughts as expressed through some hand gestures and a good stick for dirt diagrams, did the job. They agreed upon an entrapment area called "Josephine", a tiny fishing village situated within ten miles from the Spanish settlement known as, "Gonzalez". It was where the Red Sticks were embedded.

John Ross suggested a nighttime 'grab and go' tactic but Hawkins felt that would be too risky. Seekaboo did come up with the plan Tecumseh agreed with which turned Seekaboo's strategy into an order.

The Gulf of Mexico was very choppy due to a gale taking place somewhere out at sea. There were many bolts of lightning seen on the horizon. Sharp wind gusts and no moon made the prospects of success favorable.

Tecumseh estimated from the desertion tallies he had received from the tribal councilmen, there were close to a thousand boys assumed to have joined Hadjo's rebels. Most were searching for adventure and thrills but that wide-eyed gullibility, made them the perfect targets for what Hadjo needed them for.

At 1300hrs. Ross surfaced a small submarine a hundred yards off the grassy shore of "Lillian" (an Indian village). With ten pounds of bacon strapped onto Ben's and Seekaboo's backs, the two swam to shore.

Knowing full well that the Red Sticks had to forage their own food and most likely were hungry, it was theorized that a few of those naïve braves might be lured by some of "mama's home cooking".

Seekaboo built a lean-to and a small fire beneath it. The bacon was set on a rock close to the flames.

Thirty mile per hour winds caught the smoked meat's smell and took it into the direction of Lillian. Within twenty minutes, three adolescents (one Creek and two Shawnee) were tied, gagged, and transferred to the submarine. There were no tracks, no fire nor even a strip of bacon left behind.

Just at sunrise, the three prisoners were interrogated in the basket of a hydrogen balloon. At a thousand feet in the sky, Tecumseh and John Ross learned two things; first, the Red Sticks were now under the leadership of Paddy Welch and were planning a full-scale attack on "Fort Sinquefield" located at the confluence of the Alabama and Tombigbee Rivers. The second thing learned, neither the Creeks nor the Shawnee could fly.

On the ground, Ben Hawkins and Seekaboo were anxiously awaiting the results of Tecumseh's interviews. With only a cursory look at the number of people standing in the landing balloon's basket, it was obvious the inquisition had been partially productive; but, something was very wrong. Both Ross's and Tecumseh's faces were white as cotton balls.

Ross had glassed the gulf's coastline as he and Tecumseh were landing their interrogation balloon. Astonishingly, British and Spanish ships were seen coming in and out of "Tiger Point". This meant only one thing, the Red Sticks had teamed up with America's most formidable enemies.

Those circumstances equated to big trouble for the practically bankrupt United States. Wars and especially major ones, drain government coffers; the Colonists were no exception.

The Red Sticks by themselves, were not that much of a threat to this country's security but when you combine them with two world powers, gargantuan fears come into play.

If what was seen at Tiger Point was indicative of other British actions taking place throughout North America, the U.S. was in for a very rough time!

Having no other choice, Tecumseh ordered a reconnaissance detail to calculate the enemy's strength.

Seekaboo and Hawkins along with five of Tecumseh's best warriors, were to make an amphibious landing that night in the swampy area just a click north of "Warrington".

Benjamin Hawkins's men were to assess the enemy's strength and to get that information back to Tecumseh by way of light-signals. "Fort Saint Michael" was the suspected British staging site so most of the mission's focus would be there.

Providing that Hawkins's team survived and if vital information was successfully transmitted back to Tecumseh, they would be extracted the following morning. If that were not possible, they were to firebomb everything 'wooden' in sight and make their way back to "Fort Morgan" as best they could.

Seven men covered in charcoal based camouflage paint, hit Warrenton's beachhead at 2000hrs.. They were so close to Fort Morgan they could hear men's voices. It sounded as if someone were preaching.

The taskforce moved like chilled worms through the swampy undergrowth. A perimeter of Spanish soldiers encircled the outside of the fort.

British marines protected the wharfs where their massive ships were docked. The guards exchanged their posts every thirty minutes by overlapping their shifts in order to beef up the waterfront's security.

Not one single square foot of the fort's surrounding grounds was without a soldier standing on it. Still, the Americans were making progress but very slowly.

Seekaboo who had managed to conceal himself within a clump of palmetto grass, began messaging numbers of this or that to Ben.

He then relayed Seekaboo's 'counts' to the next man and so on until the needed data was flickered up to John Ross two thousand feet above them.

John then signaled Tecumseh.

At one thirty, sharp, Hawkins's last transmission was sent. Ben knew as well as the other commandos were aware, they had been snookered.

The six ship British invasion was a ruse. It had been staged as a diversion to deflect the American's focus from the British's real intentions.

Rather than the suspected town of Mobile being the invasion target, "New Orleans" was the spot, instead. Ben motioned for his men to withdraw back into the swamp.

One of them had quietly died from a snakebite. The remaining six waited for their extraction submarine to surface at dawn. A light rain began to fall.

Suddenly, the earth began trembling from the hooves of cavalry horses. Mortar shells exploded above the fort's walls.

Seekaboo motioned to Hawkins's squad the immediate necessity to find cover. The Culper knew what was coming next.

As though choreographed by a devilish conductor, flares ignited in the sky, nonselective concussion grenades dropped on the scattering people as they sought to save their lives.

Two American regiments, one charged through the swamp from the east while the other unit raced in from the west.

Horrific sounds of screaming men coupled with noises from metal things cracking against human bone, filled the early morning air. The British marines attempted to move their ships out of the harbor but were blocked by their own demolished warships.

Even the word, 'mayhem' wasn't enough to describe what happened next.

Coming out of the water as if they were walking on it, hundreds of "Choctaw" "ghost warriors" began methodically approaching the fort on foot.

Each of them identically and incandescently painted as skeletons, commenced to moan like satisfied wolves. They started stacking the dead on the beach.

In less than one hour, any sight or sound of an enemy was diminished to nothing. Bonfire crews swept a square mile of the enemy's territory as 'clean' as a hound's tooth.

The dead, wounded, and captured British, Spanish, and Red Sticks casualties were decapitated.

Three hundred and sixty three headless bodies were burned as was every other combustible thing on the peninsula. Pikes or wooden stakes were sunk a foot into the beach sand and were placed six feet apart for the entire length of Fort Warrington's coast line.

The victims' scalped heads were then placed on the skyward pointing spikes. Other than that, one would have never guessed there had been anything there to begin with. Naturally, the ghost warriors disappeared just as the darkness had done when the sun arrived.

Following an out of the ordinary isolation period for those participating in the Warrington operation, Fort Morgan's lead physician, "Doctor Edward Jenner" entered the barracks. He and his medical associates began inoculating the personnel associated with the maneuver.

Tecumseh was called to the quarantined area due to the refusals by the Choctaw ghost warriors to be stuck by the intimidating needles. Finally, a deal was struck between the great Shawnee Chief and the superstitious "skeleton men"; a highly bribed Shaman would administer the "cow-blood" injections in a manner acceptable to them.

Much to Hawkins's surprise, Tecumseh, John Ross, Seekaboo and Colonel Andrew Jackson were standing around his infirmary cot when he gained consciousness. Jackson's big ole possum grin proceeded his provocative words.

"As embarrassingly factual as it is, I too react the same way as you, when forced to accept another man's jabs with a sharp piece of metal. Unfortunately, the smallpox injections we all endured, are necessary.

It appears Paddy Welch (a Niburian 'mamba') has shared a dark secret with our enemies. Therefore, I would very much appreciate it if you and Seekaboo join me in my quarters in an hour.

I would like to send a gift to the British Supreme Commander, "Admiral Alexander Cochrane" and it would be awfully nice if the American Indian Agent personally delivered it to him.

Weather predictions claim that tonight's winds will deliver us ideal launching conditions. So, as soon as you complete your little catnap, I'll fill you in on the details." Said Colonel Jackson.

* * * * *

According to the ship models laid out on the "war table", the British command ship, "Hermes" was thirty miles off the coast of New Orleans. Admiral Cochrane's fleet of twenty three marine packed warships were docked on "Half Moon Island's" eastern side. The "Hermes" was the designated target.

Prior to the balloon's dusk takeoff, a Cerian using the name, "J.P. Blanchard" spent the majority of the afternoon instructing Hawkins and Seekaboo on how to control a parachute.

Both Culpers exercised razor-sharp focus during their instructional sessions. John Ross was to pilot the hydrogen filled craft; but, he too, participated in the training exercises.

Ross was given a map and a compass. He was to reach the altitude of two thousand feet before turning the balloon toward the west and flying it a hundred and seventy eight miles to Half Moon Island. It was expected to be an eight hour flight.

Tecumseh had arranged for crews along the coastline to guide Ross's flight by building fires set every ten miles. When John reached "Chandeleur Sound" he was to climb to five thousand feet and locate the "Hermes".

At 0300hrs., Ben and Seekaboo were to exit the balloon's basket and steer their chutes onto the warship's main deck. Once there, they were to discard their parachutes, set out in search of Admiral Cochrane's quarters, deliver Jackson's present and then hide themselves on the beach located at the extreme northeastern point of the island. A submarine would fetch them at dawn.

Miraculously, the mission was flawlessly executed. However, Seekaboo and Benjamin Hawkins did debate the idea of staying onboard the "Hermes" just long enough to watch Admiral Cochrane's face when he opened up Andy's gift.

The box in which Seekaboo had strapped to his body before lifting off from the U.S. fort, contained an officer's jacket made of the multicolored scalps collected at Fort Warrington.

In the coat's breast pocket was a copy of the "Treaty of Ghent" with the word "Void" written on each page.

No one exactly knew what Cochrane's reaction was regarding Jackson's gift but semaphore messages poured into Fort Morgan's communication depot throughout the day. Hundreds of informational snippets lead to the conclusion that the "Hermes" and twenty one other British warships, had withdrawn from Half Moon Island and were headed out to sea. This disturbed Tecumseh.

Knowing full well a "scalp jacket" would not outweigh what his intelligence people called, 'Cochrane's gargantuan ego', Tecumseh ordered a 'pack' of six submarines to follow the British's movements all the way to the Atlantic Ocean.

Less than a day later, Cochrane's warships passed through "Breton Sound", and were joined by four more English troop carriers. They briefly docked at "Breton Island".

As the sun was sinking, Tecumseh's sub pack raised their periscopes so as to gather more intel on the British's actions. Although seen at first as an innocuous landing, two submarine captains spotted a group of Red Sticks being transferred from the "Hermes" to the "Tonnant".

Among the transferees were Peter McQueen, Paddy Welch and most importantly, Hildis Hadjo.

Cochrane's stopover at Breton Island lasted about an hour; after which, the "Hermes" and the original fleet of warships, turned to the southeast as if they were headed back to London. The "Tonnant" and six escorting warships then pointed their warcrafts toward the Floridian gulf. Three submarines silently remained hot in their wakes.

After a painful three-day wait, the details regarding the whereabouts of the "Tonnant" were delivered to the anxiously awaiting Culpers at Fort Morgan. Three things were learned; first, "British Admiral Nicolls" was building a standing army of five thousand men made up of escaped slaves, rank denied Spanish soldiers, and every young Indian they could recruit.

Second, gold, food, weapons, and horses were issued to each of the 'mercenaries'.

Last, Hildis Hadjo and his entourage of Indians, were on their way to England to meet the "Prince Regent to try" in an attempt to ratify the peace treaty between the Americans and the Brits.

Colonel Andrew Jackson laughed as did Tecumseh, when they discovered the degree of trust Hadjo had in the English aristocracy. But when John Ross recited a quote from Sun Tzu's book, "The Art of War" he brought the 'house' down with rabid-like hilarity.

"If you know the enemy and know yourself, you need not fear the result of a hundred battles. If you know yourself but not the enemy, for every victory gained you will also suffer a defeat. If you know neither, nor yourself, you will succumb in every battle."

With that said by John Ross, Tecumseh ordered a few bottles of scotch to be served in the fort's war room. For nearly an hour, the men enjoyed themselves until a guard knocked on the metal enforced door. He asked for Colonel Jackson.

"Sir, you have been summoned to Washington by the Secretary of War, "James Monroe". I have been ordered to place you under arrest for the charge of "Insubordination and Failure to Follow a Direct Order" as put forth by the President of the United States, "James Madison"."

"Colonel Jackson, I am to see to it, you are taken immediately to this fort's stockade until a ship arrives to return you for arraignment. But since you have been declared an 'M.I.A.' since Horseshoe Bend, I am afraid I'll have to send this order back to the 'Secretary' marked, "Unable to Deliver", Sir!" sternly stated the second lieutenant.

"Well, "Captain", please accept this bottle of scotch as a measure of condolence for your inability to fulfill a presidential command. I wish you well in your future efforts." smirked Jackson. And that was that!

Everyone in the war room knew Madison despised Jackson. The President publicly referred to him as a "reprobate" probably because he nor anyone else in the administration, could find anything wrong with him except for the fact, he enjoyed fornicating beautiful women.

It was true, Andy had a sorted past and 'yes', it was accurate to describe Andrew Jackson as a 'mass Commandment breaker' due to his ten for ten breakage record. But no one in Washington could deny, that whatever Jackson did, he did it well and with 'style' to boot!

Nevertheless, Colonel Jackson chose to 'err on the side of caution' and return to Alabama to prepare his army for a retaliatory winter attack on the British Fort at "Prospect Bluff". He thought a Christmas eve annihilation would project a clear message to both London and Washington of his point of view!

As Jackson was packing for his morning's departure, he asked Tecumseh to invite Ross, Hawkins and Seekaboo to join him for breakfast. Using a wooden tablespoon as a gavel, he called the meeting to order.

"I am far more of a Culper than an American statesman!

For that reason, I shall make an oath to give humane and considerate attention to those who have spilled their blood for America's sake. For those who have not given us at least their sweat, I sincerely pledge, quite the opposite!

Furthermore, I stake my life and intend on giving it for my belief's sake, but as far as Washington's politicians are concerned, there are no necessary evils permissible in government; its evils exist only in its abuses!" Said Andy as he gave the Culper salute and exited the room.

At four o'clock the following morning, Tecumseh awakened Ben Hawkins. A negro slave had been pulled from the "Chandeleur Sound" by a returning submarine.

"Ben, we have had a bit of luck come our way! An escaping slave from Prospect Bluff was fished out of the gulf by one of the returning submarines that was following the "Hermes".

We have him in surgery at this minute because of his long exposure in the water. "Doctor McGuire" said his chances of survival are slim due to his loss of blood from an apparent shark attack. I'm afraid we're going to lose him before we have a chance to talk with him.

McGuire says the poor fellow does not speak English; therefore, I was hoping you might be able to make some sense out of his gibberish. No doubt, he'll still be in shock when he awakens but if we can just figure out the circumstances surrounding his escape, it will at least, be of some value to us.

Mainly, we want to find out what he knows regarding Admiral Cochrane's presence in the gulf as well as anything 'British' you can get out of him before we dispose of him.

Give it your best shot, Colonel Hawkins, and maybe we can save a few thousand American lives, not that I'm putting any pressure on you, you understand!" said Tecumseh with a glitter in his eye.

Hawkins tapped on Doctor McGuire's office door.

Ben was met by a couple of brawny assistants who led him to the recovery room where McGuire and another physician were standing over the unconscious man.

Through a surgical mask, Doctor McGuire gave Ben the lowdown on his patient's condition.

"Colonel Hawkins, I do not know how this man is still alive. We are baffled by it. When he was brought here, he had lost not only some of his blood but all of it!

Mister Hawkins, not to be condescending, Sir, but I do not believe you can fathom the remarkability surrounding this man's survival; I do know, I don't! Candidly, how this man is "living" is beyond my team's scope of medical understanding.

In other words, this remarkable young negro does not appear to be human! Not in the history of medical science has there ever been an example of a person living much more than an hour in sixty degree water; this fellow did it for three days!

And what's even more incredible, he did it with no left leg! We believe a shark bit it off."

"Doctor McGuire, has he spoken?" asked the Indian agent.

"Only a bit of delirium babble but other than that, nothing." Answered McGuire.

"Could you detect any sort of accent amidst that "babble", Sir?" pressed Hawkins.

"I did not; although, "Doctor Howe" thought he 'picked up' the word, "paddy" although, none of what any of us heard, would be of any use to you, I'm afraid."

"What are the chances of me speaking with him alone, Doctor?" Ben intimidatingly asked.

"Hey, at this point, Colonel, anything and everything is fine with me. The only request I have is on behalf of science; that is, I wish to take his body to Philadelphia for examination!" said the physician as he and his associate left the recovery room.

Ben sat down at the foot of the black man's bed and began speaking to him as though the two of them were having a beer together.

"You goddamned Cerians most certainly deserve your long lifespans! Were you able to determine the type of shark that attacked you?" kidded Hawkins.

"It wasn't one; there were six of them. They were 'Tigers'." Said the opossum-sleeping Cerian.

"May I ask you your name?"

"I am, "Radama". I came from Madagascar on orders to eliminate Paddy Welch, a 'Mamba'." Said Radama in "Malagasy" (an African dialect).

"And did you succeed?" gently questioned the Culper using the French adaptation.

"No!"

"What happened?"

"Your men attacked Fort Warrington. I barely escaped."

"What is it that I can do for you?" pleaded Ben.

"Finish my job for me. Kill Welch; he is a Niburian operative!"

"Where is he?"

"Admiral Nicolls took he and Weishaupt to London. They cannot be allowed to return to America.

A biological attack on this country's waterways is slated for December. The Europeans are in on it and…." Radama died.

Chapter Four

Benjamin Hawkins sat in his chair watching Radama's body change into a chalky white color. No one was yet aware of the Cerian's death.

Hawkins allowed the moments of reverence to serve as a reflective time for himself and for what he imagined the man's "life" was like. He said farewell to Radama.

The fort's doctors would want to examine the black man's cadaver as quickly as they could get their rubbery hands on it. But, as the Indian agent knew, Tecumseh's security concerns would clash with the scientific community's expectations.

Only a few of the American soldiers were aware of the Cerians' existence on the planet; therefore, the military physicians would likely be denied their autopsy.

There were some heated exchanges expressed by Fort Morgan's medical team when ten black suited men entered the recovery room.

Doctor McGuire was the most adamant with his well-trodden remarks on the 'for science's sake' argument; although, that debate was cut short with a little "Tatzelwurm" spray(green gas) administered by one of the black-suited body snatchers.

Benjamin Hawkins reported to Tecumseh's office as blared through his quarter's wall mounted speaker. In anticipation of a post-mortem report, Ben had jotted down Radama's statements but when he entered the great Chief's headquarters, he realized the worthlessness of his scribbling.

Seated around the war room's circular table were the same group of 'black suited' men who had zipped up Radama's body and carted it off.

When they removed the globes from their heads, Hawkins concluded, the meeting he had been called to was to confront something of far more significance than a recap of a Cerian's deathbed statements. Tecumseh was the first to speak.

"Colonel Hawkins, I believe it goes without saying, this meeting is of grave importance to the survival of America. Ben, we're in trouble!

As you and Seekaboo surmised, the British and Spanish maneuvers in and around the gulf coasts were a ruse. Their well-executed attacks were a diversion.

While we were slapping mosquitoes and chasing Red Sticks through the swamps, British forces under "General Robert Ross's" command, attacked Washington from the Maryland side and burned the Capitol to the ground. Several congressmen and other officials were killed as they attempted to flee.

The "Library of Congress" along with the "House of Representatives" were also lost. Thanks to Cerian intervention which plagued the Brits with 'lightening bolts', we were able to save most of the city.

Colonel, we have another mission for you. You'll be given the details later on today but let us be clear, it is likely, you won't return from it.

Write your last wishes on a piece of paper and I'll see to it they are consummated as instructed." Bluntly ended Tecumseh.

"Chief Tecumseh, did the "President" survive?" Hastily asked Hawkins.

"Well, Ben, why don't you ask him yourself!" said Tecumseh as "James Madison" stood to speak.

"By the look on your face, Colonel Hawkins, it seems as if you have just seen a ghost!

The truth is, Sir, you would be viewing my "goblin" if it hadn't been for the very swift actions of "Dolly" and her chambermaid. They are all quite safe now and in good hands, thanks to God!

"Ben", if I may call you by your first name, (Hawkins nodded), over the past five years, British intelligence has been sending boatloads of men and women to our country in order to keep them "informed" of our governmental doings.

These spies and there is no better word to describe them, have embedded themselves throughout our society. Parsimoniously speaking, they are everywhere!

Not only have they effected our country but others' as well!

We believe "King George III" has his sights set on world domination. Much like his father, the British Empire is the vehicle he is using to disguise those private ambitions of his.

Due to the war with his French neighbors, King George has beefed up his security forces to such a degree, it is nearly impossible to penetrate the kingdom. That, Colonel Hawkins, is where you enter the picture.

In four hours, you and eighteen other 'specialists' will set sail on the "Prince de Neufchatel" for the Florida peninsula. "Noah Brown", your captain and fellow Culper, will remain within five miles of the coastline and will continue around the tip of Florida until the ship rounds the "Keys".

Along the way, Captain Brown will occasionally fire off a volley of cannon fire when within earshot of a British port. Once he is assured the 'Neufchatel' has been reported to the awaiting "men-of-war", he will then provoke the British warships to chase him all the way to Liverpool.

When Noah's ship reaches the eastern side of Cuba our submarines will sink all but one of her trailing British warships.

The "H.M.S. Leander" will then surrender itself to the surrounding pack of surfaced submarines. It's crew will be removed.

"Noah Brown" and your men will be dressed in British naval garb as you take the "Leander" into Liverpool. The "Prince de Neufchatel" will be in-tow.

Once in sight of the Liverpool harbor, an explosion will occur in the "Leander's" hold, leaving the man-of-war in flames.

The "limeys" will do all they can to save their warship and it's in-tow prize.

But alas, another timed blast will occur; but, this time, it will happen to the "Neufchatel" which will most likely cause enough pandemonium for your men to make their ways onto English soil.

Ben, this phase of your mission is designed to create havoc; therefore, it will provide enough time for you to insert yourself. There will be no objections from Washington if additional collateral is taken. Just remember, your main responsibility is to eliminate Welch and Weishaupt!

Each man assigned to the operation has been given their own agenda. In case of capture, none of your men including you, will be aware of the others' specific reasons for being there.

Colonel Hawkins, once your team arrives in Liverpool and make their ways into London, there will be a number of explosions.

"Anarchy" among the populace, will become your only ally; wisely use it to your advantage!

Our analysts conclude, if six (a third) of your task force reach London by the fifteenth of October, a five day window will be opened for you. This is because of an annual celebration taking place honoring London's breweries.

Starting on Monday, the seventeenth, and running till midnight the twenty second, the city's taverns will open their doors to its patrons and offer free mugs of stout and porter to all!

Parades will occur hourly; therefore, movement throughout the city should be of little difficulty.

You are to meet our 'London Man', "George Crick" at the "Old Bell Public House" at noon on the "twelfth". The identification code name is, "Feather".

Your extraction point will be at "Lambeth Marsh" on the "twenty fourth" at 0500hrs.. Do you have any questions or concerns, Sir?" asked Madison with a regretful smile slitting across his face.

"None, Sir." answered Hawkins.

Tecumseh then stood. He handed an ornate metal box to the Culper. Using a somber voice, he spoke.

"This is America's gift to "King George". In this cubical are four gaming darts. Their tips are coated with a poison our Cerian friends call, "Porphyria".

Its purpose is to eradicate the "Hanover" bloodline. I wish you good hunting, my friend!"

Benjamin Hawkins was then removed from the war room by four black-suited men. He was escorted to an elevator which eventually took him to a landing pad located on the roof of a building standing at the southernmost point of the compound. Hawkins was told to be seated and to wait until, "his ride" came.

*　*　*　*　*

At eight o'clock, a newspaper was slid under Benjamin Hawkins' room's door. Ben remained completely still in his supine position. He was demanding of his senses to convince him, he was not in hell.

Following a reasonably determined conclusion, Hawkins elected recollection as his tool. Beyond sitting on the landing pad's bench, he drew a blank; although, he did recall the President's detailed instructions, quite clearly.

With courageous effort, Ben sprang from his overstuffed mattress and opened the curtains. Londoners by the hundreds, were lined up and down "Ely Place" as if they were expecting something to happen.

Drum beats and cheers seemed to heighten in volume by the minute. Ben Hawkins picked up the mysteriously delivered copy of, "THE TIMES" dated, October 12, 1814.

On the paper's first page, headlines pertaining to a captured American ship named the "Prince de Neufchatel", exploding in the Liverpool Harbor.

The article praised the navy for their exquisite marksmanship and awkwardly touted the 'no survivors' results. Someone knocked on the door.

Benjamin frantically rummaged through his suite's drawers. Sweaters, shirts, pistols, ropes, and two cases of explosive materials had been cleverly arranged in the bottom of his travel trunk.

Grabbing one of the weapons and after checking it's factual load, Ben spoke using his best "cockney" accent.

"Yes? How may I help you?"

"Sir, welcome to the "Mitre Inn"!

My name is, "O'Connor". I shall be your "good-man" throughout your stay. If I may be of any assistance to you, please do not hesitate to ring me; just give the chain beside your nightstand a tug and I'll stand ready to offer you the best service in England!"

"Thank you, O'Connor. I shall keep that in mind." said Ben as he uncocked his mare's leg shotgun.

Through his telescope, Ben saw that the crowd noises were coming from a wedding ceremony taking place in the "Saint John Baptist Church". It was directly across "High Street" from the "Mitre Inn".

According to the Inn's complimentary city map, "The Old Bell Public House" was only steps away from the Mitre.

This would allow enough time to prepare for his meeting with Mister Crick at noon. He had two hours to do it in.

At eleven o'clock, Benjamin Hawkins left the Mitre Inn and began a southward stroll down High Street. When he came to the spot where the "Lambeth Marsh" oozed into the "Thames River", he crossed the street and stopped off at "The Man" for a taste of their famous ale.

He repeated his surveillance stop-offs several times until he came to the "Fleet Street" intersection. The "Old Bell" was just ahead. The time was 1156hrs..

The area was packed with stagecoaches dropping tourists off and picking them up again when they were unable to walk to another pub.

Smells of vomit and aged urine competed with the vendors' delectable sausages smoking on their grills.

Constables did their best to control the mass of inebriated citizens but fistfights were breaking out like brush fires. Prostitutes of all shapes and colors worked their 'Johns' from the shadowy alleyways. Beggars performed their tragic skits hoping to top-off their tin cups with shillings.

The Old Bell was three stories tall. Tables on all three floors surrounded the centrally located bar. This ergonomic mishap forced the waiters to serve the tables offering the highest gratuities.

Empty crocks tossed by disgruntled customers fell like hail upon those foolish enough to miscue their position inline. 'It was a terrible place to meet Mister Crick', Ben thought to himself.

At twelve thirty five, Hawkins, who was still waiting to enter the Old Bell, noticed a lone individual standing on the balcony of a flat situated across the street and atop the "Rose and Crown Pub".

The ancient fellow raised a megaphone to his lips and audaciously began berating the mobs of thirsty imbibers below him.

That went on for a few moments until a group of men started throwing street debris at the megaphone holding agitator. Totally 'out of the blue', a policeman on horseback quelled the ruckus by whacking his 'billy-club' against Ben's head.

Two stretcher baring gentlemen carried the unconscious American into the alleyway beside the "Rose and Crown" and then up two flights of the fire escape stairs and into Mister Crick's "well-appointed" home.

The incident appeared as if nothing out of the ordinary had occurred. No one seemed concerned.

"Welcome to London, Colonel Hawkins!

Sorry, old chap, actually, I had no other choice in the matter!

The 'Black Knights' from the "Saint Albans Diocese" have been tailing you since you left the Mitre a couple of hours ago; however, they're no longer a problem.

Ah yes, I believe I'm supposed to say the word, 'Feather' but at this phase of the game, that seems a bit ridiculous if you don't mind my saying so!

Believe it or not, I have ice. Put this on that goose egg of yours while I fix you a drink. Scotch isn't it?" teased Crick.

"Why were the "Diocese" people following me, Mister Crick?" asked the recovering Culper.

"Call me, "George". Because they do that to everybody who fits their paranoid profiles; i.e., any middle aged male with the ability to pour piss out of a boot fits into their covey holes!

Actually, the real reason is because of the number of French spies fitting your characteristics, that's all. Do you have the box of darts Tecumseh gave you?"

"I do, George. But, can you tell me what I'm supposed to use them for?" questioned Ben.

"Colonel, of course I can; but, for your own sake, I shall not!

Ben, if the King's 'Watchmen' ever got their hands on you, they'd have you admitting the number of times you masturbated as a pimply faced teenager!

Those bloody boobs have mastered their craft. We just can't take the chance, ole boy; I'm sorry." Said Crick.

Ben handed George Crick the metal box. With a tool resembling a tuning fork but thinner in width, the double agent popped open the case's outer covering. Crick withdrew a pea-sized piece of squared glass of which, he placed under a microscope.

After a second or two of dial turning, George Crick asked Ben to take a look at the magnified slide. It displayed the addresses of the safe houses where Paddy Welch and Adam Weishaupt most likely were hiding.

Hawkins had before his eyes, the builders' blueprints of King George's residence, "The Windsor House". Not only did Ben have the King's house plans, he also had his travel agenda for the month. Ben lifted his eyes from the optical and turned toward Crick.

"This is incredible, George!" gasped Benjamin Hawkins.

"Thank you, Sir. It took me several months to prepare for this occasion so I hope you'll tolerate my suggestions as you ready yourself for the completion of this particular job.

To begin with, I am not in favor of suicide missions. I much prefer serving my enemies a cold pogrom; after which, 'they die not knowing who, what, or why their deaths happened'!

That being said, let me toss out for you an interesting little scheme I've cooked up. Do you know anything about the game of 'Cricket', Colonel?" chortled George.

"Not a thing." answered Hawkins.

"Splendid!"

"Are you being facetious, George?"

"Not in the least. It's just that claques (paid applauders) usually don't.

You see, you are going to be the official 'Ball-man'. You will guard the game balls." chuckled George Crick.

"Sir, you are confusing me; please explain!"

"Tomorrow afternoon, beginning at two o'clock, there is a highly anticipated match scheduled at "Lord's Field". I, being the chairperson of the "Marylebone Cricket Club", am the "Master of Ceremony". You, Colonel, will be the 'keeper of the game balls'." said Crick.

"George, I do not know anything about "Cricket". Surely you have a reason for this appointment, Sir?"

"Indeed I do, Ben. Allow me to explain.

'Cricket' is a game for only those with ties to the British Royal Families. Like most families belonging to their ilk, they do their best to 'outshine' their cousins and brothers and so on!

One of their favorite methods of doing this is through challenges made from one family to the other. Sometimes it's done through horse racing, extravagant balls, sailing and in this case, a cricket tournament.

Since a cricket match is played on a circular field, the challenging family is galleried on the north side of the field while on the south side, the same setup exists for the challenge acceptors. Each royal group then attempts to intimidate the other by ostentatiously out-strutting the other.

Elephants, orchestras, fireworks, and esteemed guests are the usual enviable instruments used on the other. Now, if you'll remember from the slide you viewed, King George will be seated in the pavilion on the north side of "Lord's Field".

His guests will be none other than two fully 'painted-up' Indians by the names of "Paddy Welch" and "Adam Weishaupt"!

Are you getting a better understanding of the game of "Cricket", Mister Hawkins?"

"Absolutely." answered Ben.

"You will be wearing an oversized French Admiral's uniform. You are to deliver the game ball to the winner's side after each of the four matches to be played.

In your gloved, I repeat, 'gloved' hand, you will present the winner's prize to the royal acceptor who will then loudly scold you for your absurdity!

Ben, did I tell you this was a 'shitty' assignment?" snickered George Crick.

"No, sir!"

"Actually it's not so bad; but, do expect to be insulted by the uppity-ups' personal strumpets.

Their wives do not attend such events; therefore, they'll be plenty of "cockfighting" going on. Meaning, the more degrading they are to you, the larger their 'penises' become in their minds. Sounds fun doesn't it?"

"I'm looking forward to it. Are you planning for those cricket balls to explode?" reluctantly asked the Indian agent.

"Heavens no! But nonetheless, it was a damn good question. Those darts you brought are in actuality, heavy duty syringes.

Just before we pull out in the morning, we'll fill the balls' cork cores with the porphyria agent your "Princeton" boys concocted.

With luck, the whole corrupt bunch, will be pissing blue streams by the new year!" cackled George.

"Will it kill our Indian friends?" pushed Hawkins.

"Not before you do, my friend!

Remember what I said about my aversion to suicide, Ben. We're just cleaning out the 'blue-bloods' for now; we'll get to our "feathered friends" next. I promise you that!"

"When do you propose we do that, George?" asked the impatient Indian agent.

"Slow up, old chum! We've got to focus on our Cricket match first. I am waiting on some information on just that, as we speak.

As soon as we find out the player lineups for tomorrow's matches, I'll have a more accurate estimation of the answer to your question!"

"Mister Crick, shouldn't I be getting back to the Mitre in case those Black Knight characters are wondering where I got off to?" questioned Hawkins.

"Unfortunately, Mister Hawkins, "your body" has already been scooted off to the public cemetery. Apparently the constable's crowning you received, was a bit too harsh for your skull's tensile strength.

You and all the rest of the celebratory week's fatalities, won't be displayed until Monday. If no one claims your body by then, they'll burn the whole lot of you poor blokes." Sardonically snickered George.

"What about my trunk?"

"Ah, that thing. It was brought here long before your arrival, Ben."

"I assume, the "TIME'S" article was nothing more than 'bologna' for my benefit! Correct?" queried Benjamin.

"Of course!" laughed Crick.

"Damn! Well, in that case, what's next?"

"We drink and be merry. I'll show you to your room."

* * * * *

At three o'clock, George Crick tapped on Ben's door.

"Good news had arrived!

The 'Surrey Boys', all bloody damn three of them, accepted our offer! They'll be on "Lord Frederick Beauclerk's" team!

What this means, my sleepy-headed friend is, ole "Douglas Kinnaird's" "Woodsmen" are going to get an excellent spanking tomorrow!" gleefully exclaimed the British double agent.

"What can I do?" groggily asked Ben.

"Let's get you fitted into your 'Napoleonic' outfit!

Here, put this on and we'll see how ridiculous we can make you look!

While I'm pinning on these medals to this oversized admiral's jacket, you can practice walking in your new shoes. I believe the green sparkles match your eyes pretty much to a tee, don't you think, Ben?" said George with a sly grin.

"What about my face?"

"That's the best part! You'll be wearing a "Little General's" facemask; it's a beauty!"

"What about the gloves you mentioned, George?"

"Actually they're mitts. With a little practice you'll be able to thread a needle with them on; but, they're really worn to titillate the royals' fancy. bellowed Crick.

As the sun was setting and George and Ben were showing signs of fatigue, a mob of drunken "ballers" gathered beneath George Crick's balcony.

George explained to Hawkins, they were professional odd's-setters and were there to get some 'insider's' viewpoints on tomorrow's match.

"Ahoy there, Captain!

Since you're the M.C.C.'s president and all, and seeing as we're just commoners, we was just wondering whom you might guess will be our "parade celebrities" this coming Monday!

We hear, ole Kinnaird is doing some 'midnight recruiting' and we wanted to know if you'd caught any wind of that?" hollered one of the professional gamblers.

"Guvnor, that would be quite irregular if such a thing were to happen, such as you said!

The rules are quite clear to both teams; that is, all participants must have been on the roster as were posted on every front door and on every tavern in this city, last week!

Shenanigans will not happen under my watch and you can bet your booty on that; however, "Jem Broadbridge" and "Benjamin Dark" are in fact, signed up on the Woodsmen's team which is certainly going to give the King's "Tigers" a run for their money!

But understand, those boys will be up against "John T. Jones" and "Geoffrey Wells" on G-three's squad, so don't underestimate either!

However, if I were to make a wager on one or the other, I guess I'd lay my money down on the......(George profusely coughed)."

He then waved goodbye to the mob below, shut the blinds, and then poured himself and Ben a big drink.

With a half-guilty smile etching across his stubbly chin, he spoke in a whisper.

"We are on "go"." muttered Crick.

"How do you know that, George?" queried Benjamin Hawkins.

"Those chaps would have never shown up otherwise!"

"So, what do we do next?" stuttered Ben.

"I'm going to sip on this excellent scotch while you practice your ball handling. Let's get you back into your full regalia and do a few runs with your mitts and mask on.

We'll rehearse with the "pre-stuck" game balls, if you don't mind?" Chuckled Crick.

That's exactly what Ben Hawkins did for the entire evening until the time came to inject the cricket balls with the dart (appearing) syringes. It was midnight.

George Crick went to his coat closet as if he were searching for his jacket. Hawkins heard keys rattling and a safe's door open. Seconds later, what looked like a dueling pistols box was laid out on the kitchen's table.

Four white leather balls with a dual set of ringed stitches surrounding each of them, were set in a mahogany presentation box. The cricket balls reminded Ben of coconut cupcakes.

Each ball was laid within a velvet indentation. The presentation case's material matched the crimson stitching stripes.

George plucked one of the darts out of the metal case. Within his gloved hands, he removed a single cricket ball from the presentation case and jabbed the heavily gauged needle point into a stitching hole until it made contact with the ball's cork center. He repeated that process on the rest of the game balls.

Crick closed the box's lid, locked it, and returned it to his safe. He nodded to Hawkins indicating that the balls were now ready for avarice handling.

"We're hot!" said George Crick with a wink of his eye.

"How do they work, George?"

"Very slowly. After a couple of weeks of setting on ole George's trophy room's shelf, the "porphyria agent" will become absorbed by the core's wrapping as well as into the balls' cowhide covers. Evaporation will then do its job!"

"So, how shall we kill the Indians?" anxiously queried Hawkins."

"Oh, we're going to drown them, Mister Hawkins!" cattily answered George.

"Drown them, Sir?"

"Monday evening!

Now get some sleep; you've a big day ahead of you!"

* * * * *

"Chipping Barnet's St John the Baptist Church's" bells announced the beginning of its Sunday morning service. Crick and Hawkins ate a hardy breakfast of boiled ham, beans and poached eggs and then got dressed up.

At twelve thirty, a six horse carriage arrived in front of the "Rose and Crown Tavern". Six minutes later, four heavily armed soldiers banged on George Crick's door.

With a consoling nod and smile, George opened his flat's front door and dramatically pointed out the "Napoleonic" dressed Indian agent to the officers.

Ten minutes following his overly animated arrest, Ben found himself chained to the carriage's rear. In his sparkling green shoes and attired in the baggy French admiral's uniform along with wearing the Buonaparte mask, the "High Street" curb gawkers had no difficulty whatsoever making Ben their target.

For two miles, despite the cheerful music being played by the royal band marching behind him, Hawkins was peppered with organic substances of all sorts.

Twice, Ben's mask was knocked off by thrown cabbage heads and twice it was refitted by the armed guardsman following him.

Finally, they arrived at "Lord's Ground" where Ben's trousers were lowered to his ankles. While competing orchestras played and fireworks hissed across the sky, Benjamin Hawkins was made to shuffle around the cricket field two dozen times.

Hundreds of Londoners applauded from outside the surrounding fence as Hawkins sped around the infield at an impressive speed considering his hindrances.

Just as George Crick had said would happen, the royals' concubines offered Benjamin no slack!

As the "Marylebone Cricket Club's" (M.C.C.) Master of Ceremony (George Crick), was presenting the match's ballplayers, Hawkins glanced up into the north pavilion's gallery. All three "sanctions" were having a gay ole time.

Once Paddy, Adam and King George were spotted, Ben Hawkins took on his 'in character' role with even greater zeal. Even though he was the butt of their defamatory jokes, the Culper beautifully performed the part of a clumsy French fool.

"Blue piss" was what kept Ben going through the whole thing.

No doubt, the first inning played would have gone until dark had it not been for Douglas Kinnaird's 'Woodsmen' walking out of the stadium. One of them found out that the Surry boys were 'illegally' bowling under fictitious names; thusly, Crick declared, a "Tie".

Consequently, Ben presented two balls to each team despite the fact that the 'Tigers' had 296 'runs' (with no batters out) before the Woodsmen even got a chance to hit their very first ball. Despite the 'foul-ish' upset, the royal party went on until dawn.

George Crick and Hawkins returned to Crick's flat around ten o'clock Monday morning. They changed into their befitting inspector's uniforms.

British law required all sellers of alcoholic beverages be approved by his Majesty's public health officials prior to any 'common mans' function where those beverages were "freely" distributed.

This meant, "Chief Inspector George Crick" and his thirty assistants, were to "mouth test" an ounce of a tavern's or inn's free samplings before being certified as "Acceptable" for public consumption.

Once a brewery or distributor was deemed 'acceptable', a medallion was hammered into the approved cask(s) which allowed it to be drawn into the thousands of celebrates' personal mugs.

Ben saw this as a fairly fun task until George Crick told him the number of establishments the two of them had to certify!

Three hundred and forty seven drink houses had to be tested before the businesses could be opened to the awaiting crock holding commoners already lined up at their doors. The parade was set to kick off the week's gala at four o'clock.

Inspector Crick sent his deputies south to cover the areas east and west of the "Tavistock Arms Company". Hawkins and he, would certify the sector between "New and Great Russell Streets".

The others' had regular metal certification medallions to hammer into the casks while Ben's and George's were made of lithium.

Around 11:30 a.m. George Crick and Benjamin Hawkins entered the extensive "Bainbridge Street Brewery" purportedly owned by "Henry Meux and Company".

The "and Company" as all those in the know would tell you, actually was King George's 'stash kitty'.

It was where he put the 'surplus gold' his navy had commandeered from pirates or from frivolous altruistic collections the empire didn't really need.

Using a ladder, Benjamin "inspected" a three-story-tall wooden vat girdled with four heavy iron hoops in which the black beer fermented. From down below, Crick instructed him as to how and where to hammer-in the water-reactive medallion.

"Ben, tap that bloody thing just above that hoop nearest the top of that vat. Be very mindful of your sweat dripping on the validation piece or they'll be fishing us both out of the "Thames River" tomorrow!"

"How much porter (malted beer) would you guess is in one of these vats, George?" quizzingly asked Ben.

"This one holds a ten month old brew which would come pretty close to a million pints of the stuff!"

"Jesus, man, this warehouse has more than twenty of these bastards spread out all over this building!" Hawkins said from twenty two feet in the air.

"Son, you're leaning up against more than five hundred tons of liquid!

If I were you, I'd focus on what you are doing. They'll be plenty of time to golly-wop when this is done!" scolded Crick.

The two men pugnaciously labored for three quick passing hours before the sounds of a military band was heard from about a mile away.

"The Beer Festival" parade was about to begin. The Culpers returned to Crick's flat.

Because there were no drainage pipes in the "St. Giles" neighborhood and due to the sad fact the parade's participants would have to walk up the cobblestoned incline, it was the ideal spot to have lit the first charge's fuse, which they had done.

It was set to go off in the "Man Inn" at 5:30 p.m..

From George's balcony, Ben could see the sharp flickers of the sunlight bouncing off of King George's renowned 'Tuba Brigade's' instruments.

The noise of squealing circus animals and out-of-control parade watchers, was deafening even from where Ben and George were sitting twenty feet above the crowd.

Behind the trapeze artists performing their stunts above the platformed float, came two more circus acts. One of them had monkeys that were reaching for the folks foolish enough to disbelieve the creatures were born as thieving felons.

On the second float was a caged box with a black bear and a kangaroo "duking" it out. Crick handed Ben a glass of scotch while he lit up a cigar. The time was 5:25.

Shortly after the clowns had handed out their remaining flyers advertising their "Big Top Show" scheduled for later that night, the cricket teams made their debut.

As they turned up "New Street", George Crick pointed out the trailing six carriages carrying two Indians, King George, and the Royal Family. It was then, a massive explosion occurred.

The force of the blast sent bricks raining over the tops of houses on "Great Russell Street" and collapsed any flimsily built structure for as far as the eye could see.

A torrent of porter rushed through the narrow lanes of the surrounding neighborhood and swept away everything in its path!

With no drainage on the city streets, the wave of black liquid had nowhere to go except straight into the citizens' homes. People scaled anything they could to escape the tsunami of beer racing toward them.

The deluge lifted everything in its surge. Carriages, cricket players, exotic animals were submerged by the frothy tidal wave of porter.

Chaos overtook good order.

Church bells from miles around, began senselessly clanging as the earth threatened to shake their stone structures down into the swiftly moving river surrounding them.

Soldiers wading in waist high grog, did their best to quiet the panicky gawkers. As they said, "they were listening for the royal survivors' calls for help!"

At quarter till six, the last malted wave made its pass down New Street. In its wake was an eerie sense of desolation and an awfulness usually felt by survivors of an earthquake.

With a sadistic tone in his voice, George Crick invited Hawkins back into the flat. He said, "he needed some help lowering a gift into the troubled waters below".

From George Crick's balcony, he and Ben Hawkins lowered into the meandering stream of beer, a miniature replica of the infamous American warship, the "U.S.S. ASP". The stars and stripes fluttered atop the model's highest mast as it made its way toward the frothy pool of debris down the street.

To Ben's surprise, Crick's face carried a look of utter despair. He began sobbing the moment Hawkins laid a consoling hand upon his shoulder.

"Ben, we killed a lot of innocent people today!" George said with chocked words.

"Yes we did; but, try to imagine the effect it had on the King!

Think of the thousands of American lives this brilliantly devised 'vendetta' saved.

Afterall, they did burn our capitol down to the ground, George!" angrily said Hawkins.

"Ben, I want you to immediately make your way to "Saint John's the Baptist Church". A Friar named, "Chris Ferris" will see to it, you make your rendezvous with your people.

He will meet you at 0100hrs. in the church's cemetery.

Colonel Hawkins, you can expect the King's men to be crawling over this place within the hour. It will be safer if you use the rooftops to make your getaway!

Take nothing in your pockets but this bottle of poison. Should George's men get their hands on you, ole chap, do not hesitate to swallow its entire contents!

It will be far better than what they would have instore for you! Goodbye, Ben."

Hawkins climbed a wooden ladder which led to the attic's escape hatch onto the roof. From Ben's angle of sight, he could see the flood's destructive pathway.

Men's voices echoed throughout the alleyways beneath. Dampened wood smoke hovered in greenish clouds making it impossible for Benjamin to get his baring.

Saint John's steeple was his only guidance marker. The murky fumes and the roofs' pitches slowed Ben's movements to a crawl.

Firefighter brigades were clanging bells and intermittently blowing whistles to signal those trapped alive. Town criers announced to the listeners, the breaking news.

Soldiers huddled around every street corner.

Seven buildings away, the Rose and Crown Tavern with George Crick's flat above it, blew to smithereens. Crick's doings were now sealed within the mushroom cloud traveling upward. 'He was forgiven', Benjamin Hawkins thought.

An iron trellises, thick with pedal less roses, served as Ben's escape ladder down to street level. He joined in with a crowd of "scavangers" searching through the wet rubbish for things of value. No one asked questions.

After a six block walk toward St. John's, Hawkins sensed he was being followed. Twice, he had noticed the same face on two different street locations. Ben ducked into a previously flooded alley.

Cautiously, a man walked by the lightless alleyway and stopped. This allowed a gas fed streetlamp to offer Hawkins a look at his tail's face.

The man lit his pipe as if preparing to continue his journey up High Street; instead, he turned into the bricked passageway and walked toward Ben's hiding place. He introduced himself.

"I am, "Detective Jack Whicher" and a friend of George Crick's. Don't worry, Colonel Hawkins, George is alive but under the circumstances, he thought it best to lay low for a little while.

Sadly, Weishaupt and Welch escaped. There will be no need to meet the Friar tonight.

I'm afraid he had an accident while attempting to repair his church's bell; apparently, the explosion within the bowels of the Mitre Inn, shook the bell tower's stairs loose and poor ole Chris Ferris paid the consequence for his missteps."

Ben remained still. 'Something was very wrong. Saint John's the Baptist Church had no bell tower; they had tortured George before they killed him!' Ben callously surmised.

Detective Whicher stood in the mouth of the alley for an elongated minute before tapping out the last ashes from his pipe on his bootheel. He then backed out of the alleyway never taking his eyes off the black cubicle he was staring into.

Luckily, through his night adjusted eyes, Hawkins noticed several vegetable boxes strewn out in the rear of his bricked hiding spot. He counted eight of them.

Doing some quick calculations, Ben figured, 'if he were able to stack the crates in such a way, he could reach the bottom rung of a fire escape ladder'.

Following what seemed to Hawkins as an eternity, he climbed to the roof of a salvage building. From the top of the abandoned structure, it became obvious that "Whicher" had expected him to run from the alley once he thought the detective had moved on.

In an eerie execution styled formation, a squad of soldiers stood with their rifles pointed at the alleyway's only exit. Benjamin felt in his pocket for the bottle of poison. Discomfortingly, it was still there.

Ben crawled around the roof's perimeter occasionally peeking over its edge to see what was below. Detective Whicher's henchmen had cordoned off the dilapidated structure. Ben Hawkins knew it was only a matter of time before they got to him.

From blocks away, the voice of a town crier announced the time. Ben had less than two hours to make it to the "Lambeth Marsh".

He heard soldiers beating down the salvage company's front door. But then, the Culper saw a discarded chimneysweep's brush head laying on the rooftop.

Knowing, British law required monthly scrubbings of active chimneys, Hawkins on hands and knees, made his way to the building's chimney top.

Iron rungs explained the broken brush head; they were the chimneysweep's ladder used to follow George I's fire prevention edict. Ben Hawkins began his forty feet of descent.

By 0420hrs., Ben had made it to the marsh's edge. The Thames River was covered with the King's patrol sloops. The marines were exploring the coves and inlets which lead into the swamp.

Ben submerged himself within the shallows of a sewage full backwash. A reed served as his only air supply. Time passed.

What seemed like a million heartbeats later, Benjamin Hawkins felt the hands of a frogman grip his ankles. A breathing apparatus was shoved into his mouth.

Three rubber suited divers guided Hawkins into the depths of the river. A metal door wheel was spun twice in a counterclockwise direction until the sub's watertight hatch opened.

A little while later, Ben found himself on the deck of a beached schooner. He was in "Nassau".

Chapter Five

Ben laid on the old sloop's deck for nearly an hour. He tried his best to recall what happened following his underwater rescue from 'Lambeth Marsh'.

Judging from the sun's position in the sky, Hawkins guessed it was around nine o'clock. There were no visible clouds in the sky which turned the miles of sugar white sand into a dangerous thing to walk upon.

Two shimmering dots wavered at a distance on the beachside of the horizon. There were nothing but birds sitting on the turquoise sea. It was windy so the waves were cresting at a man's height.

After checking his pockets and realizing they were empty, Ben climbed down the dry rotted steps into the wreck's hold. There was nothing there except for some merciful shade. Ben speculated it was ninety five degrees down there.

Once he returned to the slanted deck, Hawkins saw that the "dots" had enlarged. Something of considerable size was approaching. The only weapon he could find was a rusty link of chain.

Now hiding in the bow of the wooden hulk, Ben peeked out at what he thought to be a man riding in a cart behind a large animal of some sort. The stranger was still a half mile away.

With the benefit of a wind worn peephole, it became apparent the oncoming traveler wore a high peaked grass hat and was wearing a British naval officer's jacket. The cart was being pulled by a brahmin bull.

At two hundred yards out, Hawkins determined the driver was dark complexioned, had no visible weapons, seemed to be in no hurry and was smiling. Ben remained still in hopes the cartman had not spotted him.

That was not the case; because, the intruder began calling Benjamin Hawkins's name. He had an "island" accent.

"Colonel Hawkins, welcome to Jamaica! I thought I'd drop by to see if you'd like to join me for lunch.

Why don't you hop on and ole "Rembrandt" here, will take us to the best watering hole in Nassau. A lot has happened over the last couple of weeks and I need to fill you in on the details.

Old chap, is it true, you and Crick wiped out half of London with a bloody tidal wave of the King's own porter?" asked the curious native.

"Sir, I very much appreciate your hospitality but I already have plans at noon. Perhaps another time?" stated Hawkins.

"Laddie, my name is, "Injun Joe"!

Your apprehension toward my invitation was expected; therefore, allow me to more formally introduce myself!

I am what is known to you Culpers, as a "mole". My 'above ground' employer is "Governor Charles Cameron".

Our mutual friend as well as my 'underground' benefactor, is none other than, "Tecumseh"!

My assignment is to take you to our 'safehouse' located below "Teach's Inn". You are to meet up with my first cousin, "Seekaboo" and a, "Mister John Ross".

Those are my orders, Sir!" said the incensed Injun Joe.

"Perhaps then, you could tell me why I'm here?" pressed Hawkins.

"All I know, Mister Hawkins, it has something to do with killing "Josiah Francis" also known as, "Hildis Hadjo" or to be more precise, "Adam Weishaupt", Sir!" said Injun Joe.

"Are you aware, Injun Joe, of the whereabouts of a 'Paddy Welch'?" questioned the suspicious Indian agent.

"No Sir, I don't; although, I do know King George instructed his Secretary of War, "Earl Bathurst" to see to it that Hadjo and his 'Indian buddies' left England within the month following your beer skit!

I definitely do know they are to arrive here in Nassau later on this week. Does that answer your question?" smugly queried Injun Joe.

"How much further?"

"About two miles.

Ben, I get the impression you're disturbed about something. What is it?" sincerely asked the Indian.

"Where did you say Seekaboo and Ross were?"

"In the basement of 'Teach's Inn'. Why do you ask?" belligerently asked Injun Joe.

"What size shoe do you wear, Injun Joe?" blatantly questioned Hawkins.

"Oh, I guess about a medium for a small man. That's an awkward question coming from someone needing some help!"

"Did you know you had them on the wrong foot?" snarled Ben.

As Injun Joe was reaching for the pistol strapped to his ankle, the Culper jabbed the iron piece of chain into the imposter's eye. He then crushed the black man's larynx with his elbow.

Benjamin stripped the dead man of useful things. He took money, a knife, two pistols, and Injun Joe's shoes before setting 'Rembrandt' and his load on fire.

Afterwards, Hawkins made his way toward the town of Nassau.

The second black dot he had seen on the beach side's horizon, sent a round of lead over Benjamin's head. Ben evaporated into the midst of the bustling paradise by the sea.

*　*　*　*

British warships dominated the "Queens Harbor". Other vessels disguised as merchant ships, used the shallow water docks to resupply and make repairs.

Hundreds of nondescript sailors clogged the shops lined up and down the island's many streets. Exotic souvenirs appeared to be a big draw for the stopover guests; although, taverns with their adjoining whorehouses, got most of the seafarers' money.

"King Street connected both "West Hill and Market Streets" which seemed to Hawkins to be the city's centermost hub. It was there that Benjamin Hawkins elected to position himself. "Christ Church's" bell clanged twelve times.

After an hour of patterning the town's constables' beats that were spaced at thirty minute intervals, something interesting popped into Hawkins's mind. 'Each time a policeman passed by, "The Doubloon Inn", a young man of about fifteen years old, would run across the street and hand a one-legged beggar a box.'

The legless man would then hobble up to the Christ Church where a priest would take the box from the crutched peg leg. After symbolically blessing him, the black cloaked man sent his "mule" back to where he had previously been standing.

On the boy's fourth trip across King Street, Benjamin stopped the lad on the pretense of needing some directional information.

"Son, could you possibly point me toward the "Christ Church's Rectory"? I wish to present them a gift for their new school's building fund." Joyfully asked Hawkins.

"Mister, "Father McGrady's" funeral is tomorrow so I don't know who you would see about that. Maybe "Stubby" would have an idea as to who you might speak with about that kind of thing." Hurriedly answered the adolescent.

"I am so sorry to hear about that! The "Prince Regent" will no doubt, be stunned to hear of his death. News travels slowly to London, you know.

Do you think 'Stubby' might at least, recommend a reputable depository to me?

King George has entrusted me with a considerable amount of money. He wishes to designate it for the new school's construction.

I'm going to have to find a place to care for it until I can identify my new employer!" Bated Hawkins.

"Your 'new employer', Sir?"

"That's right!

I'll be the "headmaster" and maybe, even your teacher. You seem quite bright and exactly the type of fellow deserving of good marks!

My name is, "Professor Thomas Francis". schmoozed Ben.

'Stubby', seeing his "legs" detained by a stranger, hobbled up behind "Professor Francis".

"Is there a problem, Gulliver?" emphatically inquired Stubby.

"No there isn't; but, the church school's new headmaster is needing some advice as to a safe place to deposit the new school's building fund. It's from the King!" Gulliver announced in an oily voice.

"Well, let's talk about that after we get out of the middle of the street. If we don't hurry, we'll be runover by the myriad of drunks riding their bloody rental horses of which, our sorry-assed governor refuses to forbid!

I guess by now, my little friend, "Gully" has told you my name is 'Stubby' and I'll bet you're wondering how I got that 'nick' aren't you, Sir?" Stubby said with a grin on his face.

"No sir, I figured it was your father's name!" teased the professor.

"Well, aren't you the good sport!" cajoled Stubby.

"'The Anglican Diocese of Great Britain' has charged me with the responsibility of founding a school on this beautiful island!

But, I was told there has been an unfortunate occurrence befalling the church's rector." Said Hawkins.

"Between you and me, chum, the old booger ought to have kept his pecker in his britches, if you get my drift! How can I be of service to you, Professor?"

"Tomorrow morning at the crack of dawn, the "Hermes" will return to London. I am in need of a sixteen-man crew of velvet handed laborers, three sturdy wagons, a recommendation of a trustworthy banking depository, and four armed guards to move King George's allotment for my school's establishment!

I know that's a tall order to fill; but, if you'll point me in the right direction, I'll reward you and young Mister Gulliver, handsomely, for your troubles!"

"Guvnor, this is your lucky day. I just happened to be on my way to Christ Church at this very moment.

I'd bet my woolen sock, "Bishop Thomason" will be of assistance to you. He may even be able to put the King's school allotment in the church's safe. Follow me and let's go find out!" Glibly suggested Stubby.

Ben followed the gimpy beggar up Market Street for three blocks. Gulliver tagged behind Hawkins until Stubby fiercely turned back toward the precocious boy and told him to return to the inn.

Hawkins, wanting to tamp down any feeling of resentment, reached into his pocket and handed Gully a gold coin. After a gracious bow, the teenager did exactly what his 'pimp' had directed him to do. Stubby turned to Benjamin and spoke.

"That was a mighty big amount you tipped that boy, Professor Thomas Francis. He'll be hard to manage from here on out, I'll bet."

"I'm just grateful for your help, Stubby. Don't be concerned, they'll be more of that coming to you if we can work this out!" demurely stated Hawkins.

"Don't you worry, Professor Francis, this is in ole Stubby's hands now! With a little luck and a goodly amount of elbow grease on our part, everything will turn out just fine!" said the one legged hustler.

* * * * *

"Bishop Thomason" was standing at the top of the stairs leading into the church's sanctuary. His arms were crossed in an akimbo fashion in an attempt to cover a bulge from beneath his cloak. He nodded as Stubby and Ben Hawkins approached him.

"Father, I am proud to announce the arrival of Professor Thomas Francis to our bountiful shores!

He asked Gulliver for some directions to Christ Church among an assortment of other things that I'm quite sure you can help him with." Exclaimed Stubby.

"Stubby, I do not see the prayer box in your hand. Did you forget to bring it?" pleasantly questioned the bishop.

"Well Sir, I guess under the excitement of being the first to meet the new headmaster, I reckon it just slipped my mind!"

"My Son, the Lord never forgets to answer the pleas from sinners. Would you be so kind as to return to the "Doubloon" and fetch it for me?

I shall welcome our guest in due fashion during your absence so please do not dawdle! Said Bishop Thomason in a surgical way.

As the one legged man turned toward his employer's whorehouse, Bishop Thomason extended his right hand and offered Ben Hawkins an identifying 'limp' handshake. Benjamin reciprocated by tapping Thomason's third knuckle twice.

"I saw the smoke coming from the bayside. Were you followed?" asked the priest.

"Maybe not. Someone did fire a shot at me as I was leaving Injun Joe's cart!" said Hawkins.

"How did you catch it on fire so quickly?" suspiciously inquired Thomason.

"Lantern oil. About six pints of it!"

"Did you rob him?" pressed the bishop.

"Of course; I also set Injun Joe's brahmin's rump on fire to keep my followers occupied for a while." Answered Hawkins.

"Excellent!"

"Why was I sent here?" asked Ben.

"Two reasons really. The first being for a diversion; Paddy Welch was expecting your return to America. He lost you in London after he got what he needed from poor ole Crick.

Secondly, Tecumseh thought you'd want another shot at Weishaupt. He and Major Nichols are due day after tomorrow. Governor Cameron is welcoming him with a big hero's ceremony on Thursday."

"What about Stubby?" asked Ben.

"I'm afraid he was arrested under suspicion of Injun Joe's murder!"

"What about the boy named, "Gulliver"?" anxiously asked Hawkins.

"Just more collateral damage collected from our enemies, Colonel. Had we let those two loose with the knowledge of your presence on this island, I'm afraid we'd both be dead by morning!" said the chuckling bishop.

"Did you say arrested?" questioned Hawkins.

"Their hearts were. Now come on inside; we have some work to do."

The two men walked into the Christ Church's sanctuary and down the aisle until they reached the pulpit. With the press of a button, an elevator lowered them into the basement's strategy room.

"Wow! This is spectacular, Bishop!" exclaimed Hawkins.

"Sort of reminds you of "Fort Morgan's" war room doesn't it?

It should because Tecumseh designed them both!

Ben, my friends call me "Michael" or "Mike"; I'm no more of an Anglican priest any more than you are!

I was inducted into the Culpers fifteen years ago; I served under Colonel Benjamin Tallmadge during the "Setauket" era.

Colonel Hawkins, I am confident of Jackson's ability to erase the United States' of its European and native threats; but, neither he nor the American military, could fend off a full-blown Niburian offensive!

That, my friend, is exactly what this is all about!" proclaimed Michael in a high-pitched voice.

"Are the Niburians back to their old tricks?"

"Stronger and more devious than they have ever been, Colonel."

"Will the Cerians help us?" asked Ben.

"They're doing as much as they can. We are getting the permissible weaponry but it's not quite as simple as that. The real problem is, 'their integration into the native populations within our shores'.

In essence, the Nibs are trying to crumble our democracy. They are doing this by hiding within those groups of Americans who believe the (Niburian) promises of a "coming" 'marmalade' world!" preached Mike.

"Therefore, our "Judeo-Christian" beliefs interwoven into our country's mores, leave us somewhat helpless against 'the oppressed people of color' who in fact, are being guided by those who would, if they succeeded, have us all put back into chains?" professorially asked Hawkins.

"Bravo!"

"What is the proposal?" humbly asked Benjamin.

"Needless to say, we'll have to kill the suspects without their benefit of a trial, Ben!"

"Mike, I need a drink."

"Scotch isn't it? I thought you might want to have a few after our introductory talk; I know, I do!" kindly said Michael.

For nearly an hour, the Culpers sat in their leather covered chairs while staring at a world map dotted with red capped stickpins. Benjamin Hawkins broke the silence.

"Mike, what's your last name?"

"'Bowman'. Why?"

"Just in case, I have to chisel your full name on a conch shell!" said Ben with a scotch flavored grin on his lips.

"Well aren't you a morose little ray of sunshine!

However, keep your cutting tool handy because if our next caper turns sour, you're going to need it!" blandly remarked Michael Bowman.

"You mentioned a "hero's welcome" for "Hadjo" aka "Francis" aka "Weishaupt; apparently, I'm going to need a rifle that shoots three bullets!" slurred Hawkins.

"Are you drunk, Ben?"

"Yes, Sir." Answered Colonel Hawkins.

"That makes two of us, then. Benjamin, what would you guess is Adam Weishaupt's greatest weakness?" asked Mike.

"I'd say, his 'desire for infamy'; in other words, he wants to be remembered as being one of the greatest men of all time. Sort of on the same plateau as 'Jesus', I reckon!"

"Again, you get a star pinned on your forehead!" laughed Bowman.

"You're suggesting we use the man's 'ego' to our advantage, aren't you? Letting him hang himself with his own rope!"

"Precisely!" squealed Michael.

"Mike, I adore your thought pattern but how do you propose we do it?" soberly queried Ben.

"We'll allow the Brits to do it for us!

I'll get us another bottle while we both take a good piss and then I'll tell you an interesting story. Don't go away. You will enjoy it!" giggled Michael.

Bowman returned with a plate of bread and several smoked ostrich sausages. He uncorked the scotch jug, poured each of them a cup full of whiskey, ate a few bites of the bread and sausage, and then spun his yarn.

"One of the reasons our friend, Mister Josiah Francis left Alabama with Major Nicholls was because he was told he would be honored by the Prince Regent and recognized as the "Great Indian Prophet"!

To further believe Nicholl's line of bullshit, Josiah was told that King George would "Knight" him!" snickered Mike.

"Was there another reason for Josiah Francis's departure?" asked Hawkins.

"Oh yes, 'yes' indeed, there was!

Hildis Hadjo is petrified of Andrew Jackson!

Further, the coward is more fearful of his own lieutenants and especially one like Paddy Welch (a Niburian) who he knows, is far more adapt at orchestrating clandestine warfare than he could ever be.

Basically, the yellow-bastard is nothing more than a paper tiger having someone else operate his 'showboat'!" snarled Bowman.

"Where is Welch now?" asked Hawkins.

"He's trying to find you, Ben!

Intelligence reports state, he recognized you at the King's cricket match and has been tracking you ever since. We believe he is using Hadjo as bait!" solemnly said Michael.

"So that's how Injun Joe knew so much about Tecumseh and George Crick, isn't it?"

"I'm afraid so. The "Detective Jack Whicher" who almost caught you in that London alley, was none other than ole "Paddy" boy himself!" said Mike.

"He's a slick one, isn't he?" commented Ben Hawkins.

"Just another Nib; we'll get him, too!" consolingly said Michael Bowman.

"Who was "Injun Joe"; do you think 'he' was actually Welch?"

"Joe was just a lackey trying to earn some money. Had he been Paddy, we both would probably be shark shit by now!

No, Colonel Hawkins, Welch is waiting for you to make the first move!" prophesized Bowman.

"What is "my" next move, Mike?" nervously asked Ben.

"We're going to write a fake news article and then leave this heaven on earth. Hopefully, we'll kill him on our way out!" said Michael Bowman.

In the rear of Christ Church's sanctuary there was a small room dedicated to the publishing of the weekly church bulletins. That tiny space not only housed an archaic printing press, it also provided a relatively cool spot to stow Father McGrady's body.

"I'm afraid the good Father's ascension excluded his fleshy being; scotch will help with your tolerance, my son!" kidded Mike.

"You've already been working on the article, I see!

"THE NILES WEEKLY REGISTER" front pager is impressive; but, do you actually believe Hadjo will buy into it?

It says, "The Patriot, Hildis Hadjo who fought so gloriously for our cause in America, is to be awarded the rank of 'Brigadier General' by the Governor of Nassau, the Honorable Charles Cameron". Michael, does this even seem logical to you?"

"Colonel Hawkins, when Paddy Welch sees this, it'll take him less than thirty minutes to figure out where it was disingenuously printed. That's why you're going to wire this place up to the hilt!

I'd say, we'll be long-gone from here when he opens this door tomorrow morning. Help me put Father McGrady in the chair!" Cackled Mike.

The pair of Culpers spent several hours preparing for Welch's anticipated entry into the printing room.

While Bowman was distributing copies of the "NILES WEEKLY REGISTER" throughout Nassau, Ben was constructing an ignition device to set off a keg of black powder.

Hawkins arranged McGrady's body in such a manner so when Paddy entered the room, it would appear as though the minister was vivaciously greeting a visiting guest. (A network of olive-green fishing twine accomplished the postmortem action.)

The powder keg was buried beneath the roots of a decorative banana tree which Ben had brought down from the sanctuary. A cocked pistol's barrel was cleverly placed into the keg's spout hole.

When the printing room's door was opened, Father McGrady's right arm would rise into the air which would tighten another strand of fishing line, causing the ripened holy man's head to move.

Being fully aware of Paddy's intrepidness along with his razor-sharp intuition, Ben figured Welch would kick the printing room's door open before exposing himself to a possible ambush.

That was why the Culper placed the banana tree on top of a pedestal just to the left of the entranceway. Either way, once the door was opened, Injun Joe's pistol would fire!

As planned, Benjamin Hawkins left the basement through a tunnelway leading toward an underground dock. It was where a tarp covered skiff awaited them.

At 0400hrs. and still no Bowman, Hawkins pulled off the escape craft's covering where he discovered Mike's body. His throat had been slit wide open!

Emerging from beneath the water's surface, Paddy Welch stood up and successfully centered Ben's chest with a thrown dagger. Hawkins toppled into the murky shallows. Welch then crawled onto the dock and made his way into the church's bowels.

Having held his breath for nearly three minutes and swum underwater over a hundred yards, the Indian agent cautiously came up for a lungful of air. He removed the dagger from the silver flask he had stolen from Injun Joe.

Ben crawled onto a mound of grassy sand to regain his strength. He expected Welch to attack him at any second but that fear was squelched when the entire roof of the Christ Church was launched into the pale blue sky.

* * * * *

As the sun was rising, hundreds of British soldiers rushed toward the now fire engulfed sanctuary. Local firefighters came in by land and sea.

Now involved with their emergency at hand, the public servants never noticed one of their sloops' drifting away from its moorings.

'It was going to be a lovely day', Ben thought; 'after all, the ocean was calm and the wind was in his favor'.

Hawkins luckily found the Jamaican ship had a mounted compass in the wheelhouse. He locked the vessel into a northerly direction which freed him up so he could adjust his sails and search for something to eat.

At approximately 1800hrs., Ben saw the tops of masts diagonally coming toward him from his starboard side. Still about three miles away, Hawkins wheeled his rudder toward the portside in hopes the fast approaching schooner would ignore him.

The sun had nearly dropped behind Mexico when the first cannonball skipped across the calm waters some two hundred yards in front of him. Signaling blinks demanded that Ben lower his sails.

Given the fact, the Culper had never navigated a ship of that size and certainly had not gone up against a fully armed pirate's ship with nothing but a waterlogged pistol, Benjamin Hawkins did exactly what the invaders told him to do.

A dozen very rough looking men reiterated to the Indian agent he had made the correct decision. The pirates swung onto Ben's stolen sloop.

They accosted Hawkins and tied him to the ship's forward mast. The pirates blindfolded him while the others stripped the Bahamian sloop of its useful knickknacks. A man's voice broke through the clamor.

"Are you familiar with a vessel known as the "U.S.S. Asp"?" calmly asked a man using a Kentuckian accent.

"That would depend on what scale of familiarity you are speaking of, Sir." Obtusely answered Hawkins.

"…supposing we were referring to a ship of tiny proportions battling a flood of some extraordinary substance, who would have captained the "Asp"?"

"Sir, I'm afraid I do not know. If you are speaking of "this" ship, I won it fair and square in a game of chance and I have the papers to prove it!" Yelled Hawkins.

"I see. And what if I were to tell you Paddy Welch was blown to 'kingdom come'?" comically inquired Ben's inquisitor.

"Patty Welch? She went where, Sir?" questioned Ben.

"Alright, Colonel Hawkins, since you're a gambling man, how much would you wager against the probabilities that I have some of your cohorts standing behind me at this very moment?" prodded the unlikely pirate.

"I have no 'cohorts' but if I did, what would you be able to lose "if" such a contest were to come to fruition?"

"A "Feather", Ben!" said the inquisitor as he removed Hawkins's blindfold.

Once his eyes adjusted, Benjamin Hawkins saw the smiling faces of exactly whom the authentic buccaneer, "James Ford" spoke of; Tecumseh, John Ross and Seekaboo were standing amongst Ford's 'Ferry Gang'.

They were applauding and drinking from pewter cannisters. Ben simply cried.

*　*　*　*

"Good morning, Colonel Hawkins. They decided to let you sleep in, Sir.

I just know your ears were burning because everybody was talking about all you went through. I just don't know how you did it, myself!

Anyway, I made you some breakfast but you're going to have to gobble it down pretty fast. Ya'll have a meeting in the Captain's cabin in thirty minutes.

If you need anything just pull that cord over there and I'll square you away, Sir!

My name's, "Zeke"

I'm Captain Ford's "chief cook and bottle washer". I use to be one of his slaves but after he went into buccaneering and my wife died, he kept me on cause of my cooking and all!" graciously said the old man.

"Zeke, why is the ship jerking so much?" queried Hawkins.

"Cause we're towing the Governor's sloop behind us, that's why the ole "John's Ferry" is straining so!"

"The "Governor's sloop"?" curiously asked Ben.

"My god, man!

Didn't you even know you stole Governor Cameron's boat? You is one hard case, Mister Ben, indeed you is, Sir!" said Zeke.

"Gentlemen, let's get started. As you can see by my pointer, we are two days out from "Cedar Key". We expect the "Arbuthnot" carrying Josiah Francis and Major Nicholls to land at "Saint Marks" in ten days.

"George Woodbine", our inside man, will keep us informed as to Josiah's movements once he reaches his new headquarters at Saint Marks.

Jackson insists we allow the "Arbuthnot" to pass Cedar Key; Colonel Jackson wants Josiah Francis to believe he is no longer in pursuit of him.

Woodbine tells us, Francis's wife, son, and two daughters are already at Saint Marks and are awaiting his arrival. Jackson wants the Seminoles to become complacent but mark my words, that won't last long!

It is supposed, Bathurst's commissioning of Francis to 'Brigadier General' will influence his relationship with Major Nicholls and more importantly, with the Seminoles.

Word has it, ole Josiah Francis sleeps in his "very elaborate red uniform" which in the eyes of those who come in contact with him, will see him as the perfect 'madman'!

Jackson suspects that Governor Cameron advised Josiah Francis to make peace with the Americans and paid him a sizeable amount of money to do so. Of course, those valueless words coming from London and were only meant to appease the Indians.

British sentiments have now shifted toward "fair and just" treatment toward the Indians as well as to the runaway slaves. With their newly spun image, one could only imagine, not 'if' but 'when', they will rise up again!

However, we don't buy that malarkey; therefore, provided Josiah Francis behaves himself, Jackson will not demand their surrender until August. If on the other hand, "The Prophet" becomes frisky, as we expect he will, Colonel Jackson will invade Florida from the north while we clean their whistles from the south. That, my friends, is why we are encamping at Cedar Key!

Should it become necessary to invade the Red Sticks before Jackson's August deadline, "Colonel R.W. Scott's" marine's will attack to the west from "Fort White" while we and our northerly marching Creek forces pin their fleeing men in the "Lafayette Swamp".

Captain Isaac McKeever will prevent the Red Sticks from escaping by sea. He and four American warships are on standby at "Steinhatchee".

A peaceful outcome to this Red Sticks confederacy is most certainly doubtful; therefore, gentlemen, do not count on lounging around Cedar Key for long!

I am quite sure Lord Bathurst's gifts to Francis will 'burn holes in his pocket'; consequently, he'll likely waste no time 'rabblerousing' his old friends and looking for some mischief to get into.

Seekaboo and Hawkins are to join Jackson while Ford and Ross sail to Steinhatchee in order to bolster McKeever's marines. I'll lead my troops into Lafayette once we get Andy's go ahead.

Oh yes, and one other thing, if you have not yet been inoculated for "smallpox", see Zeke in the galley as soon as this meeting ends. There are several cases being reported throughout the gulf region so please do as I've ordered!

Finally, I wish to commend Colonel Hawkins for his superlative actions during his latest mission. Although it cost us two extraordinary agents, Ben's endeavors probably prevented hundreds of American's deaths not to mention, the successful theft of Governor Cameron's pride and joy, the "Paradise"!

We'll meet again tonight after third mess. Don't forget, Captain Ford, take your men downstairs to see Zeke. Smallpox is no joke, John; do you hear what I am saying?"

"Right away, Sir!" barked John Ford.

At 0400hrs., Seekaboo awaked Hawkins by blowing a lungful of cigar smoke into his face. He covered Ben's mouth and then whispered a disturbing message.

"We've a spy issue!"

"What are you saying?" questioned Hawkins.

"I caught Zeke signaling a message to someone on "Egmont Key"!"

"What did Zeke say when you approached him on that?" asked Ben.

"He didn't; but, the man on shore responded, 'We'll see you then'!" muttered Seekaboo.

"Have you told Tecumseh?"

"Yes! He already has Ford and his men on deck!"

"Where's Zeke?"

"In hell, I reckon." Replied Seekaboo.

By the time Seekaboo and Benjamin Hawkins had made it up to the rear deck, John Ross had Ford and eight of his men dangling headfirst in "Ford's Ferry's" churning wake.

Tecumseh from the ship's bow, chummed the waters. John Ross was interrogating the upside down men with peppering questions.

"He who first speaks the truth will be pulled up to safety! The rest of you will not!" Yelled Ross.

Strangely, the nine remaining gang members began screaming at one another. One attempted to climb up another's body to gain some altitude from the sea creatures swimming beneath him.

Ross cut that climber's suspension rope which ended up offering to the other gang men, a slight respite. John Ross then posed another question through a megaphone.

"Captain Ford, who was Zeke sending a message to?"

"God damnit! I have no idea, you bastard! Pull me out of here! I'm one of you fellows!" hollered Ford.

"That's not true! The Captain knew Zeke had made a deal with the Brits! screamed a betraying upside down gang member!

"John Ford! Did you forget to tell me something?" insolently asked Ross.

"Alright! Alright! I was just trying to pick up some extra money; I meant no harm! I was going to tell you about it!

Zeke was the one who convinced me to let "Big Warrior" know when you returned! Oh god, man, I'm sorry!" apologetically pleaded John Ford.

"How much did Zeke pay you and where did he get the money from, John?" mocked Ross.

"From Nicolls' strongbox! Zeke was one of his men!"

"I asked you how much you were paid!" teased John Ross.

"325 pounds sterling! Please pull me up!"

"Jesus brought only 13 pieces of silver, John! How come you got more?" chided Ross.

"I made a mistake! Don't kill me; I'll never do it again!" begged Ford.

"Who down there would like to pay for their life? Would anyone be willing to give me 326 pounds sterling to be pulled from the mouths of those finned beasts nipping at yall's noses?" prodded John Ross.

Soon after John Ross's command to lower the Ferry Gang's members into the sea, the sharks moved on. One assumed they were in pursuit of other things.

Tecumseh ordered Ross to take the "John's Ferry's" wheel. He would take the first watch while Hawkins and Seekaboo rummaged through the dead men's belongings. The sky promised good sailing for the coming day.

* * * * *

Seekaboo was at the ship's wheel when by the naked eye, Cedar Key came into sight. John Ross flashed a signal to the outpost in code, but did not receive a reciprocal return; not even a blink. He called for Tecumseh.

"Chief, "Captain Parton" has not responded to my signal. I sent it twice!"

"That's not what I wanted to hear, John. Any sign of activity?" nervously asked Tecumseh.

"Nothing, Sir." Answered Ross.

"Take the "Ferry" out to sea. We'll anchor down until dark. Let's wait and see what happens!" said Tecumseh.

"What about the "Arbuthnot", Sir?" questioned John.

"I suspect Big Warrior's people are waiting to ambush us. God knows what Zeke transmitted to them so we'll pretend nothing has changed."

"Do you want me to slip in there and see what's going on, Chief?" intrepidly asked Ross.

"We can't afford to lose you, John. As it is now, we've only got four men operating two ships; it would be foolish to take the risk!

Let's contact Captain McKeever when we get closer to Steinhatchee. He can afford a loss much more than we can." Stoically remarked Tecumseh.

No one slept a wink throughout the night. An hour before dawn, Seekaboo received a message from Isaac McKeever's ship. He called for the crew to gather in the wheelhouse.

"Chief Tecumseh, Captain McKeever just sent word from the "Thomas Shields". He reported taking fire from Spanish cannons at "Piney Point".

McKeever further stated, the Red Sticks were spotted near "Fowler's Bluff" and were moving northward.

Jackson has recalled his ships to Saint George Island where they are to remain until the "Arbuthnot" has safely passed through to Saint Marks.

McKeever has sent a detachment of marines under Lieutenant McKimmon, to help Colonel Scott abandon Fort White and join Jackson's division at "Wacissa".

Sir, according to McKeever, we are to make a beeline to Saint George. That's all I got; shall I respond?" calmly reported Seekaboo.

"Yes. Tell Captain McKeever we have the "Paradise" in tow of the "Ford's Ferry". We should reach Saint George by tomorrow night!" ordered Tecumseh.

"Will that be all, Chief?" asked Seekaboo.

"That will be all."

* * * * *

John Ross looked out of the wheelhouse's starboard window at the colorless swampland passing by. He bowed his head in memory of McKimmon's courageous marines.

Apalachicola Bay offered an ideal deep water port for McKeever's four warships. "Ford's Ferry" was dwarfed by them which gave Isaac's marines a target for ridicule. Downwardly thrown pieces of fruit were signs that trouble was up ahead.

Although McKeever had warned his sailors to expect harsh repercussions from Tecumseh's lot, they did not take heed. Following a barrage of challenges and 'in fun' insults, it did not surprise Captain McKeever when one of the gangways was blown out from under his exiting troops.

* * * * *

Muscogee children swarmed the newly arrived marines while the adult natives prepared a feast for their welcomed guests. Young bronze skinned women found no problems in pairing themselves up with the deep pocketed marines.

The island's owner, "John Forbes" pulled his four horse surrey up to the "Thomas Shields's" gangway as Isaac McKeever was walking down from it. Forbes immediately began bidding for the "Paradise".

"I'm surprised that thing's still afloat, Captain; are you wanting to scrap it?" purred Forbes.

"You'll have to speak with its owner about that!" baited Isaac as he pointed toward the "Ford's Ferry".

"And who might that be?" briskly asked Forbes.

"I have no idea, Sir; they were taking on water so we pulled them here. But, if I were you, I'd speak with that tall Indian fellow. He's the one with the tomahawk in his belt!" teased McKeever.

"Ain't you the joker!" squealed Forbes.

"Oh no, Sir! I haven't a clue as to whether he's the rightful owner or not; but, he was towing the vessel when we got his signal for assistance. Why don't you go and talk with him about it!" curtly stated Captain McKeever.

"Was the "Paradise" the ship taking on the water, you mentioned? What's the Indian's name?" clumsily questioned John.

"It was the "Ford's Ferry", I believe. As far as his name, Mister Forbes, I really don't know; but, I'd bet he does!" joshed McKeever.

Quite arrogantly, Forbes snapped the backs of his nearest two horses and rode up to the "Paradise's" side. He looked the sloop over and then approached Tecumseh.

"My name is, "John Forbes"; what's yours?"

"Feather." Said Tecumseh.

"Oh, my god! I thought ya'll were goners for sure. Bring your men up to the house, I've got a lot to fill you in on. Jackson's been worrying the shit out of me!" panted Forbes.

McKeever, Ross, Seekaboo, Tecumseh and Benjamin Hawkins squeezed into the back of Forbes's carriage. A bumpy mile later, they were all sitting in a Cerian submarine.

John Forbes cleared his throat before he spoke. From his heavy perspiration one could plainly see, he had a lot on his mind.

"Three hundred years ago, the Niburians wiped out the "Muscogee" populations all along the coastline in this particular section of the Gulf of Mexico. They did this for several reasons but mostly for the valuable minerals found within the waters just off our shores.

Titanium and magnesium were the most sought after; not to mention, the gold and silver. After all, this was the final stopping off point for glacial movements during the ice ages.

Consequently, this was one of the last places on earth where the Niburians found refuge from the searching Cerians. I tell you this and it is the opinion of many, the Nibs are back!" sincerely stated John Forbes.

"Agent Forbes, you mentioned the 'Muscogee' were 'wiped out' by the Niburians several hundred years ago; is there any written record of that?" asked Hawkins.

"Only by stories passed down through the generations; although, the Cerians have voluminous documentations on the matter.

Dreadfully, the Niburians killed the natives off "then" in the same way they're planning to do it now; i.e., they are spreading diseases!" chokingly exclaimed Forbes.

"We have heard of some isolated "smallpox" outbreaks. Are there others being reported?" asked Tecumseh.

"Unfortunately, yes. "Influenza, measles, yellow fever" and some we have not named yet!

Whatever it's called though, we must put a stop to it!" cried John Forbes.

"What do the Cerians say we should do?" questioned Ross.

"Round the carriers up into one place and burn their bodies!" gloomily stated Forbes.

"Are you saying, the Cerians are suggesting we exterminate the Indians?" angrily queried Tecumseh.

"Only the sick ones and those 'affiliated' with the Niburians, Chief!" reluctantly admitted John.

"How conclusive are these allegations?" yelled Hawkins.

"Colonel, that's the reason Jackson is disturbed. I'm afraid it's a Culper issue; the U.S. government has no idea of the matter."

"Anything coming from Cerian headquarters?" sarcastically asked Ben.

"They want Jackson to move the Indians to the west side of the Mississippi River!" Forbes said.

"Wait a minute, John! What do you mean, "move them across the Mississippi?", then what?" blurted out Tecumseh.

"Chief Tecumseh, with all due respect, Sir, how else can we separate the friendly Indians from the embedded Niburians? Don't you realize the Nibs are inciting conflicts against the Americans?

All the U.S. government sees, are fatality statistics 'reportedly' caused by the numerous tribes living in the east. You and I know, 'we' are not responsible for those deaths; but, there are those in 'Washington', who are!

Have you seen what the papers are printing about the "Disease hosting Cherokee!"?

It is a big lie, I know; but, the voters opting who stays or leaves office, only believe what they see in black and white!

The politicians, therefore, appeal to the peoples' whim!" weakly argued John Forbes.

"In the meantime, hundreds of thousands of us (Indians) are exterminated due to political favoritism; is that what you're saying, John?" fired back Tecumseh.

"Bluntly answered, Chief, 'yes'; however, the Cerians have offered a suggestion. While they are unwilling to "openly" become involved, the Cerians will provide us with a limited amount of clandestine assistance.

Their 'ideas' regarding mass migration of the Indian populations to the west was put forth in order to separate them from the Niburians. The Cerians in turn, will help us clean out the alien remainders. Frankly, I see their point.

As Culpers, it will be our responsibility to do exactly as they prescribe. That is why, Colonel Jackson is on his way here!

Gentlemen, the Culpers and the Cerians are about to engage in a new kind of war, one in which, 'America' will never know we are in.

On the surface, Jackson and his forces will conventionally follow President Monroe's doctrines, in the meantime, we and the Cerians will make our enemies 'naturally' disappear!" stated John Forbes.

"How do you make an enemy "naturally" disappear?" pressed Seekaboo.

"Jackson is due in here tonight. We'll let him explain those details." Said Forbes.

Chapter Six

By the time the Culpers returned to the Muscogee prepared luau, McKeever's marines were nowhere to be seen. Neither were the girls who had welcomed them at the docks.

The older folks were singing and dancing around a roaring fire while passing around crocks of agave rum. In mass, they staggered up to John Forbes's buggy.

"Mister John, you're just in time for our loggerhead stew!

Captain McKeever, those boys you brought with you are some mighty fine gentlemen, Sir. It's rare to run into young men with such an interest in the botanical wonders of our island. They should be returning any minute now." Slurred an old man.

Hearing what the aged Indian said, McKeever reached into his breast pocket and pulled out a five inch metal whistle. He blew on it with three short but loud blasts. Within seconds, eighty some marines emerged from the island's majestic foliage. Some were fully clothed and some were not.

"Now hear this! Our ships have become terribly stained by the gulf's salt enriched air. These vessels must be in pristine order by morning's light!

Return to your stations immediately. I shall personally inspect your efforts at 0600hrs.. You are dismissed!" exclaimed the Captain.

As the sailors gathered their strewn about belongings and were making their ways back to their ships, large pellets of hail began pelting the sands of Saint George's Island. Claps of thunder and violent streaks of lightening forced everyone to seek shelter.

Following the hailstorm's passing, Andrew Jackson approached the island in a rowboat. Once landed, Jackson walked toward the village as if it were commonplace for him to do so. He waved at the awestruck natives as he greeted John Forbes.

"Hello, John. It's been awhile hasn't it?

I have brought your people many gifts; they are in the skiff. Please ask the old chief to distribute them wisely. It's mostly winter clothing and footwear.

We do not have the luxury of a lot of time; so, let's get down to business right away. You can explain the cold weather gear to the Muscogee people once I have left.

Jackson took the morning hours explaining what was to happen over the coming months. He reassigned each of the sitting Culpers their new responsibilities and outlined the phases of the impending operation.

Tragically, it was learned that R.W. Scott's and McKeever's commandoes were ambushed by the Red Sticks. Jackson and the Cerians as a result of the Indians' hostility, planned on slaughtering the Red Sticks at once.

At 0615hrs., following his inspection, McKeever dispatched the warships to Piney Island. He would captain the "Thomas Shields" while John Ross manning the "Paradise", tomorrow, would close in behind the "Arbuthnot". The "Paradise" was to be the bait.

Following the attack down the "Wakulla River" and after "Fort San Marcos de Apalache" was secured, Tecumseh and Seekaboo were to return to the mouths of the Ohio and Mississippi Rivers.

The proselytes were to emphasize to the eastern tribes that the Indians living on the fertile plains west of the Mississippi would live without interference from the white man.

To get the word out, Tecumseh was to send his brother, "Tenskwatawa" into eastern Tennessee.

Hawkins was to go to Washington to reiterate to President Monroe the Cerian's model and incorporate it with congresses' wishes. Culper syndicates would see to it that Benjamin Hawkins supervised the Indians' westerly evacuation.

John Forbes's "Island of Saint George" would become an American base of operations. He was to arm and turn the Muscogee islanders into a fighting battalion. Forbes had a thirty day timeline.

The Cerians had conveyed to Jackson, they would begin tampering with the weather on the fifteenth of April. The schedule of "catastrophic events" was to be shared with Tecumseh, his brother, and Seekaboo when it was pertinent for them to know it; but, as all three of the Indian chief's knew, whatever was planned for them to do was designed to accentuate in the eyes of the attentive tribes, their "prophetic" powers.

It was anticipated, the Cherokee would send their 'message carriers' throughout the east once they saw with their own eyes, the legitimacy of Tecumseh's predictions. The intended results were to separate the "good Indians" from those wishing to upheave America's progress.

(Truth be told, the Cerians had discovered huge veins of gold in Georgia and needed the Indians out of the way. With the Cherokee gone, the Masons could mine it without their interference.)

"Operation Feather" was six weeks out, providing enough time for Jackson's generals to get into place before their attack on Saint Marks was begun. The initial objective was to "cut the body of the snake off". That is, Jackson's soldiers intended to wipe out the Red Sticks.

'Feather's' intention was to peacefully create a new home for the Indians in the lands west of the Mississippi River. There, they could reestablish a country untethered from the white mans' laws.

Benjamin Hawkins and John Forbes had become friends during the two weeks following Jackson's departure. Hawkins had helped the Indians with logistical scenarios as well as the utilization of their recently "dropped" Cerian hardware.

There had been no sign of conflict up until that point in time; therefore, targeting dummy ships occupied most of Ben's days. He awaited orders for his return to Washington.

On Tuesday morning while Hawkins and Forbes were instructing a group of women at the rifle range, John noticed there was a submarine signaling a message to them.

Five staccato blinks followed by two far spaced flashes assured Forbes he was the intended recipient. Ben wrote the encrypted letters on the back of a paper target as John Forbes called the incoming letters out.

Ten minutes later, the mile out ship disappeared beneath the gulf's surface. This is what the transmission stated:

"Mount Tambora(Indonesia) has erupted. Move Muscogee to high ground. Expect tsunami of fourteen(plus) feet in three days. Great tremors due. No sunlight and extensive snow imminent. The feather has fallen."

Following a few seconds of analysis, John Forbes spoke.

"Ben, this is bloody unbelievable! What in the hell should we do?"

"Move these folks up to "Sopchoppy Hills" and gather firewood. I have no doubt, this island will be underwater in seventy two hours. I suggest we evacuate at once!" responded Hawkins.

"Look, Ben, McKeever's ships are here!" screamed Forbes.

"How many natives live on this island, John?"

"Eight hundred or so." Wailed Forbes.

"Call them in, John!

Explain, they must change into the clothes Jackson brought them. You and I will load the armaments while the people gather their things. Tell them, they should only take items that will fit into their pockets." Sternly remarked Ben.

For the rest of the day, the Muscogee residents packed their belongings into their skiffs which in turn, were paddled to "Lanark Village" for safekeeping.

McKeever's three remaining ships took the women and children up "Saint George's Sound" to "Saint Teresa" where the marines guided them along the "Ochlockonee River" and then up to Sopchoppy Hills.

Friday morning right at dawn, the first tremor shook Saint George to the point that John Forbes' two stories tall house crumbled to the ground. Birds of all sorts, zigzagged through the bent over treetops.

The gulf waters receded leaving nothing but a slick sand bed filled with flapping fish. Waterspouts darted across the horizon.

Thunderhead clouds, orange in color, seemed to aim lightning bolts at the fleeing seabirds flailing about the sky. The sea turned to an inky green. A tidal wave rumbled toward the coast.

From Ben's hilltop perspective, it appeared as if he were sitting in a boat peering out at an angry grey ocean. Several albatross's floated on the surface apparently victims of electrocution.

Hawkins's mind drifted back to London; he thought about the flood of porter and then to Paddy Welch.

John Forbes tapped Ben on his shoulder interrupting his nightmarish remembrances. The howling winds made John have to yell out Jackson's most recent message.

"Jackson will attack "Fowltown" at 1600hrs.. I'm afraid you are to return to Washington once Saint Marks has been secured.

Ben, I don't know how to say this, but it's been a pleasure knowing you. I expect things will start moving pretty quickly; so, I just wanted to get that out of the way in case, we didn't say goodbye!" solemnly said Forbes.

"John, I share the same sentiments but I'll be damned if I'm going to leave until I see Francis's dead body!

It was my responsibility to kill the bastard and I intend to see it to its end!" swore Hawkins.

"Be that as it may be, Andrew Jackson has dispatched "Chief McIntosh" and twenty of his braves to escort you into Georgia!" quipped John.

"When?" shrieked Hawkins.

"Now, Sir." Forbes hollowly answered.

Without saying another word, Benjamin Hawkins gathered his things and left the dugout. He walked to the west bank of the "Ochlockonee River" where six long canoes were beached.

William McIntosh threw a fur jacket over Ben's shoulders as Hawkins was seated. Silently, they paddled upstream. Snow began to fall.

With the sounds of thunder long past, "Lake Talquin" came into view. Judge Toulmin and a regiment of Kentucky militiamen were waiting on its shore. Harry Toulmin greeted "Chief Billy's" party.

"Yo! Ben Hawkins, welcome to Georgia!"

There was no answer from the canoers.

"Chief McIntosh, you boys made good time! Where's Ben?" lightheartedly questioned the judge.

"He's under the bear skin!" said McIntosh.

"What's wrong with him?" asked Toulmin in a high shrilled voice.

"Ben Hawkins is dead, Harry."

"How is that possible?" angrily questioned Judge Harry Toulmin.

"Paddy Welch shot him at "Silver Passage"! He used a crossbow before escaping through the swamp. We're going after him; we'll get him, Judge!"

"Oh my god!

Ben is one of my best friends. Captain Fredricks, have a detail get him out of that boat. Bill, go get that sonofabitch!" shouted Judge Toulmin.

Four Kentucky soldiers dismounted and walked into the water to pull Hawkins's body out of McIntosh's canoe. As ordered, they dragged him to higher ground and commenced to digging a grave for the judge's old gambling buddy.

Captain Fredricks rode his horse beside of Toulmin's appaloosa. With his hand placed on the judge's shoulder, the captain soothingly asked a question.

"Sir, would you mind if I said a couple of words once we bury your friend?"

"Hell no, Captain. That man never existed and tell your men to wipe this incident from their minds; do you understand me, Fredricks?" warned the judge.

"Not really, Judge, but I'll do as you say, Sir!"

"Fine!" whispered Toulmin as he turned his horse and rode out toward the north.

* * * *

John Ross spun the wheel of the "Paradise" to the starboard side in an attempt to avoid being capsized by a ghost wave coming from the south. Twice the ship had been completely over crested by the monstrous things.

He had already lost one of his men and therefore required his remaining six man crew to use safety harnesses. Their job was to shoot the people attempting escape from Saint Marks.

Gaffs ended up being the preferred weapon because their pistols would not shoot with wet powder. Captain McKeever's ship, the "Thomas Shields" because of the schooner's size, was unable to use the harpoons therefore he fired cannisters of shrapnel at those using flotation devices.

Jackson's cavalry left the old British fort at Fowltown in charred ruins. Hundreds of bodies littered the snow covered shore.

No one was spared. Even the Spanish soldiers wielding white pieces of cloth on the tips of their sabers were killed.

Ross blinked a message to Jackson. A girl, bartering for her life, mentioned a tunnel through which Francis, his daughter (Milly),

Himollemico, and a prisoner named, "Duncan McKimmon" had escaped.

She told John Ross they were hidden in the forest north of "San Marcos de Aplache".

Bonfires glowed throughout the night all along the gulf shore. The seas had calmed enough for Jackson's plans to go live.

At 0900hrs., the "James Shields" flying the Union Jack (British flag), anchored two hundred yards off San Marcos's banks. Colonel Jackson's men had feigned a withdrawal.

Costumed in Red Jackets, four of McKeever's commandoes set out in a dinghy as if they were on a search and rescue mission. The marines played their bagpipes.

*   *   *   *   *

At the exact time the "James Shields" was attempting to lure in the Red Sticks' leader, Tecumseh and Seekaboo were starting their journey down the "Cumberland River".

Not only did the Cerians airlift the "Ford's Ferry" to "Dale Hollow Lake" they also painted the midsized schooner with a bright gold lacquer. The self-guided vessel equipped with an enhanced sound system, enabled the Indian soothsayers to speak to the hordes of tribal gawkers.

Hundreds of Indians were packed along the banks of the northwesterly twisting river anxious to see the 'flying boat'.

From two hundred feet above the yelping Indians, Tecumseh promoted the "Promise Land" awaiting those who moved to the western side of the Mississippi River.

Seekaboo schmoozed the individual tribal councilmen by correctly calling out their names and making all sorts of breathtaking promises.

Every few miles, the golden craft would rise above the river, spin around twice in the air and then resume its course. A flock of mechanical eagles dropped bags of candy to the applauding spectators.

Waterspouts, mild earth tremors and chocolate flavored raindrops were among the magnificent phenomenon demonstrated by the two "Moses-dressed" Indians.

Tecumseh's message outlined the evilness of the white mans' doings. He spoke in guttural tones of the Indians' enslavement. His eyes burned with a supernatural luster while every muscle in his body shook with emotion.

Seekaboo would augment Tecumseh's comments with mournful examples of 'whitey's' greed. Teary eyes, all focused upwards, cleared a bit due to hope.

The mighty Shawnee chief emphasized in his impassioned pleas, "unification of the tribes was the only solution!" He promised to punish the white man for 'his' incessant greed.

Tecumseh swore in the name of the "Great Spirit" whom he claimed had sent him, that every last one of the white devils would be forced into cannibalism by summer's end!

He further soothsaid, "the 'Great Spirit' will preempt the destruction by allowing 'his' believers safe passage across the east until the first of July. After which, the earthquakes, the snow storms, the disappearance of the sun and the dying of livestock, would befall the remaining people."

After a pause, Tecumseh spoke again and was echoed by Seekaboo.

"Within one year, the tribes will be able to return to their old homes. Our people will be free to restart their lives again if they so wish; but, the fertile lands to the west offer far more promise than the overly used earth in the east".

Tecumseh and Seekaboo always finalized their show with a prayer and a rainbow in the sky.

Those things happened; consequently, the Indians were comforted by their dreams.

* * * * *

The "Paradise" now hidden behind "Shell Point" and out of sight from Francis's telescopic view, the "Thomas Shields" paraded itself just off of the tip of San Marcos de Aplache.

Dressed as the spitting image of "Major Nicolls", Captain Isaac McKeever with the use of a handheld megaphone, began assuring 'all survivors' there was help on the way.

Duncan McKimmon no doubt realizing his Captain's ruse, confirmed the 'authenticity' of the British warship.

"Himollemico" a newly affirmed advocate of Josiah Francis's cause, bravely walked out of a clump of scrub brush toward the rowboat.

The fake British rescuers wrapped the young Red Stick in a blanket while serving the lad a slab of roasted beef. Himollemico waved a 'come-on' to the others still in hiding.

Milly, her father, and McKimmon cautiously joined the cajoling 'rescuers'. They too, received a hero's welcome, some grog, a thick portion of beef and a gargantuan serving of lies.

After assurances were made that there were no more survivors, the entire bunch were rowed out to the awaiting "Thomas Shields". The ship's red jacketed crew applauded them as the "rescues" climbed aboard.

Fully expecting more cuddling, Josiah Francis announced his identity.

"Gentlemen, I am, "Brigadier General Josiah Francis" of his Majesty's armed forces!

On behalf of my dear friend, King George the third, I wish to extend my gratitude to you valorous sailors for your courageous service in our time of need!

Furthermore, I ask to be treated as one of you!

Just because of my prestigious ranking, it will not be necessary...." As Francis was saying when Captain McKeever approached the 'holy man' and smashed him in the mouth with the butt of a rifle.

"Hadjo, you are under arrest!

Lieutenant Fredricks, with the exception of "Duncan McKimmon", take these scum suckers below!"

After three cannon blasts were fired from the "Thomas Shields", Jackson's cavalry rode out on Saint Mark's snow covered beach. In unison, more than a thousand rifles went off at the same time.

Colonel Jackson issued a message to be blinked to McKeever, requesting permission to board the "Thomas Shields". A boat was immediately requisitioned to fetch him.

As the dinghy was preparing to be lowered into the gulf, Jackson sent another message to McKeever. It read:

"Received word from Chief McIntosh. Benjamin Hawkins was killed. Suspend hearing. Draw and quarter the prisoners. I'll report the trial and subsequent hanging to Monroe."

Captain McKeever felt rage race through his body like broken glass. He admired Hawkins not only for his bravery but for the man he was, a gentleman.

Isaac needed to know how such a warrior died. He called his first-mate to summon the messenger to his quarters.

"Seaman Andrews at your service, Sir!"

"It's, "Thomas" isn't it?" kindly queried Isaac.

"Yes sir, Captain."

"Thomas, I have a special favor to ask of you."

"You name it, Sir!" sternly spoke Thomas Andrews.

"I need to send a private message; one that Jackson's men can't read! You and "Lieutenant Bopp" are to take a dinghy west to the tip of Shell Point.

Export a signal to the "Paradise" but you must put yourself in such a position that your semaphore cannot be seen from Saint Marks.

Invite Colonel Jackson to the execution of Benjamin Hawkins's killers. Tell Chief Ross to approach the "Thomas Shields" from the southeast thus, blocking his sighting from Saint Marks." Requested Captain McKeever.

Thomas snapped to attention and with a curious expression on his face, he asked the "Thomas Shields's" captain a question.

"Sir, it is a perilous journey across the gulf, may I suggest that Lt. Bopp do the rowing, Sir?"

"Why Thomas, that depends on whether or not you would like to be elevated to a higher paygrade or would prefer a transfer to the galley as the ship's general pot washer!" snickered Isaac.

"How shall I relay John Ross's answer back to you, Sir?" rapidly asked the messenger.

"Blink six….pause….and then two…for "Yes"." Answered the Captain.

"And if the answer is, "No"?"

"There will "not" be one of those, "First Class Seaman Thomas"!"

Isaac McKeever looked out of his window at Jackson's bonfires glowing on the peninsula's shores. He listened to the prisoners' angry voices below.

Isaac thought of Ben Hawkins, his laughter, his tears and then McKeever remembered 'Zeke'.

Captain McKeever summoned Duncan McKimmon.

"Duncan, I'm glad you made it back, son! Did you see Doctor Crimmons?"

"Yes sir, and I'm glad to be back. It was pretty bad out there!" said McKimmon.

"Those damn Red Sticks can be tough ones can't they! I've fought a few of them myself…….." said Isaac before Duncan McKimmon interrupted him.

"Captain, we weren't ambushed by Red Sticks, Sir! It was just 'one' man!"

"What in the hell are you saying!" yelled the Captain.

"Nobody could get a shot at him; he would fly in and out of rifle range without anyone seeing him coming or going, I tell you!

It was terrible how he would swoop down out of nowhere and decapitate us with a purple sabre!" hysterically exclaimed Duncan.

"Wo! Wo! Slow up, ! I am sure it was as frightening as you say it was; but, let me ask you a question, who is "Milly"?" pressed McKeever.

"Sir, she was the one who saved me!" cried Duncan.

"Maybe you should start from the beginning; I must be getting senile in my old age."

"We landed at the lower "Suwannee" just like you suggested, Captain. We picked up "Fanning Springs Creek" and took it for twenty miles to "Wannee" where we rested during the daylight hours.

Although we heard drums, we saw no sign of the enemy until we got about six miles from the fort. May I sit down, Sir?"

"Absolutely! Let me fix you a drink?" politely asked Isaac.

"I'll take some rum if you have it, Captain. Like I was saying, when we got within earshot of "Fort White" that's when we heard Lieutenant Scott's men firing their rifles. Strangely to us, the bullets streaked through the tops of the trees!

I divided my unit and came in on the left and right flanks; that's when we saw the slaughter!

We ran into the fort and formed a fighting circle but it did us no good. Welch came in from above us, killed three of my men with his purple sabre and then zipped up through the trees like a monkey!

Truthfully, I got so frightened by what I saw, I didn't take a shot at him. Even if I had, I'd of missed; that bastard was quick as lightening!

Sir, could I have another one?"

"Sure. So, when did Milly come into the fray?" asked McKeever.

"After we fixed our bayonets, I ordered my last four men to run as fast as they could to get out from under the trees. We had planned to head due east through "Lafayette Flatts" to "Steinhatchee". Only I, made it out of the woods; that's when I saw Milly.

Captain McKeever, what I'm about to tell you is the gospel truth!

That tiny little woman told me to jump into her balloon basket and then flew us both to "Hampton Springs".

From there, a group of Red Sticks took us to Saint Marks." Panted Duncan McKimmon.

Someone knocked on Captain McKeever's door.

"Sir, Lieutenant Bopp just transmitted a message to you. Shall I give you the encrypted version; because, I couldn't make heads nor tails of it?" said the seamen.

"Go ahead."

"Six flashes….a pause….followed by two flashes, Sir! That's all I got."

"Thanks. That's good news!

Lieutenant, I would like for you to send Colonel Jackson a message at Saint Marks.

'Suspected accomplice onboard. Possible Niburian. Needs your questioning.'

Did you get that?

As soon as Jackson responds, let me know immediately!" commanded Captain McKeever.

Five minutes later, the seaman returned with Andrew Jackson's response.

"Secure all prisoners with extra guards. I shall board shortly."

Duncan McKimmon was shocked when two sergeants placed him in shackles. With fire in his eyes, Duncan turned toward McKeever and spoke as the guards were securing him to the ship's main mast.

"Captain, why are you doing this to me?"

The captain did not answer.

As soon as Colonel Jackson arrived on the "Thomas Shield's" deck, he approached Duncan McKimmon who was tightly chained to the mast.

Jackson silently inspected the man's body before he walked into Captain McKeever's cabin where Andy was told exactly what Duncan claimed had happened.

"Captain McKeever, that sonofabitch outside is either the luckiest man alive or he's a boldfaced liar!

You've known the man awhile; which one do you think it is?" questioned Jackson.

"The boy's no coward, Colonel. But, I do believe he's protecting this "Milly" girl for some reason.

He swears, the Red Sticks weren't Scott's men's killers; but, a "flying" man named, "Paddy Welch" was!"

"How many marines did McKimmon lose, Isaac?" Jackson sarcastically asked.

"Seven."

"….and what injuries did 'your boy' sustain?" snarled Colonel Jackson.

"None, Sir!" sheepishly answered Captain McKeever.

"Captain McKeever, there are two 'smelly' things an eighteen year old boy's fancy might be drawn toward. One of those things would be 'fish'! sneered Jackson.

"Sir, Duncan McKimmon has been a superlative officer!" said McKeever.

"I'm not saying he hasn't been, Isaac; but, you must agree, something doesn't make sense. Let's get 'Milly' up here.

Chain her up alongside Lieutenant McKimmon and hear what they have to say." Kindly requested Jackson.

"Right away, Sir!"

By reading Duncan's facial expressions when Milly was brought up from the hold, Jackson's theory held some validity.

The captain introduced Colonel Andrew Jackson to the contrary woman in chains.

"Cutting right to the chase, Miss Francis, what is your relationship with Duncan McKimmon?"

"With whom?" questioned Milly baring a smirk on her face.

"The man 'with whom' you are sharing this mast with!" spat Jackson.

"I have no idea what you're talking about!"

"Is your father's name, "Josiah Francis"?"

"Nope." Answered Milly.

"Then, who is the man in the hold below this deck?" The seething Jackson asked.

"Which one? There are two down there, you idiot!" laughed Milly.

"They are the two, I'm getting ready to hang. Would you care to join them?"

"Whatever trips your trigger, Andrew!" giggled the Indian woman.

"Alright then, I'm going to ask you a question: 'are you in love with Duncan McKimmon?'" poked Jackson.

"Look, stupid, I don't know who you're referring to nor do I have an inkling as to why you people brought me here!

I do know, I am a Cherokee and was enslaved by the people you just slaughtered at Fowltown. So, if you want to hang me for that, go on and do it!" belligerently screamed the chained woman.

"Milly! We love each other, you said so yourself!

Tell them the truth, Darling!

Tell them how you saved me; tell them about Paddy Welch and the balloon you rescued me in. Don't do this to me!" Cried McKimmon.

Milly Francis remained silent. Jackson turned toward Captain McKeever nodded and then somberly spoke.

"Strip McKimmon of his rank and release Milly Francis on shore once we have hanged her father and Himollemico at Saint Marks.

Captain McKeever, you are relieved of your duties. Lieutenant Bopp will take command of the "Thomas Shields" and take her to Washington!

Isaac, you were given an order of which you twisted. Consequently, I shall charge you with "Insubordination" and recommend your court-martial.

Lieutenant Bopp, message John Ross.

Tell him, 'transport the condemned Red Sticks to Saint Marks. Inform him, 'report to me upon his arrival'.

'He has a Niburian to track down. Paddy Welch killed Benjamin Hawkins about which, I'll share the details of his murder following the executions!'" ordered Jackson.

Horizonal winds ripped across Saint Marks's shoreline making it difficult for John Ross to find a decent place to moor the "Paradise". Due to Mount Tambora's volcanic ash, the sun was denied its rightful duties of heating the earth's surface. Snow and sleet replaced the usual April showers.

Jackson's soldiers had constructed a tepeelike gallows out of the rafters from Josiah Francis's home. A six foot hole had been dug beneath the structure to insure an effective drop.

An army chaplain waited behind as six cavalry officers assisted Himollemico and Francis from the "Paradise's" deck. Both of the prisoners' hands were tied behind their backs.

John Ross, Colonel Jackson and Milly remained in the "Paradise's" wheelhouse. A drummer tapped out the ubiquitous beats as the division's minister began his chants.

The procession left tracks on the icy beach as they slowly moved toward their destination. Milly wept.

Jackson provided Milly Francis with a week's worth of rations, winter clothing, boots, and a map. She was let out at the "Econfina River" with no departing words exchanged.

Ross was given the intel Billy McIntosh had given to Jackson.

"Silver Passage" was the site where Welch had last been seen.

John Forbes and the Muskogee people were to exchange the "Paradise" for the supplies Ross needed for his quest. Andy returned to his soldiers.

Chapter Seven

John Forbes sent a crew of able-bodied males to pull the "Paradise" up to a newly constructed drydock. He intended on refurbishing the craft from head to toe. Its new name would be, "The Muscogee Princess".

John Ross spent four days with Forbes in preparation of tracking down Paddy Welch. Upon his northerly departure up the "Ochlockonee Trail", Forbes gave the Shawnee chief some advice.

"This Welch fellow is not like a normal human being, John; therefore, do not expect him to behave as one!

He is damn well expecting you to come after him and he's going to do his dead level best to kill you as soon as he senses your presence.

I have never tangled with a Niburian but to a degree, I have studied their ways. They seem to avoid open conflict and usually attack from positions which offer them a guaranteed escape.

'Noticeability', appears to be their greatest concern. As far as weaknesses go, if any, I would say, it is their "tunnel vision"; i.e., apparently they focus on one target at a time and then move on to the next.

Since Jackson is in Florida, my guess is, Paddy will go after a less difficult target. Chief, if I were in your shoes, I'd find Tecumseh and Seekaboo or for that matter, Tecumseh's brother, "Tenskwatawa".

Welch for sure, will go after 'someone'. Those, I named, are the three most logical 'targets', in my mind.

There is the possibility you know, that this "Milly" woman could be the wildcard in the game!

You say you put her out at the Econfina?" John Forbes asked.

"Jackson and I both did. But, you maybe right; when Andy was questioning her onboard the "Thomas Shields", she claimed to be a Cherokee!" said Ross.

"Was that not the same place Tecumseh was headed?" queried John Forbes.

"John, do you think there is a tie-in between Milly and Chief Tecumseh?" startling asked Ross.

"Not at all; but, my bet would be, there is with Paddy Welch!

Didn't Welch and Francis chum up together at one time?" Asked Forbes.

"You're correct! Damn it, that was right in front of my very eyes and I never thought about it!

I'll go to Tennessee; that's where they're going to be!

Coincidences can't be overlooked but the question still remains, 'how do I snoop around without Paddy Welch knowing I'm after him?'. Any suggestions?" asked John Ross.

"I'd make him come to you. I would have something to sell that he needs!"

"…and what might that be, you figure?" curiously asked Ross.

"Guns and whiskey!" said John Forbes.

"And where do you suppose I could find those items in such a place as this?"

"I've already packed them in your wagon, John." Said Forbes.

"How in the hell did you know I'd need them, John?" asked the surprised John Ross.

"I'm a Culper too, remember?" answered Forbes.

* * * * *

On a Sunday evening following his mandatory vesper service, Andrew Jackson took his horse out for a ride along the narrow gulf shore of "Spring Creek".

About a mile from his division's encampment, Andrew noticed a capsized dinghy that had apparently washed up on the beach.

Andy dismounted the appaloosa, withdrew his sabre from it's sheath and walked toward the wreck. When he saw a hand begin slapping against the side of the small craft, Jackson spoke.

"Before I flip this bloody dinghy over, you must identify yourself!"

"My name is, "Robert Ambrister" and my injured friend is, "Alex Arbuthnot"!

We are Scottish traders. Our ship capsized during the storm and this is where we ended up." Said Ambrister.

"Where is your injured friend named, "Alex"?" asked Jackson.

"He's under this blasted boat with me!"

"Why can't you two men toss the thing over for yourselves?" the colonel asked.

"Alex's back is broken and my legs are busted up pretty bad; please help us!" pleaded Robert.

Jackson fired one of his pistols into the air and then blew a metal whistle in four short blasts.

Within minutes, both Ambrister and Arbuthnot were in the back of a wagon headed toward the headquarters' surgical tent. Jackson waited outside until "Doctor Robinson" gave him a report.

"Andy, they're hurt but they will make it in time for their trials!" laughed the physician.

"What in Pete's name are you saying, Clifford?" asked the humorous less Jackson.

"Colonel, did you happen to see the bags of money those boys stashed in their duffle bags?

Those two men are gunrunners for starters, Andrew; furthermore, I'd bet the farm, they are British agents!" Snickered the combat surgeon.

"…And how in god's name did you extrapolate those golden nuggets of truth, Doc?"

Asked Andy.

"I simply made a deal with them, that's all, Colonel!" said the inebriated "Doctor Clifford Robinson".

"Damn it, Cliff! How'd you find out?" pushed Andrew Jackson.

"I had to set both of Arbuthnot's femurs and Ambrister's collar bone; they exchanged with me, the truth for anesthesia!" cackled Doctor Robinson.

* * * * *

Milly had traveled up the deer trails alongside the Econfina River until she reached Suwannee Springs.

Good fortune came her way when she came upon a couple of Osceola boys fishing from a canoe. They had a string of catfish dragging behind their swamp rig.

When the young men paddled into an upcoming cove, they spied a naked Indian woman stretched out on a flat rock. The wannabe braves tried to ignore her but their composure was lost when Milly motioned for them to come closer.

"I didn't think a man could catch fish in the midst of a cold front!

Ya'll must be mighty good at it; how'd you do it?" asked the coquette young woman.

"That doesn't apply to catfish!" said the boy in the rear of the boat.

"Well, what you have dangling down there looks pretty nice to me!" schmoozed Milly.

"We've caught bigger ones than this mess further up the river, before!

My little brother will testify to that!" coolly exclaimed the older boy sitting in the front.

"How do you fix them; that is, before you eat them?"

"I generally smoke them." Sheepishly replied the elder.

"I'll bet your wife loves it when you do it for her!" alluringly commented Milly.

"Oh, he's not married!" defensively responded the older boy's younger brother.

"How's that possible?

I would have bet my lucky star, he would have had at least two wives by now!" slickly whispered the voluptuous woman.

"I've had my chances; it's just that, the right one hasn't come along lately!" butted in the lying boy sitting in the front of the beached canoe.

"What are your names?"

"My name is, "Toby" and my big brother's is, "Luke"; we haven't earned our real names yet on account of our ages and all!" innocently said Toby.

"That certainly surprises me. I would have thought both of you were at least in your twenties!"

"What's your name?" courageously asked Luke.

"Bushwillow." Said Milly Francis with a lip licked smile.

"Would you like a fish, Bushwillow?" asked Toby.

"Only if you'd smoke it for me." Coaxed Milly.

"I'll start the fire, Toby, if you'll get the stringer and some wood. See if you can't find some birch while I clean this bad boy on top!" ordered Luke.

"Toby, take your time out there. Your big brother is going to teach me how to skin a catfish!

I've never done one of those before; it might take me awhile to get the hang of it!" teasingly prodded "Bushwillow".

"The first thing you want to do is be careful of the fish's whiskers…"

* * * *

Paddy Welch checked into the town of "Ramsey's" finest inn. He requested a balconied suite providing a bountiful view of the "Cumberland River".

From his riverside lanai, the "Mamba" (Niburian assassin) could take a clean shot at anything floating up or down the Cumberland's "Hartsville twist".

The downward river's flow offered Paddy a fifteen hundred yard target; but, the upward swing put Tecumseh's golden ship within range of his "'Hall' breach loader".

Upon gaging several boats' speeds passing 'down' and then 'up' the "twist", Paddy estimated, he would fire his first bullet in half of an hour.

Word on the street had it that the "magical flying ship" would pass in two days, through Ramsey on its way to Nashville.

Even the nearby "Chickasaws", were setting up campsites within spitting distance of the Cumberland River; they too, had heard of the great prophesies being told to them of what was to come.

Carnival spirited white folks joined in with their Indian neighbors. It was dually surmised that "The Reckoning" might just be really happening!

Venders of all sorts, sprang up on both sides of the river's weaving banks. An air of hopeful forgiveness seemed to mingle in with the campfires' smoke.

Disguised as a riverboat captain and decked out in the appropriate garb befitting of such a man, Paddy rented a very fine carriage under the pretense of touring the local sites.

In actuality, Mister Welch was in route to a Nashville gunsmith's shop to have a dozen brass casings recalibrated to fit his rifle.

* * * * *

"Harvey Hildebrand" looked up from his workbench when "Captain Rigsby" tapped on his shop's front door. A "Closed" sign dangled in the widow.

"Sorry, but we're closed; we'll open Monday morning at nine o'clock!" said the gunsmith using a thick Austrian accent.

"Mister Hildebrand, I have a bit of an emergency, Sir! I set sail on Tuesday for New Orleans and I desperately need an antidote for a 'pirate problem'!" gasped Welch.

"What kind of "pirate problem"?" asked Hildebrand.

"I have a "Hall Sharps 45-70 cartridge rifle" and I have to get more range. An upgraded casing to a "110", will give me what I need."

"Young man, I don't have the time nor do you have the money, to make that kind of alteration!

They're aren't but fifteen or twenty of those rifles in existence and anyway, I don't have the equipment necessary to elongate the breech. I'm afraid I can't help you and besides, tomorrow's the Sabbath and that's the Lord's day, not mine!" argued the Austrian.

"Sir, I have an ounce of gold that "says", if you reduce the bullet size, it'll fit!

Furthermore, I'm not using a lead bullet; so, for the sake of expanding your professional expertise as well as your economic wellbeing, don't you think it would be worth your while to help me with my little conundrum?" slickly stated the Niburian as he slid a doubloon beneath the shop's door.

"Ah, please come in, Captain Rigsby! Let's get your rifle out from that beautiful case of yours and let's see what we can do!

You mentioned that you were not using a lead bullet. Do you have a sample of the alternative?" curiously asked Harvey Hildebrand.

Paddy removed a slender wooden box from his peacoat's breast pocket and carefully placed it on the gunsmith's table. Welch then opened the Niburian rifle box with the strange markings burned onto its outer skin.

"What is this thing made of, Captain? I mean, what kind of metal is it? It's not steel!" amazingly queried the old gunsmith.

"No, it's not steel, "titanium", I believe is what they call it. It's a weapon the military is looking at." Said Paddy.

"You said you were a ship captain?"

"Yes, I did; but, I also do other things for a living!" Snickered Welch.

"Mister Rigsby, these 'bullets' or whatever they're called, look more like darts to me!

You say these are for shooting pirates?" suspiciously asked Hildebrand.

"Actually, they are used to blow up their boats!" laughed the Niburian.

"So, you want me to build a cartridge capable of launching an explosive warhead?"

"Precisely."

"How many feet per second is required for these little wings to make it true in flight?" inquired the analytical Austrian.

"Twelve hundred." Answered Paddy Welch.

"I see the scope; how do you achieve accuracy with such a device as this?" asked Harvey Hildebrand.

"Harvey, that's not a scope; it's a laser. Once you get the target's "signature", the dart as you call it, guides itself to that 'thing' you're shooting at."

"Level with me, Captain Rigsby, who are you?" seriously asked Harvey.

"Mister Hildebrand, if I were to honestly answer that question, I'm afraid it would endanger both of our lives; however, I will tell you, my duties are for the betterment of this world!

We live in perilous times, my friend. As an "Agent" for the American government, my duties often entail doing and using things which are not considered to be conventional nor necessarily moral. So, can we leave my explanation at that, Sir?" dramatically asked Paddy.

"I understand. Would you say a hundred grains of powder will do the job, Captain?" proudly asked the Austrian expatriate.

"Absolutely, but first, we'll need to extend the casing by a quarter of an inch. There is no twisting in the barrel; therefore, the dart's wings only have to snugly fit into the breech.

All that's necessary is the thrust, Harvey; afterwards, the smart-dart does the rest." Condescendingly remarked Paddy.

"Very well, I'll build up the shell casing, extend the length of it, crimp the end so the wings slip into the breeching perfectly, correct?"

"Exactly." Answered Welch.

"I'm going to need more time. It'll take three days to make a dozen, Captain Rigsby." Said Harvey.

Paddy plunked down three more doubloons on Harvey Hildebrand's workbench!

With a perplexed grin on his face, Paddy asked him if he thought four ounces of gold would be worth burning some 'midnight oil'.

"Captain, that's more than enough; but, stretching out brass is very time consuming!" commented the gunsmith.

"Harvey, this is a once in a lifetime opportunity for you; besides, it's a nice evening and we have nine hours left until sunrise.

I think a night's work is worth your annual salary, don't you?"

"Yes, Sir!" gleefully commented Harvey.

* * * * *

Andrew Jackson was patiently sitting between the two recovery cots where Arbuthnot and Ambrister were sleeping. Doctor Robinson pulled up a chair and sat down in front of Jackson.

He opened up a new jug of scotch and poured himself and Andy a liberal cup of the whiskey as he made some veiled suggestions.

"You know, Andrew, 'honey catches flies better than vinegar does'!

Maybe offering these chaps a little bit of kindness will allow them, in their minds, to more freely yield up the answers to the questions you're going to ask them; do you agree?"

"Cliff, I'll take your suggestions under consideration. How long before I'll be able to converse with these gentlemen?" sarcastically queried Jackson.

"Oh, I guess within the hour." Said the physician.

"Doctor Robinson, of the two, which one would you assume will be more likely to tell the truth?" questioned Colonel Jackson.

"No doubt, that would be "Ambrister"; after all, he was a former Royal Marine and a self-appointed British "agent"!

For those reasons, I would expect him to feel he should receive preferential treatment." Slurred Robinson.

Jackson called for his "Sergeant at Arms". The sergeant entered the triage tent.

"Yes, Sir. "First sergeant McGillacutti" reporting!"

"Sergeant, while Mister Arbuthnot is still under Doctor Robinson's anesthetic, I want you to take him outside and hang him!

Leave the tent's flap open. That way, when his cohort awakens and I question him, the sleepy little fellow won't be confused." Cooley said Colonel Jackson.

"Shall I have my men build a tripod, Sir?" briskly asked the first sergeant.

"Yes. Just as we did with Hadjo, Sergeant." Answered Andy.

* * * * *

At 0400hrs. a Cerian transport craft lowered John Ross and his four horse team of Clydesdales into an overgrown field southwest of "Lebanon". Forty miles north was "Hartsville", where the Cerians believed Paddy Welch's to be.

Ross's wagon was in actuality, a rolling fortress. It was painted with red paint.

The windows were not much more than gun slits with a rectangular opening for the driver to see out of. White letters, a foot tall each, advertised the mobile store's wares.

On both sides, they read: "Pistol Pete's Reasonably Priced Guns, Ammo and Whiskey For Sale."

John had bleached his hair a snow white. He wore an American army jacket, a gentleman's high-top hat and leather pants.

All transactions would be conducted through the wagon's rear window slot. Metal money was the only acceptable medium of exchange.

Neither the customers' faces nor the vendor's(John Ross) face, would be seen. It was a 'cash and carry' operation.

Ross's major objective was to kill Paddy Welch. It was hoped that whiskey and guns would do that very thing.

* * * * *

Luke's larynx was sliced open so wide that the only thing Toby could have possibly heard, was a hiss of air escaping from his brother's lungs.

Milly dragged the dead boy into the river along with a rock tied around his body. She then swept sand over the telltale blood sprays and finished cleaning the catfish.

As Toby returned with an armful of birch limbs, 'Bushwillow' lured him into the woods. The excuse she gave the eight year old for his brother's absence, was due to a bobcat prowling too close to where they were cleaning the catfish.

When Toby saw that Luke had not taken his bow and quiver of arrows, he panicked and ran into the surrounding swamp.

Bushwillow called Toby for only a few seconds before weighing the amount of risk involved with tracking him down; conclusively, she set the forest on fire.

Milly took the boys' skiff and paddled it up the "Suwanee Springs River" about a half mile and then tied the boat up. Intrepidly, the Red Stick returned with Luke's bow and arrows to the murder scene.

As dark was falling, Bushwillow hid beneath a cottonwood bush and called Toby's name just as she imagined his older brother would do. She even whistled like her father taught her. It worked. Milly returned to the skiff.

* * * * *

"Welcome back to the living, Robert!

Doctor Robinson tells me your surgery went beautifully and you'll be as good as new, in no time!

'Ole Clifford' and I were celebrating your recovery and we thought you might like to have a drink with us!

Let me pour you a mug; are you hungry?" asked Jackson in a sinister tone.

"Even if I wanted your scotch and a bodacious amount of lamb, I would be unable to accept due to the fact, my legs and arms are bound!

And what pray tell, is that in front of this tent?" screamed Robert Ambrister.

"Robert, I'm afraid Mister Arbuthnot was found guilty by our 'tribunal' for supplying the Spanish military with weapons and inciting war against the United States of America. Therefore, I hanged him." Matter-of-factly stated Andrew Jackson.

"Colonel Jackson, I am a Royal Marine of a nation at peace with your own. It is true, Alexander and I sold rifles to the Indians on properties outside of American jurisdiction but that's all, we "legally" did!"

"Here's the problem, Mr. Ambrister, you are an admitted British agent. That is, you are a spy; are you not?" charged Jackson.

"Colonel, all I have done, was help Arbuthnot move a few guns into the Spanish owned territory; you can't hang me for that!"

"I have no intention of it, Robert!" said Andy.

Jackson then abruptly stood. Once again, he called for his Sergeant at Arms.

"First Sergeant McGillacutti, would you please have four of your men remove "Agent Ambrister's" cot from this stuffy medical tent.

Prop it up against that lovely old live oak tree, the one closest to the gulf!

Kindly, ready a firing squad for Robert's execution. I shall do the 'coup de grace', myself!"

"You crazy bastard; this will be the end of your career, Jackson!" yelled Ambrister.

Andrew Jackson did not reply.

"On what grounds are you committing this atrocity?" squealed Robert.

"For aiding the Seminoles and inciting them to make war against the United States of America!" said Andy.

"And…what about my trial?" seethed the condemned man strapped to his cot.

"You were asleep during your hearing." Snickered Andy.

"This is preposterous!

Andrew Jackson, may you rot in hell!"

"Would you care for a blindfold?" comically asked Jackson.

"Fuck you!" whispered the British Royal Marine.

Jackson, without ordering the squad to 'fire', shot Robert in the head.

* * * * *

"Captain Rigsby, before I press the primers into place, I would prefer to crimp the cartridge so there will be a snug fitting for the dart wings." Said Harvey Hildebrand.

"Actually, Harvey, since the dart slides neatly into the cartridge's throat, all we need, is to accelerate the smart-dart out the end of the barrel with enough speed for the laser beam to "tell" the dart where to go." Instructed Paddy.

"There is no heat applied to the dart during assembly then; is that correct, Captain?" asked the gunsmith.

"None whatsoever. As a matter of fact, Sir, I shall only slide the dart into the cartridge seconds before I breech it."

"What happens to the target when it strikes?" queried Harvey.

"It explodes." Condescendingly snickered Welch.

"What chemical agent would cause that, Captain Rigsby"

"I'm afraid I can't tell you that, my friend. It's a "governmental" secret!"

"You're a "Culper" aren't you! I've heard about you guys!" pushed Hildebrand.

Paddy Welch ignored the Austrian's inquiry but smiled and nodded at the same time. He then gave further instructions.

"Alright, prime the cartridges, add only thirty-five grains of powder to each and plug them up. We'll test one when the sun comes up.

Harvey, you've done a remarkable job and a great deed for your country!" praised Paddy.

"It's the Sabbath, Captain!"

"That's right; I forgot. I'm sorry. I'll have to do it once I get out of the city limits."

"Captain Rigsby, it has been an honor meeting you. I'd very much appreciate hearing how our "thingamabobs" worked out." earnestly said Harvey.

"Likewise, Sir, and I'll do just that, I promise!

Do you attend that Lutheran Church just down the street?" asked Paddy Welch.

"Hadn't missed a Sunday in thirty years!" proclaimed Hildebrand.

* * * * *

Milly paddled up the Econfina River for three days until she reached the "Suwannee Basin". She would have traveled further north but she ran into a little 'luck' on the outskirts of a border town called, "Jasper".

Within earshot of the Ebenezer Church's piano, a wagon train made up of nine families in seven covered wagons, had stopped alongside the same river where Milly had beached the dead Indian boys' skiff.

Excited voices echoed off of the Suwannee's opposite bank's trees. Milly heard the word, "gold" mentioned three times.

Stealthily, Francis circled around the wagon train's rear and approached the mule team's head wagon. She paused for a few moments under the pretense of examining two of the mules' mouths.

With a professional's look upon her face, she spoke to the man sitting on the lead wagon's driver's bench.

"Sir, I'm not trying to sound presumptuous but as I was passing by, I could not help but notice your mules are likely candidates for a serious illness known as, "Bacillus anthracis"." Sternly stated Milly Francis.

"Mam, I don't know much about mules except from looking at them pulling a plow. I'm just a farmer and I've never heard tell of whatever you just said.

What was it again?" asked the middle-aged man.

"Oh, I'm sorry!

'Bacillus anthracis' in layman's terms, means, "anthrax". Mammals usually get it from insect bites that become infected.

I can temporarily treat it; however, I'm afraid you'll need to get them immunized when you get to someplace where there is a good livery stable.

Are you folks headed north?

If you are, I happen to know a mighty good one in "Dasher". Ole "Doc Phillips" up there, is probably the best horse man in Georgia!" authoritatively said Milly.

"Well, young lady, you seem to know a lot about doctoring. You think highly of this, "Doc" Phillips, do you?" queried the curious wagon train's master.

"We went to school together in "Athens" and I know he settled on his family's plantation, south of "Valdosta". He specializes in large animal medicine." Lied Francis.

"And what about you; are you an animal doctor too?" asked the team's leader.

"No, I just work with humans, mostly, pregnant ones."

"You're a doctor are you?"

"I am. What brings you folks up this way?" prodded Milly.

"We're from "Ratliff"; what's left of it!

The storm wiped us out!

We use to grow peaches but our trees froze up so we're headed up to "Helen" to join our kin.

We're Germans so it'll be nice to mix back up with our roots. I believe all of us have missed the 'old ways' if you know what I mean.

By the way, my name is, "Rudolph Mentz" and yours?" brightly asked Rudolph.

"A pleasure to meet you, Mister Mentz! My name is, "Francis Culler"."

"What miracle has brought you here, Miss Culler, or should I address you as, "Doctor Culler"?"

"My patients and friends call me, "Doctress".

A "miracle", Sir? You mentioned a miracle meeting me here?" sheepishly asked 'Doctress'.

"Yes, I did, Doctress!

We have some sick people with us. Plus, three of the women are pregnant and one of those is in labor!" whispered Rudolph.

"You mentioned sick people, Mister Mentz, what signs are they exuding for you to say that?" fervently asked Milly.

"Lesions and fever mostly."

"I see. Rudolph, do you have a good horse I can borrow?

I need to quickly ride to my office and pick up some "sulfonamide"; because of the sad fact, you've got an outbreak of "cholera" within your midst!

I'll be back within three hours. In the meantime, pull your wagons in close together and then encircle your entire caravan with fuel oil. It will prevent further "carcinogens" from entering the sick peoples' bodies.

Keep everyone within the quarantined perimeter until I get back!

I wouldn't mind taking along with me that shotgun you have beside of you; the Seminoles have been somewhat rowdy since the weather changed and I'd like to protect myself, if need be!

Do not tarry with the things I have instructed you to do. These precautions will stabilize your people until we can get some medicine in them; they'll feel much better after that!" panted Milly.

* * * *

John Ross pulled his team of horses off the road at a spot offering a shallow creek. He detached the Clydesdales from the wagon's tongue and tied them close enough to the wagon's rear slot so he could keep an eye on them.

Ross had positioned his gun and whiskey wagon on a bluff overlooking the Hartsville Twist. From there, he could see the Indians camped alongside the winding Cumberland River. He glassed the horizon looking for the optimal position a sniper would likely choose.

The only feasible shooting alley, John could fathom, was from two of the buildings in Ramsey. He then focused his attention on the taller one.

From the small window located at the wagon's front, Chief Ross examined every brick and crevice a shooter could possibly use to zero in on Seekaboo's and Tecumseh's flying ship.

Logically, Ross thought, Paddy Welch would be limited to a five hundred yard shot; therefore, he deduced that when he saw the "magic ship" pass through "Dixon Springs", he could get a 'fix' on Paddy's position.

John picked out a hemlock tree which he gaged at four hundred yards from Welch's most likely perch. 'He would use a forty-four caliber conical bullet powered by a hundred and sixty grains of black powder to 'drop' the Nib.

Darkness was setting in. John Ross elected to wait until morning to set up his tree stand.

In the meantime, he would build a bonfire, attract some customers, sell some guns and whiskey and appear to Welch as being just another huckster.

* * * *

The mood among Jackson's troops was to say the least, somber. Even the Colonel's staff officers knew when Andy was drinking, he was as mean as a cottonmouth.

If the whole truth were to be told, had Jackson not been in his cups, Arbuthnot, Ambrister, Francis and Himollemico would have had something resembling a trial; but, that was not the case.

Not one single soldier under Colonel Jackson's command would have turned him in for his "war crimes". But, if it ever got back to Washington, Jackson's numerous enemies would have him jailed!

The night following Ambrister's death, a negro woman in a frenetic like state, was found wandering around the swamp a little north of their Saint Marks encampment. Reluctantly, the sergeant at arms reported the finding to Jackson.

"Colonel Jackson, I'm sorry to wake you at this hour but the perimeter guards found a crazy woman walking around the marsh in the northwestern sector. Sir, she's in pretty bad shape with frostbite and all.

Doctor Robinson has her in the medical tent right now. The 'Doc' was wondering, Sir, if you wanted to talk with her before he amputated her toes!"

"Sergeant, I want you to give that goddamned doctor a message from me, you tell him that I am in no mood to question his patient but before he puts her to sleep, I want to know her name, where she comes from, (and) the whereabouts of her people!

If Robinson can't extrapolate that information from her, just shoot the bitch and throw her body into the bloody Gulf of Mexico." Answered the quite inebriated Division Commander.

"Colonel, Will there be anything else you wish for me to say, Sir" asked the uneasy sergeant.

"I'm not going to repeat my orders, Sergeant!

If you and he cannot find out who she is and the whereabouts of her people, then save the anesthesia for our men and kill her. Bullets are cheaper than medicine!"

Within minutes after receiving Jackson's conveyed message, the military surgeon appeared at the drunken colonel's tent. He brought a jug of whiskey with him and an armful of sausages and bread.

"Andy, you've been on a binge for two days now; it's time for you to eat something!

If you keep this up, you're going to get us all court-martialed!

The so-called "crazy woman" laying over there on my operating table is named "Elizabeth Stewart"; she is a black Seminole. Her peoples' villages are in the Spanish held, "Pensacola" area.

She says there are nearly two hundred soldiers fortifying "Fort Barrancas". Her children along with other women and their children, are there!

Their men have joined in with Nichol's and are barracked up at "Fort Angola", she thought.

Her reason for being in that neck of the woods was to bring you a message from the Governor of West Florida. They want peace, Andy." Calmly said Robinson.

"Well, what they're going to get, and I don't give a damn what they want, is lead and fire!

I'm sick and tired of fooling around with these dumb bastards!

No peace shall I give them!" raged Andrew Jackson.

"How long have we been friends, Andy?" asked the physician.

"Forever; why?" asked the astonished commander.

"Because you're burned out, my friend. You're long overdue for a rest!

As the second in command, I am hereby ordering you to return home to Nashville; besides, you haven't seen "Rachel" in over a year.

I'll order Colonel William King to finish up here. But you, Sir, are hereby relieved of your command for medical reasons, Colonel Jackson.

Kindly pack your things; you're leaving for Tennessee right now!" firmly said Colonel Robinson.

Without an objection, Jackson in an almost childlike manner, mounted his horse and rode out of Saint Marks. His escorts followed. Andy never looked back.

*　*　*　*　*

Paddy Welch checked his watch before he snapped his whip over the two horses powering his carriage. At eight thirty he reached the "Lakewood Road" and took it southeast until he came to Nashville's famous overlook known as, "Mount Juliet". Paddy pulled his team of horses off the road.

Out of what looked like a bass fiddle's satchel, the Mamba (Niburian assassin) assembled a wooden shooter's bench and leveled it on top of a mound of soft dirt. He then began glassing Harvey Hildebrand's suburb called "Green Hill".

When the Lutheran church's ground mounted bell began clanging, the Niburian once again, checked his pocket watch; it was ten o'clock on the nose. Paddy unlatched his elephant hide rifle case and proceeded to 'dry-fire' his weapon so as to maximize his comfort level.

Harvey Hildebrand emerged from his home at precisely ten fifteen and took two hundred and twelve steps toward the church's red painted door.

As soon as Harvey went inside, Welch removed one of his smart-darts from it's teakwood box and carefully seeded it into one of Harvey's customized casings. He then chambered it into the modified breach.

After making doubly sure the red door received a tightly focused signature posting, Paddy squeezed the trigger.

Following a slight 'pop', the dart traveled it's expected eight hundred and fifty yards. Hildebrand's Lutheran church imploded.

In less than one second, the stone house of worship was reduced to a sand pile. Paddy methodically repacked his lethal equipment and resumed his easterly travel. It had snowed a little bit that night but the sun was out.

* * * * *

"Rudolph Mentz" was standing on top of the driver's bench barking orders like a Hessian drill instructor. He pointed to the areas that had not yet been doused with fuel oil.

The covered wagons were bunched up exactly as "Doctress" had instructed him to do; the mules were corralled within the circular formation.

Several boys scoured the nearby forests collecting green moss from the numerous hardwood trees to feed to the anthrax infected mules.

From her well-hidden position, some seventy five yards from the jumbled up encirclement, Milly drew back Luke's bow and released a fiery arrow.

The broadhead stuck into the haunches of a mule which instantly reacted by dropping to the oily grass beneath it. The entire wagon train instantly turned into a smoky black hell.

Congregants from the Ebenezer Church pored out of their quaint sanctuary and ran to the pandemonium going on outside. One of the mules jumped between two of the intersecting wagons but caught his hindleg in between the struts of a wheel.

The people able to escape the fire licks, found their oil drenched clothing acting as fuses when they returned to help others from the places they had jumped from.

All the churchmen could do, was beat their Sunday jackets on those escaping from the blazing perimeter.

While the ruckus was going on down by the river, Milly Francis helped herself to the valuable knickknacks left on the church pews. She even swapped Rudolph's saggy backed mare for a much younger horse on which, she kicked northward.

* * * * *

John Ross had made some friends of those whom he had sold guns and whiskey to. As a matter of reckoning, he had enjoyed their company too much; for when he awakened, it was nine o'clock, his wagon had been stripped clean of its contents, his Clydesdales were gone and unbeknownst to him, a smart-dart was speedily headed his way.

* * * * *

Colonel Andrew Jackson and his escorts resupplied at "Fort Gadsden". When Jackson arrived at the fort, he was given a letter which had arrived two months earlier; it was from the Secretary of State, John Quincy Adams.

There were two things gleaned from Quincey's writing; e.g., Jackson was now a "General" and the United States and Spain were finally at peace. Andy cried.

Chapter Eight

Rachael Jackson stood on the balcony overlooking "Lebanon Cedars Road". According to the military messenger who had visited two days earlier, Andrew's arrival was expected around noon. It was half past three o'clock.

Already frayed by the anticipation of her husband's return coupled with the humbling shock of Andy Jr.'s near drowning, Hannah saw to it, Rachael got a little opium powder in her cup of coco.

It was sundown when General Jackson's carriage arrived onto the Hermitage Plantation grounds. Jackson had sworn off liquor since his near-death knife fight with a Chickamauga brave at "Tuscumbia Crossing" back in the Spring.

He had made a deal with "god"; 'if he were allowed to live through the three hour ordeal, he would give the booze up and build a church for his wife'. Although, when his entourage got to "Lawrenceburg", Andy 'renegotiated' his end of the bargain on account, he owed Davie Crockett a favor which included a brothel and some 'wicked' rum.

Jackson, as expected, continued his imbibing until he got to the outskirts of Nashville where a couple of hours were spent trying to 'walk'. That time consumption was the authentic reason he was late coming home.

Rachael was a 'dyed in the wool' Presbyterian who didn't relish the 'unsaved side' of her husband. Hannah was there along with Jacob, to get him presentable.

"Lord have mercy, General, you ain't nothing but skin and bones and praised be, you smell worse than a drunken skunk!

Thanks be to Jesus, "Miss Rachael" is fast asleep in yallsun's bed cause you ain't ready to be seen yet!" Hawked Hannah.

"You know, I love you, Hannah!

Thank you for understanding me, my angel!" blabbered the weaving general.

"Hush your mouth!

Jacobs is gonna take you to the guesthouse and get you cleaned up so you'll look like the respectable man you actually are!

We'll be serving dinner at eight thirty!" stormed Hannah.

"Yes, Mam!" answered the now ambulatorial Jackson.

* * * *

Tenskwatawa had traveled from Saint Marks and through central Georgia mostly living off the Cherokee's backs. What he presented to them, in return, was a vividly described "Promise Land" west of the Mississippi River.

The great chief also offered the questioning insight into, 'how life would be without the white man poking around their homes'. Tenskwatawa 'painted' a lovely picture.

Drumbeats sent news of the flying ship across the Allegheny Mountains and on to the Atlantic coastline. Tribes from all over the country sought out to hear what this "Shawnee Prophet" had to say.

On one particular evening in a village called, "Pocataligo", Tenskwatawa drew an audience so large, the "move to the west" meeting had to be moved into the "Sandy Cross Cavern". It was the Shawnee prophet's first opportunity to meet a real live Cerian in the flesh.

About an hour into his standard, 'pot of gold beneath the rainbow' story, the Shawnee orator noticed a green mist hanging about a foot off of the cavern's floor. A black man garbed in a white gown with a red cross stitched onto its front, floated across the unconscious mass and toward Tenskwatawa. The image spoke in English.

"I come in good spirit, Tenskwatawa. My purpose is to make you aware of the dangers your people are facing."

"May I ask you, your name?" calmly asked the Shawnee chief.

"I am, "Prince Hall" and a Cerian, wishing to impart a good measure of wisdom to your people. Perhaps with an understanding of some history involving your enemy, you may find a way to defeat him.

Tenskwatawa, for thousands of years the intelligent beings of this planet (Nicosa), have cooperated with those from Ceria. Our two worlds understand that "we"(Cerians) provide security and technologies while "you"(Nicosans) mine for us a percentage of your minerals. The Masons orchestrate the scheduled intricacies.

Sadly, another world, the "Niburians", are again interfering with our agreement. They have launched a new offensive against both of us!

I speak to you of these things not to belabor you with a history lesson but to warn you of what is to take place.

Soon, a Niburian named, "Paddy Welch" will attempt to destroy America by divisive means!

Tribal Nations throughout North America, will be the chum bait. Three different planets all with similar appetites, will come to feed.

Ultimately, the "Indian" will disappear at the hands of the white man.

The best that can be done for your people is to lead them away from the encroaching United States as quickly as possible. Gold has been found in the eastern mountains; consequently, this nation of laws, this republic, will find some statute the Indian has broken and that'll be that!

"Small Pox" hosts, known as, 'apostles', have already been sent into your tribes. Soon, the 'white man' will have a good reason to decimate the "diseased savages". You, Sir, must warn them of these things!"

"Respectfully, Prince Hall, why have you chosen this time and place and more importantly, 'me', to receive these words of cautionary wisdom?" asked Tenskwatawa.

Paddy Welch has within the last twelve hours, killed Seekaboo and a congregation of twenty seven Lutherans!

Your brother, Tecumseh also died. I know how that hurts, my friend, but you can now see 'your enemy' more clearly!" gasped Prince.

"How did my brother die?" tearfully asked Tenskwatawa.

"Explosive smart-darts took them all!" somberly said the Cerian.

"Where is this Paddy Welch now?" loudly asked the Shawnee.

"….And if you go after him armed as an ignorant man, you will join the mountain of bodies left in that renegade Niburian's wake!" Said Prince Hall.

"What makes you think I can't kill him?" screamed the wild acting Shawnee.

"Because you are a Nicosan, that's why!" whispered the Cerian.

"Then, goddamn it, give me your suggestion, Mister Hall!" spat Tenskwatawa.

"In three days, "Milly Francis" is due to arrive at a north Georgian town named, "Dahlonega". She is on her way to Nashville; that's where Paddy Welch is, Tenskwatawa.

Cerian headquarters surmises, their intentions are to eradicate the Andrew Jackson family and then on to the Washingtonians with suspected Culper associations.

One by one, the deadly set of "Mambas" will attempt to pick off the Constitutional advocates until they bring the whole institution down upon themselves and everyone else!" Remorsefully stated Prince Hall.

"Where is Colonel Jackson, now, Sir?" asked Tenskwatawa.

"The newly promoted, 'General' Jackson is 'drying out' at his "Hermitage Plantation" in Nashville. Not so ironically, Tenskwatawa, Jackson's property is less than fifty miles from where your brother and Seekaboo were killed."

"So, what is the solution, Mister Hall?" humbly asked the Shawnee.

"Dahlonega is sixty miles to the northwest of where we currently are standing. You must convince this woman to turn against her paramour, kill him and then receive something of great value to her!

It will be up to you and General Jackson to find out what that 'thing' is. Although, whatever "it" turns out to be, all those involved including Paddy and Milly, must, in the end, be destroyed.

Prince Hall reached out to shake Tenskwatawa's hand but when the Indian chief's fingers touched the Cerian's flesh, he awakened from a troublesome sleep.

* * * * *

The "Chestatee Inn" was Dahlonega's only hotel. It was the last glimpse of civilization before entering the Cherokee lands.

A surplus of men dressed in whatever they wanted others to think they were, hung around the Chestatee's lounge trying to pick up traces of rumored gold strikes.

Dahlonega's only minister interwove his pulpit stories of promises of eternal riches to his packed congregations. Believing it might bring them luck, several of the covert miners would attend "Pastor Neath's" services in hopes the ancient reverend might let it slip as to where the nuggets in the evermoving collection plate came from.

Tenskwatawa soon realized the local Cherokee were also profiting from the apparent spread of gold fever hosted by the increasing numbers of "passerby's".

Reproduced 'ancient maps' were exchanged for horses and pocket watches belonging to the demure zealots any of which, would have sold their mothers' into slavery for a thick vein of gold.

Pastor Neath in coordination with "Sequoyah" the Cherokee Chief, developed "legal documents" giving lifetime mining rights to certain stretches of the "Chestatee River".

In some cases, a "stretch" was less than twenty five yards long and marked with decomposable colored stubs.

Milly Francis had figured out all of these idiocrasies out by the time she checked into the Chestatee Inn under the name of, "Princess Pocahontas".

Needless to say, the news of Milly's arrival spread like a wildfire.

As soon as Dahlonega's mayor, "Pastor Franklin Neath" finished shoeing a miner's horse, he hustled over to the inn with the intentions of introducing himself to the extremely rare hotel's guest.

In a dark corner and sitting in a highbacked chair, Tenskwatawa eavesdropped on their conversation.

"Madam, I am, "Reverend Franklin Neath". I also have a livery stable across the street where you can board that fine little appaloosa, if you'd like.

I'll see that she gets a good rubdown and a bucket of the best malted oats in the country.

If, by chance, you were planning to stay with us for a while, I'd be honored to have you join us for Sunday service. My chapel is right up above the stable.

Maybe I can help you locate a place if that's what you're looking for. I know about everybody around these parts so I'll make sure they'll be fair with you." Said the good reverend.

"Thank you ever so much for your kindness, Pastor Neath; but, I'll be visiting your lovely town for only the day. Someone is to pick me up this afternoon, Sir." Said Milly.

"I see. What a pity. Oh well, in the meantime, I'd be pleased if you would let me care for your horse until you're ready to leave.

It ain't doing no good for her to be tied up outside in this cold weather we're having." Insistently said Franklin Neath.

"Very well, Mister Neath, but please do not overcharge me for I am not a wealthy woman, Sir!" sheepishly begged Princess Pocahontas.

"Is the person whom you're meeting from around here?" prodded Neath.

"Actually, I've never met him!" baited Milly.

"How's that, mam?" bit the pastor.

"He is a friend of one of my most trusted professors. I have been offered an opportunity in Atlanta." Lied Milly.

"Whoa here, Miss Pocahontas!

You must be careful; there are a bunch of godless folks out in this world. This "professor" friend of yours, are you sure he is a reputable chap?" questioned Pastor Neath.

"Absolutely. He is, "Doctor Prince Hall", an Atlanta physician.

I am to be his surgical nurse.

Now, Pastor Neath, if you will excuse me while I finish registering.

Give "Pandora" some extra loving care for me; she's a spirited little filly and deserves it, believe me!" gaily stated Milly.

Tenskwatawa waited until the Mamba had secured her room on the upstairs level of the Chestatee Inn before he stood. He then walked to the rear of the building and entered his first floor suite.

As he was lighting his table lamp, the Shawnee heard the sharp mechanical sounds of a shotgun's double hammers locking into the firing position. Milly Francis's voice rang out.

"It is my understanding, you have a proposal for me?

A black gentleman named, "Prince Hall" made a frightening visit to me. He mentioned your offer would be of great value; therefore, before I splatter your brains against the wall, I'd like to hear what you have to say!"

"Miss Francis, I sent "Agent" Hall to convey a message to you for a very good reason; therefore, let's not play games with the other.

I have a lucrative business deal to offer you!" softly stated Tenskwatawa.

Still training her shotgun on the Shawnee's chest, Milly indicated that she was 'listening'.

"Andrew Jackson "illegally" hanged your father at Saint Marks. Paddy Welch killed my older brother, "Tecumseh" and my closest friend, "Seekaboo".

For those reasons, we are both determined to even the score; is that a reasonable assumption, Miss Francis?"

"Go on!" Answered Milly.

"Given the fact, we represent two opposing forces and are trained on behalf of those opposite factions to see to it that our employers' objectives are met, wouldn't it make 'collaborative sense' for us to retire as despicably wealthy people?" Hypothesized Tenskwatawa.

"What's the deal?" curtly asked Milly.

"The United States government will offer you total immunity from all past crimes and provide you with a lifetime pension comparable to that of an army second lieutenant's pay.

You are to be given a three hundred acre farm of your choosing, anywhere within the boundaries of America!"

"For what reason am I offered this 'congressional embellishment', Tenskwatawa?" asked Milly Francis.

"For the heroic saving of "Duncan McCrimmon's" life and for leading me to Paddy Welch's whereabouts." Coldly said Tenskwatawa.

"Duncan McCrimmon's life was saved only because he was fleetfooted enough to jump into my balloon's basket. Had he been a mile an hour slower, Paddy would have decapitated him too!

As far as the whereabouts of Welch, I'm guessing he right now, is sitting by Andrew Jackson's fireplace sipping on some of the colonel's Tennessee whiskey. Paddy was my father's friend and confidant.

For that reason alone, the entire Jackson family must be wiped off of the face of this planet!

You see, Tenskwatawa, Paddy Welch's main focus is on destroying America's Capitol both physically and morally. He is planning to topple every building within "Washington's Square" down to the ground and light his cigars with pages from the "Constitution of the United States"!

"Proudly exclaimed Milly Francis.

"Would I be fair in assuming, you and Paddy were lovers? Asked the Shawnee chief.

"More than that, he is my husband!" blathered the weeping woman.

"I guess then, there is no reason to pursue a deal, Milly?

Go ahead and shoot if you feel so inclined, either way, our conversation is over!" Gambled the Indian chief.

"What Jackson did to my father was irreprehensible; he must be punished! Colonel Jackson disobeyed even the white mans' laws; for which, he and all of those who associate with him, must pay with their blood!

Certainly as an Indian yourself, you find his bombastic temperament dangerous?

I'm afraid my opinion is not up for debate!" Whispered Milly.

"Mrs. Welch, your position is well founded but the stakes are greater than the misdoings of one man!

We, the Indians of this country are docketed for execution if an agreement is not soon drawn!

Should an American "hero" (justified or not) end up dead by the hands of "savages", morose rationale will then fill the Washingtonians' minds; our elimination would follow!

Milly, "segregation" is our only hope of survival. Otherwise, our ultimate demise will come to us within our generation.

Extinction will be accelerated even faster if it is discovered, the Indians are the "Small Pox" hosts. I say this to you, Milly Francis, because your husband has already sent his infected 'apostles' into North America's tribes.

It is true, Jackson's methods are brutal but his ideologies are not. What he is trying to do is to create a boundary between the red and white skinned people in order to preserve both races!

Given the white man's technologies coupled with his knowledge of the gold laying beneath the "diseased tribal grounds", it doesn't take a lot of imagination to guess what will happen next.

Jackson perhaps to your surprise, hates the "Washingtonian egg-sucking cowards" more than you and I do!

And just for kicks, Milly, Andrew Jackson plans to run for the presidency. If he wins, it is said, 'he expects to imprison the Square's vermin!'" Preached Tenskwatawa.

"Paddy has an unblemished record of 'target hits'; the murderer, "Andrew Jackson" is more than likely already dead. Have you taken that under consideration?" arrogantly asked Francis.

"Indeed we have, Milly, Paddy Welch is currently being held in a Cerian safehouse!" Chortled Tenskwatawa.

"You're a liar! No one could capture my husband!" screamed Milly.

"Although we did have to pull an old warhorse out of the pasture, he was able to incarcerate ole Paddy without one once of trouble!" teased Tenskwatawa.

Milly pulled both triggers of her double barreled shotgun. It misfired.

She attempted to leap from her seat using the weapon as a club but instantly realized she was glued to her plush leather chair. Milly became vocally quite ugly.

"You've tricked me, you bastard!"

"We simply took precautions while you were talking to Pastor Neath!"

"Is Paddy alive?" whimpered Milly.

"Yep!" giggled the Shawnee.

"What do you want me to do?" pleadingly asked Paddy's wife.

"That depends upon yours's and Paddy's "death wish", Milly!

If the two of you desire a normal life together and one rich with children and pleasant memories, I suggest, you both swear your allegiance to America!

On the other hand, if the both of you insist on getting even with those whom have wronged you, your expectations of the future should be more shortsighted!" Macabrely stated the Indian chief.

"Alright, Tenskwatawa, let's say Paddy and I agree to your proposal and then betrayed you, what then?"

""Jay Ray" would harm you both!"

"Is that the man who captured my husband?" asked Milly.

"It is."

"You seem to have a great deal of faith in this man's abilities. Have you met this individual, Tenskwatawa?"

"No, but Prince Hall refers to him as the, "Eraser". "Mister Howe" as the Masons' named him, is occasionally called upon to cleanup politically sensitive messes. Other than that, I know very little about the man." Said Tenskwatawa.

"Is it possible to visit my husband?" meekly asked Milly.

"I've already answered that question, Mrs. Welch; as I said, 'You must swear allegiance to the American 'Creed' and support the promises that nation has made with the Cerians and immediately excommunicate yourself from Niburian contact.'" Stated the Shawnee chief.

"Are you implying that this Mister Howe of Tennessee would kill me if I did not oblige your offer?" sharply asked Milly Francis Welch.

"Not you, Milly!

Jay Ray Howell would simply 'erase' any child you should have born unto you!" condescendingly answered Tenskwatawa.

"Would he actually do that?" meekly asked Milly.

"Like a blacksnake swallowing biddies!"

"When can we go?"

"As soon as you are ready to commit to the aforementioned conditions." Sternly stated Tenskwatawa.

"When will I be permitted to see my husband?" tearfully questioned Milly.

"Within the hour if we have an agreement!" said the pan faced Shawnee chief.

"How is that possible, Tenskwatawa?" cautiously asked Welch's wife.

"Do we have a deal, Milly?"

"Of course!"

Tenskwatawa then pulled from his breast pocket a silver whistle and blew three short blasts on it. Prince Hall along with three other masked men entered the room. Each were wearing crimson robes.

They lifted the petrified Red Stick from her chair and gassed her. Prince Hall through Milly's right eye, injected cobra venom into the woman's hypothalamus.

Minutes later, the cloaked men placed her in the rear compartment of a troop carrying box cart. Paddy Welch was strapped to a matching gurney. Judging from their eyes, both recognized the other.

Chapter Nine

"Lieutenant Colonel Matthew Arbuckle" of the 7th Infantry Regiment gave the command for his soldiers to resume the responsibilities of delivering the federal prisoners to Fort Gadsden.

The people of "Milledgeville" clapped as Duncan McCrimmon's savior was wheeled through the fort's gates.

Tenskwatawa turned toward the ancient black Mason when Arbuckle's Infantry Regiment was out of sight. In earnest, the Shawnee Chief asked Prince Hall a question.

"Master Hall, how was it that this, "Jay Ray Howell" so quickly captured Paddy Welch?

And, who is this man?"

"It was actually Jackson's doings, Tenskwatawa.

There is much you do not know about General Andrew Jackson. You see, Andy's father was a Cerian commander named, "White Wolf".

When Jackson returned from Saint Marks a few weeks ago, he learned of his adopted nephew, "Andrew junior" almost being drowned by Welch.

Supposedly, the boy was fishing when a man emerged from the Hermitage's lower pond and attempted to pull the lad into the water!

Had it not been for Andy junior's Irish setter, Paddy's attempt would have most likely been successful.

I understand, when General Jackson was told of his "son's" attempted murder, he sprang from the dining table, saddled his fastest horse and rode directly to Jay Ray's dwelling in "Bell Buckle".

To clarify, Howell was one of White Wolf's wing commanders and good friend.

That coupled with Harvey Hildebrand's (a local gunsmith) church's destruction and Tecumseh's and Seekaboo's deaths' all occurring in similar ways, Andy knew he was dealing with a Niburian!

That's why he brought in the, "Eraser", as White Wolf called him. Does that clear it up for you, Tenskwatawa?"

"How did Mister Howell do it, Sir?"

"Very simply. Once Jay Ray figured out where the Nib made his shots from, he knocked on Welch's hotel room as if he were the downstairs restaurant's maître de and hit him in the head with a tomahawk and then injected cobra poison into his brain's 'command center'!"

"'Cobra poison', does it kill them?" curiously asked Tenskwatawa.

"No, but it'll keep them stupid for a few months!" said the Cerian.

"So what's left for me to do?" asked Tenskwatawa.

"You are to go into hiding until General Jackson calls you back into action. We have arranged a place for you in Canada." Said Prince.

"Why Canada? I know no one there!"

"Those are your orders, my friend. Anyway, things are going to get pretty nasty here and we have to keep you out of harms way!

But don't worry, the Culpers have plenty for you to do up there!

It seems the British are coercing the "Wendats" into making trouble with the "Hurons" and a good assassin is needed in those parts!" chortled Prince Hall.

* * * * *

Rachel lit the lamp that set on her side of the bed. Andy had had another nightmare. Their mattress was (again) drenched with sweat and urine.

"Doctor Maultheson" had prescribed a teaspoon of opium powder mixed in a gallon of blueberry juice. It was to be consumed daily.

But, that hadn't worked for Jackson. His failure to stop his whiskey drinking assured that outcome.

Insomnia haunted the entire household mainly because of the general's ruminations. Finally, his wife said something about it.

"My husband, it is time for us to have a talk!

You are not the only victim who has suffered during your absence. I too, have languished when you were on one of your ventures.

I have fretted every second of the day when you were at war; although, I must say, I believe this household was more content when you were away!

Since you have been back, my love, not once, have you affectionately touched me nor have you even offered to take "little Andy" on a ride in your cobwebbed racing carriage!

Both "Hannah" and "Aaron" have come to me with concerns regarding the ways in which you crossly speak to them!

As you are well aware, Andrew, you have ignored correspondences from even your closest of friends. "Eddie Gaines" even with the loss of his writing hand, has made several attempts to check on you and even went to the trouble of asking "Judge Toulmin" if you were still alive!

God forgive me for saying this; but, I'm not sure if you are in fact, 'alive'!

Don't you think for one moment, those evil Nashville bitches aren't conjuring up some stories about us!

You know the awful things they said about me concerning my being a bigamist and adulterer!

Andy, what makes you think they're not doing the same to you?

And what pray tell, kind of venal crap will they spread when they hear you have ignored "John Q's" requests for your return to Washington?

General Andrew Jackson, you have become a drunkard and a half-man; I want you to grab your rifle and take your horse into the mountains to either speak with Jesus in prayer or in person!

I am fed up with your self-pitying and I am damn sick of your sinful hedonism!

It would be best if you left this house, Andrew!"

Without a single word, Jackson put his clothes on. He grabbed his coat and squirrel rifle before going to the barn to get his horse.

Fifteen minutes later, Andrew Jackson galloped out of the plantation's gates and headed east toward Nashville.

*   *   *   *   *

Ten miles down the road and just before he came to the Cumberland's closest ferry, Jackson saw the image of a man standing in the middle of the dirt road.

In that the sun was just peaking through the trees, Andy could not make out who the determined person was. Figuring the stranger was up to no good, Andy loudly warned the (thought to be) highwayman, as he noticeably cocked his rifle.

"Proclaim your intentions, Sir!

I am armed and in no mood to tolerate shenanigans this morning!"

"Andy, I am here at your "Father's" bequest!

Get off of your horse and come to me, son!

My name is, "Prince Hall"."

"Until you further describe your intentions, I shall do no such of a thing!" said Jackson.

The old negro then disappeared!

A nanosecond afterwards, Andrew Jackson found himself on the ground.

His squirrel rifle was gone, his horse was nowhere to be seen and he, was as naked as a jaybird!

"I shan't take long to explain my message, Andrew!

Your ailment is an ancient one; but, it is curable!

As Rachel said, you have become a "half-man"!

Your selfish temper tantrums spurred on by your rapacious activities and coupled by your consumptions, have placed you in this quagmire." Said Prince Hall.

Jackson, as fast as a serpent's strike, sprang to his feet and took a powerful swing at the hologram's jaw. The reciprocally punished man found himself hanging upside down from a white oak tree.

Prince leaf-stripped a sapling and whipped Andy with it as if he were a chicken-killing stray.

"Alright, Mister Hall, what do you want me to do?" sobbed the defunct general.

"To live up to your father's expectations!" yelled the wavering image.

"What's wrong with me?" wailed Andy.

"My boy, it is guilt that afflicts you. For the past two years, Andrew, you have done nothing but kill others; as a result, you have squashed out your internal goodness!

Snuffing out the lives of others, has become a 'fix-all' for the problems facing you. To end your excruciations, you must chase out the 'evil witches' in your mind and replace them with kindnesses to those who need you!" Proclaimed Prince.

"How can I do that, Sir?" pleaded Jackson.

"Do you recall that Indian boy whose parents were killed by your army's cannons?

The one you picked up and placed on the same horse you stormed out on this morning. Remember, you turned him over to the priest at Saint Marks.

Start your recovery with him, "General Andrew Jackson"!

It will help in repairing your soul."

"Is that even possible?" asked Andy of the no longer present, Mister Hall.

As Jackson turned 'Rattler' back toward the Hermitage, he laughed when "Lyncoya" pointed out to him he was wearing no shoes. Andy hugged his new son.

*   *   *   *

"Neamathla" was nursing a puncture wound he had gotten while removing a racoon from his grandson's trap. He had ground a sliver of ginger root into a mixture of salt, honey and garlic into a paste.

As he was applying the mixture to the infected area, he heard wails coming from the other side of "Ochlockonee Creek".

'Another mother was mourning the death of a son.' he surmised.

"Cohowofooche" as a settlement, had prospered for a few years following the fall of "Fowltown" but that was because the Spaniards helped the defeated Red Sticks back onto their feet. The fecundity rates had soared.

Since the Americans had gained ownership of the territory, the Seminoles had to fend for themselves. Between droughts and diseases there were many other problems plaguing the Indians as well.

Their greatest hindrances were the white "squatters" regularly wanting a piece of land here or there. No matter what was said, they kept returning….uninvited!

As the "Chief", Neamathla did his utmost to sustain at least a dribbling of diplomacy; although, the younger tribesmen saw his peace favoring decisions as a weakness.

"He" had seen war and they had not. Therefore, the old man was the recipient of numerous shadow released defamations.

Secret war parties consisting mostly of adolescent boys, made good use of the "Econfina River" for the purposes of trading tobacco for guns and drinking whiskey with the "midnight traders".

With lethal firearms in hand, the young warriors robbed about any small group of white folks they wanted to. As a consequence, the "Cohowofooche" population saw a rise in young men's deaths. Plus, the Seminoles were getting a bad reputation!

After a year's worth of letters being sent to Andy from Washington, "President James Monroe" appointed General Andrew Jackson, "Commissioner of the United States".

He was to take possession of Florida and was given the "full powers" of the official "Governor"!

Unbeknownst to Jackson, Monroe sent the "orders" by way of a courier who was told to deliver "the appointment" notice on Christmas day.

*　*　*　*　*

Lyncoya was hiding from Hannah because of a mysterious handprint discovered on the mincemeat pie. Andy junior had actually done it; although, the promise of his brother's slingshot, enticed the six year old Creek to take the "wrap".

Meanwhile, Rachel was keeping her eye on her husband; she knew both Byron and Aaron had fabricated some lame reasons to accompany Andrew to the barn.

By Jackson's cherry red pallor, she was positive the slaves had given him some of their peach brandy. But it was Christmas; so, she let it slide.

"Judge John Overton", his wife and daughter, as well as their future son-in-law, "John Lea", were the first to arrive for Christmas dinner. "John McNairy" and his, "Nashville harpy" rode up ten minutes later.

As Hannah served dessert there was a knock on the door. Alfred answered it.

"Greetings from the President of the United States of America. I have an important letter for General Andrew Jackson!" sternly stated "Captain John R. Bell".

"Would you care to step in out of the cold, Captain?" graciously asked the shiny headed butler.

General Jackson overhearing the conversation, came to the door excusing Alfred with an appreciative nod.

"Merry Christmas to you, Captain Bell! You have a correspondence for me, Sir?" cheerfully asked the tipsy major general.

After a sharp salute, the captain handed Andy a leather valise.

"Captain, am I to send back with you, a response?" asked Jackson.

"General, my orders were to deliver this parcel to you; I was given no further instructions, Sir." Briskly stated the Army officer.

"And who was it that asked you to deliver 'it' to me on this holy day?" starchily asked Jackson.

"Senator John Q. Adams, Sir."

"Kindly give my regards to the President, Captain Bell, and wish Senator Adams a happy New Year for me!

Oh yes, and pass on to "Quincy" the good news; I shall consider him for the 'Chef's position' in the governmental palace as soon as I take the next election from him!"

"Yes, Sir!" said the Captain with a quirky smile on his face. He then saluted and left the Hermitage.

*　*　*　*　*

Neamathla heard the drumbeats coming from "Wacissa Hill"; they told him there were seventy five armed cavalry soldiers coming toward Cohowofooche.

Further, the deep vibrating message stated, the military horsemen carried a white flag; i.e., they were coming in peace!

After five staccato honks on a conch shell, twenty javelin toting braves formed around their Chief. The old man spoke.

"It appears, the Americans are coming to punish us for the actions of those disobedient youths who insisted on living out the fantasies of their fathers!

I have preached against this until I have become blue in the face! Now, we must all pay the 'piper' for their reckless insubordinations!

From this day forward, should a member of this tribe be caught with a red tipped warclub or be reported committing an unprovoked act of violence against a person or people not of our tribe, that or those individuals, shall be publicly caned and excommunicated from our boundaries for one month!

People, I too, resent the presence of the whites on our lands; but, it is too late to stop them now!

If we cannot learn to uphold their laws, we will join our forefathers living amongst the worms beneath our feet!

I do not know what this particular intrusive conference concerns; but, I fear it involves an ultimatum of which we Indians cannot abide by!

All weapons are to be hidden from sight!

When these bluecoats arrive, I want them to see a temperate people of agrarian persuasion. They are to witness a jovial and peace loving bunch. Is that understood?"

The braves nodded their heads in agreement and begrudgingly returned to their huts. Later, the women and children emerged with hoes and rakes mockingly pretending to be farmers. The men evaporated into the swamp.

Neamathla waited for several hours for the cavalry's arrival but they never came.

Realizing he was in the midst of his own 'palace revolt', he returned to his house where he remained for ten days. During that time of self-elected exile, he ate nothing, smoked opium and prayed.

* * * * *

A series of raids on southern Georgia settlements continued for which the Georgia Militia had been called out. The Red Sticks from Cohowofooche were blamed.

Belligerent bands of youthful "incorrigibles" continued to harass "the frontier" and helped many slaves escape from their master's plantations. British spies issued a call for members of "the Indian Nation" to join forces and make war against the Americans.

Weapons started pouring into the warriors' hands.

The "reinvigorated" Red Sticks attacked "Fort Scott", gutted it, and burned every timber to the ground!

Neamathla was urged to comeback as their leader of which he did with gusto.

Upon his return, the chief led an offensive on the "Ocheesee River" where he and thirty Red Sticks captured a U.S. supply boat.

* * * *

"General Gaines" who had taken over Jackson's command, had had enough of the Red Sticks. Through a series of letters to Washington, Edmund Pendleton Gaines finally convinced James Monroe to order General Jackson back to Florida to put a stop to the "Indian mischief" once and for all!

* * * * *

Andrew Jackson watched Captain Bell ride away into the sun. As he returned back to the Christmas dinner party, he felt the piercing eyes of his guests examining his expression. Rachel broke the ice.

"Who was that, Andy?" knowingly queried Jackson's wife.

"Darling, our President sent his best Christmas wishes and has extended an invitation for us to come to Washington this Spring." Lied Andrew Jackson.

No sooner had Jackson finished telling his mistruth when Rachel Jackson stood up from her chair and flung a half empty pitcher of apple cider at her husband!

After that, she grabbed the nearest corner of her embroidered table cloth and pulled the entire table's contents onto the plantation's polished floor.

Then with a salad fork clinched in her fist, Rachel went after John McNairy's wife with the intention of blinding the "gossipy witch"!

Her verbal insults would have deafened "Mother Mary". Fortunately, Mister John Lea wrestled the 'mad woman' to the floor.

Needless to say, the joyful occasion was over; but, it didn't end there. Once the guests had hurriedly left, Rachel Donelson Jackson ran upstairs to her bedroom looking for the shotgun which was always propped in the corner of her husband's dressing room.

When she got hold of it, Rachel unloaded both barrels at the McNairy's carriage which was more than a quarter of a mile away. She then collapsed onto the terrace's marble floor.

* * * * *

Knowing full well, the American government would be gunning for his people, Neamathla resettled his twenty two thousand tribesmen on the east side of Lake Miccosukee in hopes no one would look for them there.

Even though the high ground the Seminoles had settled upon was totally surrounded by the most god forsaken swampland imaginable, the Chief still insisted that there be perimeter lookouts posted every minute of every day.

He also promised to execute anyone who left the obscure hiding place without his explicit permission! (Two boys had to be hanged before the rest of the sap-full braves took his threat seriously.)

* * * * *

After nearly six months of the U.S. Army's serious wilderness combing, no results were reported. Jackson once again, called upon the services of White Wolf's trusted friend, Jay Ray Howell (a.k.a. "the Erasure"), to deliver a message to Neamathla.

In it, General Jackson gave the Chief an ultimatum:

"If your people cause no more trouble, your entire tribe will receive four million acres of land in central Florida. Added to that designation, will be metal farming implements, cattle, hogs, five thousand dollars per year, and rations enough to sustain your tribe for half of a decade".

Jackson further wrote from the Hermitage, "This will be an "iron-clad" or "irrevocable agreement" known as, "Treaty of Moultrie Creek". The United States will provide "protection to the Seminoles" for the next twenty years".

However, Jackson also went on to 'say',

"If you decline this offer or you do not subscribe to its restrictions, your people will reach the identical end as demonstrated upon the delivery of this letter."

* * * * *

"Abraham", one of the Jacksons' three hundred and seventy three slaves, knew that "Reverend Alexander Green" was "visiting" with a housekeeper named, "Naomi". They were shacked up at Green's hunting cabin on "Stones Creek".

In that the "Reverend" was also known to carry with him a plentiful amount of Chinese medicines, Abraham hopped on his horse and lit out to fetch the 'for profit' quack.

By nine o'clock Christmas night, the 'practitioner' had Rachel sitting in a chair and joking with her husband about the flock of ostriches eating the raspberries in her garden!

But, after Andy's spouse had fallen into a deep sleep, Alexander Green pulled Jackson to the side and delivered some bad news.

"General Jackson, by the looks of Mrs. Jackson's tongue and judging from it's purple periphery, I'd say her heart is improperly functioning!

It is my opinion, Sir, that you get her to a hospital where treating 'coronary infarctions' is a regularity.

The "Pennsylvania School of Medicine" is the only one I am familiar with; but, I'm not sure your wife will make it to the new year if you do not get her treated very soon!"

After gratefully paying the man for his 'spur of the moment' analysis, Jackson summonsed Hannah to his wife's bedside.

"Hannah, it grieves me greatly to inform you, Mrs. Jackson's prognosis is not favorable; therefore, I intend to take her to a hospital in Pennsylvania. I am not sure when or even if we will return in a timely manner but given the circumstances, it would be prudent to prepare for the worst.

I would be grateful if you and Abraham would keep things in order while we are gone. I'll have a talk with the boys but it will be up to you, ease the grumblings among the staff.

As far as the outside world is concerned, tell them this:

"The general and his wife are visiting in Washington and then touring the south. Their expected return will be sometime in October."

Judge Overton will be your contact should any decisions need to be made regarding judgements beyond the normal scope of the ordinary; otherwise, you are in charge!

By tomorrow's first light, I shall have prepared a letter providing final bequeaths should matters go sour. In it, for your information, Hannah, the Misses and I have allotted you and your family a hundred acres of good farming land on the southeastern side of the Hermitage as well as, a goodly sum of money.

Please deliver this document outlining those details to John upon the establishment of my demise.

Your loyalty and the mutual love we as a family have shared, has been most appreciated. Now, if you don't mind, please ask Abraham to come see me within the hour; there are some items we'll be taking with us.

I'll see you before we depart; goodnight!"

* * * * *

It was minus seven degrees Fahrenheit thus making it too cold to snow. Jay Ray Howell was concerned the water ballasts operating his elevator might be affected but they were not.

Jackson had sent another message to him during the night and he had to respond before sunrise. Apparently, Howell thought, 'something was wrong'.

By way of a chain of semaphore communications, Jay Ray jotted down Andy's concerns regarding Rachel's condition.

'This takes precedence over the "Neamathla situation"', Jay Ray said out loud.

Without delay, J.R. lifted his craft out from the hangar inside of "Deason Mountain" and as designated, airlifted the Jacksons to "Goshenville Forest" where Doctors "Morgan and Shippen" covertly moved her to "Surgeon's Hall" in Philadelphia.

Rachel Jackson's (false) name was, "Johanna Doe".

Jay Ray Howell knew by Andy's facial language, the general was aching to get back into the fight; although, the chance of Rachel's death occurring while he was at war, overrode his dark thirst.

As a consolation, J.R. promised him a full report by sundown; they were to meet at the "City Tavern" at 1800hrs..

*   *   *   *

From "Goshenville Forest" it was nine hundred and fifty one miles to "Colt Creek". That provided an adequate amount of time to pick up the materials needed to leave Neamathla a clearly "painted" message.

Jackson wanted no room left for misunderstanding.

*   *   *   *

Howell came in from the gulf side at Largo. At treetop height, he encircled "Lake Miccosukee" with phosphorous charges set to ignite at sunrise.

He then gassed Neamathla's well camouflaged bunker. Jay Ray did not want his landing to be "remembered".

At 0600hrs., Jay Ray placed the unconscious Chief Neamathla on a raft which was anchored in the center of the Red Sticks' protective lake. General Jackson's "Treaty" was glued onto the Indian's bare chest.

Howell returned to his craft and commenced to drench the five square mile hideout with a sticky type of napalm which adhered to the forest's upper canopy.

J.R. ascended to twenty thousand feet and released weighted flares. The swamp was set on fire.

The depth charges simultaneous explosions caused clashing waves to lift Neamathla's raft hundreds of feet into the sky. Like red ants, hundreds of the Chief's men dove into the lake in hopes of saving their floundering leader.

By the time the strongest of swimmers reached the place in which Neamathla was last seen, he was no longer visible!

"Tiger Tail" and a couple of other high spirited braves dove underwater in an attempt to rescue their chief. After two attempts, a boy named, "Osceola" managed to pull the half-drowned Chief to the surface.

Remarkably, the Indians managed to pull Neamathla onto a raft and push him onto the bank where efforts to resuscitate him began.

Following numerous attempts to drain the Chief's lungs of lake water, the Red Stick's Commander began breathing on his own accord.

After escaping terrifying walls of flames, the entire group of Creeks including women and children, were forced to encircle Lake Miccosukee.

It was then, J.R. Howell descended. His silvery craft hovered inches above the lake's surface.

Using the most common "Muskogean" dialect, the "Erasure" through his ship's loudspeaker, read Jackson's treaty to the awed onlookers. All listened.

* * * * *

At precisely 1830 hrs., Jay Ray Howell's two horse carriage came to the intersection of "Second and Walnut Streets".

The City Tavern's doorman saw to it that his rig was taken to the inn's stable. Howell was then escorted to Andrew Jackson's booth.

Just before reaching Jackson's second floor location, "James" the tavern's doorman, pulled J.R. to the side offering Andy's expected guest, a word of caution.

"Mister Howell, General Jackson is in pretty bad shape, Sir! He's been hitting the scotch with vengeance since noon!" said the doorman.

"Has there been any expressed reason for his actions, James?" kindly asked J.R..

"No, except he did offer a toast to his wife's "ghost" around three o'clock, I understand." Said James.

"Did Rachel pass?"

"Apparently not. According to Doctor Morgan who helped the general climb the stairs up to here this morning, Mrs. Jackson is in stable condition. I believe it's just the man's state of mind, Sir!" suggested the obsequious doorman.

Jay Ray handed James a gold piece but before he let it drop into the tavern's employee's outstretched palm, he asked a favor.

"James, would you please run over to the school and ask either Doctors Morgan or Shippen to write down for me, Mrs. Jackson's diagnosis? When you accomplish that task, James, I'll match the coin I just handed to you."

"Yes indeed, Sir, I'll do my very best! Shall I bring the note to you in the presence of General Jackson, Mister Howell?"

"Absolutely! I want Andrew to hear the truth, James. Now, please hurry, Man!" politely said Jay Ray.

Andy was slumped over the table's top as if he were dead. From the smell of things, there was a good bet the general had shit his pants. J.R. sat down.

"Mission accomplished, Andrew." Quietly stated Howell.

"How many of them did you kill?" slurred Jackson.

"Just scared the 'red' off of them, Andy, that all! But, they did get your message! How's Rachel?"

Andrew Jackson shrugged his shoulders.

"Have you spoken with her doctors?" pried Jay Ray.

"They threw me out!"

"Who threw you out, Andrew?"

"The whole goddamned lot of them, that's who!" snickered Jackson.

"Why?" frustratingly asked Howell.

"I pulled out my pistol and shot it at the ceiling, that's why!"

James timidly approached the booth. He handed Jay Ray an envelope.

Jackson became combative when Howell refused to openly share the contents of James's timorously delivered message. He attempted to reach for his already fired pistol.

To quell the situation, Jay Ray punched Andy's forehead with a move so fast, it would have embarrassed a rattlesnake. The general collapsed on the tabletop. The Cerian then read Doctor William Shippen's diagnosis.

"'Johanna Doe' has developed what is called, "aortic stenosis" or a narrowing of the aortic valve. Her prognosis is unfavorable with a terminal expectancy within twelve months. Treatment options are limited only to 'light' activities of daily living. Recommend: hypertensive-free environment. W.S. Jr."

Jay Ray Howell sat in the tavern's booth contemplating what to do with his former flight commander's alcoholic son. There were good things about Jackson; nevertheless, Howell didn't like him very much. It was a lack of respect thing, mostly.

After several moments of thought, Howell made the decision to return Rachel to the Hermitage and to keep Andrew Jackson away from her. It was obvious that 'Jackson was partly responsible for his wife's condition anyway', J.R. concluded.

Three hours later and after returning Rachel Jackson back home in Nashville and instructing Hannah as to the proper care for Mrs. Jackson, Howell transported the straightjacketed Andy to a remote swamp island in Pensacola.

While General Jackson suffered through an arduous bout of delirium tremens which lasted for almost three days, Jay Ray kept him pinned up in an underground log cage while he read to Andrew, Thomas Paine's book entitled, "Common Sense".

For sixteen weeks, J.R. Howell made Jackson perform the duties of an island governor entailing nothing much more than collecting conch shells from the gulf shore of western Florida.

On October the first, when J.R. deemed Andy "ready" for resocialization, he allowed him to return to Nashville on horseback.

Fearing more than hell itself but mostly wanting to permanently distance himself from Jay Ray Howell, Andrew Jackson before crossing between the Hermitage's gates, stopped in Nashville, rented a buggy, filled it's backseat with flowers, and then drove to his home.

Having sent a message of his evening's arrival, Andy was met by a gauntlet of his slaves lined up on both sides of the plantation's driveway. Jackson shed some tears but quickly dried them off of his tanned cheeks.

With bright smiles on their faces, the entire negro greeting party clapped their hands together and sang a happy song. At the end of the parallel formation, was Rachel.

"Welcome home, my husband! As you can see, we have missed you!"

"As I, my dear! But before I enter into the place I call, 'heaven on earth', let me offer to all of you, my family, a most humble apology!

Five months ago, I was a wretched soul! I am a wholesome person now and one who promises to be a kinder and gentler human being from here on out. Thank you!" said Andy.

* * * * *

Rachel Donelson Jackson was awakened by a clicking noise coming from downstairs. Realizing her husband was not beside her, she put on her robe and quietly crept down the circular stairsteps leading to Andrew's study.

She peeked through the keyhole before announcing her presence. Jackson was dryfiring his dueling pistol at the figure reflected in his full length mirror. His nightmares had returned. Rachel spoke out.

"Darling, shall I ask Hannah to warm you up some milk?"

"No, my dear. I was just 'walking through' a client's defense for tomorrow's trial, that's all. I'll be up shortly, precious one." Lied Andy.

"Andrew, do you still love me?" baited Rachel.

"What's bothering you, my angel? Of course, I still adore everything about you; why do you ask me that?"

"Andrew, when I'm gone, it would please me to look down from heaven and see that you were married to a beautiful lady. I have grown into a frumpy old lump in my twilight years; you deserve better."

"Rachel, enough of this nonsense, I'll blow out the light and we'll turn in together. Anyway, I'm the fortunate one to be married to a living goddess!" cooed Jackson.

"Seriously, Andy, I want you to remarry! I can tell that things aren't right inside my chest; gratefully, I feel that God will soon be calling me home!"

"Mrs. Jackson, you are the only wife I shall ever have! Now stop this ridiculous chatter this very moment and let's go to bed!" jokingly scolded Andrew.

* * * * *

Following weeks of political disarray, Neamathla finally convinced his tribe of mangled Red Sticks to lay down their painted warclubs. They were to seriously abide by Andrew Jackson's offer.

"After all", as the Chief explained, "Even, the greatest of our warriors are no match for fire breathing air ships!"

* * * * *

Without a presidential "go-ahead", Florida Territorial Governor, William Pope Duval along with his freshly appointed territorial commissioners, "John Lee Williams" and "William Simmons", rode out to the site where the explosions happened. Their carriage was at the rear of a hundred sabre drawn cavalrymen.

The blue coated troops surrounded the freshly burned periphery of Lake Miccosukee. In a "Caesar" styled manner, Governor Duval announced, 'from that day forward (October the 23rd.), the Cohowofooche Territory would no longer be availed to them'!

It was to become the site of Florida's new capitol!

Further, Duval went on to say, "'Neamathla', in the eyes of the U.S. Government, will no longer be recognized as the head of the Seminoles. Additionally, the entire Indian conglomerate must enter the "Tampa Reservation" within thirty days!"

Six hundred warriors began a war cry. But then, Neamathla stepped forward and presented to Governor Duval the inscription written by Jackson.

"Chief Neamathla, where in god's name did you get this document? Major General Jackson couldn't have possibly given this to you!" condescendingly spat the Governor.

"It was delivered to me from the heavens!" arrogantly retorted the Red Sticks chief.

"Listen here, Neamathla, I know for a fact, Jackson hasn't been here for months; what you have is nothing more than a fraudulent piece of paper!

Anyway, I am the new Governor and I only take orders from the President of the United States!"

"Then, Governor Duval, either you have been misinformed or you, Sir, are ignorant!" sneeringly said Neamathla.

"I'll not tolerate your belligerence, you goddamned savage!

What makes you think for one moment, I won't unleash my soldiers upon you?" yelled Governor Duval.

"I can think of a few thousand reasons why you shouldn't!

But before I command my warriors to scalp your paltry number of sabre brandishing boys, I suggest you read the signature below this, "Treaty of Moultrie Creek"!" Chortled Chief Neamathla.

No sooner had William Duval's lips formed the name, "John Quincy Adams", two thousand armed Seminole men, women and children emerged from the chard timbers around the Governor's military entourage.

By a one hand signal, Duval, ordered the one hundred sabre sheathed cavalrymen to turn around and leave the area as if they had wings on their horses' bodies!

Having regained the confidence of his followers, the aging Chief turned toward his worn out tribesmen. He loudly spoke these words,

"I speak to the great Tallahassee and Miccosukee people!

This "Andrew Jackson" may be a violent warrior but I believe his words are true!

Soon the whites will return with a hundredfold rifles; therefore, we must retreat to "Ocala", take their handouts, and revive ourselves until they are lulled into the belief of our docility!

When that has happened, we will rise like serpents in the grass and fill the waterways with their blood!"

After hearing Neamathla's brave proclamation, the tribally mixed Indians receded back into their hiding places and began preparing for their migration toward central Florida.

By nightfall, their joyless trek had begun. In their wakes were whiffs of peyote smoke.

* * * * *

Captain "John B. Bell" looked at himself in his full-length mirror for the seventh time. After shining his boots again, he made his way toward the detachment of cavalrymen waiting outside his quarters.

Bell had some "brownnosing" to do at Jackson's place.

"Welcome once again to the Hermitage, Captain Bell, how may we serve you this lovely November morning?" politely asked Abraham.

"I bring news to General Jackson, Sir." Answered the officer with his hat in hand.

"May I offer your men some refreshment, Captain?"

"No, Abraham, I shan't be long; but, I do need to speak with the General regarding a Floridian matter.

I'm afraid James Gadsden reports that Governor Duval has made some serious missteps regarding the 'Moultrie Creek Treaty'." Squealed the puckered up rump-kisser.

Rachel Jackson who had eavesdropped Abraham's greeting and Captain Bell's tattling, approached the front door. She pleasantly dismissed her servant and tactfully segued herself in front of the army officer while shutting the front door behind her.

"Captain Bell, are you aware of my husband's resignation?

General Jackson has now resumed his station as a 'gentleman farmer' and Senator.

I'm sure the Indian matters you spoke of, would best be managed by your superiors, Sir!

May I suggest you return …." As Rachael was saying when Andy walked up.

"Ah, Captain Bell, thank you for responding to my message!

I'm afraid I was remiss in forewarning my lovely bride of your summoning!

Rachel, my dear, I apologize.

Captain, please follow me into my library and thank you for coming on such short notice.

Rachel, would you kindly have Hannah prepare some tea for our guest. We have some old bones to pick over!" said the secretively tipsy Jackson.

With her right middle finger prominently sticking up in the air, Mrs. Jackson turned away from the two men after slamming the front door so hard that one of the sconces' lantern covers cracked.

"General, I'm sorry for the intrusion but I thought you would want to be made aware that yours' and Judge Gadsden's, 'Treaty of Moultrie Creek' was grossly ignored by Governor Duval!

He and a company of cavalry soldiers attempted to intimidate Neamathla by forcing the Seminoles to evacuate the Cohowofooche Territory and move to a section of swampland no larger than your plantation, Sir!"

"What happened?" asked Jackson.

"The Indians chased him away; but, as I am told, they have now moved to your 'treaty's region' running down the middle of the Florida Peninsula, Sir!" Snickered the smelly nosed captain.

"I see. Well, Captain, you are hereby appointed the, "Provisional Secretary of the Florida Territory" and temporary "Agent" to the Seminoles!

You are hereby commanded to take a "census" of Neamathla's followers and see to it, the Seminoles receive all that was promised to them!

Furthermore, Neamathla is to release his five thousand slaves and allow them to go wherever their hearts' desire!

Duval is to pay five thousand dollars to the Seminoles but under these circumstances: a thousand dollars of that amount, is to be evenly distributed among the Red Sticks' negroes.

As you are now their "agent", it will become your duty to make sure the Indians no longer do trade with the Bahamians nor the Cubans.

All provisions will be supplied to the fort you will build!

We'll name it after your fiancé, "Brooke", of whom you will leave behind in Nashville. You will take with you, four infantry companies in order to establish, "Fort Brooke".

I'll expect your return to my plantation within eighteen months!

I shall look forward to your updating me of your progress!

Do you have any questions, Captain Bell?" mockingly said Jackson.

"General Jackson, Sir, I only came to report an insubordinate activity to you!

I am quite satisfied with my current post, Sir, and plus, I am not qualified to handle a task of that magnitude with all due respect, General!" whined Bell.

"Apparently you thought you had more capabilities than my appointee, Governor Duval; therefore, I thought it prudent to allow you to take a swing at it!"

"General, what if I were to refuse to accept your offer?"

"It's not an offer, Captain, it's an order!

But to answer your question, I'd have you court-martialed and hanged!

Will there be anything else you'd like to discuss, Captain Bell?"

"I guess not, Sir."

"Then, I'll assume you'll be on your way?" teased Andy.

Captain John B. Bell said nothing more. He just saluted.

* * * * *

At 0245hrs., "Little Turtle" and "Blue Jacket" paddled their sloop up the southwestern side of the "Withlacoochee River". They turned into a cove where the "Black Moccasins' headquarters was based.

Rifles, whiskey, lead blocks, gunpowder and a prisoner was their payload. Anxious braves were waiting.

"Aripeka" (Sam Jones) by lantern signals, guided the 'pirates' into a safe mooring spot.

"Corporal Barnum Flats" was offloaded and hobbled.

"Coacoochee" and Aripeka carried their highjacked bounty to the cave where their leader, "Osceola" was waiting.

Upon seeing that Corporal Flats was very young, Osceola approached the lad as though he were an old friend. He spoke in flawless English.

"Corporal, may I ask you where your detachment was taking these materials?"

"To Fort Brooke." Said the corporal.

"Who is the commanding officer at Fort Brooke, Barnum?" softly asked Osceola.

"Major John Bell."

"And who is Major Bell's commander?" asked the Black Moccasins' Chief.

"Brigadier General Call." Answered Corporal Flats.

"Did General Call send the supplies to Major Bell and is "Call" the reason Fort Brooke was constructed?"

"No, sir. General Jackson did that. He sent Major Bell to build the fort."

"Why did Andrew Jackson do such a thing as that?" snarled Osceola.

"I don't know the answer to that question; however, I believe it was to protect the settlers nearby." Said the squirming corporal.

"But according to the 'Moultrie Treaty', there aren't suppose to be any settlers; isn't that correct, Barnum?

Are there white people coming on our land?" pushed the "Moccasin" leader.

"A few, I think."

"So! Does that sound as if, Major Bell, General Call and Andrew Jackson are honoring their agreement with the Indians, Corporal Barnum Flats?" arrogantly cross examined Osceola.

"Sir, I'm just a foot soldier!

I simply follow the orders given to me by my superiors. My intentions have never been to harm your people!" cried the soldier.

"Answer my question!" screamed Osceola.

"No, it doesn't seem like they are honoring their agreement; but, that's not my fault!"

"But you and your detachment were transporting items used to kill living things, were they not?"

"Yes."

"Was the gunpowder and the lead to be used for shooting the settlers or perhaps it was to be for hunting deer?" sarcastically queried the Seminole.

"No."

"It was for shooting Indians wasn't it, Corporal?"

"I don't..." Said Barnum as Osceola severed his windpipe.

* * * * *

Fourteen year old "Lyncoya" riding "Rattler", was three hundred yards ahead of his adoptive father. His almost magical horsemanship also prevented "Andrew Jr". and "Andrew Hutchins" from winning their 'high-stakes' Sunday morning horserace.

As the riders were jockeying into the last leg, a fancy carriage carrying five men was spotted in front of the Hermitage's entrance. John Overton, Alfred Balch, Martin Van Buren, General John Coffee and E.W. Earl disembarked from the leather covered car as General Jackson rode up. Balch was the first to speak.

"Good morning, Gentlemen. It appears that once again, you boys have given your papa a good tanning!

But, before you fellows take your frothy mouthed horses back to the stable, I was wondering if you might let us have a private word with the Senator?

Our visit is not intended to exclude his family members; however, it is best that your mother not be made aware of our presence. You know how she gets upset when we have political business to discuss!"

"That's just fine, "Mister Balch". The losers of our Sunday morning romps are to handover their boots to me anyway. They then have to walk back to the house barefooted!

I'll take their horses to the barn directly. "Rachel" is still at the church and won't be expected home until two o'clock. "Mum's" the word!" arrogantly stated Lyncoya.

As Andy was handing his boots over to his Indian adoptee, he turned toward "John Coffee" with a concerned expression and then spoke.

"Has the cat jumped out of the bag?"

All five of the men nodded. "Martin Van Buren" broke the ice.

"Andy, the "WASHINGTON TELEGRAPH" along with the "BOSTON STATESMAN", have both written on their front pages, some disparaging remarks concerning yours' and Rachel's marriage!

Adams' supporters have accused you of being 'a military tyrant and one who would use the presidency as a springboard for 'his' Napoleonic ambitions of building an empire!'

Senator, they brought out every skeleton in your closet; that is, your duels and drunken brawls, the Saint Marks executions, placing New Orleans under martial law, your friendship with "Aaron Burr" as well as, the 'unnecessary' invasion of Spanish Florida!"

"Was there ever witnessed such a bare face corruption in any country before?

To buy newspapers with promises of an "inside track" in exchange of their articles' flavoring, is a whack to the eye of the writers of the American Bill of Rights!

I shall therefore teach these highfaluting Washingtonians a lesson they will not soon forget!

For those who have tarred my wife's name with additives such as 'bigamist' and 'the harlot bumpkin', they will rue the day their tongues' touched the rooves of their mouths!

They will be shocked when I attach their corrupt asses to a rail and toss them into the Potomac. Those whose minds were prepared to see me with a tomahawk in one hand and a scalping knife in the other will instead, find a refined southern gentleman having superb control of himself.

Make no mistake, my friends, I shall go to Washington as a Tennessee Senator but return as the President of the United States!"

Exclaimed Andy Jackson.

* * * * *

Osceola threw the last part of Corporal Flat's body into the Withlacoochee River before turning toward his Black Moccasin lieutenants. The Red Stick confederate lifted one of the pirated whiskey jugs toward the predawn sky and made a solemn promise to his fellow rebels.

"From this moment forward, I pledge my life toward the destruction of the white man. With every ounce of strength in my body, I intend on drawing their blood!

No longer will I follow Neamathla's weak words nor will I obey the written promises jotted down by liars.

Today, marks the end of peace with those pale faced reprobates!

I do not ask the Black Moccasins to follow me for the end to this saga is death; but, if you do choose to walk in the footprints of our warring ancestors, I shall guarantee that your frightful image will become the 'star' in every white child's nightmares!

Time is up for the forked-tongued negotiators!

There are no more seconds left for those purporting a peaceful settlement, for none exists!

History may despise our actions but I swear to you, I will kill no less than one member of every white mans' family living on this earth!

Never again, will the teachings of those said to pray to the son of a god penetrate our ears for our eyes have shown us the truth. But have no doubt, beginning now, the life expectancy of the white man will indelibly be altered!"

Chapter Ten

Tenskwatawa hadn't been asleep for more than an hour when he received another visit from his father and mother (respectively, "Puckeshinwa" and "Methoataske"). In his dream which he called a "vision", "Lalawethika" (his birth name) was told of a future greatness about to be bestowed upon his name.

"Kumskaukau" (his only surviving brother of a triplet birthing) then approached Tenskwatawa and for a long time, sat quietly beside him on the bank of the "Mississippi River" before he spoke.

"My brother, I bring you good news! Our god, "Mishe Moneto" has provided you with the opportunity to save our people from obscurity; however, before your chance receives it's wings, there are certain 'devils' who must be smitten!

Lalawethika, you must return to your place of our birth and go to "Satan's Hole Lake". There, you must speak into a "lamb's pouch" (the stomach) about your past failures, defeats, and imagined short comings.

Following your purging, you are to place a stone along with your right eye into the ewe's bag and toss it into the water.

Secondly, you must come to see that the Indians' purification can only be accomplished through the abstinence of 'European ways'. These include the consumptions of the white mans' most wicked tool, 'alcohol'.

All of the settlers' ways, their clothing, tools, as well as fraternization has to be stopped. These invaders cannot be trusted and therefore are to be seen as "the children of the evil spirits"!

Lastly, Lalawethika, you are to found a powerful city-state which is to become the paradigm of Indian culture. That great city is to be located at the juncture of the "Wabash" and "Tippecanoe" Rivers. It will become the spiritual hub for all Indian Nations!

My brother, I must now return to our ancestors. Remember, these words I have spoken do not come from my mouth; instead, they are from the "Star People". Do as they have told you to do, Lalawethika, and you will save our people! Goodbye."

It was on that early May morning when Tenskwatawa drunkenly emerged from his filthy Canadian hut. He yelled out to the rats also inhabiting the "Huron" tribe's village dump.

"The sky will not lighten until well past noon!"

Several women saw his body floating in the "White River" while tasking their morning duties. They witnessed him standup and walk across the river's surface to the southern side.

Although proclaimed to be told as the gospel truth, the tribal elders wrote it off as, "old women's imagination". Nevertheless, dawn came at 1340hrs. that day.

* * * * *

Andrew Jackson's wife, "Rachel" was the daughter of "Colonel John Donelson", a surveyor, and "Rachel Stockley Donelson".

At the age of thirteen, the adolescent along with her prominent Virginia family made a touring trip through the "Cherokee Nation" in Tennessee.

It was there, Rachel learned the value of rubbing shoulders with American aristocrats such as George Washington and Thomas Jefferson.

After the Donelson family settled in Kentucky, the vivacious Rachel then seventeen, met "Lewis Robards" whom she married.

He proved a pathologically jealous and abusive husband who falsely accused Rachel of adultery despite having adulterous relationships himself. The couple separated four years later!

Following two years of attempts at reconciliation, Lewis Robards's fierce temper and violent outbursts convinced Rachel to permanently leave him. She went to "Natchez", Tennessee to stay with her mother's relatives thus leaving no trail of her whereabouts.

That same year, Robards petitioned the Kentucky legislature to allow him to seek a divorce on the grounds of 'Desertion'; although, he did not actually pursue the court action for two more years.

Mistakenly 'learning' Robards had filed for a divorce on the grounds of "Adultery" the following year, Rachel and Andy were married.

Hearing of Rachel's "illegal" betrothal to Jackson, Lewis Robards devised a well-orchestrated smear campaign and did in fact, get his divorce after milking the public's sympathy dry.

For his limp-handed 'udder' works, Jackson threatened to kill Lewis as he had done earlier to one of Robard's cronies for impugning his wife's reputation. This left Lewis Robards no option other than to spew out more shadowy lies.

Following a decade of hearing of Jackson's successes as a military hero, lawyer, senator and businessman, Lewis again raised his 'diamond shaped' head to contrive a masterful plan of 'character assignation' aimed at the whole Jackson family.

Consequently, Robards began searching out Andrew Jackson's enemies. It wasn't very long before Lewis Robards's snooping paid off.

Someone had said in a tavern "somewhere" that, "Pricilla Hobson" had 'threatened to shoot General Jackson when her fiancé, Captain John R. Bell was "screwed by the General" and sent down to Florida thus delaying their wedding for at least a year', she supposedly claimed.

After some light detective work, Robards discovered that Pricilla and her sister, "Daphne" shared a tiny flat in "Berry Hill". Their address was #8 Lafayette Street.

* * * * *

The following Sunday morning, Lewis dressed as an infantry corporal, appeared on the Hobson's doorstep.

It was ten o'clock when he knocked on the two sisters' front door. Lewis had a patch over his left eye and a thick envelope in his right hand.

"Mam, please excuse the intrusion on this gorgeous day of our Lord's!

I am desperately trying to locate an old friend of mine. I was told a, "Miss Pricilla Hobson" might know where I could drop off a package for him.

I didn't feel comfortable leaving it at the fort because of its contents!"

"I am "Miss Daphne Hobson", Pricilla's sister; won't you come in?"

"Well, Mam, that's mighty nice of you but I wouldn't want to impose on your gracious hospitality.

Anyway, it wouldn't look proper for an old warrior such as myself, to enter a lady's home without a formal invitation." Said Lewis with a Tennessean twang.

"I'm afraid my sister won't be back until the afternoon; if you would care to leave your parcel under my care, I'll be sure to give it to her!" said Daphne in a very coquette manner.

"Miss Hobson, John and I were partners in a small business before he enlisted in the army. I myself, didn't go in until the end of the war.

What I have in this valise requires his signature." Baited Robards.

"Forgive my curiosity, Corporal, but what type of enterprise were you and Captain Bell into, way back yonder?

Gosh, ya'll must have been just children then!" cooed Daphne.

"Please call me "Paul", "Paul Hampshire's" my name and yes, we were both around sixteen in those days. He and I were in the diamond mining business." Lied the one-eyed Lewis.

"So you wanted to deliver some diamonds to John Bell, Paul?" laughed Pricilla's sister.

"Not exactly; but, I do need his or his wife's signature on the 'deed' in order to sell our mining rights!"

"Oh my! I'm afraid that won't be possible; my sister and Captain, now "Major" Bell, were never married!" Daphne sadly stated.

"Why? John was smitten by 'his angel' as he referred to 'her' in his letters to me!" cried Robards.

"Because General Jackson forced him to become the 'Provisional Secretary of the Florida Territories' and 'Agent' to the goddamned Seminoles!" callously stated Daphne.

"Damn! What a crying shame!

If I don't get John's signature on this, "Bill of Sale" within the next ninety days, we're going to lose the deal!

There is no way for me to travel all the way down to Florida and back to Arkansas within that time frame!" said the crocodile teared Lewis Robards.

"Paul, may I admit something to you in absolute confidence?

Pricilla won't be returning home this afternoon; she is in the company of another man!

My sister is quite the strumpet, I'm sorry to say; but, don't despair, I may have a solution to this conundrum."

"Oh really; how's that?" surprisingly asked the fake Paul Hampshire.

"Tell me more about this 'mine' sale?

It is in "Arkansas" you said; and, who's the buyer?" greedily pried Daphne.

"John and I were restless youths in those days!

Admittedly, we did a little bit of 'this and that' when we lived in "Memphis".

Mostly, we were just small time thieves and back then, we called ourselves the, "Inland Pirates"!

One night, we were robbing what we thought was an abandoned houseboat when a man surprised us by unloading his shotgun on our skiff!

That's how I lost my eye.

Anyway, John shot the man with his pistol. After seeing he was dead, we got back on the 'flat-floater' and sunk the body into the Mississippi River.

The two of us then stole everything we could load into our boat before setting the dead man's craft on fire.

When daylight came we went through the stuff we had stolen. It was at that time, we found a deed to a piece of property that supposedly had a crater on it. That's where we went!

Our "story" was, "the farm was given to us by our deceased uncle. We got it put into our names, John went off to New Orleans as a soldier and I worked on a cattle ranch in Georgia."

Two months ago, I got word that some "Jew" out of "New York" had posted an offer of a thousand dollars for the land we had gained ownership of; therefore, all we have to do now, is sign our names to sell it and the money will be sent to…"us"!

That, Miss Hobson, is why I'm here!" said "Paul".

"Really, all you need is "John Bell's" signature, is that correct?" innocently asked Daphne.

"That is absolutely spot on!" said Robards.

"Paul, how would you like to have a silent partner?" questioned the mutt-faced sister.

"What do you mean?"

"Let's just say, if I were to get John Bell's "signature" and I mean an authentic looking one, you and I could split the money fifty-fifty!" edaciously chortled Daphne.

"How could you do that, Sweetheart?" flirtatiously queried "Hampshire".

"In about two hours, Paul, the sun will be perfectly situated in the sky for tracing my sister's ex-fiancé's name onto your, Bill of Sale!"

"What about Bell's half?" innocently asked Lewis Robards.

"How would he ever know?

I mean, 'if' Major Bell ever returns and when he finds out that his sweet little "angel" has been unfaithful to him, the last thing on his mind will be half of the money he killed a man to get. And plus, that was two decades ago!"

"What about Pricilla, Daphne?

She'll obviously notice your newfound wealth!" asked the wide-eyed conman.

"Not if she's in jail!" said the 'evil sister' out of the side of her mouth.

"That would make our caper as 'clean as a whistle', now wouldn't it?"

"And when you returned from Arkansas, Mr. Hampshire, I'd be waiting for you!" said Daphne in a sleazy sort of way.

"You mean like man and wife?

Would you even have me; after all, a half blind man ain't much to look at, Miss Hobson?" toyed Lewis.

"I'd make you a fine wife, Paul, that is, if all the other parts of your body are in good working order!"

"That's a deal, Lady!

But how do we get your sister out of the way?" blatantly asked Lewis Robards.

"Don't you worry about that; by the time you get back, I'll have our little love nest here as cozy as bug in a rug!

Darling, bring the document over to my picture window; I'll put one of John's letters to Pricilla, under it." Coyly said Daphne Hobson.

* * * *

With Governor Duval's second installment of five thousand dollars paid, Neamathla settled into the 'Ocala Reservation'. Although there were occasional but isolated clashes with white settlers, things calmed down to the point that the U.S. Government labeled Florida's 'Central Section' as, "Peaceful".

"Fort King" was built which falsely gave "entrepreneurial agriculturalists" permission to encroach on the Seminole's' legal property. Reports of missing white families astronomically mounted.

Most certainly, the Seminoles were suspected as being the culprits but Neamathla vehemently denied any part of the disappearances.

During the Spring of the Seminole's third year of their resettlement on the central Florida reservation something dreadful happened; a forest fire strangely swept across the "Ocala plains" destroying Fort King and eleven plantations.

Remarkably, the horrendous devastation missed the Seminole townships; 'not one single blade of Indian grass was scorched'.

The Indians saw it as an omen while the wealthy planters suspected the event was Red Sticks' 'devilment'!

This was reiterated in the minds of the local whites when they tallied up the numbers of their slaves missing in the fire's aftermath!

Duval was approached by the "plantation aristocracy's" oligarch, as a result of the "fiery enigma". The Governor assigned Major John R. Bell to investigate the matter.

* * * * *

On the morning of June the 5th, Major Bell, fifty cavalrymen, eleven professional slavecatchers and fourteen bluetick hounds, began a southerly bound search of "Hopkins Prairie". They were determined to find the nine hundred and seventy three negro escapees.

The Governor and James Gadsden saw the force off. From the sounds of the baying hounds, it seemed as though the searchers were hot on the slaves' trail; but, the detachment of soldiers, slavecatchers and their bloodhounds, were never heard from again.

Duval requested from Washington that a battalion of Federal troops be sent to Florida. He said, "I need fighting men wishing to earn, "Cash on the Barrelhead" for every, brown, black, or red foreskin collected on his tour."

* * * * *

Rachel Jackson and Ann Rodgers Grundy were discussing Paul's (one of Jesus's Disciples) travels to "Damascus" when "Sheriff Thomas Hickman" rode up the driveway and parked closest to the Hermitage's front porch.

Withdrawing his hat as he jumped from his carriage, he approached the two ladies in a reverent manner.

"Mrs. Jackson, Mrs. Grundy, I was wondering if "Lieutenant Donelson" was available? I need to speak with him regarding a legal matter."

"Well, Sheriff Hickman, I haven't seen you in a coon's age. I hope everything's alright?

Andy junior's down at the turkey pens. The coyotes are back so he's a-setting some traps for the rascals.!

He ain't been home but for a week!

He'll be mighty glad to see you again. He graduated from West Point "second in his class", you know!

He's put on some weight since you last seen him so don't be surprised!

When your done with your visiting, why don't you join us for supper?

The General won't be home until next month; I'll be sure and tell him you dropped by, that is, if you can't stay. How's the girls at your home?" yelled Rachel.

"Everybody's just fine at my house, Mrs. Jackson. But I'm afraid neither I nor your nephew, will be able to make supper tonight!

There has been a murder in town and I figure 'little Andy' can help me track down the victim's murderer." Said the sheriff.

"Who's that you got chained up in the back of your carriage?" blurted out Rachel.

"Oh, that's "Ben", one of "John Harding's" niggers. He's a 'witness' I have to talk to!" briskly said Hickman.

"Well, I swanney, that's one of Lyncoya's sidekicks, I do believe!" Stated Rachel Jackson.

"Yes, Mam, it is!

I'll be running on now; I'll talk with you soon, Mrs. Jackson and good morning to both you and Mrs. Grundy, now!" hurriedly said Thomas Hickman.

"Rachel, you don't suppose something has happened to your son, do you?" softly queried Ann Grundy.

"I'm quite sure it has, Ann. But God takes 'who' he wishes, when he needs them, to fulfill a purpose!

Death is something I know quite well, my dear, I just hope Lyncoya isn't too rough on the other angels!

Shall I pack your pipe with a little more hemp, Ann? It helps in these times."

"That's a splendid idea, Rachel. Perhaps Hannah could serve us some rum?"

* * * * *

For one week and maybe a few days longer, Tenskwatawa followed the Wabash River south until it joined the Tippecanoe River north of, "Buck Creek".

Not having eaten for nearly ten days and still burning with fever from his right eye's removal, the Shawnee collapsed into unconsciousness. A vision followed that event.

"Lalawethika, rise up!" said a wavering image.

""Chiksika"? Is that you?" deliriously asked Tenskwatawa.

"Yes, little brother!"

"I thought you died at "Fallen Timbers"? Is that not true?"

"One's spirit never dies, Lalawethika!

It is true; however, a white man's bullet killed my body!" wailed Chiksika.

"Big brother, I have done those things our parents and "Kumskaukau" instructed me to do. But I am still lost as to making our people see me as a holy figure!"

"'Noise Maker', as our mother named you, still fits your disposition!

The 'Star People' have sent me to show you the path to follow. Do not fret for I have come to help you!

When you rose from the dead and walked across the White River and you made the sun late in its arrival, inadvertently, you became a "holy man" in the Shawnee's eyes!

Upon your return, as they anticipate you will, you, Lalawethika, will be their "savior"; however, there is still much work to be done!"

"How can I do the things you speak of, big brother?"

"Like the trees in a forest, the white man has grown too many for the Indian to saw to the ground!

For his atrocities, we shall poison his roots with a disease his medicine men cannot heal!

'Whiskey' has been the white man's weapon against us!

You, Lalawethika, can attest to that for it has depressed and blinded you!

We as a people, if we wish to exist, have no choice but to find a method which will 'invisibly' attack our white enemies!

Sickness will quiet their cannons!" whispered Chiksika.

"What is the name of this poison?" cried out Tenskwatawa.

"That my little brother, is precisely your next quest!

You must search out Paddy Welch. He is not of our tribe but he has the recipe for the necessary pogrom!"

"Where is this man, Chiksika?"

"For now, my brother, you are to build a fire!

Its flames are to be maintained until the fawns lose their spots. You will gain a new strength from the flesh of animals living around you!

At first frost, travel to the "Apalachicola River" and follow it to the Creek village of "Sumatra".

A man named, "Osceola" will take you to Paddy Welch."

* * * * *

Andrew Donelson had grown into a strapping young man. His stature as well as demeanor, reminded the Sheriff of himself when he was that age.

Thomas Hickman rode up to the turkey pens located a mile from the plantation's mansion.

"Hello, Andy, your mother told me ya'll had been revisited by the coyotes! I've shot a few of them at my place. How have you been?"

"Why howdy, Sheriff Hickman!

Yea, we've got a goodly number to those beasts; but, I figure I'll be nailing their hides to the barn within the week's end!" Said Andrew Jackson's adopted nephew.

"How's that?" curiously asked Sheriff Hickman.

"By using an old Indian trick of bending a bamboo shoot and tying the bowed stick with string and tucking it into a ball of ground meat. When mister coyote swallows it and his stomach juices eat through the string, the bamboo straightens out and punctures the animal's intestines!

Pretty slick, ain't it?

Say, what brings you out this way?

My Pa won't be back until March; he's politicking in Washington." Said Andy junior.

"Son, I didn't want to say anything to your mother cause of her heart and all but Lyncoya has been murdered!"

Andrew fell to his knees. Then, as if splashed with cold water he stood and angrily approached the Sheriff. His fists were balled.

"Who did it, Sheriff Hickman, cause I'll certainly kill 'em!"

""Ben", over there in my wagon, says it was a woman who done it!" said Hickman.

"Ben, now, I ain't fooling!

What in 'hell's name' makes you believe a 'woman' killed my brother?" yelled Andrew.

"Mister Andy, Lyncoya was my best friend but he started fooling around with this woman in town!

I could tell by his condition, she was no good for him!" said Ben (a slave).

"What do you mean, 'condition', Ben?" asked Andy.

"I mean, he'd come home drunk, Sir, and he said, 'he was in love with her'!" answered Ben.

"Ben, are you lying to me, 'cause my brother didn't drink?

If you are, so help me god, I'll nail your black ass to that barn door!

What is her name?" screamed Donelson.

"Settle down, Andrew!

Ben's not a suspect here!" scolded Sheriff Hickman.

"Answer me, Ben!

What was the woman's name?" continued the angry Andy.

""Pricilla"....I think he said it was."

"Son, do you remember "Pricilla's" last name?" softly asked the Sheriff.

"It was "Hobson", wasn't it, Ben?" interjected Andrew.

Ben nodded.

"Sheriff Hickman, where did you find Lyncoya's body and how was he killed?" loudly questioned Lieutenant Donelson.

"On "Old Natchez Road". He was stabbed in the back with a knitting needle!

Andrew, let me caution you; by law, we can't jump to conclusions!" pleaded Hickman.

"Tom, I understand that; however, I owe my brother justice!

I won't harm a hair on Pricilla Hobson's head; but, I will find her and bring her in for questioning.

You have my word on that!" seethed Andrew Junior.

* * * * *

"Brigadier General Richard K. Call" was awakened when his aide, "Captain Herbert Winecoff" knocked on his door and handed him a directive hand signed, by the President of the United States, "James Monroe".

It called for retaliatory action against the Seminoles and the immediate arrest of their Chief, Neamathla!

Infuriated by the tone in which his orders inferred, General Call commanded "Captain Winecoff" to put together a squad of fourteen of the best Indian fighters out of his unit.

They were to be the "decoys" who would draw out Neamathla's warriors and then entrap them within General Clinch's surrounding troopers.

On the 11th of May, Captain Winecoff and his seasoned detachment, left "Fort Drane" disguised as a supply train. They hauled their 'loads' through the Seminole territory toward Fort King.

The next day, Call ordered General Clinch's seven hundred and fifty cavalrymen to surround the "Cove of the Withlacoochee". His men were to annihilate every Indian they came in contact with no matter their age or gender!

No sooner had Winecoff's soldier stuffed wagons crossed over the Seminole line when Osceola and his band of Black Moccasins, attacked the supply train!

They stripped the wagons of their valuables, stole the horses, and skinned the fifteen soldiers as though they would a mess of catfish.

The Moccasins then went over to the white man's side of the lake and burned four sugar plantations to ashes and took their slaves with them back into the Florida swamps.

Upon hearing of the supply train disaster, General Call ordered "Major Francis Dade's" one hundred and ten men to track the Black Moccasins down and push Osceola's warriors into Clinch's trap.

Two of Dade's men survived the fiasco, "Ransome Clarke" and "Joseph Sprague". They later died from infections caused by their scalping's.

General Clinch and his "crack infantrymen" reached the Withlacoochee River after six days of treacherous travel. Four of his soldiers had died along the way; one was bitten by a poisonous snake, another suffocated in quicksand while the other two, drowned.

The "Cove of the Withlacoochee" was clearly in sight but to reach it, his soldiers, horses, and equipment had to cross the river. Because they could find no place to 'ford it'. Six of the battalion's engineers constructed a raft.

Leaving thirty militiamen behind to manage the horses, the first night was spent ferrying the remainder of his fighting men to the solid land surrounding the suspected Black Moccasin hideout.

At dawn after Clinch's soldiers had rested up a bit, the Seminoles attacked.

The infantrymen fixed bayonets and charged them at the cost of four dead and fifty nine wounded. For six hours, the badly damaged soldiers ferried their way back toward their starting point.

Those left on the cove's side of the river fought hand-to-hand with the Moccasins. None returned.

* * * * *

"General Edmund Gaines" and the "Democratic-Republican Party" candidate for President of the United States, Andrew Jackson sat comfortably in the dining room of the "Blue Duchess" as it paddled its way down the "Ohio River".

Mostly, they spoke of the war years but every once in a while, Jackson would take a shot at the Secretary of State, "John Quincy Adams" (Andrew's arch enemy).

Jackson's beef with "Adams" was a personal one!

It started when the "patrician" New Englander, referred to him (in the newspapers) as a, "badly educated parvenu" or "bumpkin" whenever he got in front of reporters or the senators from the Northeast. Andrew saw those folks as "weak sisters" anyway.

President Monroe had called both Generals, "Gaines" and "Jackson" to Washington to discuss the growing Indian problems flashing up across the country. Although Jackson, General Gaines, and a handful of the Washingtonians who had actually gotten close enough to smell a "real Indian", agreed, "if the white men would honor their promises to the "infidels", there wouldn't be such issues with them"!

But, "the girls", as Jackson called them, such as "Henry Clay" (Speaker of the House) and "William H. Crawford" (Secretary of the Treasury), felt the "unchristian savages" had no right to impede America's proliferation.

It was exactly on that point, that Andrew Jackson decided to clean up the "Potomac Outhouse"!

Andrew and his closest friend, "Edmund Gaines" on their carriage ride from "Barcley's Landing" to Nashville, discussed Jackson's formal political announcement.

There were two major newspapers noteworthy enough to carry the story; however, the "TENNESSEE GAZETTE" and the "METRO-DISTRICT ADVERTISER" were constantly discrediting the other.

Finally, after their six hour road travel, both Generals settled on the 'Gazette' because of the paper's more favorable handling of the Jacksons' marital complexity.

That decision was bashed against the limestone pavement when reporters from both of the "rags" stormed the generals' wagon as they rode into Nashville's city limits.

Thomas Hickman and Andy junior (forcibly) had to manhandle the reporters so as to give the Sheriff enough time to civilly break the news of Lyncoya's death to Jackson.

Due to the reporters' chatter, the "cat got pretty much out of the bag" by the time Sheriff Hickman and Andrew Donelson reached the carriage.

When Andy junior told his stepfather what Pricilla Hobson had supposedly done, Jackson fell to his knees and wailed with sorrow.

After falsely swearing he would cause no more trouble, Jackson convinced the naïve Sheriff that he wished to personally speak with Ms. Hobson. Thomas Hickman refused to allow him to do that on the grounds of Andy's past performances.

Between the pleads and threats, Jackson did find out that 'Pricilla' was being held in the stockade at "Fort Nashborough".

Pretending to be totally crestfallen, General Jackson asked little Andy to loan him his horse and to drop General Gaines off at his nephew's plantation. He said, "he needed to be alone for a while and would arrive home by sundown".

The Sheriff and Lieutenant Donelson foolishly believed the war dog.

*   *   *   *   *

Colonel Zachary Taylor left Fort Gardiner on the upper "Kissimmee River" with a thousand men as soon as General Call sent word of Clinch's disastrous defeat.

Intelligence reports stated, "the Black Moccasins had regrouped in the "Big Cyprus Swamp" on the western side of "Lake Okeechobee".

Flush with new information gleaned from the torturing of a Seminole woman, Taylor, along with eight hundred of his Missouri cavalrymen, made a lightening swift raid on Neamathla's Muscogee village.

Ninety Seminoles were taken alive including Paddy Welch, Milly Francis and their three children.

Tenskwatawa who was within a mile of Osceola's warriors, found a safe place to hide in an old bear den. He filled the entrance hole with dirt after throwing dry leaves over his tracks.

Gunfire and screams went on throughout the night.

By morning's first light, the Shawnee prophet could hear the soldiers building a cage for the captured Indians. On three occasions a soldier passed in front of his hiding place.

He overheard one of Taylor's men complaining about missing the fight on the north side of the Okeechobee and having to guard the prisoners.

After nightfall, Tenskwatawa crept toward the place where he thought the cavalrymen had built cages. He could smell tobacco smoke.

Surprisingly, from the glow of perimeter fires, he saw a rather large fort Colonel "Zack's" men had constructed throughout the night. Someone had painted a sign naming the log structure, "Fort Basinger".

Tenskwatawa returned to the bear cave. A heavy rain commenced.

A 'hair' before noon, "Alligator" (a.k.a. Sam Jones) and his four hundred Black Moccasins triangulated the fast approaching Missourians with withering cannon fire!

The on-foot cavalrymen attempted to retreat by running through the sawgrass savannah from but were met by a couple of hundred skeleton painted slaves who butchered them like spring lambs.

Those whites who made it back to Fort Basinger lingered only long enough to mount their horses and hightail it out of the hellish swamp.

Tenskwatawa then crawled out of his hiding place, scalped a few dead cavalrymen, splattered blood all over himself, opened up the gate to the corralled Seminoles as if he were their personal savior, and then collapsed for affect!

The Black Moccasins arrived.

Pretending to be 'shook-up' from battle, Tenskwatawa raised his arms in praise as Alligator and his men scoured the makeshift holding fort for wounded cavalrymen.

Overlooking Tenskwatawa's praising antics, the grossly bloodied warrior ran over to Neamathla with his war hatchet held high into the air as if he were going to kill the Mikasuki leader.

Using the "Hitchiti" language, Osceola ordered his number one lieutenant to spare the old chief's life. He then spoke to those whom had been captured.

"While you "children" were being nailed into your safety coral, brave men were dying to protect your land!

Your cowardice however, is explainable, for a fool was your leader!

From this day forward, "Neamathla's" presence will be seen as, "nothing more than a shadow"!

The white man will soon return and when he does, his bones like 'those' preceding him, will never be found!

"We", the mighty Seminoles, shall never allow those 'pale faced demons' to plant a single seed in our earth again!

Whether their numbers are great or small, whether they come with wagons full of gold or mountain sized promises, those who step foot on our land will never return to where they came from!

All "fighters" are welcome to stay but make no mistake about it, if you do, the only interaction with the 'white man' you will ever have again, will be either killing him or burying his body!

Those of you following Neamathla from this place, may take with them: One horse and 'one' pouch of food!

All weapons are to be left behind!

Once you cross the "Olustee" and the "Santa Fe" Rivers, you are to never return!

This land belongs to the Indian!

Tell the soldiers who apprehend you these things I have said; also, as you cross through the white settlements, warn them to be gone by "Christmas Day" for the next one will not come!"

* * * * *

Rachel sat on her favorite spot on the terrace adjoining her bedroom. She was admiring the huge numbers of geese hoggishly feeding themselves in the freshly harvested cornfield.

She was thanking God for Andrew junior's safe return from West Point and his lifting the responsibilities of running the plantation from her shoulders when she saw a carriage entering the Hermitage's gates.

As the single horse drawn four seater came into view, Rachel Jackson saw that the passengers were, General Gaines, Sheriff Hickman, Ann Grundy and Andy junior.

Rachel snuffed out her pipe and went downstairs to receive the news about something she already knew. Her heart painfully thumped within her chest.

"Mama, I'm afraid Lyncoya has passed!

I thought I'd bring up Ms. Grundy so ya'll could pray for my brother's journey to heaven. I'm going to drop off "Uncle" Edmund at the Gains' place while Sheriff Hickman fills you in on what happened.

Expect me back by noon." Said Andy Donelson.

"Where is my husband?" asked Rachel.

"Mother, we're not sure yet!

We, believe Lyncoya was murdered by "Pricilla Hobson", Major John Bell's fiancé. If you'll remember, Papa sent him to Florida and messed up "their" wedding plans.

The General's checking it out now, Mom, but he did say, 'he would get home by dark'." Donelson lyingly said.

"Son, was 'Andrew' drinking?" sternly queried Rachel.

"Not, when I spoke with him!" answered Rachel's nephew.

"Alright then!

Thomas, why don't you help "Ann" down from the carriage and ya'll come on into the house. I want to know who would have done such a thing to my precious little Indian boy!"

* * * * *

Eight hundred yards from "Fort Nashborough's" main gate, was Isaac Johnson's parents' old homeplace. No one had lived there for quite sometime so the army used it to store all sorts of nonessentials such as uniforms, furniture and the like.

Once the sun went down, Jackson began setting charges made out of the keg of powder he had purchased in the same place he had gotten the whiskey from in "Goodlettsville".

After lighting a thirty-minute fuse, Andrew circled around the fort's south side and waited until the Johnson place's "distraction" popped things into action.

When the 'simulated' attack began and the fort's guards ran to their northerly stations, Jackson scaled Nashborough's wall, closest to the stockade, where Pricilla Hobson was being kept.

Following ten minutes of , "head and rat in the bag" interrogation, Andy was convinced that "Pricilla" was as innocent as a fawn; however, he wasn't so sure about 'Daphne', her sister.

Wasting no time, Andy remounted 'Rattler' and made a beeline to #8 Lafayette Street in Berry Hill.

Daphne Hobson had just blown out her lantern for the night.

Seeing that the "Hobson's" chimney still had wispy smoke coming from it's flue, Jackson quietly climbed onto the flat's roof. He plugged up the chimney top with the bedsheet he had pulled off of the clothesline.

It wasn't very long before the scantily dressed Hobson woman ran out of her apartment and into Andrew's waiting arms.

The two of them went inside.

* * * * *

Following a forensic look-over by Osceola, Tenskwatawa after coming within an inch of being skinned alive by Alligator for faking heroism and thus denied a horse, was escorted along with Neamathla's pro-peace followers, to the northwesterly trail that lead to the white man's boundary line.

"Fort King" was their destination.

During their week long journey filled with Tenskwatawa's lies, Milly Francis along with her husband, Paddy Welch and their children, bonded with the Shawnee 'tale-spinner'.

From that, forced upon, tolerance of one another, Tenskwatawa extrapolated what he came for; i.e., the "holy man" discovered how to harvest the bacteria causing, "Tuberculosis"!

With this knowledge now in hand, "Chiksika's" cowardly little brother, "Lalawethika" (Tenskwatawa), would be able to kindle the respect of the tribesmen at "Wapaghkonetta". The village was on the Ohio River.

He intended on building an empire there.

So, at the first opportunity, after stealing what he could, Tenskwatawa abandoned Neamathla's caravan and fled westward across the Florida panhandle.

Along the way, he collected the milk from dead cows.

* * * * *

Word had spread through Nashville's multi-terraced grapevine of Daphne Hobson's death. The gossip brokers speculated it had something to do with Major John Bell's death, at the hands of the Red Sticks, in the Florida swamps.

That tiny bit of "fact", of course, tied in the "bigamist" Presidential contender, Andrew Jackson.

According to the city's scuttlebutt analysts, the truth would come forth when Daphne's suicide note was made public!

It was in the hands of "Sheriff Thomas Hickman" for the time being; but, it was rumored, the "TENNESSEE GAZETTE" would soon publish its unabridged content!

Many of the "whispering gamblers" wagered their venal reputations that the self-inflicted hanging, was due to a "triangularly" shaped love affair with "Pricilla Hobson", being the lone survivor.

That version coupled nicely with the fact, "Bell's" fiancé had been arrested for the death of one of Rachel's "feral" children but was released after the authorities read her sister's "postmortem testament".

* * * * *

From the moment "Hannah Winn Robards" returned home with her enhanced story of Daphne's suicide, Lewis acquired a bad case of insomnia.

Since he and Hannah had had ten children together, there was no conscionable way for him to leave Nashville. But, if Daphne put in her "suicide note" his "Diamond Story", Jackson would surely come after him!

* * * * *

It happened two nights after Hannah brought home the Hobson tidbit.

Wearing his pistol, Lewis Robards walked out to his barn to repair the wheel on his carriage. A broken strut had caused his family to miss the Sunday's service at their Episcopal church.

As Lewis was jacking up the wagon's right rear chassis, Jackson stepped out of the barn's only stall and gently slipped a noose around Robard's neck!

Andy quickly pulled his wife's former husband's pistol out of it's holster and fired it at the barn's ceiling causing Lewis's horse to bolt out of the stall in which Jackson had shared with the animal.

Because the other end of the rope was tied around the fleeing horse's midsection, Lewis was instantly pulled out of his stable and then dragged a quarter of a mile down "Mildew Street".

Jackson followed the gravel displaced trail until he came upon Robard's dapple-gray feasting on some ripe crabapples. Andrew then disconnected both ends of his rope and walked to where he had tied Rattler and rode toward home.

Along the way, Andy picked a handful of white chrysanthemums for Rachel.

* * * * *

Fifty miles northeast of Fort Brooke and thirty-five miles south of Fort King an army of militia, Tennessee volunteers, Creek mercenaries, U.S. Marines and Army soldiers led by General Richard K. Call, encountered Neamathla's people.

By gun point, Paddy Welch and four Red Sticks were commandeered to take Call's twenty five hundred men to Osceola's hideout!

A twelve year old warrior refused and was hanged immediately.

* * * * *

The United States Government escalated the war against the Indians for two reasons, the first being, the Indians throughout the North American continent were protecting their "legally owned" lands and killing the white intruders like flies.

Secondly, it was a presidential election year; meaning, John Quincy Adams (a New Englander and a Washingtonian "Elitist") was running against Andrew Jackson (a Kentuckian "ruffian" and a firm "Constitutionalist") who believed in keeping his word even with the Indians.

But when the Native Americans began stealing the negroes from the plantations and turning them into formidable fighters, Adams claimed that Jackson was a "traitor" who intended to destroy the American economy by allowing the "red savages" to filch the workforce (slaves) from the people who paid for them.

"James Monroe" the 'lame-duck' or outgoing president, due to his being blackmailed over some past indiscretions, allowed folks like Henry Clay and other "patricians" to persuade him to unleash the idol generals loose on the Native Americans.

*   *   *   *   *

On Christmas day, Osceola's six hundred Black Moccasins (tribally mixed Seminoles) and two hundred Maroons (enslaved Africans who had escaped from their bondage) kidnapped "Wiley Thompson" (an Indian Agent) from Fort Brooke. They prepared him as if he were a roasted pig and ate him.

Under the leadership of "Osuchee" and "Yaholooche", the combined Maroon and Moccasin forces swept through the state like a scythe cutting high grass.

On saddleless cavalry horses, the red and black warriors attacked farms, settlements, plantations, Army forts and even burned the "Cape Florida Lighthouse" down to the bedrock it rested upon.

They cut supply routes, poisoned the whites' fresh drinking water, and spread measles throughout the state by releasing infected prisoners into the midst of towns too well defended to burn!

Many white settlers fled northward and almost every fort was evacuated.

*   *   *   *   *

"Major Benjamin A. Putnam" found himself and his sixty five soldiers, surrounded by a larger number of Maroons and were forced to defend themselves in the "Bulow Plantation's" sugar mill. They did it by stacking wetted cotton bales around them.

They held off the skeleton painted negros for two and a half days.

All that was found of Putnam's company was a note; it read:

"The government is in the wrong, and this is the chief cause of the persevering opposition of the Indians who have nobly defended their country against our attempt to enforce a fraudulent treaty. The natives used every means to avoid a war, but were forced into it by the tyranny of our government."

* * * * *

"Major Ethan Allen Hitchcock" discovered the remains of Putnam's company, he forwarded the 'found quotation' to "Major General Thomas Jesup" who in turn, by courier, sent it to President Monroe.

* * * * *

When Andy Jackson caught wind of it despite Quincy Adams's attempts to destroy Major Putnam's 'testament', Jackson read the quotation during every political speech he gave during his run at the U.S. presidency.

Sadly though, in late February following "Putnam's Christmas day massacre", Major General Jesup (U.S. Quartermaster) was "punished" by the influential Washington bureaucrats and ordered to take full command of the "Indian War" in Florida.

* * * * *

"Either whip the Indians or don't come back" was the spirit in which his orders were written!

In a rather coy fashion and through Jackson's "private" advice, General Jesup put a new spin on Indian fighting!

He concentrated on wearing the Seminoles down rather than sending out large groups who were more easily ambushed!

To do that, he got Monroe to send him nine thousand men. What differentiated Jesup's request from like requisitions by previous generals, had "Old Hickory's" thumbprint all over it; e.g., Jesup ordered volunteers and "Revenue-Marine" personnel (mercenaries for hire) to patrol the coast and inland rivers. What he got was exactly what he needed….nonpolitical killers!

* * * * *

Rachel Jackson and Ann Grundy had had Abraham construct a military tent over Lyncoya's grave. Within that ten by ten feet of canvas covering were most of the trappings both women were accustomed to.

There were two comfortable beds, lots of beeswax candles, chairs with inserted chamber pots, a barrel full of fresh spring water and assorted cuts of dried meats.

When Lyncoya's body had been brought to the Hermitage, Rachel demanded that her son be taken to the hill where the Creek boy use to sled down after a good snow.

She and Ann dug the little Indian's grave as soon as "Felix Robertson and Thomas Critcher" trucked him up to where he was lying in repose until the women made the proper preparations.

Andrew Jackson came home three days after he and General Gaines arrived back from Washington. Rachel strongly suspected his tardiness was due to his respite from sobriety.

She proclaimed, "she" had taken her last name of "Donelson" back!

In other words, Rachel decided, "from there on out", 'she and her husband' would live a celibate life, "forever"!

Her new home, she swore, would be the army tent on the hill where Lyncoya was interred!

The only acceptable communications with the outside world would be through written correspondence which was to be delivered by only one of three people: Abraham, Hannah, and Andy junior.

Visitations were restrictive in nature but not solely inclusive to Ann Rodgers Grundy, Presbyterian ministers, her personal servants, or any other invited guest provided they were not a politician or a "Catholic", were welcome. (Andy was not)

There was one caveat added to Rachel's new 'standard'; that is, "Andrew" could write letters to her at her new address, "but should not expect any sort of response, immediately"! she added.

This situation went on for three weeks until Nashville, Tennessee experienced the deepest early snow, in rememberable history!

By the time a team of field hands had dug a trench up to "Lyncoya's Hill" to check on Rachel, something wonderfully strange had occurred.

Rachel thought she had heard her son (buried beneath the Turkish rug and four feet of dirt) suggest to her, 'Mommy, forgive my father for his drunkenness. Return to him with forgiveness in your heart'!

* * * * *

When Tenskwatawa reached "Wapaghkonetta", he was met by some five hundred Shawnee hailing him as the, "Guiding Spirit"!

They had waited for more than a year to see the 'holy man'; the 'one' who 'walked across the 'White River' and caused the sun to not shine'!

On the second morning after his arrival, "Grey Bear" the village's 'Shaman', awakened "The Spirit Man" with a tipoff!

"White newspapermen were gathering in the "Council Circle" awaiting the speech he was scheduled to deliver that day.

Hearing this, Tenskwatawa demanded that the finest of the tribe's clothing be brought to him. He told Grey Bear to find a colorful headdress for him to wear!

Clad in what would be called, "hyper-Shawnian" attire, Tenskwatawa came out of the tribal chief's hut and walked through a gauntlet of flower throwing squaws and down the hill toward the 'council circle'.

Before stepping up to the "Sayers' Stone", two white men by the names of ,"Andrew Reeder" and "Lewis Cass" approached him. Lewis Cass was the first to give his pitch.

"Great One, we are all anxious to hear the wise words you are about to share with your people. What I am about to say, will offer gladness to their hearts for I bring good tidings from the President of the United States, John Quincy Adams!

In an offer of good faith and fair wishes, 'Mister Reeder' and I have been given the authority to place in your hands, the irrevocable deed to ten thousand square miles in the "Argentine District" of the "Kansas Territories"!

Furthermore, your people will receive two thousand dollars per year for the next twenty years!"

Andrew Reeder then stepped forward with an ornate box in his hands. He reverently bowed before he spoke to Tenskwatawa.

"Grand Chief of the Shawnee, I too bring you good tidings from your brothers in Washington!

Within this presidential giftbox, is the sum of one thousand dollars, an agreement signed by President Adams himself, and a "Certificate of Recognition" granting you in the 'eyes' of the American Government, the inalienable authority over the entire Shawnee Nation!"

"….and if, I might add one other point to our President's generous offer, "King Tenskwatawa", these fertile acres, your subjects are about to receive, has been placed in the "Washington Registry of Deeds" under 'your' name and therefore appropriately listed as, "Prophetstown"!" schmoozed Cass.

With tears streaming down the sides of the "Shawnee King's" cheeks, he stepped onto the Sayers' Stone and opened his arms to his people. In a deeply resonating tone, Tenskwatawa spoke.

"I have missed you, my brothers and sisters!

Since my departure when I walked across the White River under the darkness caused by the belated sun, 'Mishe Moneto' came to me and asked if I would travel with him into the stars.

As frightening a proposal as it was at that time, the 'Creator' assured me of my safety. It was then, I was shown his masterful plan.

Together, The Great Spirit and I saw many things from which I gleaned an understanding of his magical intention for us!

You see, my people, 'we', the Shawnee, are "his" chosen ones!

We have been given the most special place in his heart!

Although it was difficult for me to grasp at first, Mishe Moneto taught me the purpose of the white mans' presence on this continent. "They" were sent here to learn from us!

I realize it is difficult to fathom; but, think about it, they were fleeing a land from cruel and unrelenting rulers! We saved their lives!

Because of our benevolent ancestors' kindnesses, 'they' allowed them safe harbor here with us!

But due to their poor understanding of our ways and the misinterpretation of our hospitality, the time has come for us, to draw the line!

Starting now, the 'red man' of all tribes, must cross the great northern rivers and start anew. We, then, will have done our part for "goodness's" sake. We shall rebuild our world into an enviable civilization and an even better one than the white mans'!

What Mishe Moneto told me, I shall convey to you:

'The white man's flaw lays in his proclivity towards codifying the differences between rights and wrongs. Ultimately, he will destroy himself due to the perceived murkiness separating the two'.

In closing, let us rejoice as we journey to our "promise land" but shed a tear for our guests. We should wish them well and thank our god for the opportunity to purify ourselves in the waters that will forever divide us!"

The majority of Shawnee did not understand what Tenskwatawa had said in English but they applauded anyway. They had simply done what they saw the large group of white dignitaries do.

At his speech's conclusion, the newly anointed celebrity ordered (in Algic) the best chefs in the settlement to prepare an 'authentic' Shawnee dinner for the attending visitors.

Following a couple of "ritualistic" dances and a hatchet throwing exhibition, the diplomats and the newspapermen were served steaming platters of fresh vegetables, wild game meats, assorted fruit delicacies and the dead-cow milk Tenskwatawa had collected during his journey back to Ohio.

As the white men departed, the Shawnee hosts waved 'goodbye'.

* * * * *

By the end of May, Jesup's mercenaries started to achieve more tangible successes by capturing or killing numerous Indians and runaway slaves!

At the end of June, some Seminole chiefs sent messengers to Jesup, to arrange a truce.

In August, a "Capitulation" was signed by several chiefs, including "Micanopy". It stipulated: "the Seminole could be accompanied by their "allies" (their negroes which they considered as bona fide property), in their relocation across the Mississippi."

On October the eighteenth, six chiefs surrendered to Jesup's men much to Osceola's displeasure.

Eight days after that, Osceola and Sam Jones (Alligator) along with two hundred Black Moccasins and fifty Maroons, raided Fort Brooke's holding camp and led away the seven hundred Seminoles who had surrendered.

Jesup had lost his trust for the Indians. He vowed to kill them off.

* * * * *

Following his hard fought loss to John Adams, Andy returned to Tennessee as a bitter man. For over a year, few Nashvillians laid eyes on the man.

Despite attempts to raise his spirits, Jackson stoically refused to associate with even those reaching out to him. His own family, practically, never saw him.

Now living in a self-built primitive shack on the furthest point from his house, the demoralized Andrew Jackson went to great pains to avoid the interaction with human beings. He trapped squirrels and rabbits so as to not use up his powder and lead.

Jackson's reclusion came to a screeching halt when 'Judge Harry Toulmin' awakened the 'defunct' presidential candidate with harsh whacks of his cane! Harry then lambasted Andy with angrily spoken words.

"As I was watching you slumber in your quagmire of self-pity, I was wondering where this country would be today if it's founders had slid into the 'quitters ditch' that you have chosen!

I guess we'd all be picking cotton for the King of England!

Have you taken a good look at yourself, Andrew? Your appearance not only is atrocious to the eye but to the nose as well!

Do you believe you are the only 'swinging-dick' who was cheated out of an elected position?

I can't tell you the numbers of times, I rinsed out Jefferson's crying towel; I was his campaign manager, you know.

'Madison' had even more problems than 'T.J'.; although, the public never saw it, they sure as hell admired him for how he weathered his foe's relentless attacks!

How would you guess, those same "voters" might view you?

Can't you read your 'epitaph' now, 'Here lies a man who defeated battalions of British soldiers but was destroyed by a handful on limp wristed New Englanders!'.

For heaven's sake, man, burn this 'house of narcissism' down!

Come with me, Andy; I'll show you how to whip those aristocratic bastards!

We'll do it the way Jefferson beat both "Burr and Adams"; we'll appeal to the wealthy mans' bottom line by attacking Washington's (the government's) control of the monetary system!

You, 'Andrew Jackson', will become the "people's candidate" whose arch enemies are the elitist thieves loitering along the back alleys of the Potomac!

Andy, you beat "Quincy" fair and square in the first match; now, just imagine what you will do to him by fighting him with stones in your fists!

Son, if you'll tolerate my lead, we'll clean up Washington from wall to wall!

So, Andy, knock over that barrel of mash, grab the things you want to keep, strike a match to this place and never return to this 'sad trap' again!"

* * * * *

Jesup organized a sweep down the peninsula with multiple columns pushing the Seminoles further south. On Christmas day, "Colonel Zachary Taylor's" column of a thousand fighting men, forced Alligator's Red Sticks into a hammock located on the north shore of "Lake Okeechobee".

On Jesup's orders, "Brigadier General Joseph Marion Hernandez" commanded a force of "Firemen" who encircled the island believed to be the Moccasins' headquarters.

Slipping in on flatboats loaded with barrels of coal oil and protected by crack riflemen, Hernandez's marines emptied the fuel on the sunbaked sawgrass protecting the Seminole's hideout.

Osceola had prepared for such an attack in case the situation came down to a last stand effort!

Surrounding the Moccasin's dirt and log fortress was an encircling moat filled with multiple feet of mud and water, making horse travel impossible. The Indians had sliced the grass to provide an open field of fire and notched the trees to steady their rifles.

Their scouts were perched in the treetops so as to announce every movement the attacking troops made.

When General Hernandez gave the order to, "fire the island", Osceola's tree-perched marksmen opened fire dropping the torchbearers into their own flames!

Merciless cannon ball explosions disintegrated Hernandez's flatboats thus trapping the firemen between the wall of billowing flames and the alligator rich swamp lake.

Throughout the morning the Seminole snipers remained busy.

At half past noon, with the sun shining directly overhead and the air thick with smoke, Taylor initiated a sneak attack with the use of a crack unit.

The Seminoles allowed Colonel Taylor's men to unload without a defensive shot being fired at them. They were all on foot.

In the first line were the Missouri volunteers. As soon they got far enough into the knee deep marsh and out of sight from the five companies belonging to "Colonel Gentry's" Sixth Infantry, Osceola's Moccasins sprung from the surrounding foliage and soundlessly killed the twenty six young men with knives, arrows and hatchets.

When Gentry's Missourians failed to 'whistle' the "all-clear" signal, the Colonel ordered his men to spread out and slowly move across the island in a deadly sweep.

After hearing not one shot nor any other sound from Colonel Gentry's regiment, Colonel Zachary Taylor's cannoneers blanketed the island with rocket fire.

With one hour of sunlight left, Colonel Taylor called a ceasefire.

Even through the officers' telescopes, human movement was undetectable.

The once leafy island had been turned into a half square mile of charred timber.

There were no birds, no soldiers, no animals nor Indians, just a whole lot of smoking debris.

A lone canoe bumped against a cypress stump before the current took it away.

Chapter Eleven

'Lalawethika' climbed up the timber sized base of the crucifix on which his father was nailed!

Green worms weaved in and out of the hollowed skull appearing and then disappearing through the bone globe's sockets.

Despite "Puckenshinwa's" postmortem condition, he lambasted his son for his naivety while carrying on a teeth flashing argument with his wife also affixed to the opposite side of the wooden cross!

The eight year old Shawnee could not pull the impaling spikes from his parents' feet with his bare hands!

That's when, in unison, they told their son of the existence of "binary worlds"!

"Tenskwatawa, there are two caves high upon a hill, one filled with blessings for following the 'Master's' will. The other, offers misery and pain for those who live beyond the tribal ways!"

With a deep throated scream that echoed off of his hut's mud walls, 'The Prophet' awakened from his dream.

He was relieved to find, his nightmare was just 'that'; but, the Shaman also knew, his long dead teacher, "Penagashea" had sent him a message!

Two hours of darkness had to pass before Tenskwatawa was able to execute his plan. He changed into clothing artifacts once belonging to white soldiers along with mementos collected by ancestral warriors.

His intentions were to 'rebrand' himself. The "prophet" wanted to be remembered as a man with connections to the 'Creator' himself (Mishe Moneto)!

Therefore, when the blue jacketed holy man stepped out on the morning's amber colored ground, he blew a loud honk on his acquired

U.S. Cavalry bugle. His people needed to hear about his freshly delivered epiphany!

When an ample enough crowd had gathered beneath Tenskwatawa's treehouse podium, the Shawnee Shaman laid out his long-term plan for them.

Basically, their 'spiritual guidance' as told to him by way of the previous night's vision, outlined the necessity for the Indian people to separate themselves from the "children of the Evil Spirit" (the white man)!

Purification was the only way!

"His chosen ones" (The Prophet's actual followers), were to reject European habits, such as alcohol consumption, and were to return to their traditional mores.

He wanted his "new aged population" to reject the white mans' customs by forbidding interracial marriages, eating Euro-American foods, wearing their clothing (unless through postmortem theft) and the utilization of any and all manufactured goods!

Tenskwatawa demanded that his people return to their traditional gender roles; i.e., women were to do the farming and all home maintenance while the men hunted and protected the villages.

He threatened harsh punishments for those rejecting his vision-obtained teachings and promised execution for his detractors!

Any association with the settlers, the discussing of Christianity, or doing trade with the whites without his authorization, would be subject to a public execution on the grounds of 'heresy'".

For Tenskwatawa, the dissidents remained the most active agents of the evil spirits on earth!

He sought to identify and destroy them!

* * * * *

After Lyncoya's death from which Rachel Jackson never recovered, the Hermitage's vibrance dimmed.

Rachel was often seen revisiting her "little Indian boy's" haunts along with toting his youthful toys to and from his room to the hilltop, he was buried on top of.

Graveside seances were commonplace.

The days to 'Rachel', passed unabbreviated with joyless happenings!

She rarely spoke with Hannah nor anyone else on the plantation grounds. With her husband's rigorous second presidential campaign grinding on, her intermingling with those still living, almost never took place.

Depression and helpless anguish made the dates on the calendars' pages wash together into meaningless blurs.

It was "Charles Twinning" (the postman) who inadvertently drove the final spike into Rachel Jackson's heart when he handed her the Hermitage's mail pouch!

Since Jackson's second bout with Adams was at the tooth and claw level, Andrew junior had taken over the management of his stepfather's businesses and properties.

Because, he was tending to a slave's medical issue in Nashville, Rachel got hold of Mister Twinning's pouch and began reading every piece of mail in it!

Mostly there were letters from supporters but some were from folks just wanting something or another. Unfortunately, there was a five day old copy of "THE PHILADELPHIA GAZETTE" in the bag.

On the "Gazette's" very front page, in big and bold letters, was a quote coming from her husband's political archenemy, "John Quincy Adams"!

The following was as much as Rachel Jackson read before collapsing into the Hermitage's famous goldfish pond.

"Ought A Convicted Adulteress And Her Paramour Husband, To Be Placed In The Highest Offices Of This Free And Christian Land?"

It was Abraham who pulled the near dead woman off of the ice covered pond's surface!

Her face was as blue as a skin boil. She had also chipped her eye teeth.

The seventy two year old house servant, threw Rachel over his shoulder and ran her all the way to the big house.

Hearing Abraham's calls for help, a handful of field hands who were dragging in a Christmas Tree, ran to help get "'Mastress' Jackson" stretched out on the dining room table!

Hannah pronounced her, "dead on arrival"!

* * * * *

News of John Quincy Adam's defeat spread like wildfire through the military installations across America!

Finally, one of their own would take command of the armed forces!

The military would now get the supplies needed to do what they were supposed to do with them!

Too long, had they lacked the weaponry to fight the ever improving enemies of this country.

Even the Indians, at times, had better battle equipment than the U.S. Army.

With the "1812 hero" at the helm (Jackson), Europe would be stopped from supplying the country's adversaries.

With faster and more heavily armed attack vessels, the British, Spanish and French warships would be sunk before they got within sight of our shores!

Without realizing that Jackson had not yet taken over as "Commander and Chief", Major General Thomas Jesup, without Washington's permission, pulled in three additional regiments from southern Georgia and Alabama!

With that overwhelming number of soldiers, the Seminoles on the east side of Lake Okeechobee were forced to retreat southward into a trap in which Jesup had set in the "Loxahatchee" flatlands.

Reactively, "Tuskegee" and "Halleck Hadjo" (two Seminole chiefs) approached Jesup (under a white flag) with a proposal to stop fighting. Their one request, was to remain in the area south of Lake Okeechobee rather than relocating west.

Believing that "President" Andrew Jackson would 'approve', Jesup called for a ceasefire until a final treaty was declared by Washington.

The Chiefs and their followers, camped near the Army while awaiting the reply.

With only forty five days remaining before Andrew Jackson took office, Adams chose to muck up as much as he could prior to the victor's 'seating' in the "big chair"!

Therefore, by the stroke of his turkey feathered pen, "Quincy" not only rejected a peaceful climax but fired Jesup, as well!

The 'short-rowed' president replaced Jesup with "Zachery Taylor".

Taylor's first executive order was to seize the Seminole warriors (600 of them), put the Indians in chains, march them across the Mississippi, and drive them into the appropriated Oklahoma territory.

His second decision was to separate the leaders from their followers. He did so and executed all of them!

* * * * *

Ann Rodgers Grundy, John Hardin and Sheriff Thomas Hickman were the first to arrive at the Hermitage after hearing of Rachel's death.

Andy junior rode in from Nashville about two hours later but was denied seeing his stepmother's body until Ann Grundy got Rachel's hair presentable for viewing!

Sheriff Hickman asked three Nashville councilmen, "Thomas Crutcher, Jackson Baker and Felix Robertson" to ride up to "Campbellsville" to break the bad news to President Jackson.

They were to take with them, a jug of whiskey and plenty of rope!

* * * * *

"In a free government, the demand for moral qualities should be made superior to that of talents. Therefore as your President, it will be my sincere and constant desire to observe toward the Indian tribes, within our limits, a just and liberal policy, and to give that humane and considerate attention to their rights and their wants which is consistent with the habits of our Government and the feelings of our people." Said Jackson on the front steps of "Governor Robert McAfee's" home.

Members of the Kentucky legislature applauded as did the crowd of Republican-Democrat supporters until they noticed three "solemn men" sitting in a carriage some twenty yards behind them.

Thomas Crutcher stepped out of the black coach and approached America's seventh President.

Whispers and sighs snuffed out the gaiety as if everyone knew what was coming. Crutcher reached out his arms to Jackson and hugged him while he softly explained why the carriage was there.

Andy's face greyed as he bowed his head and cried out loud!

As if queued, Felix Robertson and Jackson Baker sided the widower and escorted their friend toward the carriage; but, just before Jackson seated himself into the curtained coach, he turned back toward the joyless Kentuckians and spoke.

"I am now the President of the United States and in a short time I must make my way to the metropolis of my country; and, if it had been God's will, I would have been grateful for the privilege of taking Rachel to my post of honor and seating her by my side; but, Providence knew what was best for her. For myself, I bow to God's will, and go alone to the place of new and arduous duties…"

Ten miles south of Campbellsville, Kentucky, Jackson asked Felix Robertson to pull off the side of the road in order to relieve himself within the privacy of a cluster of rhododendrons.

Four hours later and after some serious tracking, Felix found Andy in the village of "Greensburg" attempting to purchase a horse and a rifle from a farmer.

Following a slew of guilt provoking parables, Felix finally convinced the incoming "Commander and Chief" to give up his murderous quest of killing "THE PHILADELPHIA GAZETTE's" owner, "Samuel Keimer"!

Jackson swore he would peaceably return to Nashville but when he got to Washington he'd see to it, 'the man lost his typesetting fingers!'.

*　*　*　*　*

On the day (December the 24th) of Rachel's funeral, some ten thousand people turned out not only from the areas around Nashville but also Jackson's political supporters rode in from across the country.

Hundreds of mourners filed through the plantation house to pay their respects to the "people's president's" wife.

The "Donelson clan" had to stand guard around the silver casket to stop the "respecters" from snipping pieces from the gown Rachel had planned to wear at her husband's inauguration.

White and black, wealthy and poor were noted in the gathered crowds awaiting their chance to say goodbye to the first lady.

Upstairs, while the people were passing through the "viewing room", Jackson's friend and business partner (Judge John Overton) was trying to sober Andy up enough so he could 'presentably' attend the ceremony.

Among the pall-bearers was Tennessee Governor "Sam Houston" who led the procession to the Hermitage's gardens, followed by Jackson and the plantation's servants.

Sheriff Hickman and a crew of eleven appointed deputies, forbade any newspapermen from coming near the burial site for fear of Jackson's reprisal!

Nashville's church bells rang throughout the day.

*　*　*　*　*

Under Tenskwatawa's stern leadership, the new village attracted thousands of "Algonquin" speaking Indians.

Although the village endured hardships such as food shortages, epidemics, and tribal disagreements, "New Prophetstown" became an intertribal religious stronghold within the Indiana Territory. Three thousand Native Americans populated the massive reservation.

An estimated, fourteen different tribes comprised the "Confederation"; but, the majority of its inhabitants came from the "Shawnee, Delaware, and Potawatomi" nations.

Suffice to say, with those numbers of different tribal groups scattered out over tens of thousands of acres, communicative leadership became a problem!

One effect of the increasing pan-Indian alliance was steady pressure from the territorial governor ("William Henry Harrison") and the U.S. government in their attempts to establish land-cession treaties which Tenskwatawa had not approved!

While warriors continued to congregate at Prophetstown, Tenskwatawa remained adamant about maintaining their independence from the United States.

British and Canadian spies began seeping into the Indian villages bringing war materials and whiskey!

George Augustus Frederick (King George IV) was biting at the bit to have another whack at America!

When word got back to the Capitol of King George's "cloak and dagger" activities, President Andrew Jackson ordered a thousand seasoned Indian fighters out to "Fort Harrison"!

To add some teeth into Territorial Governor Harrison's attempts at negotiation with Tenskwatawa, Jackson sent a "special" message naming a 'place and time' for a meeting between 'Harrison and him' to happen!

* * * * *

Upon the receipt of Jackson's (Indian-skin) "ultimatum", Tenskwatawa (after some deep gulps of mescaline tea) consulted with the spirits!

Acting on the received 'celestial' guidance, he sent a war party of his most skillful warriors to kill Harrison within the fort's walls!

That "hit" might have successfully been pulled off had it not been for one guard relieving himself behind the horse stables, who managed to get a warning shot off before his throat was cut!

All thirty of Tenskwatawa's assassins were executed.

Their bodies were sent back to Prophetstown with a note nailed to "Screaming Owl's" skull. It read,

"Should one more arrow or even the handle of a tomahawk be found within the confines of a U.S. Government compound, your people and the land they stand upon, will become indistinguishable from the other!"

Not heading the advice of the majority of pan-Indian chiefs and not remembering Jackson's earth-scorching mentality from way back in the "Horseshoe Bend" days, Tenskwatawa summonsed a few hundred young braves to attack the fort the following morning.

He promised to lead the warriors into battle (himself) and assured the "immortal" braves they would be immune from the opposers bullets if they painted their faces with a "spirit rendered" green paint!

At sunrise the next morning with Tenskwatawa holding back some five hundred yards behind his green-faced warriors, they attacked Fort Harrison with loud zeal. None survived.

Seven hours later, Jackson's Indian hunters reported that Prophetstown was no longer in existence!

Each mercenary claimed to have discarded at least one part off of Tenskwatawa's body on their way back to Fort Harrison.

Narrowly surviving Jackson's "Indian hunter's", Neamathla and less than a hundred Red Sticks hid out in the "Olpe Caves" for twenty seven days.

When spring arrived and the rivers were filled with melted snow, the eighty year old chief and his "Hitchiti" speaking survivors, built small boats and floated them down the "Verdigris River" into the "Oklahoma Indian Territory".

Milly Francis, Paddy Welch and their two living children, were among the refugees' flotilla.

* * * * *

Still grieving the loss of their two "green-faced" boys, Milly's and Paddy's relationship became intolerable. Finally after a knock-down-drag-out fist fight between the two, Neamathla along with four of his rather stout councilmen, forced Paddy Welch to leave their tribe!

On September the third of that same year, Paddy Welch wandered into the village of "Winchester".

The Virginian community served as a Washingtonian outpost as well as a place for senators and their mistresses to frolic in the many hideaways dotted along the Shenandoah River; therefore, finding work was easy!

Welch's first opportunity for employment was advertised in the kitchen window of the, "Red Lion Tavern".

They needed a chamber pot cleaner as well as a floor sweeper. Paddy offered to take both positions for the salary of just one of them; if, the tavern would provide him with room and board!

"Peter Lauck" took him up on his offer and sent him to "Hill's Keep" to get situated before returning back to the Red Lion for that evening's shift.

Paddy Welch was soon praised as the hardest working man in Winchester!

It wasn't long before other business owners began soliciting Welch to work for them. One of those was the town's mayor, "James Dowdall" who surreptitiously operated "Cocke's Tavern", a place where anything on earth could be bought for the right price.

Paddy was offered a spacious flat above the tavern and ten percent of every night's take.

*   *   *   *   *

For reference sake, Jay Ray Howell had been quite efficient with his syringe; although, it would be completely erroneous to surmise that an injection of cobra venom into the hypothalamus has the same effect on Niburians as the operation would on Nicosans (Earthlings); it does not!

Although, J.R.'s work would be commendable by any upstanding surgeon's standard, it only decreased the Nib's mental acumen by thirty percent still leaving Welch the comparable abilities of an earthing scholar.

Peter Lauck and Paddy Welch began raking in mind boggling amounts of money.

High stakes gambling, prostitution, gunrunning, political tale spinning and of course, bulk vote stuffing were the hottest commodities on the Cocke's Tavern menu.

Soon after Lauck's and Welch's partnership was formed and this should not be shocking, Paddy Welch started up a side business.

One hundred ounces in untraceable gold would make any U.S. "unpedigreed citizen" disappear; however, the higher up the "food chain" the 'mark' went, as did the cost of the assassination!

To keep his overhead as low as possible, Paddy did most of the local work himself; although, jobs requiring more than a day's ride, he often used the mail.

Poisoned whiskey was the premier agent used for men. For women, arsenic tainted dilaudid seemed to do the best job on them.

"Murders" contracted on active military personnel or individuals living in less sparsely populated areas, were farmed out to the "outcasts" abandoned by their tribes.

Paddy Welch's favorite was an old "Iroquois" drunk who went by the name of, "Whippoorwill". He was called that due to his incessant whistling especially when he was deep into his cups.

James Dowdell and Paddy Welch prospered for nearly two years before a "Detective Cranch" from the "District of Columbia's Police Department" investigated the murders of three senators all of whom, had ties with or regularly frequented, 'Cocke's Tavern'.

This put the "quietus" on the tavern's less than legal activities thus influencing Dowdell to shut down the 'drink house' and turn the establishment's building into his home; but, this did not quell the detective's investigation.

Senators Alexander Smith (Virginia), Robert Adams (Mississippi) and John McLean (Illinois) had been murdered in the same town (Winchester), at the same time (three o'clock in the morning) and by the same method (poisonous injection)!

Respectively, the most likely suspects were Peter Porter (a Virginian), Thomas K. Reed (from Mississippi), Nenian Edwards (John McLean's successor), all of whom, were high-stakes gamblers known to play games of chance at Cocke's Tavern.

Detective Cranch found one common denominator, "Paddy Welch".

* * * * *

James Dowdell was totally caught off guard when Detective Cranch and four of the Capitol's security officers came to his home in the predawn hours of a Sunday morning.

With a search warrant clutched in Cranch's hand, Winchester's Mayor was quite sure he was "busted" for not paying his taxes on his tavern's unadvertised extravaganzas and yet, he said nothing in his defense, when the Capitol Policemen knocked on his door!

"Mayor Dowdell, I'm very sorry to disturb you on this sabbath day; but, the matters of our visit are of grave concern toward this nation's security!

May we come in, Sir?" politely asked Detective Cranch.

"Certainly, but what's this all about?" sternly quizzed the mayor.

"Well, Sir, as I am sure you have read in the papers, we have lost three "Senators", apparently murdered, and all within the last twelve months!"

"That's right! But what does this have to do with me?" angrily spat Dowdell.

"Mayor, that's why we're here; it seems the deceased senators were frequent customers of yours. Isn't that so, James? Attacked Cranch.

"Gentlemen, as you, I'm sure, already know, I closed "Cocke's Tavern" seven months ago!

I did so, for precisely the reasons you say you are here for; that is to say, practically every politician in Washington came here to, I suspect, blow off a little steam!

Frankly, it was getting out of hand so I felt compelled to shut the operation down; so, what does that have to do with the three senators' deaths?"

"That's what we wanted to ask you, Mayor!

Do you know a man by the name of, "Paddy Welch"?" coyly asked William Cranch.

"Of course, I do. He managed my now defunct tavern for me; why do you ask?"

"When was the last time you spoke with, 'Mister Welch'?"

"I believe it was two weeks ago; no, it was four weeks, why?" pressed the mayor.

"I was under the impression he lived here, Judge Dowdell!

Is "he" no longer residing in this house?" queried the Washington "dick".

"When I closed the tavern, he moved!

And 'NO!', I have no idea where he moved to; although, he did say he had family in "Tennessee" but there is no reason for me to think he went there!

Fellows, I'm not trying to be rude; but, I have a lesson to teach for my Sunday school class. I need to prepare for it; so, if you don't mind….."

"Would you care if we take a look around, Mayor?" rudely interjected Cranch.

"If you feel compelled to do so, then help yourselves; but, watch yourselves, these walls have been freshly painted!" said Dowdell.

"Yea, thanks for the warning!

I can see you're doing quite a bit of work here. Where did Welch stay; I mean, which room did he live in?" abruptly asked Cranch.

"Detective Cranch, look…I know you have an immensely important job to do but, so do I!

Therefore, I'm going to speak with you, as I would to my own son!

Not to overlook the necessity of preparing for 'my' doing "god's work", I'll address the issue you are unsuccessfully skirting around!

I haven't seen nor heard from Paddy Welch within the past two months!

If you do run across the 'scoundrel', I'd be much obliged if you would arrest him for 'lifting' five hundred dollars of my money, before he vanished!

Plus, if I get my hands on the 'cockroach' before 'you' do, you'll never find him, I promise you that!

Any man who would steal from his partner, ain't worth the cost of the rope to hang him with; although, he is worth a bullet!

Do I make myself clear, Sir?"

"I guess so, Judge Dowdell, I'm just trying to be thorough!"

"I don't know where your man is; frankly, I just want my money back. But, if you do catch up with Paddy, tell him, I'm 'lookin' for his hide!" said the judge.

"Judge, I have an idea, why don't you work on your 'Sunday school lesson' while my men rummage through 'ole Paddy's' flat!

I'll sit down with you while you're working on it and who knows, I might even be of some help to you. My "mama" use to be so proud of the way I would recite the 'Scriptures' to her.

Say, didn't Mister Welch work at "The Red Lion Tavern" before you hired him?

And, did he not bunk-in over at "Hill's Keep" at the same time he was employed by the tavern?

Is it not true, there is a passageway running beneath "Loudoun Street" which connects from (the closed down) Cocke's Tavern to the Red Lion?

Doesn't that same underground tunnel go directly under "Miller's Drug Store"?

Is that the place, Welch got his "dilaudid" and other concoctions from?

Aren't you one of Benjamin Miller's three partners with his drugstore?

You see, "James", we believe you have been complicit in the murders of numerous politicians; consequently, once we match up certain chemicals with the victims' blood samples, we'll be one step closer to dropping "you boys" through the gibbet's shoot!

Judge, if you wish to evade the gallows, I suggest we become the best of friends!

By the way, we also know you haven't darkened a church's door since your wife died three years ago!"

"Look, Detective Cranch, granted, I did lie about the church thing but so help me god, I don't know where Paddy Welch's whereabouts are!

All I can truthfully say is, 'it's my belief that my ex-partner was into some "midnight" side deals with an unsavory few of our politically inclined guests'."

"What were Welch's work hours?

When did he come to work and when did he leave?" whispered the tenacious cop.

"Cocke's Tavern was a "Members Only" establishment. Our guests pretty much set their own schedules.

Actually, when I think about it, Paddy normally opened the tavern around 'three' in the afternoon and shut her down around midnight." Clamored the judge.

"Where did Paddy stable his horse?"

"That's funny you should ask that question, Mister Cranch; because, I just realized, he didn't have one!

He was a quiet man and one who never discussed his personal life with anyone!"

"You never saw the man after the tavern closed?"

"Before he took the room upstairs, never; but, he would walk back to Hill's Keep every night. He had his own keys; that's why I never heard him stirring around." Said Dowdell.

"Did he have any girlfriends?"

"None that I saw. Like I said, Detective, Welch wasn't the social sort. I never did really get to know the man!" Judge Dowdell said.

Four policemen came back downstairs after going through Paddy's room. They apologetically shook their heads; meaning, they found no clues.

The five "slew foots" were handed one of the tavern's parasols after they dawned their rain jackets and broad billed hats.

In preparation to meet a wind-blown deluge, each of the detectives carefully opened their umbrellas so that a swift blast of wind wouldn't turn the Cocke's Tavern's multicolored seal, "bassakwards".

As Detective Cranch was the last Washingtonian to bid the Judge an acidic farewell, he glanced down into the gamps' receptacle and saw a brass tube with a tuba's mouthpiece soldered onto its end!

The judge attempted to reach for it but was prevented from doing so by Dowdell's lightning fast handshake!

With a wisp of whiskey on his breath, the Judge spoke.

"Ah, you noticed my little "tomfoolery toy"!

Sometimes when the weather gets hot and the flies smell the dab of bacon grease I smeared on the living room wall, I'll stick those buggers and leave them dangling, I will!"

"Which wall did you master the art of "blow gunning" upon, Sir? Slyly asked Cranch.

"Why, the one behind you, Mister Cranch!

I believe, you can see 'my' tightly patterned work behind my wife's portrait. Have you ever lost a loved one, William?

"Death" does curious things to a man's mind!" humbly babbled Judge Dowdell.

"My, my, my!

Look what I just found in the bottom of the empty umbrella container!

I'll be darned, it's a syringe-dart kit!

Judge Dowdell, you are under arrest!"

* * * * *

"'Beyond the great Mississippi, where a part of your nation has gone, your father has provided a country large enough for all of you, and he advises you to move to it!

There, the white man will not trouble you; they will have no claim to the land, and you can live upon it, you and all your children, as long as the grass grows and the water runs, in peace and plenty.'" Said the seventh President of the United States to his full length mirror at the foot of the bed.

Andy was preparing for a speech he was slated to give to the "Senate" that afternoon.

Andy and Hannah had been lovers for many years but now the stakes were even higher!

If the papers caught wind of their relationship, or for that matter, "Jackson" (their four year old son), living in America's Presidents' house as a happy family, "it", would incinerate any chance of a second term!

"Andrew, in southern Mexico there is a small village overlooking an emerald green sea.

A good day's work there, consists of catching enough fish to contribute to the town's evening feast. It is in such a place, my love, you would discover a better way to live!

I fear you will die if you linger in this 'snake pit' much longer. My god, honey, you worry all of the time!

People are mostly liars here and frankly, it's just a down and out, dirty place to be!

We have nothing to stay here for; why don't we leave, dear?" pleaded Hannah.

"Can't do it!

If I jump ship now, the Cherokee will become 'fair game' for every prospector wanting to pan some gold on Indian lands.

Hannah, how long do you think it would be, before the U.S. Army was called into action over a miner's scalping?"

"Not very long, I'm afraid. Whatever happens to the "Red man" will take place because of what is decided within the dark chambers' of it's Czars!

For our longevity's sake, let's get out of this evil town!" Purred Hannah.

"There is no doubt in either of our minds, Hannah, the immense love we have shared. Long ago, I signed the papers authenticating your release from my ownership; furthermore, you have been deeded a substantial portion of the 'Hermitage' upon my demise.

You were Rachel's saving grace, an angel, who made her last days better. It was you, who tried to blow life back into her body. She loved you!"

"Andrew, Rachel knew about our son. She told me the day before she died.

Actually, she said, 'it put her mind at ease, in case her heart gave out, to know "I" too, would take care of you!"

"I had no idea she was aware of that!" gasped Jackson.

"Oh, Andy, women know when another one comes prowling around!

Maybe it will offer you some relief to know that your wife and 'Ms. Ann Rodgers Grundy' had a love affair throughout the last ten years of her life!

We cannot undo the knots we wove in our earlier lives; we must try and avoid the naughty strands pleading for entanglement, next time!

My love, I vote for freeing your soul so it can soar above the dunes and splash into the salty waves. Let time go; stop trying to get a rebate for it. Just accept the sun's warmth as payment! " tearfully exclaimed Hannah.

"I dismissed the romantic portrayals of a "lost Indian culture" as a sentimental longing for a simpler time, quite some while ago. The demise of Indian tribal nations is inevitable and the white mans' infatuation with 'legal' land purchases will be the reason for it!

Progress requires moving west; there is no other direction to go!

The only thing I can do is postpone their extinction. And you're right, Hannah, I would certainly love to do what you suggest and I am sure it would double my life expectancy; but, I can't live with the thought of my having a hand in the Indians' elimination!

If the aborigines do not peaceably go to the vast regions on the other side of the Mississippi, the New Englanders' 'philanthropic sham' will crumble like burnt grass!

Don't forget about the gold in Georgia and North Carolina; the hot spots seem to be on the Indian's side of the boundary!

All I can do is stall the greedy wheels from running over those few groups of remainders who simply wish to be left alone!

Quite candidly, it'd be my preference to divide America into three parts. Anything west of the Mississippi would be for the Indians.

There would be a line drawn from the northern tip of Missouri through the bottom of Pennsylvania until it dropped into the Atlantic. This would separate "us" from the New Englanders.

All three would "be" their own sovereign nation and would run their governments accordingly!

With the deep valleys separating the ways in which we see things, there is very little chance that peace will exist among us. Wars and many of them, are surely on the horizon!

It is my duty, Hannah, to do as much as I can to stop that from happening not so much because of my being the "president", but for the Indians' sake!

If I had my druthers, I'd swap out the New Englanders for the Indians in a heartbeat!

I'd make those spineless bastards leave their homes and move across the Mississippi and then we'd see what they had to say about that!

I hate those goddamned people!" Said Jackson.

* * * * *

"Indian Key" is a small island in the upper Florida Keys.

Chief Chakaika's scouts, over the past two nights, had counted the munition boxes offloaded onto wagons destined for "Tea Table Key". It was where "Brigadier General Walter Keith Armistead's" joint Army-Navy amphibious base was chiseled into the bedrock.

Naval Lieutenant, "John T. McLaughlin" was General Armistead's "wild wolf" of whom was unleashed every time a bunch of Indians needed killing!

That was why Chakaika and a dozen of his Black Moccasins were there; they intended on taking the lieutenant and his sloop's crew out to sea and dropping their bodies into it.

"Early in the morning of August 7, a large party of Spanish speaking Indians sneaked onto Indian Key. By chance, one man was up and raised the alarm after spotting the Indians.

Of about fifty people living on the island, forty were able to escape!

The dead included, "Dr. Henry Perrine", former United States Consul in Campeche, Mexico who was waiting at Indian Key until it was safe to take up a 36-square mile grant on the mainland that Congress had awarded him." As the report read from Lieutenant McLaughlin's hand to General Armistead:

"Sir, The Naval base on the Key was manned by a doctor, his patient (White Wolf), and five Culper agents; they were Cerians! Before being slaughtered, the facients mounted a cannon in the entranceway of the surgical quarters and managed to kill a dozen or more Red Sticks with a load of musket balls." Sternly reported McLaughlin.

"At what point during the skirmish did you strike, John?" asked the general in a fatherly way.

"General, when we heard the cannon blast and that was the first sound we did hear, my men and I moved toward the center of the island. Although we had secured the perimeter around the base, the Indians no doubt, slipped by us.

In hindsight, I should have put a boat on the creek. I believe that's how they got in!

But then, out of nowhere and from up high in the sky, came a thunderous roar and a blast of the brightest light I had ever seen!

I ordered my men to lay face-down and flat on the ground!

Thirty minutes later when we moved onto the scene, all I could see was a crater filled with smoking ash.

Absolutely nothing recognizable remained, Sir." Exclaimed Lt. McLaughlin.

* * * * *

It was "Richard Lawrence's" thirtieth birthday. The young man sat on the sharp slant of the "Wayside Inn's" roof recapping his life's high-points!

Most of them involved people being kind to him.

Even after living in America for seventeen years, "Dickie" retained his cockney accent. He was a risk taking artist, the kind who painted things most other laborers would be afraid to do!

Richard Lawrence worked on tall structures. Church steeples and flagpoles were his call to fame; but, repainting the "pyramid" at the "Belle Grove Plantation" was to be his greatest feat yet!

The gold paint was to arrive at "Larrick's Tavern" in a couple of days. In the meantime, Dickie had to be content with tarring the Wayside's roof in exchange for his room and board.

But, on October the 31st, he never worked; because, it was the nitwit's birthday!

From Winchester to "Toms Brook", Lawrence was the man to get in touch with whenever something like a lightning rod needed to be put up or a leaking water tower required a patch. Seemingly, the man showed no fear whatsoever of heights.

Everyone in "Middletown" knew it was Dickie's birthday because every month that had 'thirty one days' in its calendar, would give cause for him to sit on top of the Wayside's roof and dawn a pair of stilts!

"Dressed to the nines" and sparkling like a firefly, Richard would walk up and down the village's only street, three times, while singing and dancing his foolish heart out!

He always threw the children candy.

* * * * *

Paddy Welch entered 'Larrick's Tavern' a little after three in the morning; he was to wait for "Paula and James" to come fire up their ovens.

"Thursday's Special" was always a sauerbraten sandwich made with freshly baked pumpernickel. Paddy crouched behind a stack of silver birch kindling.

He had chosen a five pound hammer to work with due to its swiftness and tidiness!

Afterwards, he dragged their bodies down into the springhouse; 'they'd remain fresher there', he thought. That was when he saw 'Richard Lawrence' for the first time; he was tossing chocolates down to the dirty little hands waving in the air beneath him.

On stilts, Dickie's head was ten feet off the ground. Paddy ran outside to speak with the high-stepping craftsman.

"If your name is, "Sir Richard Lawrence", I have a very important message to deliver to you!

It is from your employer, "Major Isaac Hite"." Hollered Paddy.

"I'll be done in a minute; I've got to go sit on the inn's porch roof in order to get these walking sticks off!

What'd you say you was looking forward to doing?

These kids is making an awful racket and I can hardly hear what you was saying!"

"Look! When you're done, meet me at my tavern; there's no need of yelling back and forth, just come on over!

You'll be my special guest; I'll even close the place down for the day so I can explain the "position" my father has made for you!" Smoothly stated Paddy Welch.

"And your father's name? timorously asked Dickie.

""Major Isaac Hite, Junior". The golden pyramid guy. I'm "Jost", the Third!" lied Paddy.

Richard Lawrence speedily stepped toward the Wayside's porch roof.

He spoke to the mob of "varmints" beneath him.

"Dickie has a lot on his mind as of this minute and I can't be bothered right now!

Maybe next birthday, you'll get some more candy!" he said to the children.

* * * * *

"Welcome, Sir Richard!

You know, that's a mighty nice thing you do for the kids, Mister Lawrence. I can certainly see why "The Major" picked you for the job!" greeted Paddy.

"Where are the Larrick's?

They always have a chicken pie for me on my birthday!" Dickie asked with a pouty look on his face.

"I'll explain their whereabouts in a moment, Richard, but first, I need you to be sworn in; please raise your right hand!"

Dickie did as, "Jost III" asked him to do.

"As the Belle Grove Plantation's "Potentate", do you promise to protect and preserve the many hundreds of acres surrounding the "Great Pyramid of Isaac" and will you accept the responsibility of patrolling the grounds nightly by air balloon? If so, say, "I will"!

With the look of a man badly needing a bowel movement, Richard answered "affirmatively" but then, asked "Jost" a surprisingly intuitive question.

"Mister Hite, is what I'll be doing, going to mean that I'll be working for the United States Government?"

"Paddy placed his forefinger over his lips as if he were warning Dickie not to speak loudly. He then explained.

"The Major was right, you are a genius!

"Yes", to your question; your 'code name' will be, "Lightning"!
I'll fix us a cup of tea and then go into the details of your mission."

"When will you teach me to fly, Mister Jost?" pleadingly asked Richard Lawrence.

"Well, aren't you the eager-beaver; how about tonight?" coyly asked Welch.

"I have to finish tarring the inn's roof before going on fulltime!" stuttered Dickie.

"Here's your tea. It's got honey and chocolate in it. Cheers!" gleefully said 'Jost'.

"That's good. It also has mint in it, doesn't it?" childishly queried Lawrence.

"It is the coca syrup which lends to the tea its 'spirited' flavor. Would you care for another, my friend?" slyly asked the Niburian.

"Man, this stuff is great; it makes my body feel … wonderful!
What is that you're winding?" asked the dunce.

"Richard, it is a metronome!
Watch the hand go back and forth and feel yourself floating down a beautiful creek. See the moss hanging from the live oak trees. Feel the warm breeze pass over you as you rise into the sky. You are warm and safe as you float atop the billowing clouds. "Lightening", do you wish to fly now?"

"Oh, yes! I want to fly!" garbled Lawrence.

"Then, open up your arms and let the gusts of wind lift you into the heavens!" cackled Paddy Welch as his five-pound hammer crunched through Dickie Lawrence's skull.

Chapter Twelve

Andrew Jackson looked out from the third floor balcony of Rose Hill's finest room, "The Presidential Suite".

The horizon reminded him of the days when he would be looking for Red Sticks hiding in the same clumps of trees.

The downwardly cast mumblings from his supporters gathering in the "Lockerly Arboretum", brought Andy back into the present!

He had a speech to give to the, "Southern Association of Human Rights Advocates". They were drinking champagne and politely nibbling on small sandwiches.

Tromping over the bodies of a fallen enemy was Jackson's ejaculatory level of glorious pleasure; but, speaking to crowds of liberal minded backstabbers, was the epitome of purgatory to the man!

In simple words, he hated them and they hated him!

As Jackson opened the doors to the awaiting "advocates" seated below, they stood and clapped. Gleaming white smiles looked up at a president of whom, they were convinced was out to kill the Indians off!

Therefore, Jackson threw away the prepared script written by a "leftwing advisor" and decided to speak from his heart; after all, the "President" had nothing to gain, by speaking about "a something" he saw in a certain way.

The seated "humanitarians" hushed their amorphic criticisms when "Old Hickory" broke tradition by removing his hat and loosening his tie. He leaned forward like any ole country boy would do if he were trying to sell something, and spoke.

"I have chosen to break away from protocol for one parsimonious reason, I would like to share with you, what I actually know to be factual!

I shall be brief.

Folks, the demise of Indian tribal nations is inevitable!

One can only look toward our country's "northeast", to find a European's farm now superimposed over a "Mohican" village.

It is where the white man's plow horse, at this minute, is busting up their once beautifully painted jars!

My "New Englander" critics are nothing more than 'hypocrites' given their history!

"Up there", tribes have become nearly extinct. Hunting grounds have been replaced with white-owned dairy farms and 'State' law has replaced 'Tribal' law!

If the Indians of the south were to survive and their culture be maintained, they will face powerful blocks of people willing to speed up their end. And, just as I said earlier this morning to Hannah, 'the romantic portrayals of lost Indian culture as a sentimental longing for a simpler time in the past, must be abandoned'.

Progress, my good people, requires moving forward." Concluded Jackson.

Some of the people stood as they applauded; still others, especially the frail men, clustered together and whispering about the President's mentioning of "Hannah's" name!

At that moment however, Andy's mind was on the man standing beneath the rose covered alcove. He was wearing a black hat and had on a pair of sunglasses.

Andy returned to his suite to get his telescope but before he could reach for his satchel, there was a knock on his door!

From his waist holsters, Jackson withdrew two matching pistols and loudly made a statement.

"I was not to be disturbed! State your business and be done with it?"

"Andrew, open the door. It's "Jay Ray Howell"; I've got some bad news to share with you.

On a brighter side, I have a jug of scotch and a handful of opium powder to give to you!"

"My, you have a way about you, J.R.; you scared the living shit out of me!"

"That was a very nice talk you gave, Andrew." Matter of factly said the Cerian "Eraser".

"What's happened?" fretfully asked Andy.

"White Wolf is dead!

He was killed by the Red Sticks at our base on "Indian Key". Your father was undergoing heart surgery when Chakaika's Black Moccasin warriors struck." Emotionlessly said by Howell.

"Did they get away?"

"No, my dear boy, they did not!

It's "dust to dust", Andrew; you know the deal."

"Thank you for letting me know. Have my brothers been told?" Jackson asked.

"All but "Running Hawk"; he's away on assignment.

Andrew, Paddy Welch has shown up in the Washington area!

Various data sources tells us, we need to prepare for whatever might be thrown our way. An "assassination" of the U.S. President isn't out of our parameter's concern!"

"Jay Ray, I need to be left alone now. I appreciate your personal interest in me but this is something I must work through, myself!" sniffed Jackson.

"If you need me, Andrew, run an advertisement for selling, 'hickory axe handles' in the newspaper. Use "Franklin's Code". So long."

Jackson filled his lungs on long draws from his pipe; the opium dust mixed with cured tobacco, made the memories of White Wolf softly come into focus.

Arabian horses, space flights, target contests and big fish, all became part of a whirling collage of seconds the two had spent together!

Sadly, even those thefts from the past could not stop Jackson's hatred of the "Indian" from growing.

* * * * *

"Mayor" or "Judge" James Dowdell, one and the same, began "singing like a bird" when his cell's iron door was padlocked!

He told Detective Cranch every detail he could remember about Paddy Welch along with the "combination numbers" to his personal safe.

That way, all the Cocke's Tavern irregularities were forgotten!

Detective Cranch and his black suited goons, snickered as they left the Mayor's house.

James Dowdell, on the one hand, was elated due to the fact, he was still alive; but, on the other hand, the judge knew he was now Cranch's "bitch" and that troubled him, very much!

Not wanting to do it; that is, asking for help, Dowdell after three nights without sleeping, signaled his Culper 'upline' for help!

"Major Scott Bowman" and he were to meet at the "Burnshire Dam" at 0200hrs.. It was one o'clock in the afternoon.

Dowdell poured himself a massive amount of scotch. He went through his home collecting his firearms, cleaning rods, powder, patches and balls.

Most of the afternoon was spent putting his pistol, shotgun and hunting rifle into good working order. At fifty yards using any one of his weapons, James could mess up a dozen apples in short order!

He had turned down "four" assignments and in the Culpers' organization, that was something one shouldn't do!

James had 'fallen' to the temptations provided by wealth and ego enhancement. It had been all wrapped up into a nice political position; therefore, doing something 'good' for the world had to take a backseat.

Judge Dowdell was hoping "the Major" would understand.

'Maybe, if he could be tasked with killing Paddy Welch himself. That way, he'd atone himself and show the "company" he was still one of them.' Dowdell thought.

But, what he really wanted was, 'exoneration' from the crimes he committed while in cahoots with Welch!

Judge Dowdell knew full well, Welch was up to something; he could smell it in the air!

He was aware of Paddy's part-time jobs but this particular one, James Dowdell surmised, had submerged his old crony into some evil doings!

'Paddy was going for the 'title' of, "First Presidential Assassin"!'.

* * * * *

"Why hello, James. I expected an older looking man; the years have been good to you, I see!

Pardon my abruptness, I had a scheduling pinch and decided, it would be better to meet you in your stable rather than have you make that long journey all the way to the dam!

I've been looking at this report and......." As Major Bowman was saying before Dowdell interrupted him.

"Major Bowman, I don't know if you have ever gotten off kilter before; because, for the past ten years, I have allowed others to "buy" bits of my soul!

As a 'Judge', I took money from the 'guilty'; as a mayor, 'bribery' built this house!

My wrongdoings are many; but, so help me god, when I saw my partner, Paddy Welch molt into the devilish organism he became, I reached out to you!

It is true, we as a couple of 'shysters', committed every single sin in the "Good Book" but killing "Jackson" goes beyond my moral limits!

That is the reason I needed to tell you about Paddy." Pleadingly said Dowdell.

"Who paid Welch for, 'the hit?'" whispered Bowman as he pressed the barrel of his pistol into the mayor's forehead.

"Sir, all kinds of politicians came into the tavern and many went into dark corners with Welch!

I was more or less, a silent partner in the Cocke's' operation!" Diminishingly cried James.

Major Bowman moved the judge to the front of the barn so the men could see one another, eye to eye. Scott Bowman with a wide grin on his face, spoke.

"Judge Dowdell, you will have ten seconds to recall "five names" of people with whom you think might have spoken with Welch concerning an assignation!

Look into my eyes, James!

Ten-Nine-Eight......"

"Warren Davis, John Calhoun, George Poindexter"......I can't remember anymore; there were so many!" squealed Winchester's mayor.

"Four, Three, Two, One...."

A bullet then zipped through James Dowdell's brain!

Bowman dowsed Dowdell's body with lamp oil and burned him, the barn, four horses, and the house to ashes.

The Culper jumped into his wagon and took off toward Washington.

* * * * *

The Larrick's were beginning to smell like rotted eggs. Soon, Richard Lawrence's carcass would make it worse.

To compound Paddy's challenges, several dozen of the tavern's 'regulars' were starting to tap more harshly on it's front door.

Those more adamant even began tampering with the lock. The bodies in the springhouse had to go!

With the evening sun to his back and from the tavern's rooftop, Paddy Welch apologized to the mob loitering below Larrick's Tavern.

"Guys, I apologize for the tavern's closure!

We have had a monster of a sink hole occur in the cellar. If you will bear with me, I'll have it filled in, by this time tomorrow night!

The first of ten guests to 'come back' when we reopen, "your drinks", will be on the house!"

Throughout the night, Paddy removed everything of value from the tavern. He stacked kegs of beer and cases of whiskey into the back of the Larrick's covered wagon.

In the basement, three bodies formed the base of the massive amount of kindling stacked on top of them. Any and all things flammable, such as tables and chairs, made entry into the basement an impossibility.

A line of gunpowder served as the ignition fuse.

* * * * *

"Senator George Poindexter" of Mississippi, was to drop off his and "Calhoun's" final installment at Larrick's Tavern that night. They had already paid Welch half of the ten thousand dollar fee, 'to send Jackson to hell'.

Once the money arrived, Paddy Welch's would move into the 'execution' phase.

In order, to lure the President into 'point-blank' range, Jackson would have to be "invited" to some important person's funeral!

In that scenario, his guards would be seated, 'Andrew' would then, be an easy target while reverently bowing his head.

At eleven thirty, Martin Van Buren, Senator Poindexter and four armed cavalry officers (all on horseback) rode up to Larrick's Tavern and stopped.

A "Lieutenant Sparks" dismounted, untied a leather bag from his horse's haunches, gently placed the cowhide sack against the establishment's front door and then remounted his government issued horse and rode off along with the others, at a quick pace.

Welch, hidden in a stand of trees, watched the whole transaction from across the street. As soon as Paddy got his hands on the sack and removed the final installment from it, he lit the gunpowder fuse and returned to Richard Lawrence's room located in the basement of the Wayside Inn.

Paddy laid on Richard Lawrence's floor pad and looked up at the only ray of moonlight jabbing through the basement's door. He could hear the vibrations of horses' hooves and the heels of men with clanging buckets traveling from "Cedar Creek" to Larrick's Tavern.

It was a nice sound; also, one that sort of had a rhythm to it.

At daylight, Paddy Welch was awakened by two things: choking smoke and Richard Lawrence's youngest sister, "Laura Lee" banging on his door!

By pouring a goodly amount of whiskey on his bandanna, which he used as a mask, Welch spoke through the 'moon hole'.

"What's going on out there? What do you want?" gruffly asked Paddy.

"I was worried about you, brother!

We heared about the fire and "Pa" wanted me to see how you wuz adoing!

I drove the wagon here myself. You know, I just turned twelve don't you?" spouted Laura Lee.

"Sweetie, there is a lot you do not know about me. You remember me as, 'your industrious good brother' but there is something no one has ever told you!

"My" father and "your" father were different men!

'Yours', is the one we grew up with, while mine was, "King Richard II"!

You see, my dear, our mother was what one would have called a, "Chippy" back in those days!

The "Prince" was the sperm donor; they were both about fifteen years old! Our Pa took her in; because, 'her side of the family threw her out into the street'!"

"Richard Lawrence, if you don't stop telling tales like you are, you're gonna turn to salt!

I've a good mind to turn my cart around and head right back to Winchester and tell Pa what you just said!

By god, he'd whip some reverence back into your butt!

What's gotten into you? Why don't you want to open your door; ain't it smoky in there?" Questioned Laura Lee.

"Listen, Sis, people whose names, I shall not repeat, are preventing me from returning to my "Kingdom"!

If Jackson weren't in office, "Vice President Martin Van Buren" would establish a "National Bank" and allow 'Congress' to pay me for my estate claims!" Loudly prophesied Paddy.

"I can tell, Richard Lawrence, you have lost your marbles; therefore, I'm going back home and bring back with me the sheriff and enough of his deputies to put you in a place where there are others babbling identical nonsense!" screamed the girl as she spun back up the basement's stairs.

"Wait a minute! Don't you want to see the music box I bought you?" Welch said as he opened up his pocket watch making a musical chime drift up the sandstone steps.

"I'm still gonna tell everyone what you said but seeing as you were thinking about me while you wuz seeing the world and all, maybe, I'll milden up my tattle tailing, if you brung me something that plays music!" artfully said Laura Lee.

"I was just funning with you, little sister!

Let's turn your wagon around and head home; it's been more than a month of Sundays, since I last saw Maw and Pa!"

"Cover your head as you come through the door, a lot of water is coming down from the ceiling.

Forgive the mess, I quite foolishly allowed a friend to stay here while I was on a mission in Philadelphia. He sure did make a mess, didn't he?" played Welch.

"You ain't my brother; you're a foot shorter than he is!

Who the hell are you, mister?" yelled Lawrence's youngest sister.

"Listen to me, young lady, I am handing you fifty dollars because my father would want you to have it. Considerate it a slight tidbit of what is to come!

I need to borrow your wagon. I'll bring it right back here in six hours. There is so much to tell you, sweetheart, but for now, you'll just have to believe me.

I am owed thousands of dollars by the U.S. government; therefore, by using your buggy to transact a little business in "Strasburg", I'll be that much closer to being able to hire a ship and get back to ruling my people!

You are not to leave this basement for any reason!

If you do and "you" get arrested, they'll probably hang you right out front!" said the macabre lipped Niburian.

"So, what am I supposed to do while you're gone?" asked the girl.

"Did I, not just give you fifty dollars?

Why don't you earn it by cleaning up the place!" quibbled Paddy as he sprayed a green dust into the air as he opened Dickie's basement door to leave.

*　*　*　*

Jackson had hidden his odious feelings toward the Indians. Not even Hannah knew how or why, he was torn between his country's expansive progress and a people, partly his own family, making a beeline toward obliteration.

Should he let the generals loose on "them", like the southerners wanted him to do? Or, would it be best, continuing to play the same game of, "Promise and Renege" throughout his second term?

This was Andy's dilemma but when they killed White Wolf, the scales were tipped toward the lead slinging side!

"General Armistead" was a man Jackson held in high regard. In Andrew's mind, ole "Lo" was the perfect picture of a "Southern gentleman", even down to his sharp pointed mustache and goatee.

But, as a fighting man, Andy preferred the less "chivalrous" sort!

That's why he was going to fire him but not until after sending 'Lo' out on one last mission.

Within his "Indian Resolution Plan", Jackson devised a two pronged attack to begin in May.

On the fifth, Armistead was to approach the chiefs of the remaining Red Sticks hunkered in on the east side of Lake Okeechobee.

In the grandest of ceremonious fanfare, Lothario Armistead was to dole out $55,000 to use for bribing the war chiefs into surrendering. His first payout went to "Echo Emathla", a Tallahassee Red Stick and his thirty warriors.

His second, went to "Coosa Tustenuggee" and his thirty some fighters. Every warrior got $30 and a rifle; tribal chiefs received $200 while the bigtime war mongers like Tiger Tail, Echo, and Coosa, were to get $5,000 each!

All but Tiger Tail and his Black Moccasins took the buyout which was exactly why President Jackson ordered a fellow Culper and full bird colonel, "William Jenkins Worth" to command a brigade of "Indian Killers".

They were to come in on the west side of Lake Okeechobee and eradicate those rejecting Armistead's "conscience levying" offer.

Those who accepted the cash, had to be out of Florida and on the way to Oklahoma by the first of June!

As Armistead had stated, "All Indians are to evacuate the territory; for afterwards, it will be cleansed of them!".

The Red Sticks who declined Jackson's "Last Offer", were to be hunted down like sick hogs and slaughtered!

* * * * *

Colonel "Jenk" Worth and seven hundred blood hounds, along with the same number of their handlers (experienced bear and Indian hunters), camped outside of the fort.

Some had jackets made of scalps taken from previous battles while others, painted themselves up like skeletons.

Something they did have in common was, 'the mass of men were "un-chatty" while incessantly cleaning weapons and sharpening their tomahawks'.

They were loners and yet they moved harmoniously, almost skillfully, around one another. Watching them interact was likened to seeing alligators tear a fawn in half.

When Armistead gallantly galloped away from his Florida 'crusade', he sent by way of 'runners', the news, "his job was done"!

"He was retiring to Washington".

Thirty minutes after Worth's crew got the go-ahead, like a caravan of tarantulas and with their muzzled companions at bay, the Indian killers inflated their hot air balloons.

The winds were coming out of the east making an attack on Tiger Tail's band of cutthroats, a thumbs up.

A handful of the government's mercenaries stayed on the ground with the dogs while others teamed up into the large baskets setting beneath the balloons. Once the dogs were unmuzzled, the pilots followed the blinking lights attached around the dogs' necks.

Within each squad-carrying cockpit was a capable pilot, a spotter, and three snipers!

When the dogs got onto an Indian's scent, the pilot would steer the vessel toward the dogs' blinking lights.

Each of the four balloons had skulls painted on their bulbs and carried ten men, five hundred rockets, ten fire bombs and a plethora of grenades on board.

Flares and laser beams made the ground alive with things escaping below the canopies. The dogs wailed with their smorgasbords of victories while the shooters were at a 93% 'headshot' count.

* * * * *

"Coacoochee" waved a white flag as a "death-headed" balloon hovered above him. Warriors lined up with their backs against five miles of lake water!

Forty six men threw their weapons onto the sand beneath their feet and everyone of them were instantly killed by a cantaloupe sized fire bomb!

This same scenario went on for three days. Cross winds met the fourth morning and therefore the end of the mission; but then, one of the dog handlers signaled up to his team's pilot!

He had spotted a couple of dozen of Tiger Tail's Moccasins hiding out on a tiny little island about five hundred yards off the gulf coast!

With a great white flash followed by a "waterfall sounding gulp" and then a period of electric bolt jousting, the acre sized island disappeared. No bodies, no debris, just swamp water that even the seagulls were uninterested in!

There was nothing left to eat, anyway.

* * * * *

Jenk Worth ordered his men to pile up their deflated balloons along with their armaments, cut their horses' throats, roll the wagons into the burnable mound and ignite it!

A congratulatory speech was given and "that" action along with the memory of "it", were forever extinguished.

A Cerian evacuation craft arrived for the contingent.

Colonel Worth asked the pilot to circle the area so his men could make an accurate assessment of their work; but, the Culpers chose to sleep since the seagulls weren't flying that day.

* * * * *

President Jackson looked out at the rose garden's abbreviated clusters of cherry trees. He watched Armistead's aide jump down from the driver's bench and scurry around the carriage to open the door for his "general" to step out upon the Capitol's steps.

Painters had to move their ladders away from the side entrance's columns in order for the servants to carry in a box of Red Sticks souvenirs.

Lances, arrows and a sack full of Indian scalps were gifts for the Commander and Chief. They were a warrior's spoils being delivered by a 'disperser of payoffs' to a man who was sickened by 'that kind of crap'!

Primitive weapons used to defend the last inkling of their land against a foreign invader who took from them…everything.

General Armistead saluted President Andrew Jackson before he gave his report.

"Andy, you're looking mighty chipper these days. I'll tell you, it's just not the same without hearing ole Rachel's cheerful greeting!

How are you doing with that, my friend?"

"Sit down, Lo. I'm doing as well as can be expected and I thank you for asking.

General, I'm pulling you out of Florida for good. As a matter of fact, we're all getting out. This world is changing as are the ways we fight our enemies!

Our days of honoring an opposer such as allowing them to collect their dead, has been replaced with boobytraps and ambushes!

Lothario, I have transferred you to West Point; those lads there, are still wet behind the ears and are in need of a good Commandant!

The cadets need to learn from our mistakes!" Said Jackson.

"God damnit, Andy, I don't want to rot in front of some chalkboard. I want to kill Indians!" stammered Armistead.

"Lothario, my friend, in the days when I was in the field, I too, looked at the body counts, the stacked up victories and so on; but, from this country's President's perspective and presiding within a democracy where congressional haggling takes place, America feels that the $40,000,000 we have already spent along with the 1,500 soldiers who have died, is enough!

They want us to get the Indians east of the Mississippi, "out or buried"!" Warmly stated Andy.

"Is that why you sent "Jenk" and his merry band of Indian murderers in after me?

Andrew, did you see what he did to those people?" yelled Lo.

"I ordered the Culpers to exterminate Tiger Tail for killing my father!

The fact that White Wolf's murderers were 'Red Sticks', was coincidental.

That is the way in which the U.S. military intends to deal with her future enemies. From here on out, American foes will be met with overwhelming force intended to extinguish any form of defiance!

Surrender will no longer offer them quarter!

The days of a "warrior's ethic" has passed. Today, it's a, "kill them all" mentality.

Even our Army's generals' promotions are determined by weighing their casualties against those of their enemies, no matter the gain or loss of real estate. It is time we let a newer generation do it; besides, I like the idea of retirement!" spouted Jackson.

* * * * *

Major Scott Bowman watched Detective William Cranch as his dapple-gray backed the two-seater carriage into the barn.

Cranch rewarded his horse with an apple he had withdrawn from his pocket and then proceeded to unbridle the pedigreed beast when he felt the cold mouth of Bowman's blunderbuss against the back of his hatless head.

"Do not turn around. Do not fear; we work on the same side of the law!

Detective Cranch, let me be clear….you will have some questions to answer! Should you lie to me, I'll kill you and your beloved pony, deader than four o'clock!

Do you understand what I am saying to you?

And do you believe that I am sincere about killing you if there is even a 'hint' of mistruth in your answers?" slyly asked Bowman.

"Yes, but don't you think we could get more done by sitting at a table and sipping on some of my finest whiskey?" asked William.

"Actually, 'no', Detective Cranch. You see, I have already subdued your wife and baby!

They are safe as long as your words are "straight"; otherwise, you know the way of the Culper. Your body and your family's will go up in smoke!

Alright, remember there are, 'no', "do overs"!

Let's start with an easy one.

Were you the one who cleared out James Dowdell's safe?"

"Yes, I did."

"Were you intending to turn the contents of Mayor Dowdell's deposit box over to the higher authorities? Be careful here, Mister Cranch, this question is a slippery one!" Threatened Bowman as he cocked his blunderbuss.

"No, I was not!" Cried the Washington gumshoe.

"With what you found in the safe, would you have had enough to charge Winchester's Mayor with a crime?" Scott playfully asked.

"'Tax evasion' and 'odds tampering' would have been about all."

"How much cash was in there?"

"Seventy-five hundred dollars and a bag of precious metals was what I kept. I gave two hundred dollars to each of my men, as well!" chocked Cranch.

"Here is a thought question: 'Since there were no markings on the pig iron safe, you must have been given the combination numbers. Now here it comes, 'what did Dowdell sell you beyond your keeping mum about his business escapades?'" toyed Major Bowman.

"The names of the men who contracted the "assassination" of President Andrew Jackson!" laughed the arrogant sleuth.

"You may live to see another day, after all, William!

What are the names of these men?" coldly asked the Culper.

"What guarantee do I have that if I tell you his name, you won't kill me and my family?" bartered the Washingtonian.

"Billy, I will unequivocally promise you, I most certainly will destroy the entire "Cranch family" if you so much as hesitate another second in giving me the answer to my question!" yelled the major.

"Paddy Welch." Gasped the federal spook.

"And the names of the financiers of the, 'hit'?" snarled Major Bowman.

"I wrote their names down in the book in my breast pocket. If you will allow me, I shall hand it to you!"

"Alright, Detective Cranch, raise your left hand into the air!

With your right hand, reach into your pocket and extract your notebook and put it on the carriage's seat!" Cooley ordered Bowman.

Cranch did precisely what Major Bowman asked him to do except for one small detail; instead of pulling out the detective's note pad, William Cranch drew from his breast pocket a derringer and shot Scott Bowman in the head with it.

Immediately, he hoisted the agent's body into his carriage's passenger's seat and harnessed his dapple-gray up again.

After untying his wife and their two year old son, Cranch headed out into the wilderness area south of where he lived. There was a dumping spot he often used when witnesses or collaborators disagreed with his arrestee's guilt; it was where the Potomac River met the Atlantic Ocean.

* * * * *

Paddy Welch pretending to be the halfwit, "Richard Lawrence", reconstructed the scaffolding beneath the Capitol Building's columns just as his boss had told him to do.

"Maxwell Weldon" made "no bones" about his displeasure with General Armistead's untimely delivery of the Red Sticks' artifacts when he was doing his dead-level best to refurbish the west alcove's ceiling after a summer plagued with muddauber wasps. He took out his frustration on his 'new hire'.

""Dickie-boy", the next time you allow someone to intimidate you into tearing down something that took us half the bloody morning to build, you have them come see me!

Only a dumb knucklehead such as yourself, would have not seen that the 'high fangled' general was at the wrong goddamned entranceway!

Your stupidity will cost you a pretty penny, it will!

I'll not pay you for work done over. I've got a good mind to…" yelled Weldon when Paddy jammed a mortar trough into his throat.

Welch lifted the bullyish man's body and dropped it into the back of their work wagon and disappeared into the Capitol city's traffic.

Paddy had found exactly what he had come for; he discovered where the President's bedroom was and how to gain access into it.

Chapter Thirteen

The "For Sale" sign had impotently hung on the "Bailey-Coble building's" front door for most of a year. It was Christmas Day so neither of the "Mill House" owners anticipated a buyer.

Since the "Henson Creek" flooded two summers ago, "Jeff Bailey" and "Benjamin Coble" did everything they could to recover their losses. They never did!

The two men, had to turn their business over to "Oxen Hill's" Sheriff, in exchange for not going to the 'work farms' for back taxes. Both of their wives had left them, parenthetically, making Jeff and Benjamin bunkmates in a shack they had slapped together.

After researching the shutdown flour mill, Paddy Welch found out where the "busted" pair lived!

There was no number nor a formal address; because, it was the only "shanty" under the "Brinkley Road Bridge". Paddy knocked on their door.

"Merry Christmas!

Please excuse the intrusion but it's my understanding, you gentlemen, might be in need of a wealthy partner!

My name's, "Lawrence", Richard Lawrence."

"Please come in, Mister Lawrence, and forgive the mess!

That sorry-assed "Bailey" laying over there on the floor, hadn't gotten around to cleaning the place up yet!

What may we do for you, Sir?" said Benjamin Coble.

"For starters, you might offer me a seat. Then, let's all scoot up around this table and enjoy a sip or two off the jug of rum I brought you!

Let's see if we can work together and get the "Mill House" up and running again!

What do you say?" pushed Paddy.

"Mister, I don't mean to be rude but why in the hell, would you want to include us in the deal?

"Sheriff Sasser's" had the goddamned thing up for sale for a long time. The waterlogged wreck ain't worth the taxes due on it!

Why don't you just pay Sasser off and be done with it; anyway, there ain't much left of it!" curtly stated Jeff Bailey.

"Gentlemen, I am placing this envelope on the table. In it, is "five hundred dollars"….for each of you. Your tax bill is forty-three dollars!

As for my end of the bargain, all I want is, to set up shop on the mill's top floor. This is a "governmental project"; therefore, I can't stress enough the importance of secrecy!

And remember, any slip of the tongue regarding a 'Culper operation' always equates to a death sentence!

Am I understood?" threatened Welch.

Benjamin and Jeff looked at one another in disbelief. After a few seconds of "sidebar" conferencing, the bankrupt owners approached Paddy with two hands ready to shake.

"Congratulations, "Partners", shall we have a toast?" gleefully chatted the Niburian as Bailey and Coble bottomed up their "strychnine infused" cups of rum.

Minstrel-type well-wishers, all practicing their Christmas songs from within a straw filled wagon, passed over the bridge.

The 'clickety-clack' of the wheels rolling across the planks overhead served as a distraction from the convulsing Mill House defuncts.

It took forty five 'headbanging moments' for the two men to expire; however, Benjamin Coble lasted eight minutes longer than Jeff did.

When the night came, Paddy slid the Mill House owners' bodies down the steep incline into the creek. Given the recent rains, Welch estimated their arrival to the "Potomac River" would take at the outside, two days.

With no noggins, it would be nearly impossible to identify them!

"Oxon Hill" whether the townsfolk wished to admit it or not, was a 'river town'. It was similar to "New Orleans", only smaller.

Drink houses bulging out the seams with ill begotten monies, served as a mecca for the 'bottom feeders' to flourish. Everyone carried a gun there!

To top that, it was the ideal "spot" to hire some bad people!

Welch chose the "Golden Pony" to set up his recruitment campaign.

The "working girls" were old which meant the saloon's clientele didn't have a pot to piss in!

'Desperate men come cheap' thought Paddy as a buxom barmaid came to his booth to take his order.

"What will it be, sweetheart?" asked the graying redhead.

"I'll take a jug of your good corn whiskey, mum." Requested Paddy using his best Scottish accent.

"That'll be one dollar!"

"If I paid you ten dollars, would you tell me your name?" politely asked Paddy Welch.

"Honey, not only would I give "it" to you for that, I'd take "yours" to boot!" laughed the waitress.

"Ah, madam, you're much too flattering!

My name is, "Richard Lawrence" what's yours?" toyed Paddy.

"It's "Guinevere". Just like Sir Lancelot's "squeeze"; what might I get you?"

"Now, I'm really intrigued, Guinevere!

Besides, I was wondering if a "hundred dollar gold piece" might help me find a crew of mentally unhealthy individuals?"

"Mister, I'd love to chat with you longer but as you can see, I have other 'bull shooters' to serve!

I'll bring you your whiskey when I see your money on the table!" hollered Guinevere at the top of her lungs.

The barmaid opened her mouth to the size of a peach when "Richard Lawrence" slapped a golden coin against her forehead. The stunned woman took the coin in her hand.

As she clutched it against her hiked up bosom and with a grin stretching to both sides of her face, she laughingly spoke.

"If I were a betting woman of which, I am, I'd wager this gorgeous piece of gold that "one" woman, could do more for you than a whole slew of men!

Besides, you're not stupid enough to solicit the kind of "helpers" you're looking for, in a tavern!

Therefore, my assumption is, you picked me out for some reason. Is it fair, Richard, to ask you, "why"?" queried the sun wrinkled waitress.

"Because your "government" needs you!

The President of the United States is in dire danger!" loudly exclaimed the Scottish stranger.

After biting the hundred dollar gold piece several times and then sliding it between her flesh and her corset, Guinevere sat down in the booth across from the man she was told was, "Richard Lawrence".

She beckoned Paddy to lean closer toward her because she had a secret to tell him.

"Look, 'Mister', whatever your name is, do you see those two men standing beside the front door?

If I, so much as look at them in a certain way, they'll impolitely drag you out of "my" tavern by your heels!

I reckon, you either start enjoying the ambiance of 'The Golden Pony' or get the hell out of here!" said Guinevere.

"Excuse me for a moment, my dear." Blandly stated Welch who then stood up from his booth and walked over to the two 'wiseguys' Guinevere had spoken of.

Following a brief conversation with the men, Paddy returned to the booth. He was grinning.

"Darling, you're in luck!

I have managed to arrange a "crew" to move your belongings to wherever your little heart desires!

Guinevere, why didn't you tell me your "bouncers" were, in fact, here to foreclose on this fine establishment?

I would have helped you; instead, you attempted to intimidate me into giving you that gold piece without your earning it!

Do not despair, I have arranged for your arrearages to be paid in full; however, I'm going to need a little something from you in return." Said Welch.

"….and what would that be, Mister Lawrence?" she modestly inquired.

"Other than my residing upstairs, there will be no changes. You'll continue to manage the tavern as you have done, until I tell you to do otherwise, understood?"

"I'll agree, but you haven't answered my question yet; what is it, you want me to do in "exchange" for your bailing out my tavern?" pleaded Guinevere.

"I shall return to the Golden Pony in three days. By then, I will assume your things will have been removed from my quarters?" snorted Welch.

"But, I have no place to go!"

"May I suggest that you store your things in the barn and put a cot up in the kitchen. That way, we can open for breakfast earlier!" snickered Paddy.

"Perhaps, during your absence, I can come up with a more compatible idea for the both of us!

Is there anything, in particular, you might "want" upon your return?" purred Guinevere.

"As a matter of fact, there is!

Sunday afternoon, I shall announce to the townspeople of Oxon Hill, my plans to turn this 'river village' into the hottest gaming spot in the northeast!

Would you be so kind as to see, we have adequate seating for the members of this community?

We'll need them lined up, in front of the Mill House. Space the chairs, precisely, four inches apart.

At three o'clock, I shall unveil for all to see, the reason why every single citizen of Oxon Hill will soon be wealthy beyond their wildest imaginations!" Paddy said from horseback.

"Anything else, my Lord?" cattily retorted Guinevere.

"I expect you to do as you are told and to "watch" your tongue!" sparred Welch.

"Yes, your 'Highness'!" said Guinevere from atop the apex of her curtsy.

"Make sure everyone attends!

Anyone "absent" will be excommunicated from my kingdom!" said "King Richard III" as he rode his steed into the mist.

From the look in Paddy's eye, Guinevere could see that Oxon Hill's new "Mayor" wanted to experience her mysteries. She threw him a kiss 'goodbye' of which, he returned.

For a miserable three hour ride through a mixture of sleet and rain, Paddy Welch was rewarded with the sight of a road sign showing a busty "Pocahontas" on it. The "Brown's Indian Queen Hotel" was one mile ahead and at the corners of "Pennsylvania" and "16th" Avenues. Paddy got ready for the next scam to uncoil.

The "White House" was so close, a man could throw a que-ball through its front window. Pennsylvania Avenue was muddier than most pigsties.

Ironically, there were gentlemen escorting ladies and literally, sharing a covered walkway with a feral hog.

The "Indian Queen" stood above the other nearby hotels by a "country mile". It was like finding a doubloon on the beach!

There were plenty of (cocktail holding) "rich types" standing around the lobby. Paddy Welch approached the front desk.

"Welcome to the Indian Queen!

How might we be of service to you, on this dreadfully dreary day?" greeted the Brown's Indian Queen Hotel's owner named, "Jesse Brown".

"I would like to lease out the entire upper floor of your hotel.

So we won't act like a couple of monkeys trying to ride a watermelon, why don't I just plunk down on this fine oak desk, $500 worth of gold nuggets?

For the next six months or at least until the end of April, a "Governmental Assayers' Laboratory" will be occupying the upper most floor!

I shan't go into detail about its use; although, I can mention, "my town" is the grateful recipient of something discovered there!

Anyway, I didn't come to bore you with those kinds of minutia!

For now, I just want a room with a scalding hot bath in it along with an appointment scheduled with you tonight at eight o'clock…in your restaurant!

We can discuss the financials then; if, it would please you, Sir." Intimidatingly stated Paddy.

"That would indeed 'please' me; however, my evenings belong to my wife and children!

Perhaps, if you can bare the warmth of a roaring fire and a glass of very old scotch, maybe we could chat in my office, right now?

I'm sure, the two of us can cut through the ubiquitous "red tape", as they say." Smoothly responded Jesse Brown.

"I totally understand, I have a couple of 'rug rats' of my own back home. They sure can pull a man in a thousand different directions, can't they?

Your spectacular vision of the two of us sipping that decades old scotch in front of a crackling fire, appeals to me very much. Show me the way!" humorously remarked Welch.

"Please have a seat, Mister….. Oh dear, I must be slipping!

What did you say your name was?" graciously asked Jesse Brown.

"Forgive my manners, Mister Brown. I am, "Sir Richard Lawrence, "Mayor" of Oxon Hill".

My purpose for coming here must be kept under wraps, do you understand? If what I'm about to tell you were to get out to the public, it'd mean curtains for the both of us!

"Culper Intelligence" reports that "you" are considered to be a trustworthy patriot!

Would you say, that's a correct statement?" Harshly asked Paddy.

"Sir Richard, I am a business man operating the finest hotel in a city laced with intrigue and secret rendezvouses. My concerns are of a financial nature only, I'll assure you!"

"Jesse, there are "eleven" rooms on the Indian Queen's third floor. As clearly posted in front of the registration desk, a month's rent is 'thirty-five dollars' per month. Therefore, if you multiply that (per monthly) fee times eleven (number of 'third floor' rooms) and then times four (months), you will come up with the grand total of, 'fifteen hundred and forty dollars'. My offer to you is just that!" quipped Welch.

"Richard, although your math is spot-on, you are not taking into consideration the costs of accommodating the security personnel necessary to protect the type of high-level metallurgical operation you're describing. Frankly, I'm not sure if 'double that amount', would be enough to cover my risks!" bartered Jesse.

"I think to be fair to the American taxpayer as well as to you, two thousand dollars' worth of gold nuggets would be just!

Besides, the U.S. Cavalry troopers will be crawling around this place like ants on a dead June bug; after all, they've got to eat, sleep and drink somewhere, don't they?

Jesus, man, you'll double that two grand in the first month, just on your girls'; so, don't horse me around with your 'extra expense' malarkey. I'm a business man too!" huffed Paddy Welch.

"Be that, as it may be, Mister Lawrence, I must know the disposition of the materials you will be bringing into my hotel!

Things like "explosives" are the types of items I'm referring to, Sir Richard!" squawked Jesse Brown.

"May I be completely candid with you, Mister Brown?" asked Paddy, tearfully.

"Well of course you may!

All I ask is, 'everything' going on in the Indian Queen be at least, an 'inch' above 'deep water'! Truthfully,

Richard, tell me the things I need to be aware of regarding the government's usage of my hotel?" spat Brown.

"Jesse, I have found a cube of solid gold the size of this room!

No one knows about it except for me and now, "you"!

A few months ago, I purchased a piece of business property which had been badly damaged by flood waters. Upon inspection of the dilapidated grist mill's subterranean floor, I discovered a golden block.

Here's my problem, if I am to turn this fortune over to my bosses on the "Hill", they'll accuse me of purchasing the building for my own personal interest's sake!

After that, and because they're mean bastards, a "special assembly" will charge me with some petty crime and then absorb the precious monolith into their own coffers!

On the other hand, I was hoping to partner up with someone who might have the wherewithal to cut the gold block up into sections, melt it down into transportable ingots, and then, spend the rest of their life in mindboggling luxury!" Coaxed Paddy Welch.

"Sir Richard, don't you find the 'shape' of this rather 'odd find' somewhat perplexing?

Have you questioned the reasons "why" someone might have melted that much gold into a room sized cubicle?" Openly surmised Jesse Brown.

"Indeed I have. It's my opinion, the "old mill" was used as a treasure vault by pirates." Emphatically said Welch.

"Mister Lawrence, did you notice any particular markings or numbers stamped on any side of this gold cubicle you discovered?" pressed Jesse.

"Now that you mentioned it, there was a line of odd symbols pressed on it's top side. It looked like "Egyptian hieroglyphics" to me but I'm certainly not a linguistics specialist. What do you think it is?"

"Sir Richard, I am returning to you your more than generous show of good faith. If that "thing" is what it sounds like it is, I don't believe anyone having possession of that block, will live very long!

Should the stories of the "Masons" and the "Cerians" be true and this gold of yours happens to belong to them, I would say no one, within a mile of 'it', would survive their wrath!"

"You're turning my offer down?" surprisingly asked Welch.

"I'm afraid so but before you go, may I suggest that you drop by the "Grand Lodge" at the corners of "9th" and "'D'" Streets. It's the only purple building in the "District".

I'd bet a king's ransom, they'll be able to help you and who knows, you might even get a hefty reward for finding it!"

"I am grateful for your wise counsel, Mister Brown. I shall heed to it but first, I must return to my people for their agreement. Maybe, I can return next week to do as you suggested; of which, I wholeheartedly agree!

The 'nugget' I left on your desk is a token of my appreciation of your frank advice. Thank you!" Said Paddy Welch as he left the Indian Queen Hotel.

Next to a shooting star, the fastest phenomenon on planet "Earth", is a "secret" spreading across "Washington's Square"!

Paddy reckoned, his "Cerian gold story" had already reached Jackson's ears. 'Hopefully, "Andy's" curiosity would get the best of him and he'd come down to Oxon Hill to take a peek for himself', the Nib thought to himself.

* * * * *

As Paddy returned to Oxon Hill and when he came closer to the town's city limits, he strategically laid out numerous ambush scenarios.

'The trick would be, to strike and then escape, with the operative word being, 'escape''. Thought Paddy.

*   *   *   *   *

Plain clothed policemen were combing through Oxon Hill like red ants. Paddy Welch had to come up with a foolproof plan, one that would 'guaranty' maximum casualties and assure his (substantiated) innocence!

There was no doubt in Welch's mind, 'Jesse Brown' was a Culper. Already, Paddy imagined, 'there were agents on their way to Oxon Hill'.

There were several things he needed to take back with him; therefore, he bought a horse and wagon.

"Guinevere, forgive my abrupt return. I need for you to ring the "Fire bell" immediately!

Our delightful little village is about to be visited by the, "President of the United States!"" proclaimed Paddy.

"Sir Richard, my darling, I see you've come back early for some of mama's good loving; I've missed you!" laughingly teased Guinevere.

"This is no time for falderal, woman!

Get your ass down to the town's square and ring that goddamned bell like I told you to do!

Wakeup Sheriff Sasser and tell him to pull his auxiliary deputies together; because, there's going to be an onslaught of Washingtonians arriving in his town the likes of which, has never been seen before!

Remind the sheriff, the Governor is on the 'look out' for "solid detective timber" and he'll be watching to see how well our, "Lieutenant Sasser" handles pandemonium!

Newspapermen from across the country will, soon, be banging on our gates; therefore, the manner in which the insurgence is managed, well or dismally, will be read by thousands of Americans!

Be sure to mention to him, "only the Washington crème de la creme will be permitted in the rows of seating, beneath the Mill House's upper loft". It is advisable that Sheriff Sasser place his 'biggest' men in front of the mill's entranceway.

No one but President Jackson and his multiple staff members, will be permitted to view the contents within the bowels of the Bailey-Coble building. I'm sure 'Old Hickory' will want his soldiers to control the situation after the finale but until that time, the sheriff had best perform at the peak of his capabilities!

Guinevere, I want you, personally, to see to it, a split rail fence, four feet tall, be constructed around the mill's perimeter. Once, the wagon load of gifts has been unloaded, there are to be no more people allowed to pass beyond that point!

One guard is to be at the juncture of every length of railing!

It'll be daylight in seven hours and we need to be prepared for what surely is to come!" ordered Paddy from his wagon's bench.

"Sir Richard, may I ask you, what's all the commotion about?

I'm excited about it, don't get me wrong, but I'm sure the few hundred of us Oxon Hillians', would like to know what all of those highfaluting Washingtonian's are coming to our village to see!" sassed Guinevere.

"In time, my dear, in time!

Soon, you, and all of America will learn of a splendorous gift bestowed upon our town's people by an angel from heaven!

It would be ashamed to spoil the surprise by telling you, what you will find out tomorrow afternoon!

Hurry along, darling, and by the way, if you ever answer me again with a sarcastic remark, I promise you, I'll cut your nose off!" barked Welch.

As Guinevere ran away (in tears) toward Sheriff Sasser's house, Paddy Welch gallantly walked into the Golden Pony and fetched himself a jug of whiskey.

Two men, both in their mid-eighties, quietly sat in the rear of the tavern. They were playing chess. Paddy spoke to them.

"I need a couple of "veterans" who know how to successfully fulfill a military operation!

I'm prepared to offer you a "mercenary's" annual salary of $100.00 for one night's worth of you gentlemen's expertise!

We need to offload the contents of this wagon and move them 'piece by piece', throughout the areas of the mill house property. The goddamned Army wants it done in such a way that doesn't always make sense to me; but, what in hell do I know?

I'm just doing what the "brass" tells me to do!

Can we count you boys in?

America sure could use your help!" Staunchly asked Paddy Welch.

"Mister, that's a pretty tangy offer you just made we, "Tipton boys"!

My name's, "William" and my twin brother's name is, "Roger"; now, was you just funning with us or is it a fact, a general sent you here?" challenged William Tipton.

"General Andrew Jackson sent me to recover something of "priceless value"!

If'n you gents are in on this with me, I'll tell you, what I think it is!

Boys, it's my belief, we are standing on a solid gold slab!" slobbered Paddy.

"You saying, the President sent you here, to tell us about this gold thing? " asked Roger.

"No, Sir!

I'm saying, I discovered the gold block shortly after I purchased the Mill House from Misters Bailey and Coble, of which, had been repossessed for unpaid back taxes!

My intentions were, to open it back up and start making whiskey but as fate would have it, I discovered that one of the spring cellar's walls was made of solid gold!

Tomorrow, when the hoity-toity folks arrive here from the "Government Palace", I shall divide the nation's reward money among every resident of Oxon Hill!" braggingly bellowed Paddy.

"You mean to tell us, you're going to share all that 'gold' with every person living in our town?

What about those of us who come here a lot but live a mile or two outside of Oxon Hill, like me and Willie do?"

"Roger, if you are 'at heart' an 'Oxhillian' then by all means, both you and your brother, will be among the recipients!

Afterall, you men were the first to stand up, just like you did during the war for the American cause!

I guess, once a valiant patriot, always one!

Your willingness to be the first to charge into the steely jaws of death is the kind of 'trait' which has made you men, the heroes you still are to this day!

That, gentlemen, is why I selected you!" schmoozed Paddy.

"Gee, Sir Richard, you make it sound like we were the equals to "Jackson" and "Washington"!

We just did our duties, that's all!" said Willie Tipton.

"It was men like you, who sent the "Limeys" back across the Atlantic. Your sacrifices will forever be hailed by those who acknowledge their freedom!" slathered Welch.

"We're honored to be of service, sir!

How can we, once again, serve our country?" Willie shouted after taking three gulps off of Paddy Welch's jug of whiskey.

"A wagon load of mining supplies must be carefully taken to the Mill House's storage bin.

Once safely secured, the "U.S. Government Metallurgical Corps" will utilize the offloaded materials and relocate the priceless hunk to the capitol's treasury vault. Then, our delightful natives will be showered with evenly divvied out amounts of money!

Needless to say, ten percent of the town's reward will be split by the two of you!

The remaining ninety percent of Oxon's good people, will receive their 'fair shares' based on the total number of citizens present!

We have many crates to unload and a very short time to get it done before the sun rises!

We don't want the whole town goggling at our doings. As much as I adore the fine folks of Oxon Hill, I am aware that gold has quite an effect on humans; therefore, it is prudent to use extreme caution and to not antagonize the greedy devils living deep within their souls!

Plus, this is a military assignment and we 'all' know what that means; 'if Jackson ain't happy, we're headed for a heap of trouble'. Right?" Stoked Welch.

"Right on, Commandant!

Just show us where to start; we'll be the best unit you've ever had, Sir!" said the twins in unison.

"Do you see this diagram of the grist mill's rooms?

You will notice, each useful space on the sketch is painted-in with one of four colors; e.g., red, green, blue or yellow. They will match that same 'color' painted on the wooden crate's handles.

Your duties entail, stacking the various sized boxes into their appropriate places. I shall return here within the hour!" ordered "Sir Richard".

Taking with him the only two boxes with white handles, Paddy Welch disappeared into the bowels of the Bailey-Coble grist mill.

Tubes of blasting powder with ignition fuses already attached, found neat little hiding places within the semi hardened bags of damp corn flour.

A coat of golden paint covered each individual charge, of which, there were many.

Using an old wagon bed and a significant number of finely woven flour bags, Paddy turned the wheel-less bed upside down and spread out the flour bags so as to make the bomb's hiding place, unrecognizable!

More golden paint followed.

Following twenty minutes of creatively sloshing three buckets of metal flaked lacquer over the wagon bed, Paddy Welch's "painted" cube looked pretty much like the real thing.

After discovering the Tipton brothers had satisfactorily stacked the boxes where they were supposed to be put, Paddy cut their throats.

He allowed "Henson Creek" to take their bodies away.

* * * * *

Streaks of copper colored bars of light elongated the tree shadows across the road leading into Oxon Hill. Morning arrived with the sounds of squeaking wagon wheels approaching the village.

Paddy had just completed wiring up the mill's loft when he heard his "name" being called from the floor below. It was "Guinevere".

"Sir Richard Lawrence!

Sir Richard, an old friend of yours, a "Mister Jessie Brown" and four well-dressed gentlemen, are here to speak with you!

They're at the Golden Pony; they say it's a friendly visit but from the sidearms they were wearing, I'd say them men ain't looking to catch up on old times!"

"Where did you say, I was?" sharply asked Welch.

"I told them, you were still out of town!

I hope that was the right thing to do!" whined Guinevere.

"Where's Sheriff Sasser?"

"He's rallying his deputies together; they're starting on the fence just now!"

"Did you get an idea of how many people are due to come?" frantically questioned Paddy.

"Mister Brown didn't exactly say; but, from the looks of the regiment of cavalrymen surrounding our village, I'd say there are some mighty important people anxious to get a look at "something" they believe, is buried here!"

"Would you be kind enough to invite the town's residents and the entire slew of visitors, to be seated in front of the Bailey-Coble millhouse at twelve o'clock noon?

Keep them occupied for as long as you can; but, announce that I shall unveil a surprise of such magnitude, that the "American people" will forever remember "Oxon Hill's" name!" yelled Welch in a high-pitched voice.

"I'll, of course, do what you ask, Richard; however, I cannot promise I can stop them from barging into the mill looking for you!" said Guinevere.

"Go back and tell Jesse Brown that you remembered to tell him, "Jay Ray Howell" will be the "Master of Ceremony" during this afternoon's decloaking. Mention to Mister Brown, 'Jay Ray' and I will soon arrive by balloon!"

"What if, they insist on inspecting the "place" anyway?" asked Guinevere.

"Pull Sheriff Sasser aside, explain the situation, then inform him that "Cerians" outrank "Culpers" by a thousand paygrades!

Once, he swallows that bitter pill, inform him that 'Mister Howell' is not a Culper!" sharply advised Paddy Welch.

"Will you be coming home after the ceremony, Richard?" sheepishly inquired Guinevere.

"Of course, I will. Just don't let those guys into the town!" shouted Paddy as he hammered the reins on the rumps of the two mules pulling his emptied wagon.

* * * * *

Dressed as a monk whose face was shadowed by his hood, Welch raced his way toward the "Old Forest Heights" cannon battery. His hot air balloon was hidden there.

At eleven o'clock and with five knot winds coming out of the northwest, Paddy Welch rose above the Oxon Hill community. Flight conditions were perfect.

A hemp sack and hat tied to one of the guide ropes, made a "manikin" of 'J.R. Howell' appear as if, the Cerian himself, were standing beside "Sir Richard Lawrence".

From a thousand feet up in the royal-blue Maryland sky, Paddy could see hundreds of ant sized people lined up between the Golden Pony and the Mill House.

Barely inside the picket fence were no less than fifty high-top hatted gentlemen clustered below the mill's loft.

Faint banjo twangs reached Paddy's only good ear. 'A military band was down there', concluded Welch.

The Niburian pumped more gaseous flames into the balloon's bulb forcing the craft to rise higher.

Due to the unfiltered sunlight, the audience (beneath) could only see the eclipsed image of the balloon and it's basket carrying "two" very important people!

With a megaphone pressed tightly against his lips, Paddy pretending to sound like "Jay Ray Howell", began his oration.

"Greetings, great people of Oxon Hill and to all Americans, I bring you good tidings!

On this grand day, I'll deliver to you, a gift from your "Creator"!

For the pain and suffering you brave citizens have endured throughout the years, in payment for the integrity demonstrated by your country's leaders and the respect shown toward "us", we hereby grant those residents of this village, permission to divide the many tons of bullion amongst you!

This treasure, is a token of our gratitude and presented to you in hopes of another two millenniums of harmonious symbiosis!

Therefore, in keeping with the Egyptian tradition of honoring our pact, I shall ask your mayor, "Sir Richard Lawrence" to ignite the "Torch of Thanks"!"

Paddy laid down the megaphone and dropped a weighted spool of tightly wound cord onto the Mill House's fuel drenched roof.

A hydrogen filled bladder was released to allow Paddy time enough to detach himself from the firebomb's guide wire.

As Welch's balloon rose into the sky, he lit a finger sized wick attached to a phosphorous grenade.

The people below were still applauding when the downward traveling device obeyed its guidance system.

An explosion vaporized all "organic things", three inches or higher, off the ground. A mushroom cloud dissipated into the atmosphere.

Paddy Welch glassed the area which had once been Oxon Hill. He saw no movement below.

Chapter Fourteen

Semaphore blinks telling of bad news, continued throughout the night. Culper communications created oddities for the locals to puzzle over. This went on all the way down the "Appalachians".

'A plow propped against a stone wellhouse', 'blue candles placed in windows of public buildings', 'church bells ringing in intervals of 'seven strikes' followed by silence', sent a chilling 'tallying' of the body count from the explosion at Oxon Hill!

The final numbers were promised at 0600hrs..

With White Wolf gone, "Jay Ray Howell" now held the responsibility of directing the most qualified Culper agents to the hot spots breaking out throughout North America.

He had made the wrong choice, no doubt about it; all those "in the know", agreed. The information of a gold transport block 'tripped off' him sending, "Jesse Brown" to the rumored discovery site, ended up being a miserable blunder!

After all, Jesse was one of the best Culper agents in Washington and since he had already made contact with a man calling himself, "Richard Lawrence", Jay Ray thought "#706" was right for the mission; but, he was wrong!

This was reiterated when the 'body count' came flying in on the back of a carrier pigeon!

"Oxon Hill has been reduced to ashes…..Charges set with Niburian blasting caps….Known dead: 193…..Unknown: est. 446….."Richard Lawrence" logical suspect." as read out loud by Jay Ray Howell.

With his back against the pigeon coop's wire mesh door, the Cerian Commander bowed his head and wept.

With flesh ripping screams intermingled with air jabs aimed at his tormented self, J.R. stood up with the intentions of getting a jug of scotch and a pistol.

'It was true, he had forgotten about the frontal lobe oddities encapsulated within a Niburian skull. 'He should have followed the manual.'

'At the conclusion of an event, every strand of evidence must be transposed into ashes. Instead, the old warrior(he) had "selfishly" administered cobra injections to Paddy Welch and his lover, "Milly Francis".'

'I sometimes became a bit sadistic with my treatment of those whom I had a bone to pick. In my case, it was "Benjamin Hawkins's" murder!'

'The real reason, I did not destroy the couple; was, I wanted to every once in a while, go by and admire my work.'

'To me, it was much like visiting a museum filled with my own trophies!' thought J.R..

Following three good gulps of whiskey, the humiliated Cerian stood up so as to look out into the darkness. Already, he could feel the psychological effects from his being stalked by, "this planet's" top carnivore!

Jay Ray imagined, amidst the outside's colorless night, a flicker of orange flame which, for a nanosecond, made Jay Ray glow with a warrior's death-accepting pride!

But then, "nothing" happened; although, a bullet did pass some four feet above his head!

* * * *

Using official documents signed by the President of the United States, Vice President, "John C. Calhoun" plus his four assistants, "Martin Van Buren" with three secretaries (one of whom was his mistress), and "George Poindexter" who had only one aide boarding the "Hector" at the "Baltimore Harbor".

"Captain Williams" escorted the Washingtonian elites to their second balcony suites. Hannah bunked in with the kitchen help.

Two simultaneous events had happened; e.g., "Senator Warren Davis's" death in the explosion at Oxon Hill and the gluttonous "King George IV's" demise by choking on his alcohol infused vomit.

The United States had to represent her "values"; therefore, the "happy-face game" had to be played on both of the Atlantic's shores, at the same time.

It was Hannah (during their last week together) who convinced Andrew Jackson to bring in an outsider. 'Someone' he could trust; a person who had not yet been licked by the forked-tongued lobbyists offering gollywhopping bribes!

Jackson was drinking again; therefore, he grew increasingly more depressed. 'Life' to Andy, had no color nor joy. Structures were dimensionally flat and the world seemed unfairly dangerous.

The yearning for war had again come. This time, it was an urban battle against an enemy dressed in "sheep's" clothing!

In 'Washington', no one could be trusted; 'honor' and 'loyalty' were valueless antiques!

With the deaths of "White Wolf", "Rachel", "Lyncoya", and a host of others quite dear to him, Jackson's state-of-mind sunk from an "acceptable" diplomatic platitude, to that of a mass murderer!

As Andy had said to Hannah, 'I think it quite odd and far more than coincidental, that within the walls of four years of time, almost every one of my most intimate associates have been murdered'.

That was why, the President sent her to Europe.

Hannah was to make contact with, "Sir Francis George of the Walkers".

* * * * *

Although, Jackson had, long ago, "freed" Hannah (she always carried the papers to prove it) but when the funeral procession met the U.S. Diplomats on London's "Tobacco Dock", Hannah was not invited.

King George IV was being buried in two days and "coloreds" were not allowed within the "Winchester Cathedral's" holy gates.

Once "Calhoun, Van Buren, and George Poindexter" were whisked away like fairytale goblins, "Captain Albert Williams" (a.k.a. "Neptune" or Culper agent #1004), prepared to take the "Hector" back out to sea.

The weather was good so they'd have no trouble making their rendezvous point in time.

The "crow flying" distance as Captain Williams said, between "London and Glasgow" was 345 miles. Generally speaking, in a week, one could expect to arrive at "Port Glasgow".

Hannah and her Cerian submarine crew did it in five hours!

At 0625hrs. Hannah dressed as a bearded fishmonger, parked her 'cod wagon' at the corner of "Kilanock and High Streets".

She was to wait for the "Ayrshire Distillery" to open.

The password was, "Square Bottle".

When the sun did finally rise, it met a thick bank of fog rolling up from "Dumfries".

Hannah lost all sense of direction; her map of "Ayrshire", Scotland was useless!

A man's voice cut through the whiteness.

"Hannah, kindly, do not turn around!

Please step backwards, four paces!

Now, reach out and take my hand as I seat you into my carriage; lay down in the backseat!" Said "Sir Francis George of the Walkers".

"Sir, be forewarned, I am armed! threatened Hannah.

"Alright, then, "Square Bottle"!

I mean, you have a guy call your name out in the midst of a cloud thicker than Irish stew, and you want a secret password?

It's as if the world has become paranoid; no one seems to trust one another anymore!" Teased Sir Francis.

"You try being a 'bearded black woman' and see how you feel, Sir Francis. Andy told me, 'you were as ornery as a castrated rooster!'" Sighed Hannah.

"Worse than you could imagine, my dear!

Now, please give me the 'scoop' of what's troubling Andy!

We've got a long ride; so, there will be plenty of time to tell your old "brother-in-law" exactly what has gone awry in America!"

"Brother-in-law, Sir?" playfully asked Hannah Jackson.

"Don't tell me you've already forgotten the "jump the broom" ceremony you and my brother participated in, the week after Rachel's death?

It was in Nashville, was it not?" asked the pan faced Scot.

"Oh Jesus! I thought no one but Andrew and I knew about that!"

"Except for his brothers and now deceased father, you would most certainly be pleased to know, not a single other person knew!

You see, Hannah, I am quite well aware of why you are here. Andy had to get you out of Washington!" said Sir Francis.

"And why was that, Sir?" asked Hannah.

"Because a very bad man is trying to kill you!"

"Why? Who would want to do that?" alarmingly asked Hannah.

"His name is, "Paddy Welch". Look, Hannah, I don't know how much you know about Andy's past; consequently, I'm not at liberty to discuss something he might have preferred you not know!"

"We hold no secrets from the other!

Is this "Paddy Welch" a Niburian?" assuredly asked Jackson's bride.

"Ah, so you are aware of Andrew Jackson's gene pool?" cautiously responded George.

"…And of your father's insatiable thirst for wanton Nicosans!" giggled the sassy negro woman.

"As I was saying…Paddy Welch and your husband go back before "New Orleans". Paddy was a Niburian spy.

Andy caught him and killed his lover's father. He destroyed the Red Sticks who were the "beginnings" of his great army!

To add 'insult to injury', he had "J.R. Howell" inject "his" and Milly Francis's hypothalamuses with cobra venom which made it very difficult for Welch to execute the chaos planned for this country!

That, my dear, is "who and why" Welch is determined to destroy those associates of Andrew's!" humbly stated Sir Francis George of the Walkers.

"Well, Sir Francis, it appears as if our, 'Mister Paddy Welch' doesn't take a joke very well. Why don't you blokes just kill the bastard?" sarcastically asked Hannah.

"He's a slippery one, Hannah!

We don't have a clue as to what he even looks like; all of "those" witnesses are dead!" spat the Walker.

"Who could point him out?" angrily quizzed Hannah.

The only person who could recognize him, would be his former business partner, "Judge James Dowdell".

Not only is he a 'Federal Judge', he is also the 'Mayor of Winchester', Virginia; but, the probability of his still being alive are between slim and none!"

"You say Dowdell and Welch were partners?

That doesn't seem to fit. A 'Judge' and a 'Niburian spy' in business together?

What were they into?" asked Hannah.

"The "rackets" mostly; although, there have been suggestions that Welch had a little 'murder for hire' business going on the side!

It's only logical to assume, Welch picked up his clients at Cocke's Tavern which, to answer your question, Hannah, was the name of the 'shell company' the two owned together."

"Do you believe we can stop Welch, Sir Francis?" innocently asked Hannah.

"Only if I'm lucky; but, there is no 'we' to it!" said the Walker.

"Sir Francis George of the Walkers, please excuse my abruptness; but, Sir, I did not ask for your permission to protect my husband!

I did follow his directive by speaking with you 'personally' and asking for your help!

There is no doubt in my mind, my assistance would be invaluable to you!

If you choose to either ignore your brother's request or to operate independently, that's your prerogative. But, whatever your decision turns out to be, rest assured, I'll do whatever I can, to eliminate "Paddy Welch"!" coolly argued Hannah.

For an exhaustively long minute, Sir Francis analyzed every inflexion in Hannah's face. He then spoke.

"You are every bit the "grand lady", "Andy" said you were!

Forgive my introductory callousness. I, very much, would appreciate your assistance in finding this "rodent"!

Tell me everything you know about this Niburian, Hannah. Please try to recall every detail Andrew might have mentioned about Paddy.

In the meantime, I'll make contact with, "North American Intelligence" to see 'if', "we" can get an idea of 'who' and 'where' this guy is!" apologetically stated the Culper.

"Alright then, tell me what I need to do next, Sir Francis."

"Return to the "Hector". See what you can glean from the "three musketeers" on your voyage back to the United States.

Probe into their most recent visits to the Cocke's Tavern in Winchester. Pretend as if, you were "professionally" acquainted with the tavern as well as its owners, "James Dowdell and Paddy Welch".

It seems, Paddy Welch is here to do a very specific job; that is, to destabilize the literate world's governments. Like "Atilla the Hun", this Niburian, destroys institutions for no other reason than, 'he likes to do it'!" pensively spoke Sir Francis George.

"What if something goes wrong; how can I reach you?" stuttered Hannah.

""Neptune" will look after you!

He's one of our best agents. He'll let me know if something goes awry, I promise!" declared Sir Francis George of the Walkers.

Hannah deeply exhaled with relief when she saw that the dignitaries had not yet returned to the "Hector".

Captain Williams and she had more than an hour to work up their plans.

* * * * *

"'Neptune' was to play the 'straight man' while Hannah was to be introduced as, "Lady Catherine Walters", the wealthiest shipping mogul in New Orleans!

She was on the run from a situation involving the owner of the, "Bisso Shipping Enterprise, Ltd.".

Supposedly, she and "Daddy Bisso" had gotten married by one of the company's ship captains. They were on a private cruise around the Gulf of Mexico.

As a "wedding gift" to his new wife, "Captain Joseph Bisso" titled over the "Leo" (the yacht they were honeymooning on) to her.

The ship was a seventy foot pleasure craft, 'Papa Joe' had built for his "child bride".

As scripted, Captain Williams was to let slip, "Within a week after Catherine Walters' and her, astonishingly wealthy, husband's wedding, Hannah sold the "Leo" to one of her husband's competitors!

With no cash involved, she exchanged the "Leo" to smuggle the "nuptial-escapee"(her) out of New Orleans and to Baltimore in absolute secrecy.

Because of the infatuation shared with (Paddy Welch) and after a year of letter writing, Catherine and Welch were to reunite at Cocke's Tavern, marry, and live happily ever after!

But, with all the blind accusations going around, the two, put their plans on hold!

When Paddy "disappeared" and the Washington detectives started their snooping, poor "Miss Walters" was forced to go to London to pick up the treasure she had ransacked from Captain Bisso's townhouse!

She and Paddy Welch planned to buy an island with the loot she had stashed onboard the "Hector"."

If executed correctly, Captain Williams and Hannah would have extrapolated enough information about the Niburian(Welch) to transmit to Sir Francis.

With luck, the missing "parts" would lead to the assassin's death.

What they planned to do, was to act naturally and play the "Bisso" story up to the hilt!

* * * * *

The Atlantic was as calm as a bathing pool.

Following after dinner drinks, "Captain Williams" stood to address the homeward bound Washingtonians.

"All indications lead us to believe, we are in for 'smooth sailing' from here to the Caribbean Islands!

'Friends, let's forget about what's facing us back home!

I say, to all, live today, as though, it were your last!

* * * * *

After slaking each passenger's curiosity until the wee hours of the morning, Hannah handed the "Hector's" Captain a three page summary of the dates, places, times and collected fees for Paddy Welch's rendered services.

It was all there and much more than supposition. Paddy was their guy!

* * * * *

The days on the "Hector" dragged on.

To rectify the situation with the objective of preventing a duel between George Poindexter and Vice President Calhoun, Hannah and Captain Williams created a masterfully planned "experience" for the diplomats and their attaches.

Sir Francis George of the Walkers after receiving Hannah's synopsis of Paddy Welch's last three years' of activity, sent a message to the "Hector" by way of the semaphores that dotted the western coast of Africa.

"Sao Tome' Island" was to be the resupplying port before crossing into the Caribbean currents. Sir Francis would meet up with them there.

* * * * *

On Sunday morning, the "Hector" docked at "Skitts Bridge". "Commander Busigo' Cumel" the harbor's 'Regent', impatiently waited to collect Puerto Rico's recently enacted, "Docking Tariff".

He became very nervous when the seven foot tall, Captain Williams hurriedly walked down the gangplank toward him!

Several of the Washingtonians were on the "Hector's" deck listening to their Captain's interaction with the Puerto Rican Naval officer. Cumel winked at Williams giving the signal to make their initial confrontation seem authentic.

"Good Morning, Sir. May I see your ship's manifest please." Barked Cumel.

"Gladly, Commander. Here they are."

Matter-of-factly said Williams.

"How many passengers, not crew, do you have onboard the "Hector"?

"Eighteen, Sir!" quickly responded the ship's captain.

"Any cargo?" sharply asked Commander Cumel.

"None other than the fifty pounds of cotton seeds, I promised you!" whispered Captain Williams.

"Any niggers on board?"

"One passenger, and five crewmen all of whom, are 'freemen'!" Arrogantly replied Williams.

"They do have papers don't they, Captain Williams?"

"Yes, sir, they do!"

"Captain Williams, Sir Francis George of the Walkers has instructed me to escort you and Hannah to the bridge house at half past noon!

I am to quarantine the "Hector" due to your passengers' exposure to "Cholera"; unfortunately, they must remain quarantined for a month!" Said the dock officer in a low mumble.

"So, I guess, Hannah and I are under arrest, is that the game?" snickered Williams.

"Precisely!" said Commander Busigo' Cumel before blowing a whistle.

A company of uniformed soldiers rushed up the gangplank with bayonets attached to their rifles.

"You, no doubt, are aware of 'who' my passengers are?

Let's hope they return to Washington unscathed!

I'd hate to imagine the political fallout, if England were blamed for a mishap at sea!" loudly stated Captain Williams.

Hannah and the "Hector's" captain were chained together and led off by four pistol toting noncommissioned officers toward the bridge house!

The diplomats along with their staff members were lined up against the forward deck's starboard railing. Their clothing had been removed and were being scrubbed down with a lye based disinfectant.

Words could not describe, the messages being expressed on the aristocrats' faces as the hair on their bodies were being shaved off!

'Seventeen', naked as 'jaybirds', American diplomats looked like newborn piglets as they watched their Captain and Lady Catherine Waters, wearing neck collars, being escorted away!

Hannah got a brief moment to see Calhoun and his two crony lawmakers, being branded!

The letters, "R.A.C." were burned into the smalls of their backs. 'It' signified that each of the "unsold breeders" had been deloused and were ready for the block!

Commander Cumel of the "Royal African Company"(R.A.C.), had been brokering slaves for sixteen years. Since, the United States was paying him his annual salary (in upfront gold) to educate the diplomats on the innerworkings of the "human cargo industry", Busigo' was determined to do his best to show them the skills involved with being a, "master slave seller"!

The women came next. Each was marched back and forth across the "Hector's" lower deck. The R.A.C.'s commander allowed his "rough hands", twenty in all, to exteriorly touch the passing-by cargo!

The harbor's deckhands made all sorts of proposals before the ladies were put into their viewing pins!

Excitement was building; because, as the Sao Tome' regulars knew, predelivery cargo could be "leased" from the Royal African Company for all sorts of purposes!

The (in transit) usage fee (for a particular slave), was determined by Commander Cumel; however, neither the soldiers nor the 'rough hands'(crewmen) were permitted to do anything which might hinder their pulling top dollar on the bidding stump!

Pregnancy was not considered a "hinderance".

Sir Francis George of the Walkers greeted Hannah and Captain Williams as soon as Commander Cumel brought them into the bridge house.

"It appears to me, our Washingtonian friends are getting a birds eye view of what goes on behind the scenes in the world of slave trading!

Perhaps the lawmakers will listen to what these, "white lilies" have to say about the treatment they received on Sao Tome' Island. Maybe they'll think about that before they propose the extension of buying humans for America's economic benefit!"

"Sir Francis, with all due respect, it would take a whole lot more than three such experiences to make that "congressional gang" in Washington sacrifice their careers by voting against our nation's labor force!" argued Hannah.

"I'm afraid you're right, madam, but for now, we must focus on fixing a less complex issue!

Folks, we have a renegade Niburian who has taken it upon himself, to erase from America's future recollection, any semblance of civilized governing!

Paddy Welch is set on wiping out our Republic's leaders and leaving in his bloody tracks, nothing but an anarchistic wasteland!" Said Sir Francis after staring out the bridge house's windows.

"With regard to the "Diplomats", Sir, shall I dispose of them at sea?" coldly asked the "Hector's" captain.

"Not yet. We've got a while before a decision is made on their fates!

When Hannah and I finish our investigations, I'll signal the details to you. In the meantime, enjoy the sunshine of Sao Tome' and before you know it, you'll be on your way back home!" Humorously stated Sir George.

"And, Sir, what if for some unforeseeable reason, I should not receive your messages?" nervously queried Captain Williams.

"Then, give the 'diplomates' to Commander Cumel!

Let him sell them on the Asian market!" responded the Walker with a toothy smile.

"Aye-aye, Sir. What shall I tell Busigo' Cumel has happened to Hannah?" quizzed the captain.

"Explain to the Commander, "Lady Catherine Waters" escaped from the bridge house and is believed to still be on the island!

A couple of his 'hard hands' are suspected of holing her up!

When she is found, Miss Waters is also to join the Americans and share with them, whatever their futures hold!

Those responsible for breaking her out of confinement, should also join in with the Washingtonians and thus enrich Commander Cumel's pockets considerably more; i.e., whites bring tenfold of what the Africans sell for!" Briskly said Sir Francis.

With no further words spoken, Captain Williams nodded to Hannah a pleasant farewell and saluted the Walker.

When he exited the bridge house, Williams rang the emergency bell alerting his soldiers of Lady Catherine's escape!

A search party was formed. The submarine's periscope was lowered.

The last glimpse of Sao Tome' Island was that of torchlights against the backdrop of a buttermilk sky.

Sir Francis George of the Walkers and Hannah were on their way back to America.

Based on the comments "Miss Waters'" extracted from the Washingtonians, Paddy Welch was hiding out in "Winchester", Virginia.

Chapter Fifteen

Following an eight hour 'crawl' up the "Potomac River", the Cerian submarine emerged four miles northwest of the charted rendezvous on "Glen Echo Pointe".

Hundreds of skiffs manned by lantern carrying marines, combed over the Potomac's banks looking for something. It was 0300hrs..

Sir Francis George and Hannah upon stepping off on Maryland soil and disappeared into the marsh paralleling, "River Road". After an hour's worth of briar full travel, Hannah raised her arm motioning for Sir Francis to stop!

There was a man sitting in a two horse carriage atop the bridge they were about to cross under!

Unsure if they had been detected, both Hannah and the 'Scot' remained as still as river rocks.

Finally, Colonel Robert Townsend exposed their failed attempt at invisibility.

"Hurry! Get below the bridge! Someone's coming!" loudly whispered Townsend.

Temperatures in Washington hadn't risen from the teens during all of January.

Feelings in the toes, had stopped about a minute after they had slipped into "Cabin John Creek". Sir Francis and Hannah had passed the shivering stage.

They fought to stay awake. Hyperthermia was advancing.

The noise going on above them, sounded like soldiers' voices!

Every second, elongated into an hour; pain became a reminder that they were still alive!

"Hold it right there!

Raise your hands high into the air where we can see them!

Identify yourself!" antagonistically demanded "Captain Marx" of the Capitol Police Department.

"I am, Colonel Robert Townsend." Replied Townsend from atop the bridge.

"Well, "Robert", I reckon you're going to tell me, "next", you were taking a morning ride in order to get a jump on the day?" mockingly slurred the policeman (showing off for his two accompanying lieutenants).

"Actually, Captain Marx, I happened to be checking up on you!" condescendingly remarked the Culper.

"What in the hell do you mean?

I am directly under "Detective William Cranch's" command; anyhow, what you got in the back of your mighty fine carriage there, Bobbie?"

"Captain Marx, you and those two drunken 'also-rans' snuggling up to your horse's butt, are hereby under arrest!" Laughed Colonel Townsend.

"You know, mister, at this time of morning and way out here in the boondocks', a smartass such as yourself, might just have to be taught a lesson!

"Luke", go around to the rear of the good colonel's ride and see if there's anything worth taking!" yelled Marx.

"Son, I shall warn you but once; back away from this bridge and leave this minute!"

Neither Hannah nor Sir Francis George of the Walkers heard anything else; although, they did see the illuminations of the burning policemen!

Colonel Townsend allowed Hannah and Sir Francis practically thirty minutes to warm their bodies. Afterwards, the two were swept away before the sun caught them out in the open.

* * * * *

"Tenleytown" as Colonel Townsend explained, was the highest point on the 'District's' topographical layout; therefore, when one wished to enter or leave the 'Capitol House' unseen, they could do so by taking the underground railway.

Townsend drove his dapple-grays into the center of "Uncle George's Livery Stable", jumped out of the carriage and shut the barn's doublewide doors.

Sounds of rushing water and metal teeth biting into other gears ushered in a mechanical marvel!

Uncle George's stable floor was neatly fitted into a train car. The horses were the only mammals not amused by the effortless transport.

The boxcar quickly broke through inertia with 'hissing' ease. The three passengers were forced against Townsend's padded seats.

Loose items floated upward toward the carriage's ceiling. They then arrived at their 'stop'.

"Aaron" (Hannah's husband) gently opened the coach's door. He was sporting a smile larger than a slice of moon melon.

Andrew Jackson laughed. Sir Francis George of the Walkers was forced to speak.

"Andy, for god's sake, get me out of this "bullet"; and, where in the hell is the privy?

Oh, I almost forgot; I'll be needing a bottle of scotch upon my return!"

"Certainly, my brother. Abraham will attend to your requests!" snickered Jackson.

Four hours passed as quickly as did, the feast, drinks, and the 'catchups' from days gone by!

Rumored Culpers' deaths and the whereabouts of those still alive quite naturally shifted the impetus of the gathering, to a deadly intent!

Colonel Townsend was the first to speak.

"On the day before yesterday, a man using the name of, "Richard Lawrence" made an attempt on Andy's life!"

"Hell, man, how did that happen? Didn't you blokes have our people there?" angrily quizzed the tipsy 'Scot'.

"Sir Francis, we did; but, somehow the "Capitol Police Department" failed to investigate the backgrounds of a handful of repairmen; of which, 'one' was "Lawrence"!" coldly stated Townsend.

"In defense of the Culper's, Sir Francis, let me say, they have done an extraordinary job putting the pieces together. Paradoxically, it has turned out, "Richard Lawrence" is in fact, "Paddy Welch" (a Niburian)!

To make things worse, there is evidence the assassination attempt was a "hit" paid for by people within my own cabinet!" said the President.

"I'm afraid it's one of those old fashioned "palace revolts" you Europeans have experienced for centuries, Sir Francis!

Ridiculously, it is happening over here which comes as quite a surprise; since, America "thought" by handing over the fate of their country to its voting citizens, that kind of nonsense would not happen!" Lamented Robert Townsend.

"Andy, where is Richard Lawrence's body?" asked Sir Francis.

As if caught masturbating by a priest, the Culper leader and Jackson stared at each other with mutually painful looks. Robert Townsend came clean.

"At the conclusion of South Carolina Representative Warren R. Davis's funeral at the Capitol and as the President and his attending cabinet members were being shuttled through the East Wing's portico, a man claiming to be, "King Richard III" appeared from behind one of the pillars and attempted to fire two shots at your brother!"

"What does, "attempted to fire two shots" mean?" shrieked the now standing Walker.

"Both of his pistols misfired!" curiously smiled Townsend.

"Horse shit! Someone's jerking yall's chains! Two different pistols?" mocked Sir Francis George.

"The President and I were together so we never exactly saw what happened! After we were escorted away, Kentucky Representative, "David Crockett" practically beat Lawrence to death with his walking cane.

The Capitol Police (for safety reasons) did not disclose where they took him; however, we are now being told, "the accused" is missing!" Robert Townsend more than seriously stated.

"Gentlemen, it appears we are knee-deep in a nest of vipers!

Andy, was there a trial?" asked Sir Francis.

"Indeed there was; but, my men nor I, ever got wind of it!

I swear to you, living here, is worse than being on "Nat Sackett's Island"!

We even have to burn our own garbage!

I'm telling you, they're more spies within "the square" than there are in North America!

What kills me, most of them were born here!

Boys, to tell you the truth, if I hadn't promised myself to eradicate those slimy bastards who killed Rachel, I'd be back at the Hermitage perfecting my bourbon. I despise it here!" Said President Jackson.

"So, Colonel Townsend, how did the trial turn out?" asked Sir Francis.

"The D.C. 'City Hall' found Richard Lawrence "not guilty by reason of insanity" for the attempted Presidential assignation!

The prosecutor, F.S. Key settled for "life" in a facility for the 'criminally insane'!

Although, no one believed Lawrence's "Richard III" routine, to show the country's softer side, "Senator John Calhoun" and a select group of his 'butt-buddies' pressed for Lawrence's escape from the gallows!

From the Culper's perspective, that ridiculous ruling was not only intended to be a political kick in Andy's teeth, it was also proof, in my mind, that Paddy Welch and a handful of "Washingtonian Whigs", just sent a warning to the Democratic-Republican Party!" Blared Townsend.

"And what message might that be, Colonel?" ribbed Jackson.

"'Ya'll get on back to the sticks and leave the business of running the government to we aristocrats', is what I believe, they are sadistically messaging to us!

Gentlemen, I am sure, the Niburians have finally infiltrated into our government!" answered Robert Townsend.

"Of course they have! That's what I've been saying all along! Not only are the Nibs filling our federal slots, they are infiltrating "state governorships" as well!

Should they ignore the wise counsel from the Masons, the Cerians, if shorted their due, will simply move Nicosa a thousand miles away from the "Sun" and then return for their gold, a couple of years later." Calmly said Jackson.

"Colonel Townsend, let's identify the 'rotten eggs' and dispose of them!" Said the Walker.

"George, that'd make the entire district look as if it had been struck by the bubonic plague!

I'm telling you, my brother, this is the new and improved "Sodom and Gomorrah"; truthfully, I'd say ninety percent of the adult population in this town, are as straight as bent nails!" chuckled Andy.

"Seriously, why can't we kill out their leaders and just move forward?" bleated Sir Francis George.

"Because that would make us, "Europe"!

We are a "Republic"; America is a nation of laws!

If the rules do not apply to all citizens this thing we call "freedom", will be as precious as a rat turd. Either we all live by the same 'ethos' or "we" as a country, will sell off its soul. No longer, will people be "allowed" to live their lives in the way they wish to!

If we cannot turn this anaconda like squeeze on our principles into a unified effort in making this land into a great one, it will be sectioned off and sold to our enemies!

All of the 'oldies' like France and Britain not to mention Spain and the Dutch, would be on our shores like a red tide!" Gasped Jackson.

"That being as it is, Mister President, if in fact, Paddy Welch and members of your cabinet have conspired to kill you, we have no choice as Sir Francis said, "we must identify the most venomous serpents and chop their nasty little heads off!

My question to you, Sir, is, 'which nest of them do you want to start with first?'." Excitedly pressed Townsend.

"It is no secret that I have many enemies, Gentlemen; the two bullets floating around in my body will testify to that!

However, if we follow the crumbs toward those of whom would have the most to gain by my demise, I'd say Paddy Welch, is our most eminent threat!

Since Warren Davis died, leaving the three we shanghaied to Africa, I can't think of anyone other than 'Welch', who would attempt such a monstrous thing!

The remaining questions still unsettled in my mind, have to do with "Detective William Cranch" and the whereabouts of his psychologically deranged suspect, "Richard Lawrence".

Robert, what do we have on Cranch?" asked America's seventh president.

"Sir, Judge William P. Cranch was John Quincey Adams's confidant and legal advisor during his stint as "Secretary of State". Cranch was promoted to the position of "Superintendent of Capitol Security" during Adam's final year in office.

From what we have gathered from his profile, Detective Cranch is a staunch "Federalist" and one who loves to rub shoulders with the "in office" elitists.

His call to fame is that of a "smut-digger"; i.e., William Cranch uses his army of investigators to find disparaging information on his cronies' opponents and then uses his powers to defame his buddies' opposition.

For payment, Cranch got appointed to various committees providing him uncountable opportunities to skim money from the swift flow of government contracts zipping through his office!

Andy, had you lost your second term run, 'ole Willie Cranch' would have been the, "Federal Land Commissioner"!

We suspect, Mister President, Cranch was the broker who negotiated with Paddy Welch the "fee" for your assassination!

As for those footing the bill for the contract's fulfillment, as best we can determine, it looks as though, the "New Englanders'" and the "coastal slave states'" representatives, all chipped in!" meekly stated Townsend.

"If that's the case, why did Lawrence's two pistols misfire?

Any fool capable of masterminding a complex murder certainly would not neglect the potency of their chosen weapon!" Exclaimed Sir Francis George of the Walkers.

"You're exactly right, Sir Francis!

Unless it was "intentional"!" Said Townsend.

"What?" screamed both Jackson and Sir Francis at the same time.

"Unless.….Paddy Welch is "blackmailing" the "contractors" and Detective Cranch is in on it!" gasped Robert Townsend.

"Colonel Townsend, are you suggesting that Cranch and Welch are in this together?" coyly asked Sir Francis.

"Yes, I am; but, I don't believe either are in it for the 'hit' money!

Welch is a Niburian outcast trying to make a name for himself. He hopes someone will offer him a place to live!

Detective Cranch on the other hand, is your typical Washingtonian status seeker; his 'dog in this fight', has to do with "ultimate" fame!

No matter their motives, the duo make for a formidable foe. Therefore, I propose, Mister President, without alerting the others,

Sir Francis and I, root out these scoundrels and burn them to a crisp!" proclaimed the senior Culper.

"Hold your horses, Colonel; this country has already lost hundreds of good people at the hands of this psychopathic Nib. And besides, who else in this godforsaken district, can I trust enough to bounce strategies off of?

I think it best, to somehow lure them from their hiding places and then allow the situation to determine their outcomes!

Robert, do we have any clues as to where those coyotes are holdup?" sternly questioned the president.

"Respectfully, gentlemen, I'm still puzzled over the double-misfires!

Have either of you, calculated the probability of that happening at the hands of a seasoned assassin?

I could be mistaken; but, it is possible, those 'misfiring pistols' was a signal of some sort!

Maybe Welch is calling for an amnesty pact or perhaps Detective Cranch is a real cop and by doing his job, prevented the death of our nation's 'number one guy'!

Do either of these men have any friends or family members we might speak with?" debated Sir Francis George.

"Only Cranch!

Welch is a genuine Niburian spy; we believe he 'turned' and went rogue shortly after arriving here from Nibiru.

'William Cranch' has one son, "Edward"; his wife died of cholera three years ago." Recited Townsend.

Suddenly Jackson's face turned an ashen grey. With a jittery voice he spoke.

"I just remembered something; Paddy Welch and Milly Francis escaped together from Fort Gadsden during our "Apalachicola" action against the Red Sticks!

Milly Francis's father was none other than, "Hildis Hadjo", the Red Sticks' "great prophet" at that time.

Colonel Townsend, what are your thoughts of baiting those two into 'our' arena rather than tracking them down like rabid dogs? If our allure is sweet enough, boys, they'll walk right into our trap!"

"Andy, are you suggesting we "pickup" Milly Francis and Cranch "Junior" and take them to someplace where their "longing" loved ones, can view them?" sardonically queried Sir Francis George of the Walkers.

"Sir, Hadjo's daughter is with "Tenskwatawa's" old tribe at Fort Gibson. Intelligence informs us, Milly is mentally impaired and that her duties within the old Shawnee tribe, are meager.

Young mister Edward P. Cranch 'Junior' is an instructor at the "Columbian Institute for the Promotion of Arts and Sciences".

"Eddy" is said to be an excellent ballet teacher but is subject to long bouts of melancholy apparently because of his father's distain for the choices he made during his adolescence!

To clarify, Edward looks, dresses, and acts like the ubiquitous stage star. "She", is known to be quite a "pistol", Sir!" Reported the Culper.

"Colonel Townsend, with Cerian assistance, how long would it take for your people to get those two in our company?" Asked Andrew Jackson.

"Borrow any complications, Sir, forty eight hours!"

"Very well. Robert, go get Milly and bring her here. I'll be more specific with the exact address as her delivery time draws nearer.

Sir George, you're to become a perky-cheeked newspaper writer. "Eddy" of course, will be your 'feature story'; but, during your long and shared hours of closeness, the two of you will become drawn to the other!

Gentlemen, at 1500hrs., this coming Sunday, three days from now, we shall meet again at Tenleytown!

Please have your "escorts" dress for the 'occasion', as they will be, our guests of honor!" Said the President.

Chapter Sixteen

Cerian Flight Commander Richard Alter banked his X-47 attack carrier so as to slip between two stone pillars at the south entrance of the "Ozark Plateau".

The commander touched down long enough for Sir Francis George of the Walkers and Robert Townsend to offload an "official" war wagon.

Two black stallions and six Culpers dressed as U.S. Federal Judges, also stepped out onto the Oklahoma sand.

Like hardwired scorpions, the squad of commandos quietly clamped metal plates onto the sides of their wagon. The horses were clad with ankle and forehead armor.

Two cannon barrels protruded from both sides of the metal covered land vehicle. The turret rising above the wagon's iron roof, sported a pair of howitzers capable of propelling cannisters up to a mile away.

An American flag offered the onlooker a single hint as to what the strange thing was to be used for!

At sunrise, Colonel Townsend's detachment crossed the "Three Forks River".

Predators normally pay the closest attention to their hunting zones during the first hour of sunrise; therefore, Townsend had his squad of Culpers pull off the road and throw branches over the armored war wagon.

The horses were fed.

Sir Francis and a Culper 'newcomer' named, "Stick" were on watch while the others slept. Two U.S. Cavalry troopers were approaching on slow walking mounts.

They were the point men of Colonel Hitchcock's 9th Cavalry Unit!

Their "Unit" was coming back from a flareup between the "Creeks" and "Seminoles" over the damming of a creek. It had escalated to a level that "talk" on the night drums, spoke of 'all-out war with the whites'!

"Stick" awakened Colonel Townsend.

"Colonel, in ten minutes, a hundred or so of Hitchcock's "Ninth", will be coming up on us!

The 'Scot' has the 'point-men' tied up to the tree closest to the wagon!

He wanted me to ask you, 'if you wished to introduce yourself to them?'."

"Tell "Blue Team" to construct the field gallows!

Additionally, set up the "Judges' tent"!

We'll do our court-martialing right here!" said Townsend.

When Fort Gibson's "'A' Company" topped the hill marking the two-mile point to the fort's gate, what "Lieutenant Maddux" saw, was an unimaginable spectacle!

A full-fledged courtroom had been set up at the entrance of the only covered bridge crossing the "Verdigris River"!

Behind a ten foot polished table, sat seven 'Federal Judges'.

The red cloaked presiding lawmaker (Townsend) was flanked by three black cloaked judges on each symmetrically pleasing side of his seat. Hoods and masks protected their identities!

Other than the back-to-back (tied) point-men, Sir Francis George of the Walkers was the only clearly distinguishable human being available to speak with 'A' Company's commander.

The table of judges surreally posed as if, 'frozen'!

Sitting in a cane rocker and rocking back and forth atop the battle wagon's dual gun turret, Sir Francis spoke.

"Greetings, from the President of the United States!

General Andrew, "fucking", "Old Hickory", Jackson sincerely sends his best regards to the valiant soldiers of Fort Gibson!

However, we are here to "charge, arrest, and hang" those commanding officers, "aiding and abetting" a gang of native American criminals!"

"How about you, putting your hands up in the air, mister!

I don't know who in the hell you think you are but out here in Oklahoma, we don't cotton to orders given from roadside showmen!

Now, untie those men and move that goddamned heap of metal off the bridge's ramp!

You got one minute to do as I say or these men will shoot you and your wax figurines all to hell!" Barked Lieutenant Maddox.

Slowly, the two-gun turret Sir Francis George was sitting upon, turned toward the gung-ho officer. Sir Francis George of the Walkers stood in preparation for his oration.

"Gentlemen, I'm afraid you misunderstood me!

We are here to place under arrest, charge, and hang those "Belonging to" or "Sheltering from Justice", the "Tuckabatchee Hadjo's war party" which resides within your fort's jurisdiction!"

"Listen here, dick-weed, either you move that junk heap off of this road or I'm going to blow you and your statuesque buddies to kingdom come!" ferociously screamed the "shave-tail".

"Son, how old are you?" kindly asked Sir Francis.

"That's my concern! Detail!....draw your weap......." Yelled the young man nanoseconds before a howitzer round exploded inside of the horse he was sitting on.

Hot hair and horse flesh, at an enormous rate of speed, splattered the cavalry unit standing thirty yards behind what was once where their company commander's horse stood!

The soldiers dismounted!

With a show of "truce" (removing their hats), the cavalrymen stacked their weapons with the business ends pointed toward the ground.

Waiting their fates, the soldiers stood in their ranks preparing for the "consequence" Sir Francis George of the Walkers was about to pronounce!

The seven hooded judges remained motionless as Sir Francis spoke.

"Tonight at precisely six o'clock, your Commander, "Lieutenant Colonel Ethan A. Hitchcock" along with his five staff officers, are to stand trial before "The United States Supreme Court"!

These men have been charged with "Aiding and Abetting an enemy of the Republic"!

Also, to be at this hearing, will be, "Tuckabatchee Hadjo's Red Sticks"! Every man, woman, and child from that gaggle must be present!

Failure to adhere to these orders will cause the dismantling of Fort Gibson in an "unordinary" sort of way!

To conclude, I shall demand that each of you, remove your boots!

While I bid you gentlemen a farewell and as you and your horses walk past me in a single file manner, let me offer a piece of advice to your "commander". Tell him, 'if he wishes to avoid a deadly entanglement, deliver Milly Francis and her belongings, to this courtroom by 1700hrs. today!'

If what I ask is done, this "experience" will end and these and all future charges, will be dropped!

One more thing which will take the sting out of our uncanny meeting, kindly share with Lt. Col. Hitchcock, 'provided he cooperates and delivers the Creek "Pocahontas" to this courtroom by five o'clock this afternoon, he and every man at Fort Gibson will receive a "Presidential Citation" and one level upgrade in rank'!"

As the last man passed beneath Sir Francis's perch atop the battle wagon's turret, he turned around and then looked up at the Walker. With a grimace reminding one of eating a green persimmon, he stopped.

His horse's reins clutched in his gloved fist, the middle aged soldier turned and raised his chin toward Sir Francis George of the Walkers!

He stood on his toes as he leaned as close to the 'Scot' as he could possibly get; he then spoke.

"Sir, I am, "Lieutenant Colonel Ethan Hitchcock".

Now that it's just, "us men", how about you jumping off that wagon of yours and come get your ass whipping!

Those boys you killed, happened to be returning from their final exercises before their graduation from "Officer's Candidate School"!

Maybe "you" can write their mothers the news of their sons' murders!"

"Ethan, Ethan, Ethan. Listen to me, you had no business allowing your candidates to engage in an 'uncontrolled' confrontation!

Sadly, some boys lost their lives today but that "ownness", belongs to you!

What military officer in their right mind, would….." Spouted Sir Francis until he felt the wide barrel of a blunderbuss touch the back of his skull.

"Stand down!

Colonel Hitchcock is our inside man!" sharply stated Stick.

Then, like a magician's "post-cape" residue, the remaining 'frozen' judges hopped down from their judicial stage and encircled the halfdead mole!

"Ethan, by my calculation, you have somewhere between one minute and forty five seconds, to explain what agent 'Stick' said to interrupt Sir Francis's interrogation of you!"

"Sir, what Colonel Hitchcock's purpose was, all started….."

'Agent Stick' was getting ready to say, when Colonel Townsend reached out his left hand holding a boot knife, and sliced Stick's windpipe open!

Only a bubbly hiss completed the double agent's sentence.

"As I was saying, Ethan, you now have less than fifteen seconds to answer my question; that is, 'who are you'?" calmly asked Townsend.

The petrified cavalry officer did his best to act as the type of brave man he had always imagined himself to be, if ever captured by the enemy; however, Ethan's sphincter muscles betrayed him.

"Sir, I am Lieutenant Colonel Ethan A. Hitchcock of the United States Arm….." Hitchcock was saying, as two robed Culpers tied his legs and hands together!

A leather hood and noose followed.

The log tripod settled with a groan as Ethan stepped onto the trapdoor covering a six foot hole.

With a shoulder tap from the executioner, the condemned man was made aware of the consequence of his answer.

"Lieutenant Colonel Hitchcock, you are hereby sentenced to be hanged by the neck until you are dead!

Do you have anything to say, before your sentence is carried out?" Macabrely whispered Colonel Townsend.

"You fools have been snookered by your own people!

Milly Francis was taken from here more than two weeks ago by the "Capitol Police Force"!"

"Ethan, did you recognize any of the members of this so called, 'Capitol Police Force'?" shrilly asked Townsend with a smirk on his face.

"Only "you" and the Vice President!" muttered Hitchcock.

Following a loud laugh, Robert Townsend leaned down to pull the leaver operating the gallows' trapdoor but couldn't; because, three Culpers stopped him from doing so!

Sir Francis George of the Walkers took control of the uncovered "chink".

After removing Hitchcock's hood, Sir Francis ordered the now thumb-tied Culper commander to be brought forward to face his accuser.

Colonel Townsend attacked!

"Toad" was the only Culper killed in the efforts to neutralize the expert assassin!

The 'Scot' placed Stick's blunderbuss at the base of Townsend's skull and said a few uplifting words to his former instructor before splattering his brains into the Oklahoma sky!

Sir Francis then faced Lt. Col. Hitchcock with a very sad expression on his face. As the Walker slowly made his way toward the tied soldier, he dropped Stick's spent blunderbuss and removed his sidearm.

Sir Francis spoke at the same time he cocked his long barreled pistol.

"I would assume you have heard of the "clean-up" efforts made following a Culper operation, have you not?"

Ethan Hitchcock nodded as Sir Francis placed the pistol's muzzle between his eyes.

"Ethan, do you solemnly swear that Milly Francis was taken by "Van Buren" and others claiming to be the Capitol Police Force?" asked the 'Scot'.

"Yes, I do!" answered the visibly frightened cavalry officer.

"You may return to the fort!

Remember this, "Congress has awarded the Creek woman named, "Milly" the "Citizens' Medal of Honor" for an act of bravery!

She is to receive a pension of ninety-six dollars per year for the rest of her life!

Is that understood, Lieutenant Colonel Hitchcock?"

With his boots in hand and no horse, Ethan Hitchcock hightailed it back toward Fort Gibson.

After hearing an explosion, Ethan turned back toward the place of the incident; he saw a black disk slowly rising above the flame engulphed scene.

* * * * *

Jackson wept when Sir Francis George of the Walkers recapped the events occurring in Oklahoma. It was Townsend's heart ripping betrayal that seemed to get to him the most.

"Sir George, my guess is, Robert Townsend's intolerance to indescribable luxury became tolerable!

I've learned a lot over the past twenty four hours; ironically, Townsend's true colors were beginning to bleed through when he fiddled with the investigative reports implicating Calhoun's and George Poindexter's complicity in my assassination!

Hannah saw him remove them from my desk!

When you tie-in Judge James Dowdell's business partner, Paddy Welch and a long string of 'contract for hire' murders, in with Martin Van Buren's promise to appoint our allusive Detective William Cranch to the position of Federal Land Commissioner once he became the eighth President, 'something' stinks!

My brother, I have something dreadfully important to tell you!

On the day of South Carolina Senator Davis's funeral, as I was leaving through the East Portico, Paddy Welch stepped out from behind a column and snapped his two pistols as if he were attempting to shoot them at me!

What was not seen but later remembered, was Detective Cranch sticking me on the back of my neck with his ring!

Since then, I have been running a fever and suffering from muscle cramps which have frankly prevented me from walking at times!

Sir Francis, I'm sure, I have been poisoned!"

"Andy, have you verified your suspicions with anyone other than personal judgement?"

"Rachel's physician, "Shippen's" his name, gave me a full exam including a blood analysis and found nothing!" pensively said Jackson.

"What about the Cerian doctors; have you made an effort to get their help?" pugnaciously hammered Sir Francis.

"Jefferson's (Thomas Jefferson was a Cerian) in France; I don't trust anyone else!

He's due back in April. I'll just have to 'bite the bullet'!" sneeringly stated Andrew Jackson.

"If you get an earlier opportunity to take the matter in hand, I'd certainly jump on it, sooner than later. Viruses especially exotic ones, have a tendency to lay dormant until they gain enough strength to harm you!" expounded the Walker.

"Believe me; I will!" responded Jackson.

"So, my dear brother, how shall we smite this multiheaded dragon?"

"I'm afraid conspirers such as Van Buren, Calhoun and Poindexter are "ever-presents" in this town!

They are much like the swamp rattlers are to the Everglades. Kill them all and within a day's passing, they're back with even more resolve to destroy those rooting for evenhandedness!"

"Are you recommending, we only go after Paddy Welch?" asked the 'Scot'.

"I'm afraid ole 'lady luck' would have to be on our side in order to accomplish that feat. That Nib is one treacherous character!

'No', to answer your question, Sir Francis; but, William Cranch is a much softer target and will be easier to flush out!

Why don't you ride over to the "American Antiquarian Society" and pay Edward P. Cranch a visit?

In the meantime, I'll prepare a small 'father-son' get together for tonight."

"Where shall I bring 'Junior'?" asked Sir Francis.

"Room #711, at the "Willard Hotel". Will nine o'clock suffice, George?"

"Indeed!

What will the dress code be, Andrew?" heckled Sir Francis.

"Awe, Sir George, it'll be casual; but, you might suggest that "Eddy" wear a warm skirt!" laughed America's seventh President.

*   *   *   *   *

"The Columbian Institute for the Promotion of Arts and Sciences" was surrounded by an eleven foot iron fence.

Wearing white jackets, shiny black boots and red pants, a pair of mechanical midgets stood on both sides of the institute's driveway.

"Pardon me, Gentlemen, I am looking for the 'American Antiquarian Society'; I hope to interview a, "Mister Edward P. Cranch". Can you help me?" asked the Walker.

Like spring wound toys, the human looking gargoyles raised their lanterns at the same time and both pointed toward a road leading into the property's forested area.

A sign reading, "American Antiquarian Society" claimed the distance to it was a half mile away.

Sir Francis George of the Walkers snapped his riding crop against the side of his spit shined boot to prompt his white stallion to prance down the dreary lane as if pulling a chariot!

Cinders kept being slung onto his carriage's seat. Sir Francis saw 'that' as a message from his deceased grandfather!

Not surprisingly, since the "Walker Clan" was known for its fine distilled whiskey, there was a long running "custom" needing attention to.

'If "one" were to ever have road cinders fall onto his seat, "that chap", must stop and have a swig or two', which is what he did!

After relieving himself and neatening up, Sir Francis proceeded into a tunnel like passageway formed by contiguously joined chestnut trees. Echoes from the stallion's hooves sounded as if, there were many horses behind the roadster.

"African green monkeys" began swinging through the chestnuts' upper canopy. This opened the way to the institute's first sighting.

'None of the monkeys crossed beyond the tree line', he thought to himself.

The Walker gazed through an instrument measuring the height of the structure's scaffolding looming above him. It was the beginning of a 555' monolith!

"So, what do you think of him?" came a voice from behind the slim lined wagon.

With the speed of a viper's strike, Sir Francis George withdrew his pistol from its holster and pointed it at the forehead belonging to a gorgeous young redhead!

With difficulty, the Walker uttered a few words.

"Lord, woman, I almost shot you!

Why do you call "it", a 'him' and what is it?"

"They're many answers to your 'what is it?' question; but, I must say, one would have to be as dumb as a rock to imagine that, 'it', was a vagina!

You aren't an ignorant man are you, Mister (Pause)?" Eddy coyly asked.

"Apparently, "I" am!

It was just that this monstrosity stole my attention to the point of forgetting my manners. I am, "Sir Gilbert Duprez" the Chief Arts Writer for, "THE ALBION CRITIQUE".

My mission is to interview an, "Edward P. Cranch" on behalf of "William Dunlap", an entrepreneur!

He is in search of a 'Stage Manager' for New York's first ballet theatre. It is to be named, "Park Theatre". Eloquently said Sir Francis.

"Sir Gilbert, as well meaning as your intentions appear to be, I would strongly advise you, to leave these premises at once!

Entanglements with my father should be avoided at all costs!

"Detective William Cranch" is perhaps the most ruthless 'man' living on this continent!" panted Eddy.

"With whom do I have the infinite pleasure of speaking with on this lovely morning?" asked Sir Francis George of the Walkers.

"Oh, please forgive my rudeness!

I am "Elizabeth Austin" but I go by the name of, "Eddy".

You see, Mister Duprez, because my mother and the other slaves were apportioned as part of a legal settlement awarded to the 'devil' Cranch, I have been imprisoned on this miserable plantation for years!" cried the 'woman'.

"Are you saying, 'William Cranch' is not your real father and your actual name is not, 'Edward Cranch'?" strongly asked the Scot.

"Sweetheart, perhaps you have been afflicted by 'gun-ear'; so, read my lips, 'I am a slave belonging to William Cranch'!"

"Then, where is "Edward", Miss Austin?" politely asked the Walker.

As though 'Elizabeth Austin' had been hit in the head with a brickbat, she jumped up on the back of Sir George's roadster and made two perfectly executed pirouettes.

With a twisted grin on her face, Eddy with her left hand, raised the front of her bellbottomed skirt. Daintily with her other slender hand, grasped 'his' penis, urinated on Sir Francis George of the Walker and then jumped to the ground while cackling all the way into the forest!

Observing the ritual of old Johnnie Walker's 'cure' for being 'peed' upon, Sir Francis George weighed out the 'should' or 'should-nots' as to whether to go after Edward Cranch!

Listening to the monkeys howl however, tipped the scale toward a more diabolical solution!

The Walker lingered several moments while sipping on his ancestors' scotch. He was contemplating "how" he was going to get the "crazy boy" to the 'Willard Hotel' alive.

Sounds of someone splitting-out kindling turned Sir George's attention toward the five and a half storied monolith.

Once again, he snapped his riding crop against his boot to prompt the stallion to move forward. He saw a middle aged woman swinging a maul over a pile of leg sized logs.

"Madam, please forgive the intrusion!

Perhaps you may be of some assistance in helping me locate a, "Mister Edward P. Cranch"?

If it's any trouble, I'll handsomely pay you for your efforts!" said Sir Francis George of the Walkers.

The woman slammed her wood splitting maul into the chopping block, removed her gloves, straightened up her red hair and approached Sir Francis.

"I didn't hear you ride up. Please jump down from that very fancy carriage of yours and come on inside!

I've got some tea on the stove; let's get to know each other!

By the way, my husband and I, are the "chief cooks and bottlewashers" around here!

We're called "Superintendents" but that's ole 'Willie Cranch's' schmoozy way of paying us as little as morally plausible!

What do you take in your tea? I have honey and fresh cream.

By the way, I'm professor, "Annie Grigsby"; my husband, "Oakley", and I are from Edinburg.

Six years ago, we were commissioned to design a 'garden landscape' around this monstrosity. Oakley and I liked it here; so, we just stuck around.

Now, you mentioned you were looking for Cranch's son, 'Edward'?" delicately stated Annie.

"Yes, mam!

My name is, "Sir Gilbert Duprez" an arts columnist for "THE ALBION CRITIQUE".

Not only would I like to do a story on this talented young lad, I also wish to invite him to meet my employer, "William Dunlap, Esquire", in New York!

'Mister Dunlap' is opening the northeast's first ballet theatre and is interested to know if Mister Cranch would enjoy being 'The Park Theatre's' Stage Manager?" matter-of-factly said Sir Francis.

"That simply boggles my mind, Sir Gilbert!

How would anyone outside of the institute's grounds even know Edward's name, much less, some ballet theatre on "Manhattan Island" wanting to hire the boy?"

"Mrs. Grigsby, I am only following my boss's instructions. I have little to 'no' information on those of whom, I deliver his messages to!

Factually, just this week, I dropped off two other proposals for similar positions. Mister Dunlap was hoping to fill his "staffing" before the Park's April debut!

Not to sound presumptuous, Annie, is there something I should know about this 'Edward Cranch' that 'William Dunlap' might need to be made aware of?

If there is, please tell me; because, if I withheld anything 'earthshattering' from him, I'd end up feeding the catfish in the Hudson Bay!"

"Sir Gilbert, "Edward Cranch" is my little brother!

He was ten years old when we were brought here!" whispered Annie Grigsby.

"Brought here, Mrs. Grigsby? Asked Sir Francis George of the Walkers.

"Yes, all in all, there were "fifteen of us" shipped here from "Charleston".

After Mister Cranch won a suit against a London ship company that lost fifty of 'his' slaves in transport from Africa, the court awarded the "evil bastard" my father's entire holdings which included, his family!"

"Where are the others?

Where's 'Oakley'; are your father and mother still alive?" Sir Francis kindly asked the flurry of questions.

"Sold off; that is, except for my "brother" and me!"

"But, you're white!" exclaimed the Scot.

"Mister Duprez, are you really that naïve?

The market for 'whites' on the "Cairo blocks" are begging for "them". Fertile white women, I am told, bring three times the price of black ones!" huffed Annie.

"So, why don't the two of you, leave?" clumsily asked the Walker.

"Because of the poison monkeys, Sir Duprez."

"Poison monkeys?"

"Do you always repeat someone's statement, Gilbert?" smart mouthed Annie.

"Do I always repeat ...." Sir Francis laughingly mocked Annie Grigsby before he came within inches of her face. After grabbing her shoulders and coaxing her to lock eyes with him, Sir Francis asked her a serious question.

"Would you actually want to escape from here, if you could?"

Annie nodded.

"Tonight at nine o'clock, there will be a semaphore code sent from the top of that monolith to the President of the United States!

In its message, I shall expose through your testimony, the real truth about this venal man named, "William Cranch"!

After that, we'll get you and your brother safely out of here!

Speaking of him, where is "Eddy"?

I may have already met him when I rode in." said Sir Francis George of the Walkers.

"You met my brother?" asked Annie.

"Now who's repeating questions?

After I came through the front gates and greeted by a pair of mechanized lantern carriers, I rode less than a mile down the driveway toward this pinnacle. Monkeys began swinging through the trees as soon as I entered the forest but they never followed me beyond the grove of chestnuts.

It was then, I met a person who called 'herself', "Eddy!"" pleasantly commented Sir Francis.

"How did "he" look?" asked the haggard woman.

"Much like yourself; that is, a beautiful "lady"!" cooed Sir Francis.

"Where did he go after he spoke with you, Sir Gilbert?"

"After peeing on me, "he" ran into the forest cackling like a "sprite"." Stated Sir George.

"So, that's what saved you!"

"From the monkeys?" squealed the 'Scot'.

"Their saliva is deadly poisonous!

One bite and the recipient is infected with a disease which after a few weeks, leads to death!" sadly explained Annie.

"Eddy ran into the woods where they were!"

"They only attack on the other side of the chestnut grove, Gilbert!"

"You're saying, that someone exiting through their habitat would be bitten?"

"Exactly, it's the monkey saliva Cranch uses to kill his political enemies!"

"Annie, have you ever heard of a man named, "Paddy Welch"?" asked Sir Francis George of the Walkers.

"Of course. 'Uncle Paddy' has been the "Institute's" greatest contributor and William Cranch's business partner, for as long as I can remember!

Why do you ask?" said Annie Grigsby.

"Because Paddy Welch made an attempt on President Andrew Jackson's life, but now, I'm not so sure it wasn't Cranch who committed the dastardly act!

When was the last time you saw either Welch or William Cranch?

Also, Annie, is it possible to get Eddy to come inside the monolith?

I have a 'plan' to spring both of you out of this place tonight and we'll need him to be close by, when it's time to leave?" confided Sir Francis.

"Both men were at the Institute's science laboratory less than five days ago, they left together and to my knowledge, they have not returned since then. As far as getting Eddy to leave his treehouse in the forest, I'd say the chances of that, are slim to none!

You see, Sir Gilbert, when Eddy was a very young boy, the medical men at the institute tampered around with his monozygotic sister. They were supposedly creating the genetically perfect ballet dancer; unfortunately, they ended up with a woman's torso and a man's trunk?

The psychological effects on poor Eddy have been horrendous!" cried Eddy's only living sister.

"Would it be better to leave him behind, Ms. Grigsby?" timidly asked the Walker.

"Even if he wanted to go with us, I doubt if the monkeys would allow it; but, I'll ask him." Flatly responded Annie.

"How can you do that?" sharply questioned Sir Francis.

"Every night, "Elizabeth Austin", Eddy's stage name, exits the forest and twirls toward the monolith. The performance lasts for one hour, flat!

Nine monkeys always sitting in the same trees, applaud when "Miss Austin" leaves the vaulted stage. That's when, I'll ask her!

I have fresh cut flowers for Eddy following her every performance!" proudly stated Annie.

"Are there only nine monkeys living in that forest?" queried the 'Scot'.

"That's plenty enough, I'd say, Mister Duprez, wouldn't you?" asked Annie.

"Well, it's better than a hundred, I'd guess. Say, don't you have some dried out gourds laying around here someplace?

I noticed when I came in, you had put up some "nuthatch nests" around the pond; I was hoping, you had a few spares put up somewhere?" asked Sir Francis George of the Walkers.

"I sure do but what are you going to do with them?"

"I'm simply going to catch nine furry "critics" so Eddy can makeup 'her' or 'his', own mind!"

A dozen gourds were carted into the fifty five stories tall monolith and the Walker began his work on the monkey traps. Annie started reminiscing of her days in Edinburg.

She spoke of her father's work at the university; he was an "immunologist", she said.

This made it practically impossible for the Walker to remain in character; because, the man she spoke of, her father, was a colleague of his.

"Doctor Tessler" and he, were graduate students together; although, "Benjamin's" department, was in "St. Cecillia's Hall" while "his" (at the other end of the campus) was the "Teviot Row House".

"The Columbian Institute for the Promotion of Arts and Sciences", appearing as a university with ivy covered walls, was in actuality, a biological research center!

The scientists knew quite well, they were working for a very rich and powerful entity; but, they did not know who it was!

Project funding seemed bottomless provided the weekly reports proved out to be significantly hopeful in finding a 'virus' that promised to eradicate human life on any chosen continent!

The District of Columbia was the "test site".

"Annie, how come you and Eddy weren't "Sold" ?" humbly asked Sir Francis.

"I guess, because I am an 'old' woman and 'they' had already fiddled with Eddy; therefore, we were not 'selected' to be members of the institute's, "Samplers Club"!

Anyway, only 'males' between the ages of twelve and thirty were participants." Answered Annie Grigsby.

"When we first met, you mentioned there were people whose ownership shifted to William Cranch as a result of an unfavorable court ruling, against your father. Were there no other 'females' in the group?" pried the Walker.

"You see, Sir Gilbert, those were the days when my father, still in his prime, set out to cure the "African" people of their diseases!

On sabbatical and with not much cash, "Pappa Ben" as I called him, contacted the "Royal African Company" and arranged for his family and other volunteers with medical backgrounds, to purchase a ticket on one of their slave ships to "Port Ouidah" in western Africa.

Once their tickets were in hand, the 'medical aid group' began their preparations to set up a hospital in order to combat a plethora of raging epidemics! Now, Sir Gilbert Duprez, 'here', is where it gets interesting, Paddy Welch was among 'other' fare paying passengers on that same ship!

As my mother told me, I was only "ten" at the time, Welch finagled it so, the 'Ouidah authorities' disallowed my pappa's medical team to disembark!

It was said, Paddy Welch went to the local gravediggers and paid them a "Flowing Hair" (silver dollar) for each dead person they could load onboard our ship.

When we landed in Charleston, Welch and a few of his cronies, pressed charges against my father and three other Edinburgh physicians, based on the offense of "Involuntary Manslaughter"!

"Judge John Drayton" believed Welch's testimony, claiming that he had paid for the university's humanitarian effort; although, their expense payments were contingent upon the "guarantee" of delivered "disease free" slaves!

Paddy claimed, the immunization injections his thirty five negroes had received onboard the Royal African Company's slaver, killed them all!

For settlement, Judge Drayton awarded Paddy Welch "twenty years of servitude" from the university's onboard medical team!

Sir Gilbert, I believe you can fill in the rest of the story!

Obviously, William Cranch was conveniently standing by at the conclusion of Judge Drayton's 'kangaroo' hearing; consequently, he bought us, paid Drayton, and the rest is history!"

"What happened to the others, Annie?" asked Sir Francis.

"I do not know for sure; but, I suspect the younger men were subjects used in the institute's studies!

The faculty members, I assume, are still doing their research but again, I can't be positive of that. One thing is for certain, though, anyone who enters the Columbian Institute's grounds, never returns!" hissed Annie Grigsby.

"When was the last time you saw "Oakley", Mrs. Grigsby?" gently asked the Walker.

"My husband and my father were both scientists; no one has seen them since our arrival eight years ago!"

"Have you and Eddy tried to figure out a way to escape from here? I mean, the Capitol is only a stone's throw from where we are right now!

I would imagine, you have, at least, configured an inconspicuous route to leave the property?" Asked Sir Francis George of the Walkers.

"Cranch's monkeys are always watching us!" softly said Annie.

"Do they ever leave the forest?"

"Only during 'Elizabeth Austin's' ballet performances but that's only for fifteen minutes, give or take, a minute or two. Why do you ask?"

"Because, while tonight's performance is taking place, we're going to lift our furry primate friends to unimaginable heights!

Mrs. Grigsby, if we're fortunate enough to keep the beasts at bay for ten minutes or so, do you believe Eddy will leave with us?" asked Sir Francis with a strained expression on his face.

"I wouldn't count on it; Eddy is mighty close to those animals, Mister Duprez. For the last two years, my brother hasn't spent one night in the monolith; I believe the boy feels he is their 'king'!"

"Annie, a question, are Paddy Welch and William Cranch the same person?"

"That's a helluva query at a time like this, Sir Gilbert!

I'll assure you they are separate men; of whom, I have known for six years!" shrieked Annie Grigsby.

"No offence meant, my dear; but, it was a serious question!

Think all the way back to the days when you and your father were shanghaied by Paddy Welch and that 'pricey' South Carolina judge. Try to remember, when you actually saw the two men standing within an arms-length of the other, Annie?"

"Seriously, Sir?

Well, let's see, there was the time when we were delivered here to the Columbian Institute!

William Cranch was the man who 'brought' us here, if you remember me explaining that to you?

It was the first time we met the man!" defensively stated the monkey guarded prisoner.

"Did you physically see the men together (and) at the exact same time?

Is it possible for you to dance back through an old memory ravine and restage the 'precise' manner in which you and your 'fellow slaves', were introduced?" pushed the Walker.

"Let's see, we rode into the Cranch property in the back of a covered wagon. I remember that quite clearly!

It was early in the morning, I'd say four or four thirty, when we rumbled down the same cobblestone driveway as you did today.

Welch jumped from the wagon master's bench and ran into what is now, the institute's "Science Building". The wait was agonizing, as I recall.

Being fair, I guess we sat there in pitch darkness for two hours. As soon as the sun came up, "William Cranch" introduced himself in high style!

First came the usual kudos publicly offered to his chef's staff; but, then the heartwarming words of welcoming from our new 'master', made us feel nothing like prisoners. Instead, it was more like being chartered into a nice club!

We had a grand feast and were shown our luxurious quarters. Each of us were given a hunk of cash to go into town and buy whatever knickknacks we needed to make our "homes" more comfortable.

By the time we returned from our shopping tour of Washington's Square, a "Doctor Davenport" gave us the news of both Paddy's and William's departures. Davenport whom we never heard from again, explained, our "owner" would return by summer's end.

The assignments Doctor Davenport spoke of, were to be posted on the scientists' office doors at the beginning of each week; although, that never happened, my father told me." Refreshingly exclaimed Annie.

"So, did you or did you not, see Welch and Cranch in the "flesh", together?" mildly cross examined the Walker.

"My god, you're right!

I never witnessed the men together; what a foolish assumption I have made throughout these years!" whined the scarlet headed woman.

"When did William Cranch return to the Institute?" asked Sir Francis.

"Oh, this time, it was neither!

A man named, "Hillis Hadjo" whisked in from nowhere. In other words, no one saw the Indian 'enter or leave' the Columbian's campus.

During his, no more than three hour visit, the rumored, "Creek Prophet" graded the scientists' work. He executed the faculty's 'deadwood' but rewarded the productive ones with elaborate gifts and provided each family an acre of land to do whatever they wanted to on that property!

At the end of his visit, I remember it as clearly as if it had happened yesterday, breakfast had just been served when this prophet, "Hadjo" rose from his place at the communal table and ascended to the very top of the Columbian Institute's vaulted ceiling!

Only inches from the ceiling's mural depicting "Moses" escaping the "Philistines", the Creek chief unloaded a seaman's bag full of U.S. paper dollars, bid us a farewell on behalf of William Cranch, and flew away!" emphatically expressed Annie Grigsby.

From above, came a whirring sound tempting both Sir Francis and Annie to look upward into the open sky!

Anxiously, Annie pointed out to the Walker a parachuted box which had just set down some ten feet from where they were standing.

"What is it, Annie?"

"This week's rationings. Are you hungry, Sir Gilbert?" asked Mrs. Grigsby.

"Absolutely famished!

I've got some fabulous scotch and a smidgen of "laughing bush" in my pouch. Those items used in tandem, would make an old boot taste like a delicacy!"

"Hurry inside and stop talking, Mister Duprez!

The monkeys move in closer to the fall line after the delivery drones leave. I don't know how they survive out there in those woods; but, I know it's a capital crime to feed them!" said Annie.

"And why do you suppose that is?" smirkingly asked Sir Francis George of the Walkers.

"I have no idea now that you mentioned it. Why do you think they're not to be fed?"

"Because hungry monkeys are easier to catch!" whispered the 'Scot'.

"Why would they want to catch them, Sir Gilbert?" asked Annie.

"Because Paddy Welch, as you said, is harvesting their saliva for biological warfare usage, Annie!

Let's finish up this gourd work and get out of here as soon as possible, shall we?

What kind of fruits are packed into those boxes, Mrs. Grigsby?

We're going to need about fifteen pieces of whatever is in there, that smells fruity to them!"

"How are you going to coax them out of the chestnut trees?

The monkeys only come out when "Elizabeth Austin" performs upon the scaffolds surrounding the stone pinnacle!

She'll be performing soon; after all, it's twenty past six!

Gilbert, that gives us practically no time to prepare for whatever you have up your sleeve, for those critters out there!

Maybe we ought to give it a try tomorrow night; what'd you think?" frantically asked Annie Grigsby.

"Is there any way you can communicate with "Edward", Annie?

I've got an idea which just might, do the trick!" excitedly said Sir Francis.

"Those furry bastards will be biting at their bits to grab a good seat during "Eddy's" performance tonight; I think, it's prudent that we not 'upset the applecart' and leave things be!" gasped Mrs. Grigsby.

"Why don't you announce, 'tonight at eight o'clock, President Andrew Jackson and his Cabinet members will be watching her performance from the White House? More than a hundred 'telescopic eyes' will view Elizabeth's eloquent movements from afar!'

Tell her, 'there are a host of theatre critics just waiting to plaster her reviews on every wall within the district. Semaphores will broadcast to the "city" exactly who she is and where that 'triple threat' is headed to!

Stardom will await her in New York City at, "The Park"!'"

After repeating almost verbatim what Sir Francis George of the Walkers had suggested, not surprisingly, a throaty voice broke through the dusky tinted surroundings.

"I have my "subjects" on a very regular schedule, you know!" snipped Eddy.

"Are you in character, my dear?" softly broadcasted Annie.

"Of course, darling; my show opens in ten minutes. I'm warming up right now."

"Look, Elizabeth, I'm not trying to make your decisions for you; but, 'Sir Gilbert Duprez' whom you've met, has come a long way to offer you a position as 'Stage Manager' for the newly opening, "Park Theatre".

Secondly, Sir Gilbert was in the middle of inviting you to tonight's audition for a major part in the ballet, "Prima Donna" but your actions precluded any chances of that!

You were Sir William Dunlap's (the Park Theatre's owner) first pick for the protagonist's leading role; however, you 'pissed' away that option by being a 'bitch'!" Bellowed Annie Grigsby.

In what most people would call a child's voice, Eddy through lung jerking sobs, spoke.

"Mister Duprez, I humbly apologize for my vile behavior but please understand, I didn't know "you" from 'Adam's housecat'. I 'acted-out' in order to scare you away!" came Eddy's oozing words from the forest's darkness.

With Annie Grigsby's megaphone pressed against his mouth, Sir Francis George of the Walkers sent out a vocal message aimed at an 'out of place' clump of brush.

"Miss Austin, with great sadness, I must tell you, your window of opportunity has past!

'Sir William Dunlap', I'm afraid, is packing as we speak; he will be taking a voyage to France to fill the role in which, he would have offered to you!

With a mirthless feeling running throughout my mind, I just want to say before I too, get underway, just how great you would have been as the "Prima Donna".

You are both beautiful and talented, Miss Elizabeth Austin!" Said Sir Francis as he slipped away from the firelight.

"Hold it, Mister Duprez!

I know, I haven't portrayed myself in the most ladylike fashion; however, I'll be goddamned if some wimpy assed errand boy, is going to shortchange me out of this grand opportunity!" yelled the talking bush.

(Sir Francis for theatrical reasons, had already hitched his white stallion to the sportscar. He did not answer Eddy's plea for a retry.)

This time, the 'hermaphrodite' stood up from behind a dried out blueberry bush and pranced across the grass carpeted divide, separating the chestnut trees and Sir Francis George of the Walkers who was sitting in his speed wagon. Eddy spoke.

"Sir Gilbert, with all due respect, it seems counterproductive for you to have come all of this way in search of the 'world's greatest ballet performer', only to have failed at your quest because of a temper tantrum?

For heavens' sake, man, get a grip on yourself!

Had I known of your true intent; that is, if you had had the courtesy of sending me a post announcing this honored occasion, I would have prepared for this earth shattering event!

Instead, you leave my hopes bashed upon the rocky shores of despair, all of which, was sparked by the nefarious introduction of yourself!

Frankly, it felt like you were up to something, the minute I laid eyes on you!

It seems to me, Sir Gilbert Duprez, the least you could do considering the degree in which you value your, to date, untarnished reputation, would be to signal President Jackson and my soon to be employer, Sir William Dunlap of the fact, my show will go on stage at eight!" shrieked Eddy.

"Assuming you are chosen, Miss Austin, will you miss your monkeys?" empathetically asked Sir Francis without a megaphone.

"My dear, Mister Duprez, I'm afraid you, my big sister, and "I", shall never leave this campus. Truly, if I ever do get the chance to leave, I'm not sure, I would!" tearfully said Eddy Tessler.

"Your tears of misery would not be for your furry friends would it, Elizabeth?" asked Sir Francis in a fatherly way.

Eddy shook her lowered head.

"Does "he" love you as much as you love him?" gently questioned the Walker.

"Yes, he does!" sobbed the adolescent.

"If that's the case, why would you wish to audition for the Park Theatre's stage manager's position?"

"Because I want him to be proud of me. He'll let me keep my monkeys then!"

"What, if, you could take the monkeys with you when you left for New York?" asked Sir Francis.

"It wouldn't be the same; we are a family, you know!" shrieked Eddy.

"Who is a family, Miss Austin? Do you mean you and the monkeys?

"No, silly! I mean "Billy", my sister, and my animals!"

""Billy"? I'm afraid I don't know who that is, Elizabeth. Gently poked Sir Francis George of the Walkers.

"William Cranch, you dufus!

Now, explain to me, what this, "Sir William Dunlap" wishes to see me perform?" fired back Eddy.

"Very well then, Miss Austin. In one hour, there will be a gathering of dignitaries meeting on the twelfth floor of the, "Willard Hotel"!

They will have just completed their dinners and being served after dinner cocktails, when the dining room's windows will open!

Your performance will be their post conference entertainment!" matter-of-factly stated Sir Francis.

"Sir Gilbert, who will be present at this gala affair?" sheepishly asked the 'in character', Miss Elizabeth Austin.

The Walker pretended to shuffle through a stack of papers in his valise. When he located one particular sheet with lots of writing on it, the Scottish distillery heir began rattling off the names of those thought to be complicit in Jackson's assignation attempt!

"Elizabeth, I'm afraid I can't read all of the invitees' names because some of them are "secret agents"; however, those "I" can call out, are mostly public figures you are already familiar with.

Of course, the President and his Cabinet, three former Vice Presidents, Edward and William Cranch, Samuel Culper, and most importantly, Sir Gilbert Duprez, all of whom, will be watching your performance!"

"Sir Gilbert, do you think, I have a chance?" timorously asked Eddy.

"It's hard to say, Elizabeth. You're up against a lot of talented actresses who too, are 'triple threats'!

Realistically, your competitors can sing like birds, dance like flamingos and make you believe who is on stage, is real!

Frankly, unless, you were to present a spectacular audition, one filled with extraordinary props and titillating lighting, you really don't stand much of a chance!

Sadly, I must admit, you should probably just give it up!

Anyway, you, more than likely, wouldn't be able to control your monkeys making your efforts, in vain!

I am sorry, Elizabeth, but I can't take the risk of having a show, one with my name attached to it, crash and burn in front of America's most influential art critics!" Toyed the Scottish fisherman.

"I can tell you one thing, if you refuse to help me achieve my lifetime dream, I'll command my animals to eat you!" Screamed Eddy.

"You listen to me, young man, Sir Gilbert has gone to great expense in time and effort, to offer an opportunity to you!

You, in turn, decided to do everything you could to make yourself into the least attractive candidate in the running!

After you peed on his head, hid in the woods for half a day, insulted and now threatened him, what in the hell would you do if "you" were in his shoes?

Eddy, I'd beg our kind guest's forgiveness and ask him for his help!" Scolded Annie Grigsby.

Through cascading tears, Eddy looked up at the Walker and spoke.

"Sir, if there is but one ounce of forgiveness left in your heart, I need it!

I am aware of my abominable behavior but please try to understand, my sister and I, are desperate people; we've gotta get out of here!

Could you please, Sir Gilbert, show me how to win this life changing contest. I'll do whatever you say; just give me a second chance, please!"

Following a 'Schadenfreude moment' (and two slugs of scotch), the Walker stood up in his harnessed speed wagon.

Following a pensive pose and an animated throat clearing, Sir Francis George of the Walkers rendered his verdict.

"Alright!"

"Thank you! panted Eddy.

"The emissaries using their theatre binoculars, will be gazing at you from a quarter of a mile away; therefore, the use of lighting and semaphore communications will be the only way we can let them know of the prolific story you are about to play out!

From the tiptop of the pinnacle, there is a heavy-duty pulley wheel. My stallion will pull the cable operating the upwardly moving stage.

Elizabeth, you are to play, "The Flame". Each scene and there are three of them, will depict a period in your life!

In that we have no stage lights, we'll use the inside of the monument as our golden lit backdrop; the Washingtonian elites will see you in glorious "silhouette"!

"Scene One" will begin with you (a slave) being brought to the Charleston docks and sold.

"Scene Two" is of the wonderous love affair which ignited between a wealthy plantation owner and his house servant. It is at that time, your monkeys will be brought into the performance.

But!...."Flame's" lover forbids your pets from remaining inside his mansion!

Consequently, you and your "white" lover fight but, in the end, the two of you make passionate love.....

In the "Final Act"(Scene Three) due to a celestial intervention, a spirit appears, giving each of yours' and your master's "children"(nine monkeys), the opportunity to fly away to a land drenched with milk and honey!

How do you like it, Elizabeth?" Sir Francis asked.

"It's beautiful!" exclaimed Eddy.

"Elizabeth, can you handle the role?

"You're darn tooting I can but tell me, Sir Gilbert, how does the "third scene" end?"

"That all depends on your faith!

If you truly believe; then, your hopes and dreams will always come true!" prophetically stated Sir George.

"What do I do, first?"

"We've only got an hour; why don't you go get your leotards on and get your furry little cast members ready for the show!

Elizabeth, in the meantime, your sister and I, will build the set."

Once Edward Cranch reentered the chestnut forest, Sir Francis and Annie Grigsby wasted no time hooking up the stage riser cable to the bumper of the Walker's sports wagon.

The actor's platform consisted of seventeen tiny seats, a long table, and an arrangement of gourds with a one inch wide hole drilled into each one of them.

Between tokes of laughing bush and deep swallows of ninety-proof scotch, both Sir Francis and Annie worked feverishly to place lanterns onto the inside of the monument's scaffolding.

Upon completing the lighting task, Annie stuffed the nailed down table gourds with every bit of the strawberry jam that was delivered in her airdropped provisions.

It was then showtime!

On ground level, "Flame" opened the audition by drudgingly standing on top of the table while the African green monkeys pretended as if, they were rowing a slave ship.

Elizabeth's acrobatics along with her displayed dancing talent, astounded Sir Francis. It was much better than he anticipated!

Up top, at the very tip of the monolith, while Sir Francis George of the Walkers was tending to his white stallion, Annie was semaphoring a message to Andy. Her communique had been scripted by Sir Francis.

"Captured!... Send evacuation team with fire... Location evident... Two survivors...Cranch and Welch are the same person...Definite assassin...African green monkey saliva was toxin used...Strike now...End."

The stallion was guided down a prearranged path (fifty yards) causing the stage platform to rise to one hundred feet into the air!

"Scene Two" was about to begin.

An easterly wind had picked up to more than ten miles an hour. At times, Eddy's stage would bang against the side of the unfinished stone pinnacle creating a hazard for the "act's" acrobatic performance.

The monkeys had already found the jam inside the stationary table gourds. Their frustration at being unable to taste their discovered delicacy was reaching an obvious level of concern for (in character) Eddy.

At one point during the pretend like Christmas dinner, three of the African greens managed to grab onto a few others' tails and started biting them!

Disturbing squeals rang out across Washington's Square. The stallion walked another fifty yards causing the stage to rise even more!

When "Act III" arrived, pandemonium had reached its defined limit. 'Monkey bashing' were the 'new words' used to describe what was taking place halfway up Cranch's pinnacle!

Elizabeth was out of her mind with terror as several handless "greens" attacked her!

A whirring sound coming from above sent a very strong message to Sir Francis George of the Walkers. He quickly signaled to Annie of the impending danger; tragically, it was too late!

One lone disc opened its belly full of "blue balls" onto the Columbian Institute's campus. After a few seconds, deep sounds reverberated beneath the earth's surface.

Amazingly, Sir Francis witnessed Annie Grigsby with her leather britches in hand, use the pants as a zipline handle to slide safely down to the rear of Sir Francis's wagon.

Quickly, Sir Francis George of the Walkers and Annie cut away the wagon's connecting strands of bridle leather. They mounted the white stallion and rode it as fast as they could toward the Willard Hotel.

After looking back only once, Annie Grigsby saw what the Cerians had done to the institute's grounds. As tragic as it was, Annie felt an inward emotion of pure elation; she was alive and free!

When the stallion reached the Willard's stables, Annie reached out for Sir Francis's hand. After looking into the other's eyes for some time and without saying another word, they parted.

Chapter Seventeen

After tapping on Room #711 three times, pausing for three seconds, and then lightly kicking the wall with the toe of his boot, Andrew Jackson opened the door. The pungent odor of sulfur and garlic was the second disturbing thing Sir Francis George of the Walkers sensed when he was admitted; the initial reaction was Andy's appearance.

Weighing not one ounce more than a hundred and thirty pounds, Jackson after a grimacing smile, guided his brother through a labyrinth of hallways which eventually led to an elevator. A minute later, Sir Francis witnessed for the first time, the "Cerian North American Headquarters".

The domed ceiling provided a dimly lit screen for the communication experts to interpret and then transmit back, to the glowing dot on the outlined world map above them.

People speaking odd languages, could be heard beneath the whirring mask of white noise. Red and blue pin lights blinked on and off.

"Sir George, much has happened during the past twelve hours!

Your communiques from atop Cranch's pinnacle, gave us the "Rosetta Stone" needed to find out who this, "Paddy Welch" really is; you won't like what we learned!" gasped the seated Jackson.

"How's that, Andy?" sharply asked the Walker.

"Not only is, "Paddy Welch" and "William Cranch" the same person, 'Welch' is also an ordained Culper known as, "Samuel Culper"!

He "is" and has been, a double agent for over thirty years!"

"I always thought that "Samuel Culper" and "Robert Townsend" were the same person; is that not true?"

"Sadly, 'no', Sir Francis. He killed 'Townsend' just like he did our father and a whole host of ,"our own"!

'Who', we thought was just another renegade Niburian, has been identified as the "Master" assassin for the "Mambas"!

He has methodically picked off every single Culper, he searched out!" exclaimed Jackson.

"How did you find that out, Andy?" snapped Sir Francis.

"That poor unfortunate hermaphrodite, "Edward P. Cranch" was forced to take the unit's commander to the "American Antiquarian Society's" records vault!

Welch's "book" of Culpers, was found. It listed every agents' numeric code, real name, plus their city of residence!

Robert Townsend must have gotten an eyepopping amount of money for that damn thing; there were only four of them printed!

What has been learned to this point is, Paddy Welch more than likely, was responsible for George Washington's death!

The Cerians have done their best to alert the affected Culpers; although, there is no word yet, as to whether they have made contact with "Thor" and "Running Hawk". I'll let you know, as soon as I hear something." Said the frail American President.

"Andy, do we know where Paddy Welch is now?"

"Maybe!"

"Surely, since Milly Francis is with Paddy, it would seem logical that his ability to slip through "cracks" is now more likely, to find a tighter squeeze than expected!

Those blinking lights on the ceiling; do they have anything to do with Paddy Welch's whereabouts, Andrew?" asked Sir Francis.

"Tragically, those flicks of red light represent some type of Niburian initiative.

George, our greatest fears have become a reality; the Nibs have infiltrated the United States' government, at every level!

From American cities on the Atlantic coastline and all the way west to the Mississippi River, our churches and schools have been filled with the bastards!

Here's the irony, thousands of patriots gave their lives and property to provide their grandchildren with the privilege of choosing how they wished to live their lives!

One might ask, "what's the fallout, when those naïve young voters elect a self-serving or worse, a "narcissist", into a position of leadership?"

What happens to our successors' freedoms when the objective of our government is to maintain a lavish lifestyle? Who pays the "lawmakers" to utilize our tax dollars as a personal 'money tree'?

To ask an even darker question, how do you depose an evil ruler or a whole nest of them, if there are no Culpers? Who will referee, a 'fixed game', Sir Francis?" panted Jackson.

"Andy, how do the Cerians weigh in on this? Have they proposed a solution?" Snapped the 'Scot'.

"Well, first of all, the Cerians believe that a democracy is like giving a room full of children, a loaded pistol. Secondly, their concerns only go as far as when the next shipment of gold is scheduled to be sucked out of our mines!

Their way of handling such an issue as this one, is to simply execute all of the suspects and let "history", sort out the innocent!

Unfortunately, this is America's problem; that is to say, the Cerians' primary focus is and always has been, to supply its people with Earth's (Nicosa's) minerals.

Frankly, from their point of view, all they want, is what they have been promised. To block or retard that process would be like, multiplying all of our country's wealth times "zero"!

Fore, in the end, after about a half second of radiation blasts, America would become a lifeless desert!" grumbled Jackson.

"I wouldn't know how to work the muscles in my brain in order to attempt to understand, what makes people sacrifice their scruples for those things. Prideful beliefs like making the world a safer place, are what I think, make good men who they are!" said the pan faced 'Scot'.

"That's absolute horseshit, my brother!

"You", have never existed on this earth, not even at a minute old, when your net worth didn't exceed that of any small Scottish city!

However, if a poor man and especially one with an esteem issue, is given a thousand pounds of gold, they'll usually turn into the "person" they despised the most!" prophetically prodded the Walker's younger brother.

"Andrew; do you really believe that men like "Townsend" can actually be 'turned' by money?" sincerely asked Sir Francis George of the Walkers.

"Yes. Factually, I know it did!

I can even go so far as to say, no less than forty percent of our elected officials are on the Niburian payrolls!" yelled Andrew Jackson.

"So, where's the prize money coming from? The last I heard, America was still reeling from her seemingly incurable war addiction!" sarcastically snapped Sir Francis.

"Those blinking blue lights indicate the numbers of gold strikes popping up all over the northern hemisphere!

The problem with that scenario is, once the Masons' report their findings, the Niburians (dressed as Indians) attack the mining sites; thus, perpetuating the "Indian Wars" into the nineteenth century!

The irony is, we already had the problem whipped by allowing the "Mississippi River" to police our segregation agreement. But now that the Appalachians have become a gold mining hotbed, the Cherokee are doomed!

You might ask yourself, 'how do the Congressmen (etc.) get their hands on the money, in order to shell off their devil's dues?'.

The answer is, through the "Bank of the "fucking" United States"!" wailed the nation's sixth president.

"Therefore, you're saying, this bank belongs to the United States?" quizzed Sir Francis George of the Walkers.

"The 'Bank', is a quasi-public corporation chartered by Congress to manage the government's finances and provide a sound national currency. I personally believe the "golden goose" is not only "unconstitutional" but an outright threat to our liberty!

Regretfully, it is the rich and powerful, who too often, bend the acts of government to their selfish purposes. Thus, when a "farmer" sells his crops and deposits his 'paid in gold profits' into an account, in order for him to buy a new plow horse, that same citizen, must pay a fee in order to get the script to pay for that damn animal!

But here's the real kick in the teeth, once that "redneck" deposits his metallic earnings into the Bank of the United States, he may no longer receive withdrawals in any way but, in "printed money"!

Even an idiot can see the fallacies in that system. Can you imagine the number of fingers dipping into that pie?

When a country's lawmakers control, sift through, snip a "point"(%) or two off the balance, monitor and tax a working man's money, the bulk of that person's mobility is greatly influenced by the whims of those 'dishonest' politicians!

Considering, all "legal" transactions are paid in paper script, one has to marvel at the amount of control that same governmental entity, has over its citizens!

That is why, I have been "Censured"; I tried to break up the federal banking system by allowing each state to manage their own territory's finances. The result I proposed, was for each particular state and not the federalists, to benefit from the toils of their own citizenry!

None of that will come to fruition, I'm afraid. The Niburians have already gnawed their way into the very girders holding up this great land of ours!

So, when an enormous gold strike say, in Georgia, is filed with the "U.S. Assayer's Office", the Washingtonians in essence, become the "owner" of that mine until a "reasonable" tax is paid.

The end result, the mining company produces taxable gold and the state gets nothing!

To make the situation even more awful, those Indians who were appropriated thousands of acres of land (where that successful dig was discovered), are now dead!

They were killed out by the same "virus" Paddy Welch infected me with; i.e., 'the monkey spit sickness' which, by the way, has decimated their population!" seethed Andrew Jackson.

"With the Culpers now breached, I can't see how the American government can survive without some kind of "overseeing mechanism" providing a check against that sort of subversion.

Within every nation, there has to be some sort of intermediating control implemented; so, no matter what, wise counsel prevails!

How do the Cerians and the Masons weigh in on this obvious crisis, Andy?

Aren't they the ones with the two thousand year old agreement: 'to scratch one another's back'?" angrily queried Sir Francis George of the Walkers.

"Ideally, you are correct, Sir Francis; although, there are two very important realities you are overlooking!

First, the Mason's just like the Culpers, have been infiltrated by incorrigible characters. But, more importantly, the Niburians have appealed for a "Peaceful Amnesty" in exchange, for the management of this nation's mineral extrapolations!

What this really means after you take a close look at it, the Nibs insist they can double the gold production, cut the Mason's out of the deal altogether, and 'guarantee' the Cerians seamless extraction schedules for the next century!

I am sad to say, Sir Francis, it looks like the Cerians are going to accept their offer!" softly stated the President.

"So those blue lights are actually communications from the Niburians, signaling to the Cerians, telling where the mineral deposits are ripe for the pickings?"

"Isn't it crystal clear as to how the Niburians have 'turned' so many good men, into maniacally ferocious beasts?

Imagine, a state's representative supporting a certain bill in Congress and is "paid" for his support by being awarded the legal ownership of that same state's mining rights!

The Culper "membership log" as a case in point, got Townsend, Georgia's mines!

I believe it's easy to see how the Niburians quite masterfully have managed to 'rope-off' this country for their own purposes and drawn their "disciples" in with the promise of uncountable wealth!"

"Easy to see, maybe; but, the only real question left is, 'how are we going to put the quietus to this crap, Andy?'"

"I can't leave the Willard, George; these Cerian doctors have me quarantined in this germless vacuum. My treatments occur every four hours (around the clock) which includes, a complete transfusion of a special blend of Nicosan and Cerian blood. We can thank "White Wolf" for that!

Anyway, I couldn't run from these responsibilities of mine. I volunteered for this job and I intend on completing it to the best of my ability!

To answer your question, I am going to fight 'tooth and nail' against the "Whigs" and their banking plans; while, you go and cut off the head of the Niburian serpent!" chuckled Andy.

"How is this, "Paddy Welch" going to be smitten when no one can find him and much more importantly, when no one can identify him?"

"Sir Francis, we know where both "he" and Milly Francis are hiding or at least, where they were last seen together!

I exercised my executive power by assigning you, a pilot!

He has the language skills and the terrain knowledge you're going to need." Proclaimed Andrew.

"Where might that be, Andy?" asked the Walker.

Chapter Eighteen

Sir Francis awakened when it was time for his vitals to be checked. He could see through his cabin's only porthole, diamondlike planets streaking by.

From the beeping sounds, Sir Francis George knew the drips would start again. This time, a "film" about "The Gilded Man" was to begin as soon as the chemicals did their thing.

As the 'Scot' blinked-in the correct number of rapid eye movements, the legend of "El Dorado" came alive with flashes of waterside scenes!

Naked "Muisca" ladies were throwing gold trinkets into a glacial-fed crater called, "Lake Guatavita". They were choosing a new King!

Exaggerated colors trespassing their supposed boundaries, hypnotically placed the 'Walker' in a cave with a man preparing for 'his' coronation.

He had water but no salt; nor, a woman. His rigors lasted for seven days.

When the day came for the "Omnipotent One" to meet his people, he singlehandedly commandeered a giant raft to the center of the crystal clear lake!

The raft (made from reeds) was laden with treasures of gold and emeralds. On all four corners there was an incense burner; the 'scent' was "mosque".

The flatboat's essence mingled with the tribes peoples' additional, thousand or so, burning bundles of sweet smelling sticks.

Clouds of smoke greatly added a mystique to the ceremony. Drums and musical instruments blared out perky numbers which rippled around the shore of Lake Guatavita.

With gestures similar to those of a "Shaman", the royal man flung off his jewel studded robe as if it were on fire. In a second or two, when the air bubbles gave up the fight, it sank.

Standing on the deck's highest point, the naked King raised his arms and in an amplified voice, beckoned the "Muisca" to praise their ancestors, in hopes for his long and prosperous reign.

Once again, the surrounding instruments sent sounds clashing throughout the volcanic bowl!

Magically, a titanium ladder rose from the center of the King's floating platform. It extended itself thirty feet into the air.

The music and praising came to a swift halt. The naked lad made his way up to the weaving platform above him.

Without hesitation, the anointed one impressively dove into Guatavita's ice cold depths. The Muisca's nervously awaited their potentate's resurfacing. Time clicked onward.

At an unidentified "someone's" command, the tiny natives began throwing their gold plated possessions (ranging from plowshares to shields) into the translucent waters.

All the gold they had, whether used regularly or not, was to be sacrificed to the ancients. That way, when the "spiritual beings" tallied the peoples' 'allegiance alms' and it was deemed sufficient, the underworld antagonists would release the ransomed King, from their strangling grip!

The climax of the ceremony came when the golden winged King himself, emerged from the frigid waters and flew high into the heavens!

Because the musical instruments had also been sacrificed, all the Muiscas could do, was sing and clap their hands to rejoice their new King's ascension.

* * * * *

"Welcome to "Padre Island", Sir Francis George of the Walkers!

While we decompress, it takes about an hour, let's spend some time getting to know one another.

Understandably, you might be a little groggy. After leaving the Willard Hotel and while you were still under the influence of our infamous green gas, the Cerian physicians removed a piece of shrapnel lodged in your thigh.

More than likely, it was of no real bother to you; but, you know how the Cerians' are, 'everything must be precise'!

By the way, I am, "Lord Horatio Alvarez of the Nells", the guy Andy told you about, the "pilot", remember?"

"Ah yes, the multitalented Irishman who baffled his Oxford professors with his personal theory of "trajectories"!

It's evident, this adolescent scholar, also a Culper, mesmerized his audience to such a level of disbelief, this same "dilatant", exchanged the 'solution' to a 'military rocket maladaptation' for a university diploma!

Additionally, an authentic "Knighthood" (awarded by King George III) was bestowed upon this "stupefying" young man!" quibbled Sir Francis.

"Front and center, Sir!" said the grinning pilot.

"Lord Horatio Alvarez of the Nells, …"

"My friends call me, "Nelson". Like "George", that name is parsimoniously transmitted which can be of significant value in a pinch; if, you know what I mean?

As, I am sure your curiosity is about ready to cause you to bust out of your britches, let me preface my overview, by being up front with you about the facts!

Paddy Welch and his wife (Milly Francis), along with nine thousand Indians under his command, are burrowed inside a hundred square miles of the "Coahuila Mountains".

From what Intelligence has gathered on his Niburian stronghold, we suspect it holds the "El Dorado treasures" within its limestone tunnels!

I believe, you were educated on the "Muisca's" proclivity toward throwing solid gold items into "Lake Guatavita", were you not?

Apparently, the Nibs discovered the hidden trove some time ago and have thus constructed a subterranean strongbox beneath the "Coahuila Mountain Chain".

It is guarded by Welch's army!" said Nelson Alvarez.

"What is our objective, Lord Alvarez?" bluntly asked the 'Scot'.

"To coerce Paddy Welch into a trap and chum the Gulf of Mexico with pre-cut bits of his body!"

"And, what about Paddy's seven thousand man army?"

"Let's hope we can spare as many of their lives as possible. Those people have been through enough!" pensively stated the Nell.

""Who are they, Nelson?"

"A better question might be, 'who aren't they'?

While, the U.S. government thought they were clearing out the Indians by moving them west, as quickly as the refugees crossed the Mississippi, Paddy and his lieutenants were shipping them back down south (by the boatloads)!

Right under the noses of North America's watchdogs, the Niburians bedded up with the South Americans!

Given the Spaniards' voracious appetite for gold and a fresh supply of hungry workers, Paddy Welch and a Spanish general, turned rebel, became business partners.

"Agustin de Iturbide" and Welch (after Agustin became the Mexican Emperor) scientifically went about debunking the myth regarding the Muiscas' "Gilded Man" story.

With the brawn of thousands of North American refugees and the possession of a Cerian aerial gold detector, the two men went to work!

What had taken hundreds upon hundreds of years, for the Spanish "mineros de oro" to fail at finding the El Dorado gold, one hot air balloon with Iturbide and Welch as passengers, found "Lake Guatavita" in less than five hours!

What the two men did not realize at the time, the volcanic lake had a false bottom; which, when dived down to and then opened, would lead to a cavern which apparently had no end to it!

On the backs of thousands of men representing every known Indian tribe and race on the planet, Iturbide and Welch transported more than five hundred tons of treasure from Lake Guatavita to "Piedras Negras", Mexico.

What's amazing, Sir Francis, they did it on foot and mostly through caverns which stretched out for three thousand miles. Even more incredibly, they moved it all within eight months' time!"

"Why don't the Cerians just gas them and go in and suck their spoils up and be done with it?" clumsily asked Sir Francis George of the Walkers.

"Because they don't know about it!" Cattily said Lord Alvarez.

"What about the spaceship and all that Cerian hullabaloo back at the Willard? What are we supposed to do?"

"George, the Catholics, the Masonic lodges, the Culpers and the 'seats' filled by many American bureaucrats, have been compromised; therefore, "trust" is the rarest of all the U.S. commodities!

Sir Francis, this mission is not one sanctioned by anyone other than ourselves; in other words, a handful of 'we' loyalists are going to steal the 'Gilded Man's' gold!

Perhaps, this would be a marvelous time to leave this 'spaceship' and retire to my office where we can drink some scotch and take a good look at a map of Piedras Negras.

"Eagle Pass" will be our "Base of Operation" but for now, let's focus on your grandpa's malted whiskey."

"Tell me, Nelson, what am I supposed to be looking for on this map?

I see nothing that jumps-out making me suspect Welch and Iturbide had anything to do with this unprosperous village!" Queried Sir Francis George of the Walkers.

"Exactly!" yelled Lord Horatio Alvarez of the Nells.

"From your response, I'm assuming I'm overlooking something obvious; what is it?" asked the frustrated Walker.

"If you hold the map up to the light, you can see the (subterranean) network of caverns connecting Piedras Negras to Eagle Pass!

The section named, "Sponge Rooms" is where the tunnel passes beneath the "Rio Grande River".

From inside the barn located on the town's far western side, where the cavern's entrance is, Paddy and the Red Sticks stashed the El Dorado gold!

Jackson estimates the worth of the South American treasure at a billion dollars (plus)!" stated the Nell.

"Yes, I can see that; but, what about this 'eastern part' of the caverns?

It doesn't appear that Welch and company pass through the 'Sponge Rooms' stretch. You reckon it's because of the Rio Grande running overhead?"

"I asked myself that very same question, Sir Francis!

My theory is, 'they don't know the cavern continues beneath the river' or maybe, 'they are aware of a booby trap laid by the Aztecs or the Spanish'!

Whatever the case, Andy thinks we ought to lure the whole bunch into the depths of the "Crystal Palace's" peninsular dead-end. We'll let the water from Halo Lake drown them.

The more I think about it, the better I like his idea; consequently, once we're done with them, we'll just seal them off for an eternity!" exclaimed Lord Horatio Alvarez.

"We're going to need some help with this caper, Nelson. Where do you suggest, we recruit a small army of professional spelunkers? queried Sir Francis.

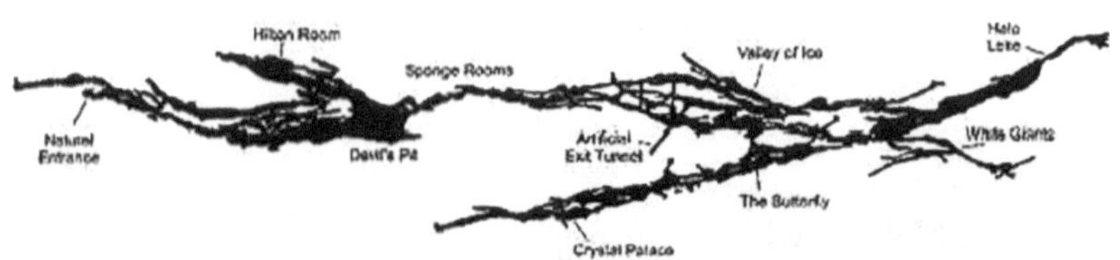

"Jackson assured me, he would send us a couple of cavalry companies by the end of February!

Anyway, the work ahead of us doesn't require an army. What will be necessary to trick those goddamned renegades into the "Crystal Palace", will be one eloquently "executed-execution"!

"So, when do we get started?" asked Sir Francis.

"I thought we'd travel up there tomorrow night. We could both use a little sleep!" said Nelson.

"Captain, if it's all the same to you, I'd just as soon get on with it!

It would be doubtful, I'd get a single wink given that I am riddled with excitement over my brother's 'sleight of hand' genius!" Sourly stated the inebriated Walker.

"Don't be so "dour", Sir Francis. There are ten of us in on this "dido"; each of us have risked our lives in the name of the Culpers and have done so on behalf of America!

Frankly, if the United States doesn't start filtering out those likely to become corrupted by smiles and cash, they, like a sack of canister worms, will ultimately starve out the associations' incorruptible!

To put it bluntly, George, we're not heisting the Colombia gold for the Masons and Cerians nor are we planning to turn it over to the U.S. government, we're stealing it for ourselves!" Giggled the Nell.

"Are we saying, we are "now" among the 'corruptible'?" prodded George.

"Not that we'll do it for free; but, Jackson's intention is to move the Dorado gold into a place where only the "inner sanctum" of trustworthy Americans can utilize it for the world's betterment!

In today's political climate, it is difficult to distinguish, who is the 'good' or 'bad' guy; consequently, until the time comes when "we" can recognize "who is who", we'll store it for safekeeping!" Said Lord Alvarez.

"How can this be kept from the Cerians, Nelson?"

"Andy claims, the Cerians believe they already have possession of the El Dorado gold. As a matter of fact, they are convinced the 'gilded man story' is pure bunk and therefore, are casting their interests at the glut of Niburian strikes happening throughout North America!

Jackson surmises, Welch and Iturbide have kept the Lake Guatavita "myth", at just that!" slowly said the Irishman.

"Lord Alvarez, you mentioned "ten men" some of whom, I suspect, are other Culpers, will we be joining them soon?" questioned the Walker.

"We won't be meeting up with those men until the mountain snows have melted. The President will have the unit in place before our plan begins somewhere around the "ides" of March, as best as can be figured.

At sunrise, you and I will be in "San Antonio" visiting the local assayer's office. We'll be spreading the news of a tunnel "we" discovered. We'll tell them about it holding cases upon cases, of gold artifacts!

Our inside man, "Porfirio Diaz" (the territory's only assayer) will see to it, the "priceless discovery" gets out to the "literate" public.

* * * * *

At seven o'clock sharp, Lord Alvarez and Sir Francis George of the Walkers tapped on the front door of "The San Antonio de Bexar General Store". A sign on the inside of the front window pane 'said', "Closed for the Sabbath".

Piano and guitar music echoed off the frontal facades of the Mexican town's two stories buildings. Bored cavalrymen meandered around the riverbank walkway.

Some of General Cos's soldiers fished but most waited their turn at "Polly's Porch" (Porche de Polly).

As far as saloons went, there were three to choose from. "El Gallo Rojo" (The Red Rooster) looked to be the most lucrative from the standpoint of information extraction; because, it's clientele were mostly made up of the English speaking locals.

The bartender's name plate read, "Lock". Sir Francis ordered two drinks.

"Good morning, Lock. Give my partner and me a couple of "Palomas" please!"

"Sure thing, gentlemen. Will that be with a lime?" pleasantly asked the Texan bartender.

"While you're at it, make it a double with squeezed lime juice on top; but, first, kindly rim our glasses with salt and do not stir!

We've got a lot to celebrate so why not share the wealth?

My buddy and I, would be honored to buy everyone in this establishment a drink!" jovially chattered the 'Scot'.

"Well, that's mighty generous of you boys; I'll pass the word." Said Lock.

As expected, the Red Rooster's patrons slid their stools closer to where the two Culpers were sitting.

Smiles, nods, and air-toasts preceded more spontaneous efforts to quench their curiosities. Four white men walked over to where George and Nelson were seated.

"We are the, "Reagans"!

I am, "Frank" and these blokes, are my brothers: "Jim, John, and Lee"!" squealed the oldest of the four Reagan brothers.

Sir Francis looked into Lord Alvarez's eyes searching for a clue as to "who" these pugnacious people were!

Seconds afterward, Nelson answered that question.

"Have you heard? They found "Nigger Bill's" body!" Exclaimed Nelson Alvarez.

"Who found it?" asked Frank Reagan.

""Andy" did." Answered the Irishman.

Suddenly, the twenty some patrons of the Red Rooster Saloon stood up from their seats and walked toward every window and door as if it were their individual lookout station!

Porfirio Diaz approached Lord Alvarez.

"Did you bring the money?" blatantly asked the Mexican official.

"I have it close by; it is $10,000 worth of twenty dollar greenbacks, just as you requested. Are the papers completed?" inquired Nelson.

""The Halo Lake property" has been signed over to the "William Broderick Cloete Mining Company" and the 'backdated' "Mining

Permit" was issued to "Abraham Wattenberg" and "John Young" of "The Alpine Ore Mining Company".

Everything is signed and sealed. That is, of course, pending the receipt of your payment!" Expounded the bribed "Coahuila" Commissioner.

"Are you aware of the spring well located near the southernmost entrance to this village?" asked Alvarez.

"Yes, it is very close to my home; why do you ask, Senor?"

"Because of the troops, I didn't carry the box through town. If you'll have one of your minions go pull it out from under the wellhouse steps, we'll consummate our agreement with another round of palomas!"

"No bother, only a fool would betray an encircled army and furthermore, I believe these men are genuine; they have strong hands and thick necks!

Now, I believe you have something you wished for me to appraise?" kindly asked Porfirio Diaz.

Lord Alvarez withdrew from his jacket's inner pocket, a three inch tall golden monkey. The territorial commissioner's musclemen came around the table to look at it; although, Porfirio permitted only two of them to touch it and none to hold it!

"Where did you find this?" asked the practically speechless assayer.

"Our 'employer' asked me to show it to you, Sir!

He wanted me to ask you, 'if you have any idea of what "it" is or where it might have come from?" lied Nelson.

"It certainly is pure gold but as far as what it is or where it comes from, I can't even begin to guess!" clearly stated the double agent.

"Oh well, it was worth a try. Perhaps we'll have the opportunity to meet again?

Oops, I almost forgot, "Mister Cloete" asked me to leave the monkey with you; it is a "gift" with a string attached to it!

Should you discover the gold monkey's origin, kindly let him know; otherwise, the trinket is for your enjoyment!" Said the departing Lord Alvarez of the Nells.

"If I should run across the answer to this 'monkey-riddle', where might I reach you?" sincerely asked Porfirio.

"We should be surveying for the next couple of weeks. After that, we'll be headed back to London.

For the time being, I reckon, we'll be camped near Halo Lake. Although, if the weather turns bad, we'll be coming back here to civilization!" Quickly stated the Irishman.

"I don't believe, I got your names!" prodded Diaz.

"That's right." Calmly stated the Nell.

"Alright, alright, I get it!

Before you, fellows, head up into the mountains, help me figure out this gold monkey puzzle!

How far away from where I'm standing, was the "monkey" found?

Sir Francis looked at Nelson as a big grin sprang across their faces. The Walker answered the man's question.

"Approximately seventy feet below the soles of your boots!"

With a sharp snap of a coachwhip, the Culpers pulled away from the quaint village of San Antonio. Some of the soldiers made faces at the "gringos" as they rode by them for the... first time!

On the second and final pass and done for spite, Sir Francis George of the Walkers and Lord Horatio Alvarez of the Nells swept back through the main part of town with their naked butts sticking out of the carriage's passenger windows!

None of the cavalrymen had the opportunity to get off a shot; because, the pair of Arabians pulling the carriage, were extraordinarily swift.

*   *   *   *   *

"Father Miguel Hidalgo" rang the bells of his small church in "Piedras Negras". He was announcing the arrival of a single horseman crossing the "Rio Grande".

"General Agustin de Iturbide" jumped from his bed and swiftly walked to the window to check on his troops' readiness.

The exterior buildings surrounding Piedras Negras's central part, was connected with brick walls creating a fortress protected by Paddy Welch's battle hardened band of runaways!

Every ledge, window, roof, and door, had a rifle sticking out from it. Each man holding one of them, were experts with it!

*   *   *   *   *

"Captain Jose Menchaca", under gunpoint, was ordered to dismount his horse before given permission to enter into the village's square. Eleven feet to the left of the public's central wellhouse, was a guillotine.

Four Cherokees "escorted" the Mexican officer to a holding cell. A mixture of Iturbide's Spanish deserters and Welch's negro and Indian desperados gathered around the mission's makeshift jailcell.

Milly Francis approached the cell's door.

In buckskins and dressed as a Shawnee squaw, Milly timidly tapped on the Mexican captain's cell door before entering. She had a purple box tucked under her left arm.

After provoking a sigh of relief from the prisoner with one of her compassionate smiles, Milly placed the purple box on the table in front of the chained general.

Like the words coming from a nursing mother, Milly explained the reason for her visit.

"Hello! My name is Milly. I am here to measure the circumference of your noggin!"

"Mam? I see no reason under the sun, as to 'why', you would need to do that!

I traveled here to provide some important news for General Iturbide!

He knows me. I use to ride with his regiment!" said Jose.

"Sweetheart, I don't pay much attention to my client's 'hither and yon' recollections; I just go about my job 'whistling' while I work!" gleefully exclaimed Milly Francis.

"Look, lady, cease with this nonsense immediately and get this goddamned stinking box off this table!

"Client", my ass! Who do you think you are?

Get me, "Agustin de Iturbide" at once, you silly trollop!" screamed the Mexican officer.

"If you continue with such outbursts, you'll need to be anesthetized. I just need a few questions answered, okay?" asked Francis in a sly manner.

"Get this fucking box away from me and get me General......"

Captain Menchaca was yelling when he heard the buzzing noise of a diamondback's rattlers.

As the purple box's lid was lifted, Jose's eyes immediately sought out the source of the alarming sound.

Four inches behind the pit viper's head was Milly's left hand gently holding the serpent's wrist sized body!

In her right hand, was the snake's last nine inches of tail!

Laughingly, Milly began teasing the soldier.

"Jose, are you familiar with the diamondback?"

"Go to hell, slut!"

"When "Tag" bites, 'Tag's' his name, he normally injects enough poison into a man's body to kill him off within an hour!

Coincidently, this happens to be your lucky day. I just fed him this morning and 'dry bites' can be awfully merciful!"

Tag's head thrusted forward with surprising strength, when the officer attempted to lunge at Milly!

The viper's fangs left two conspicuous injection sites on Jose's right cheek!

"Ready to settle down, now, Captain Menchaca?

I only have a few more preliminary questions before my husband comes in to visit with you!

It was noticed by "Father Hidalgo", you rode in from the northeast; where did you come from?"

"Go straight to hell!" cried Jose.

Tag struck again!

"Last try, Jose, where did you come from and what do you want?

I'm not playing, man; answer my questions!" hatefully scolded Milly Francis.

"I came from "San Antonio de Bexar". I serve under "General Martin Perfecto de Cos's" command.

Last week, while sitting in the "Red Rooster Saloon", I overheard a conversation taking place regarding a "tunnel discovery" beneath that very same village.

Two Britishers "picked up" from Governor Porfirio Diaz's own hands, the deed to some lake property and the "mining rights" to somewhere else, I wasn't sure of. One of the 'Brits' even gave the Governor a little gold monkey their boss had found nearby!" gasped Menchaca.

"Captain, try and keep your head up for as long as you can. Hanging it down like you're doing, will inhibit your oxygen intake!

That's how those darn rattlers get you; the venom paralyses the muscles needed to expand your lungs so the air can fill them!

Captain, just one more question and then we'll be done. Your lips are turning a little blue; therefore, I'll be brief.

Was Porfirio Diaz paid anything by these British agents and if so, how much?" motherly questioned Milly.

There was seemingly no life left in the hunched over interviewee. Milly Francis made sure the Mexican officer wasn't playing possum by pouring a tablespoon of lantern oil into his lap and lighting it.

Jose Menchaca sprang back to life!

"Ten thousand dollars in greenbacks, you bitch!" said Jose with struggling breath.

For a little bit less than a whole minute, Milly let Tag blow off a little steam. She allowed the diamondback to pepper the Mexican officer with strikes to his unresponsive face.

Afterwards, Milly Francis placed Tag back into the purple box, returned it to the crook of her left arm and hurried off to wake up her husband.

She couldn't wait to tell him what 'a little birdie' had told her!

* * * * *

Against Paddy Welch's suggestions, General Agustin de Iturbide chose to use Captain Menchaca's 'head' as an intimidating weapon!

The Mexican emperor sent a company of his most "STRAC" cavalrymen to San Antonio de Bexar!

Jose's most memorable appendage was to be delivered to the "Coahuila's Territorial Governor", (Porfirio Diaz) in a purple hatbox. A message was attached.

Because the "Emperor" had fashioned himself into the "living-self" of "Napoleon Bonaparte", a simple "dropping off a head" would have fallen mighty short, of what Agustin imagined the people of Mexico expected of him. Iturbide therefore, provided a "formal" military parade for the San Antonian's amusement!

At the conclusion of the cavalrymen's' exhibition, there came the part in the ceremony, where the 'opposing general' was supposed to come onto the battlefield to discuss the rules of engagement. No one showed.

Disgusted and probably confused at the same time, Emperor Iturbide summoned his staff to establish their battle plan. A cotton white wall tent was set up beside a blazing and yet, comfortable fire.

The drill team's band played, "Beethoven's Symphony #6" (Pastorale) while the officers dined.

When the after dinner drinks were served and just as Agustin was getting down to 'hardtacks', Porfirio Diaz's snipers commenced firing!

From the silhouettes projected onto the wall tent's cotton white roof, the Texas buffalo hunters (six of them) turned the inside of Iturbide's meeting area into a slaughter house!

Due to the distance from where the shooters launched their rounds, the five man 'symphony' did not realize the horrid incident had happened until the officer's tent went up in flames!

Miraculously, the emperor and two of his lieutenants, survived. Upon gathering his wits about him, Agustin Iturbide ordered his bugler to 'blow' the "Attack Command"; but, since his blue-chip drill performers only carried lances, he changed his directive to the "Retreat Command".

Out of the ninety nine men who gallantly left out of Piedras Negras, twelve hours earlier, only nine (badly injured) returned. Of the living, "9", each soldier had a different and almost conflicting, account of what happened in San Antonio.

Realizing that her husband's business colleague was an embarrassment and that Paddy could rightfully be criticized for choosing an idiot to partner up with, Milly Francis and Tag paid a visit to the compound's infirmary!

With the Emperor dead, so went the laws mandated during his decade long rule. The tumultuous struggle for control of Mexico's "presidency" began to show its talons!

But now that Iturbide was gone, his 'namby-pamby' feelings toward Mexico's expansion into America, became a burning affixation!

Milly saw that scenario as a very dangerous threat to her husband's standing within the "Mexican Federalist Party".

Before Paddy Welch got himself "drowned" in the shifting sands of war, someone with both political and military power, had to be bought!

If the El Dorado gold tunnel, in truth, continued its path beneath San Antonio, she had to identify a "Spartacus" among those already high up the military chain of command!

Milly needed a man who would mount a grand steed and charge into the jaws of death to protect her and a third of the world's worth, beneath her throne!

As the 'Queen' of Coahuila, Mexico, Milly would then be, the most powerful woman alive!

Chapter Nineteen

After an eleven-year struggle, Mexico gained its freedom from Spain. Much like the American war with Britain, many heroes were born from those revolutions but so too, were those still loyal to their royal motherland!

The now deceased, Emperor of Mexico (Agustin de Iturbide) had allowed the American colonists to settle in "Texas". About the only condition he placed on his Anglo guests was, "they had to become Catholics".

Consequently, it wasn't long before the Mexican territory of "Texas" was bought up, fenced off, and filled with men and women who could shoot well. In addition, they liked living in Mexico.

With a "war challenge" such as having the boxed up head of one of their own officer's delivered to Coahuila's governor, the petri dish was perfectly prepared to spawn a new breed of protagonist.

The village's boys developed woodies at the thoughts of the 'last night' before marching off to war!

So, there it was, the liberal-leaning "Federalists" and the dictatorial "Centralists" fighting with clawhammers, over a thousand miles of desert.

* * * * *

Perhaps it was "power" the winners were after; nevertheless, it was time for Paddy Welch to figure out a way to clean out the north running tunnel before 'someone's' army found out about it. Milly had the answer.

Throughout the evening, Paddy Welch schooled his spouse on the "do's and do nots" of intermingling in a city the size of San Antonio!

He cautioned her about the slave chasers who were known to snatch up attractive squaws here and there!

Mostly, the Niburian and Milly spent their last few hours together going over the terrain map of the "Halo Lake property".

Welch's directive was for Milly to search out the Coahuila Territory's Governor (Porfirio Diaz).

She was to find out everything there was to know about the two agents from London. Once the governor was located, she was to kill him and dispose of his body.

Only minutes after Milly left her husband's study, she deliberately disobeyed his "orders"; instead, the "lady" chose to arrive "uptown" in style!

Milly slid on her red dress.

* * * * *

Gaging from the looks Milly got when she galloped into "San Antonio", one would have thought the forty-year-old woman was a "blue-blooded" Spaniard!

She rode into town (sidesaddle) on a coal black stallion.

As San Antonio de Bexar was under military rule, four of General Cos's twelve hundred troops, assisted the crimson clad lady from her horse's side.

A striking young captain welcomed her to "General Antonio Lopez de Santa Anna's Headquarters".

Having read everything written in the 'military files' on Santa Anna, Milly was prepared to weave her way into the man's heart. Afterall, besides being gorgeous and rich, the "general officer" had the power to protect her from Paddy's reaction when he realized she had double crossed him!

An oriental woman introducing herself as, "Ming" approached the meticulously groomed Milly Francis. The dainty servant gracefully poured a cup of tea for the awaiting subject(Milly) of the encampments' trash talk!

In her mind, 'it was the ideal setting for the laying of leathery eggs filled with deadly mistruths'!

The first 'hatchling' slithered out when Milly introduced herself as, "Maria de los Delores de Tosta"!

"It is indeed an honor to have you here in San Antonio de Bexar!

As, I am sure you can imagine, the General is very busy; therefore, it would be my pleasure to present to my "master", the nature of your visit?

Perhaps in the spirit of time consciousness, I may be able to convey certain considerations you wish to share with General Santa Anna.

In essence, Madam, how might we be of service to you?" politely asked Ming.

"At the risk of sounding pythonic, Ming, I would recommend you swiftly shuffle your bowed-up feet into "Master Antonio's" quarters and tell him that he has an "American spy" in his waiting room!

Also explain to General Santa Anna, 'I have the names of those mounting a "coup" against him and it would be prudent if we met in an 'alone' setting'!

The reason I ask for the privacy is for his own safety; because, at this very moment, he has three separate forces burrowing their ways beneath this city!

'Ming', tell the General, 'Maria de los Delores de Tosta holds for him and only for him, the keys to his North and South American reign!'" boldly stated Milly.

When Ming darted away, Francis took it upon herself to "photographically" memorize the mass of information she could get close enough to see.

As soon as she heard the clicking of spurred boots coming toward her, the "Shawnee" inserted her right forefinger into her vagina and lightly dabbed the essence behind her ears.

While Milly waited for the Mexican statesman to come for her, she listened to the vibrations of whispering voices, scraping shoe soles, and neighing horses. It sounded as if, the building was being evacuated.

Enduring an agonizing three seconds of listening to the masculine 'clinks' of spurs tapping against wood and leather, "Antonio de Padua Maria Severino Lopez de Santa Anna y Perez de Lebron" entered the main foyer where Milly Francis was seated. Their undisguised eyes locked into the others'!

"Ming mentioned, there was an attractive lady wishing to speak with me; however, she neglected to say, that once this mystery woman was viewed, her host would risk his own life just to see her again. I am Antonio Lopez…..."

"If you don't mind, Antonio, let's skip the "gumming" and share a hug together!

It has been a long time since you felt a 'real' woman close to you, no?" said the hard breathing Red Stick.

"Indeed!" answered the visibly erect Mexican general.

"It has been so long since "Lopez" and "Manuela" have seen their son; they say to me, "We are sorry for the dissuading attempts to uproot your military career!".

Manuela wanted me to tell you, "your children are well and happy. Their mother's death has only expedited their maturity.

Both Manuel and Antonio have enrolled as cadets in the, "Fijo de Veracruz Regiment"" just as you did!

Your daughters, "Maria" and "Mariadel" have become scholars in their own rights; they are nuns now!

I am here as a "gift" from your mother and father; "we" were married two months ago, I understand!" Blushingly said Milly.

"This is quite a shock!" breathlessly said Santa Anna as he stumbled backwards into a seat.

Milly kneeled in front of her groom and skillfully performed fellatio. Following a morning of pelvic bludgeoning, the General and his bride, 'Maria de Los Dolores de Tosta' announced from the headquarters' front porch, their formal marriage plans!

Santa Anna ordered a steer to be slaughtered, "Priest Miguel Hidalgo y Costilla" to perform the ceremony, and Cos's entire regiment to freely imbibe from several casks of ales to be rolled out onto the parade ground.

The military band would perform for those officers and their companions, invited to the ball following Father Costilla's "ostentatious" ceremony. Milly glowed with joy.

It was during the first months of Milly's and Santa Anna's marriage, control of Mexico's "up for grabs" presidency was of utmost concern to the General's wife!

"General Martin Perfecto de Cos" (Santa Anna's brother in law) was the only qualified contender; therefore, Milly had to remove him from the running!

Without her husband's consent and following a 'steamy' encounter with a captain, "Maria de Tosta" ordered a message to be posted on the village of "Gonzales's" courthouse door!

It "officially" announced, "All immigrants (those not holding Mexican Citizenship) are to leave the country within ninety days!"

To upset the town's eighty percent American expatriates even further than they already were, Milly demanded, under General Cos's signature, the townsfolk demolish the statue of Mexico's previous president, "Augustin de Iturbide"!

The townsfolk had commissioned the brass image to honor the president who put into the Mexican "Constitution", "land bought by Americans automatically granted them citizenship"!

Maria de Tosta's dalliance partner, "Captain Juan Ramirez" dragged the thing sixty miles back to San Antonio where Iturbide's monument was reconstructed on the business side of the compound's gallows!

It looked like the hooded "Augustin" was ready to "drop" upon command!

Unaware of his wife's subterfuge, Santa Anna was awakened by three simultaneous cannon blasts!

When the General arrived at the front gate's wall, there where hundreds of Gonzales village's armed men demanding entry into the bricked up Mexican capitol of San Antonio de Bexar!

They were hoisting a 'white flag' above their leader's head.

From between the timbers of San Antonio's reinforced gate, "the Man of Destiny", the reference Santa Anna's first wife used to describe him, opened up a dialogue with the man holding the 'flag of truce'.

"I am, "General Antonio Lopez de Santa Anna" of the Mexican Army!

You and your men have committed an egregious crime by approaching a military compound with hostile intent!

But laying that aside for a moment, what is the reason for this squirrel rifle brigade's presence in San Antonio de Bexar?

Don't you realize, with the simple flick of my wrist, I can order your men 'cut to ribbons'?" Questioned Santa Anna in a firm way.

"Most certainly, General Santa Anna; however, as you and I know, you, Sir, are a man possessing scruples!

More importantly, you are an intrepid soldier and thusly, you know what a hostile force "does not" look like!

I am, "Colonel Ben Milam of the Texas Volunteers". We are here to present to the Mexican government a document designed to convince the Federalists that "we", the Texans, desire, only, to preserve the "1824 Constitution" guaranteeing the "rights" of everyone living on their bought and paid for soil!

Our intention, is to avoid conflict if at all possible; although, we will defend our land as legal Mexican citizens with lead and steel, if we must!

Therefore, I shall return your purple cap box with "our publication" at the base of this gate; it is entitled, "The Declaration of Causes"!

In it, you will see the needs and complaints of those whom for decades, have been your neighbors, friends, husbands and wives!

It is our sincere wish to live in harmony with you and "our" fellow countrymen."

"Colonel Milam, I shall deliver the "Declaration" to "General Jose Joaquin de Arredondo" tomorrow. Should he have a response to the Texans' requests, where can you, be contacted?" politely asked General Santa Anna.

"To the same place you sent Captain Jose Menchaca's 'head' and from where you dragged off Agustin de Iturbide's 'statue'!

'Gonzales' is where I shall be, General!" gruffly stated Milam.

Without any delay, two hundred Texans turned their horses around as if they were connected by leg chains, and rumbled off toward the west. Through the slits in the compound's front gate, the man, Antonio Lopez watched the Texans ride away in a cloud of dust.

Still stunned by Colonel Milam's accusations concerning a "head" and a "statue" of his former commander, "being dragged off", General Santa Anna called a formation.

When Santa Anna recognized the purple box the "Declaration of Causes" was delivered in and noticed the aforementioned statuesque theatrically teetering on the gallows' trapdoor, he cancelled his earlier "troop formation" order and sternly demanded that 'all' of his senior officers meet with him in his quarters!

Because "Captain Juan Ramirez" was not a senior ranking officer, it was not difficult for Milly to lure the young man into an empty barracks. Once again, her undulating throat muscles bought her another favor.

This time, it was for a handful of sharpshooters who were to circle around Colonel Milam's company of volunteers, ambush them, kill "Ben Milam", and then return to Santa Anna's headquarters as if nothing had happened.

Milly's thoughts were on, 'she and her husband (Santa Anna) escaping the inferno which was about to blast over every square inch of San Antonio'!

Once General Santa Anna dismissed his staff officers, he entered his quarters to find a tub of tepid water awaiting his submersion into it!

'Milly' scantily dressed as a housemaid, rubbed him down with oatmeal soap and a sea sponge. The Red Stick then announced a surprise she had prepared for him.

After a good long puff of opium and two mouthfuls of corn whiskey, Milly led her blindfolded husband up to the roof of his adobe styled billet. Carefully, she helped him into a fully inflated hot air balloon and off they went!

A warm wind was blowing in from the Gulf of Mexico at six miles per hour. The stars were out and twinkling at a quarter moon. No one from below noticed their liftoff.

Following a long kiss, Milly showed Antonio a map of where they were flying to. Since 'Piedras Negras' was a five hour ride, they had lots of time to mentally count their 'golden eggs' before they were greeted by the man (Paddy Welch), Milly was anxious for him to meet!

* * * * *

'Paddy Welch was rumored to be, the most powerful man in both Americas!

He was the curator for a 'godawful collection' of fighters the American NEWSPAPERS said, "was a 'threat' greater than "Britain"!

Welch owned the 'southern' three hundred mile ,tunnel's worth, of the El Dorado gold and was willing to join forces with Santa Anna(him) for fifty percent of the northern half of the tunnel's value.' Or at least, that was the "shibboleth" permeating Milly's and Antonio's conversations during their redeye flight to Piedras Negras.

Dawn welcomed the sight of a silvery ribbon snaking to and from the horizon. They were forty nine minutes from touchdown.

The weather prognosis: an uneventful landing atop the "Serranias del Burro Plateau".

* * * * *

More than a thousand torches surrounded the landing zone. Each one was held by either a Red Stick or a person who for some reason or another, had a quarrel with the Americans.

All were dressed in Mexican infantry attire!

A circle of brass cannons, fifteen in all, and each pointing away from the '"X"' marked' landing site, fired a volley of harmless smoke rings across the "Nuberian Headquarters" and the Rio Grande River.

The "Texas-Mexicans" across the river at, "Eagle Pass" gleefully applauded and set off fireworks as the balloon touched down.

"Bocanegra's", "Mexicans, at the Cry of War" blared out from the tent set up, on the northernmost corner of the plateau; it was the "Mexican National Anthem"!

Wearing a Mexican admiral's uniform, Paddy Welch saluted the dazzling newlyweds which was then duplicated by the columns upon columns of sharp and ready soldiers, honoring the, "Napoleon Bonaparte of the Americas"!

A red carpet was rolled out, the band started up a rib-rattling tune, while precious bronzed skinned girls tossed flower petals onto the path, "The Queen of Coahuila" was to walk upon.

As Milly approached her throne, little children swarmed around her like cubs suckling a honeycomb.

Drumrolls announced, "Admiral Welch" was about to speak. Spotlights spun around the plateau's surface stoking the soldiers up for a show that was to be put on for the crowd proclaiming "Welch", "The King of Mexico"!

* * * * *

Even with Lord Horatio Alvarez of the Nells' map of the "Sonora Caverns", it took him and Sir Francis George two days to find the entrance into it!

Finally, the tunnel's opening was discovered behind a waterfall that crashed directly into the "Medina River" and which, fed "Halo Lake"!

Armed with "Davy Lamps" to prevent "minedamp" flareups, the Culpers inched toward the southeast, traveling about fifty yards an hour. The windmill Sir Francis constructed, pumped only the minimal amount of oxygen needed for the men; but, it was safer with a partner even if there wasn't a plentiful amount of air.

Nelson and George intended to reach "Crystal Palace" in three days. Water and steep crevices were the most feared obstacles; however, poisonous gas certainly came in "high" on the "danger chart"!

As Andy had said, "Take the load of pyrite knickknacks and begin lightly dispersing them when you reach "The Butterfly". Make it appear as though the heavier and thusly more valuable things, were deposited in the southern split of the "Crystal Palace".

Organize the "glittery" pieces in such a way, so that, Paddy's soldiers will believe that they have found the last portion of the entombed, "El Dorado gold"!

After 'treasure seeding' the lower side of the 'palace', set your charges at both of the exits coming from the "Valley of Ice" and the mouth of the "White Giants". When the moment comes, the water from "Halo Lake" will drown them like river rats!"

Seventy two hours after finding the entrance into the Sonora Cavern, the 'Scot' and the Irishman returned to the earth's surface. No sooner had they polished off a bottle of scotch when out of the south, they heard the sounds of someone hard riding a horse their way!

It was Governor Porfirio Diaz and he was yelling something as he rode into hearing range!

"Gentlemen, praise the lord, I found you. Much has happened since our meeting at the "Red Rooster"!

There was a spy (Captain Jose Menchaca) in our midst while the transactions regarding the Halo Lake mineral rights were taking place!

He told General Iturbide about it, who in turn, decapitated the Captain and sent, rather ceremoniously, the poor man's head to "me" in a purple box!

I have just received orders from the newly acclaimed "dictator" of Mexico, "Antonio Lopez de Santa Anna" to remove all "nonbirth citizens" from the country!

Paddy Welch and his wife, Milly Francis have finally surfaced in 'Piedras Negras'. They, along with Mexico's newly 'elected' "President", 'Santa Anna' have unified their armies and are bent on attacking America!

From an 'interviewed' Mexican lieutenant, we learned, 1,200 of General Cos's cavalrymen have been moved into San Antonio de Bexar which, by the way, has been placed under military law!

"Wanted: Dead or Alive" posters have been nailed on every flat wooden surface in the "Coahuila Territory". Our "heads" carry a bounty for a measly thousand bucks a piece!

Jackson has ordered me back to Washington. I am on my way there now!

He requests, the two of you, meet up with agent, "Ben Milam" at Gonzales this Sunday. Milam will be at the village's central well at noon.

Andy's orders are to destroy Cos's troops, burn their bodies and level San Antonio to the ground!

Afterwards, Ben Milam is to move his men east to, "Fair Oaks Ranch" where "Colonels Neill, Houston, and Bowie" will join up with them at the, "Cascade Rapids".

According to Jackson's 'prediction', the Mexicans will push no further north than San Antonio de Bexar. But, if they do, the "Invisibles" and the "New Orleans Greys" are to annihilate them, in total!"

* * * * *

At the precise millisecond that Governor Porfirio Diaz raised his hand to bid his Culper partners' a farewell, a single bullet passed through his brain!

Nelson looked at his watch; the distant rifle's report came five seconds later. A sniper was stalking them!

"This guy's a pro, Sir Francis!" whispered Nelson Alvarez.

"You're damn right he is; that was a thousand yard shot!" exclaimed the 'Scot'.

"Fourteen hundred!"

"By the looks of Diaz's head, the shooter used a small caliber bullet. Judging from the exit wound, this guy was going for 'distance' rather than a 'knock-down' hit!

As you can see, the 'entrance and exiting' holes have the same circumferences. Nelson, I believe our hunter is using silver bullets!"

"Because of the consistent bullet track?" asked the Nell.

"That, and the ricochet splash left on the edge of this wagon wheel!

Look for yourself, you'll see that the residue is not lead but in actuality, 'silver'!"

"Well, Sir Francis, if you are correct and I have no doubt of your assertion's accuracy, then we, my friend, have a Nib on our tails!

We're either going to have to kill him here or escape and hope we can bushwhack him if the sonofabitch continues to follow us!

Which is your choice, mi amigo?" politely asked Lord Horatio Alvarez.

"I have been pondering that myself, Lord Alvarez!

My first impulse is to put some distance between us and the shooter; contrarily, my experience insists, we catch him and drain out every bit of the information he has locked up within his skull and then send him to hell!"

"Given, our being pinned down by a Niburian marksman of the highest order, that sounds like a marvelous plan! What'd you have in mind, Sir Francis?"

Suddenly a buzzing sound whipped above the crouched down Culpers. Five seconds later, another one followed.

Their wagon's horses fell to the ground without a twitch from either! Forehead shots had taken them both.

"Do you suppose, he's perched somewhere or moving toward us?

Between Diaz's killing round and those shots dropping our horses, I'm guessing, the shooter is not in a fixed location. I think, he's about a thousand yards to the northwest of us." said Lord Alvarez in a whispering voice.

"And he's firing from a mountain top...." Sir Francis was saying when it simultaneously dawned on them, there were no "higher elevations" surrounding their location!

At the same time, they saw the same thing; the hydrogen fueled flame (viewed from the ground) centered in the underbelly of a hot air balloon!

The pilot dropped a sparkling grenade from the passenger basket.

Like beached tadpoles making their way back to a puddle, the agents slid into the "Medina River". They dove very deeply into the depths of the slow moving water.

At twelve feet below the Medina's surface, the concussion made their noses bleed.

Culpers learned during "SERE" school to use their leg dagger's scabbards as underwater breathing tubes. For only a dot of a second, Sir Francis saw through the translucent river water, their pursuer. It was Milly Francis!

* * * * *

Northwesterly winds brought a mixture of freezing rain along with two hundred of Colonel Ben Milam's armed horsemen. The Texas volunteers started firing their pistols at Milly's rising balloon.

Pieces of the passenger's basket began falling to the ground. Droplets of blood marked snow provided the direction of the Red Stick's escape.

Milam and his men only stayed long enough to see that the "Europeans" made it out of the "Medina" alive; before, they attacked Cos's troops in San Antonio de Bexar.

Spies had said, 'General Martin Perfecto de Cos's staff officers were billeted in the village's mission known to its congregation as the, "Alamo"'.

The fighting in Bexar raged with a house-to-house assault unlike anything the Mexican army had before experienced. Cos finally flew the white flag of surrender from his Alamo compound on December the ninth.

More than a third of his regiment were either dead or wounded; therefore, the General signed papers of "Capitulation". This "gave" the Texans all public property, money, arms and ammunition in San Antonio!

By Christmas Day, the Mexican Army was back across the Rio Grande.

* * * * *

Milly Francis was in bad shape. She had been struck by nine bullets, two of them, still remained lodged in her body; but, it was the loss of blood that had practically killed her.

Although, now off "death's doorstep", there was a strong probability her left leg would have to be amputated!

Irrespective of Milly's condition, again, Paddy insisted they go through the details concerning the men "she failed to kill"!

He especially wanted to know about the equipment Milly "should have seen" in the back of the Europeans' wagon!

Twice, the treating physicians had to forcibly remove Welch from the recovery room due to the effect he was having on the infirmary's other patients!

The third time, the chief surgeon called for the guards on duty; however, they refused to ruffle the feathers stuck into their supreme leader's flesh!

In an act born from utter frustration or maybe just out of pure stupidity, the Lisbon born physician, reached down and grabbed Paddy Welch by the scruff of his neck and threw him out of the operating room!

Soon afterwards, that same surgeon was standing (blindfolded) in front of a firing squad!

When the volley of rifle fire rattled the town's windows with their thunderous roars, Santa Anna dismissed his head maid and then dressed up in his "Napoleonic" replicated uniform.

Promptly after reaching the corner of the parade field where the gunpowder's smoke was still hanging in the trees, he saw Paddy walk up to his battalion's only surgeon and unnecessarily shoot the already executed man in the head!

For fear of antagonizing his "host" any further than he already had, Santa Anna diplomatically proposed a working lunch for the two of them in the "Captains Mess Hall".

There was one stipulation to that request: Both men had to immediately challenge the other to a drinking contest!

Once Paddy gulped down his third glass of corn whiskey, he mellowed down a bit; but, Antonio Santa Anna still found he had to 'walk on egg shells' during their staggard conversations.

"Paddy, General Cos lost slightly over two hundred of his men day before yesterday. He's under a suicide watch and locked up in the stockade, as we speak.

Speaking of tragedies, it is my understanding, at the hands of an aerial mishap, my precious "Maria" (Milly) suffered a pretty sharp spill!

The dead surgeon over there behind the drill field, prohibited me from visiting with her; thankfully, you ridded me of that "problem"!

How is she?" asked Santa Anna with a coy grin on his face.

As though he had just dropped in from the moon, Paddy Welch finished off the inch deep bottom of his whiskey glass and turned toward Mexico's dictator with an angry looking stare.

Antonio was asked a deadly serious question.

"Who, in your estimation, is the most lethal soldier in your army, General?

I'm talking about a fighter who can shoot the eye out of a flying sparrow while cutting the head off of a sidewinder, sort of guy!

Antonio, do you know a man such as this?"

"I most certainly do; his name is, "Illinois Johnson"." Quickly responded Santa Anna.

"Where is he right now?" coolly asked Welch.

"I'm sure, he's nested up in some tree just outside the compound. Why do you ask, Sir?" asked Santa Anna in a shy way.

"Antonio, never question me again!

I want Big Warrior to take command of the Red Sticks and what remains of Cos's regiment. You and your gaily dressed staff of pansies, can head up the northern march; although, the Shawnee chiefs will 'spearhead' the attack!

Is that completely understood?" rudely asked Welch.

"When will we have the opportunity to explore the tunnel, Paddy?" Cooley asked Santa Anna.

"In this battle, you understand, there will be no prisoners!

Should any of your' or Big Warrior's men return, then, and only then, will that obnoxiously stupid question, be relevant!

You have 8,000 men to lose, General; that is, if you are not victorious. Should that be the case and all of those brave warriors are either dead or laying in a hot field crying for their mothers, remember, my friend, you must die, as well!

Yet, on the other hand, if the opposite occurs and you invite me to visit your "conquered city", we together, I promise this, will venture into the northern tunnel and pluck golden trinkets up as if they were fallen pears!

That indeed, will be a glorious day, now won't it?

I shall expect your scouting party to leave the compound by midnight. Also, send me this "Johnson" fellow.

Does he go by any other 'first' name rather than, "Illinois"?"

"Just, "Illinois Johnson". He claims to have grown up in the wild!

"Word" has it, some local "Iroquois" called him by that name. Anything else, Admiral?" curtly asked, Santa Anna.

Paddy shook his head with a dismissing air. He returned Antonio's salute but only after the two men's eyes were examined by the other.

Both men knew, the other, hoped for the other's, early death!

The harsh commands coming from the Mexican officers mixed with the "clip-clop" sounds of oxen pulling tons of supplies, almost blotted out the foot taps at the base of his office's door. Paddy knew it was Big Warrior.

"I shan't come in, Paddy. We are pulling out now!

"Tiger Tail" and I will travel up the "Nueces River" until we reach "Choke Canyon". There, we will split our men into two battalions and circumnavigate San Antonio in opposite directions.

We'll attack from "Fair Oaks Ranch" after General Santa Anna's army arrives. They are following the "Hondo Creek Road" and will launch their offensive from the south.

I plan to put fire to the city the first week of February!

With a little luck, we should be sipping white wine and tasting their women by the fifteenth of that month. So farewell, my friend!"

Welch watched the old warrior mount his favorite warhorse. Tiger Tail raised his right hand high into the air, circularly spun his finger around three times, and then with his left fist, raised his scalp laden lance toward the heavens!

Sparked by the Mingo's silent command, 6,000 Red Sticks lightly trotted away!

Santa Anna, the self-styled 'Napoleon of the West', marched at the head of his massive regiment of 2,000 lance carrying cavalrymen.

They blew horns and beat drums as they left the barricaded village of Piedras Negras.

As Paddy Welch was closing the front door to his office, a sparrow hawk flew through the swiftly closing opening and clamped her talons into the Niburian's face!

The fowl's beak dispatched tuffs of Paddy's hair as it tried to crack into his skull. A whistle's shrill blast stopped the hawk's attack.

""Princess" I'm afraid, went a little overboard on you, Admiral. She's been cooped up too long, I recon!

Anyway, she'll sit right here on my shoulder and behave herself. I'm "Johnson". You wanted to see me?"

"Goddamn! That's a dangerous weapon you have there, Johnson!"

"She's pulled me out of some mighty tight spots. Princesses' momma was even better than she was, though!

What'd you want from me, Admiral?" bluntly asked Illinois Johnson.

"Son, have a seat. May I get anything for you or Princess, Mister Johnson?"

"We're fine." Answered the feral human.

"Tell me, 'Illinois Johnson', what is the most important "thing" in your life? In this big wide world, what means the most to you?" asked Paddy.

"I think, it would be, 'my being left alone; I don't like people but I do, animals!'"

"Are you familiar with the, "Sonora Caverns" beneath "Halo Lake", Johnson?"

"I've been there." Briskly answered Illinois.

"Did you know, I own it?" questionably pushed Welch.

"No, I didn't."

"If it were yours, what would you do with it, my brave young soldier?"

"Probably, never leave it!

I'd, well, me and my animals, would stay out of everybody's way and 'mess up' anyone who'd bother us!" yelled Johnson.

"Do you read, Mister Johnson?" asked Paddy in a priestly manner.

"Never needed to learn. I can count real good!"

"Would you be able to sign your name on a "deed" if I awarded you an underground plantation?

You could do whatever you wanted to do with it!" sharply said Welch.

"I reckon, I'd do about anything for a shot at that offering!

What'd it take so we could make our marks on that deed?" innocently questioned Illinois Johnson.

"Until last month, signing over the "Sonora Caverns" would have been no more complicated than taking a quick jaunt up to San Antonio and paying Governor Porfirio Diaz for his seal.

Sadly, Illinois, our friend, "Porfirio" has chosen to side with the "Anglos" and sell "your" ranch to a pair of Europeans for a "song and a dance"!

Frankly, I'm not sure our men can beat the Texans in their own backyard! Plus, if America were to wade into the boundary dispute, all those bored patriots who would prefer to take a bullet rather than face life's last stretch, would pick up their dusty sabers and rush down here just looking for a fight!

And if the U.S. Navy decided to join in on the fray, Mexico would eventually be divided up into 'manageable' states and become the prison colonies of North America!

So..., if you want the cavern for your very own, you will have to enter 'it' somewhere around, "Lake Halo". There is no way to know how complex the cave system actually is; hopefully, the map I'll give you, should solve that conundrum!

Basically, this is 'our' agreement, "you diagram the cavern's network, kill the two Englanders and Governor Diaz, bring me their foreskins, a legible schematic of the cavern's infrastructure, and the deed is yours!

Do you have any questions, Illinois?"

"Only one. Where will we meet to collect my papers?" bluntly asked the deadly marksman.

"An excellent question!

It is believed, the Sonora Caverns extend beneath the Rio Grande River. If that is so, and you emerge west of "Eagle Pass", the world will then become your oyster!

Not only will I deed the property over to you, I'll also throw in a troop of nine monkeys!

Illinois, "Governor Diaz" could easily point them out to you but my guess is, he's hightailed it as far away from San Antonio, as he can ride. He knows damn well, war is imminent!

Additionally, for your information, in all likelihood, those "Europeans" are U.S. Secret Agents. It is also probable, as we speak, those two Culpers are somewhere close to Halo Lake!

Poke around and find the farthermost entranceway into the Sonora Caverns. Once you find it, you are to make your way to the "west" for as far as you can go!

When you emerge on this side of the Rio Grande River, my assistants will bring you back here for the formal signing of your property's deed!

It is supposed, your information gathering journey will take you thirty days. Mine nor Santa Anna's forces will attack the Texans until you are safely out of the cavern.

In the meantime, get packed up!

I'll be ballooning you to Halo Lake in six hours, Mister Johnson?"

"Alright."

Chapter Twenty

The siege of Bexar and Cos's surrender had embarrassed Santa Anna. With 'blood in his eye', Mexico's commanding general marched northward toward Bexar determined to teach the insubordinate Texans a lesson. He said he would exterminate them!

Although it was midwinter, Santa Anna pushed his army mercilessly toward the Alamo. The frigid, wind-battered deserts of northern Mexico took their toll.

Men and animals died by the hundreds; their remains were buried in the snow covered ditches along the way. The brigades straggled apart separating integral companies by miles.

When the big siege guns bogged down in a particularly nasty quagmire, Santa Anna for the sake of expediency, had them spiked and left there. Nothing was going to stop him!

"Colonel James Neill" had assumed command of the Alamo "garrison". The Culper and eighty of his men, had fortified the village so as from any direction the enemy came, "triangular fire" would cut them down!

The Texans' plan of defense was simple and deadly; e.g., once the Alamo's gate was breached, Santa Anna's soldiers would rush in where "Captain William Carey's" "Invincibles" would fire (at pointblank range) a barrage of 'double-ball and chain' cannons at the attacking men's' legs!

The "Orleans Greys" led by "Captain William Blazeby", with blistering crossfire, would then drop those still standing!

While the "Greys" and Carey's men were reloading, "Captain Robert White's" marksmen would shoot those attempting escape.

"Repeat and repeat", were Colonel Neill's orders. If they were effective, the system would continue until the darkness came.

* * * * *

Sir Francis George of the Walkers and Lord Horatio Alvarez remained very still while 'Illinois Johnson' rappelled from Welch's balloon. He skittered into a patch of woods a little southeast of Halo Lake.

Heavily packed and with a sparrow hawk fluttering around his head, the spritely man disappeared into the underbrush. Sir Francis whispered a question.

"What would you say the distance is to that balloon?"

"Seven hundred and fifty yards. Are you itching to take a shot?"

"No!

We've been waiting for this moment for far too long!

Do you really believe, I'd ruin our chance to pull ole Paddy and his merry band of scoundrels into their watery graves, Lord Horatio?" teased Sir Francis.

"One thing's for certain, wherever that strange fellow is headed for and where he ends up, will be the place in which our trap will have to be set!

It would be better however, to turn him to our side rather than kill him; do you agree?" Alvarez queried half out loud.

"I doubt if that ole boy is tamable, Nelson!

I had him under glass for several seconds and from what I could make of the man, he appeared to be as rough as a cob!"

"Wasn't that a sparrow hawk fluttering around his head?" asked the Nel.

"It sure as hell was; the guy couldn't have been over four feet tall and was carrying a backpack which must have weighed more than he did!

Nelson, he may be "catchable" but killing him appears to be our single best option at this juncture in the game!

What are your thoughts?" gruffly questioned Sir Francis.

"I say, while he's farting around in search of an entrance, let's get on down to "The Butterfly" and 'net him' while he passes beneath the "Valley of Ice"!" Answered Lord Horatio Alvarez of the Nels.

* * * * *

Although it took six hours to relay by semaphore, correspondence between 'Washington' and the "Texas revolutionary army", it was sufficient enough for their commander, "Sam Houston", to be warned of the Red Sticks' and Santa Anna's forces moving toward 'San Antonio de Bexar'!

General Houston set out immediately to scour the "Texas Territory" for enlistees. Before he left, he sent "Colonel Jim Bowie" and twenty five other Culpers, with orders to destroy the Alamo fortifications and retire westward with the captured artillery to, "Fair Oaks Ranch".

Bowie and Neill agreed, it would be impossible to remove the two dozen Mexican cannons without oxen, mules or horses; however, they deemed it foolhardy to abandon that much firepower especially since Captain Carey's 'Invincibles' were known to be the deadliest artillerymen in all the world. Therefore, the Alamo would be the battleground!

Knowing that General Houston needed time to raise a sizable army to repel Santa Anna, Bowie set about reinforcing the Alamo after Neill's leg was amputated on account of gangrene.

Luckily, Colonel William Travis and his posse of slave hunters, were bribed with so much "phony money" they agreed to stick around until the advertised 'skirmish' was settled.

This brought up the number of San Antonio's defenders to one hundred and thirty men.

Spies told Travis, "the Mexican brigade had already crossed the Rio Grande", he did not think Santa Anna could move his soldiers the hundred and seventy five wind torn miles of desert, before Spring.

While Jim Bowie's volunteers built barriers and dug trenches, Travis's band of cavalry regulars scattered out over a two days' ride trying their dead level bests, to muster up some fighters to join their cause!

They found fourteen Tennesseans which brought the garrison's defensive number to one hundred and ninety four.

Among the "Tennessee Mounted Volunteers" was a close friend of Andrew Jackson's, "David Crockett". He was there, the day "Richard Lawrence" attempted his presidential assassination and was now the only person in Mexico, who could identify Paddy Welch!

As Travis's recruiting unit rode into view of San Antonio, they along with Crockett and his roughriders, drew their horses to a halt. The Tennesseans were flabbergasted by what they saw!

Thousands of white tents and campfires blanketed the village's surrounding hills. Smells of roasting meat hung in the groves of trees.

Time was up!

* * * * *

Because he drew the shortest straw, "Captain Albert Martin" stood up from the officers' dining table, saluted his compatriots and promptly left the Alamo's sanctuary.

With him, was a "plea" written to anyone who "cared" and could shoot a rifle. It read, "To the People of Texas and All Americans in the World…I shall never surrender or retreat….Victory or Death!".

Captain Martin was knocked off his horse by a single bullet; the shot was fired from a distance in excess of a thousand yards. No one came to check on the body so the horse returned to the Alamo.

* * * * *

Milly Francis could have chewed nails when she realized "Piedras Negras" had been evacuated. Her gunshot wounds had almost healed which was why, she was so angry!

Paddy had "spiked" her medications with powdered "valerian root". The Niburian's concoction made her sleep about three days longer than she was supposed to. Milly's suspicions grew darker.

According to the town's blacksmith named, "Tom-Tom", Santa Anna's two thousand man army, pulled out for San Antonio on "Tuesday", he said.

As it was Friday, that left only one more question for Tom-Tom to answer.

"Admiral Welch and a mean little sonofabitch going by the name of, "Illinois Johnson" took that "shot up" balloon of yours and followed the Red Sticks who took the easterly route toward Bexar!

They left the night before the 'General' did!" Nervously muttered Tom-Tom.

The livid Red Stick spun out of the blacksmith's shop and marched directly toward her palatial housing. When she opened her closet doors, Milly's heart sank; Paddy had stolen her shoes, every pair of them!

Now, more than ever, Francis was sure that "Welch" was cutting her out of the northern tunnel's treasure!

With a week's head start and provided she had some breaks, her only chance of catching up with her husband was to enter the "Sonora Cavern" from its southwestern entrance and make her way (underground) to the "Sponge Rooms".

She would ambush him at "Devil's Pit"!

After scrounging through the Red Stick's barracks, Milly found enough gear to pack on a couple of horses' backs. The other two pack animals were loaded down with a "ton" of gunpowder.

Milly smacked the reigns as she sped off toward the cavern's only known entrance. Tom-Tom genuflected on both knees as "loco-queen" rode off.

* * * * *

Andrew Jackson was having another bout of insomnia. For the fifth night in a row, his nightmares had dumped him into a state of frenetic unconsciousness.

Deliberate activities such as fetching the latest semaphore postings from beneath the mail slot, comparatively, was akin to him, fist fighting underwater!

Welch's infliction was doing its job; Andy was dying.

Hannah had learned from years of living with the man, when Jackson had those jags, a glass of milk, a quarter cup of pure honey and a pint of whiskey (generally) would settle him into an unconscious state.

His mind was on Texas!

"Sweetheart, it's four o'clock; come on back to bed!" sleepily exclaimed Hannah.

"I'll be there in a minute; I'm going to stoke up this fire and jot a quick note to Sam Houston!

In lieu, of all the hell coming his way, I thought it might lighten his spirits to know, I shall be sending him a "seasoned cavalry company's worth of help"!" Answered the president in a distracted manner.

"Well, Andrew, that doesn't seem like it would be much trouble to find a couple of thousand 'bored out of their minds' soldiers willing to fit that bill!

Afterall, America hasn't been at war for at least six months; so, I'm sure her armies are itching for a fight with someone!" Sarcastically stated Hannah as she handed him a jug of whiskey without the previously mentioned sides.

""Cocoa", because of tax free and dirt cheap land, thousands of southerners have moved into the Texas territory. With Mexico's "Napoleon" running the show down there and threatening to expel those "Tejanos" from their own country, they're wanting military protection from us!" said Jackson.

"You haven't called me that since the Hermitage, Andy!

'Hot Cocoa' and the 'Tennessee Stud', kicked up quite a ruckus at times, didn't we?" cooed Hannah.

"Yes we did, my angel."

"Andy, why don't you simply "annex" Texas into the country? It sounds like the ranchers have enough political clout to carry a state's voting right?" Questioned "Cocoa".

"The 'Whigs' and northern "Abolitionists" refuse to allow another slave state into the Union; therefore, as a lame duck, I can't do much to assist them!" said Jackson.

"Then, where will you get the troops you promised Sam Houston?"

"The Cerians!" Answered the President.

"Andrew, it is my understanding, the Cerians nor the Niburians are allowed under the agreement made in eighty-eight (1788), to have any form of standing force underarms. Isn't that correct?" humbly asked Hannah.

"That is so; but, what I messaged to Houston was, 'I am sending to San Antonio a unit of cavalry soldiers', "worth of help", tomorrow'. In actuality, only one Cerian will be needed!"

* * * * *

More folded pieces of high rag paper dropped through their suite's mail shoot. Atop the Willard, a messenger ran down the stairs and back up again, only to repeat the process throughout the night!

Andrew Jackson looked bad. At 0545hrs., the message Andy was waiting for finally hit the suite's floor!

With a sigh of relief, Jackson turned toward Hannah with a smile, he spoke.

"The Cerian has made contact with "Scotch" and "Blarney"!

'Will stall Santa Anna for three more days. Houston and 1,000 to arrive. The Red Sticks will follow their scout into the eastern entrance.' He states.

"Further, this fellow, "Stephen Austin" says, that he, Sir Francis, and Lord Alvarez will lure the Mexicans into the cavern's western side.

When that is done and all the 'drowned rats are in their holes', he claims, the contents of the entire stretch of the El Eldorado tunnel system will be legally transferred over to the Cerians. He is waiting for my reply!"

"And then what?" abruptly asked Cocoa.

"And then….Santa Anna's army will be gone!

The Red Sticks will be gone. Texas will be freed from Mexico's grip and as always, the Cerians get the gold….that's the deal!

Should I sign it?" laughingly asked Andy.

"Do you have any other choice, Mister President?"

"No." answered Andrew Jackson as he sent the messenger running back upstairs.

* * * * *

Sunday morning arrived in San Antonio. Two remarkable things were happening on that azygous day: it was snowing and the sun never rose!

Church bells clanged without little bellboys riding them upward. Then came a third unexplainable phenomenon, a star rose high into the heavens!

And from the east, came three "wisemen" (dressed in hooded robes) riding camels. On the "Saspamco Mountain's" tiptop was a barn with some onlooking farm animals in the background.

From a distance, it was the most ubiquitous manger scene ever made. A blue-white star even hung seventy some feet above the stage prop's roof.

Rumors spread through the Mexican troops like a bad smell. Some said a child had been born up on the "Saspamco"; while others swore, "it was the beginning of the "Rapture"!"

Either way, the Cerian (Stephen Austin) had caught General Santa Anna's attention!

Thousands of the soldiers then realized, they were witnessing an honest to goodness miracle taking place. The camels stopped in front of the "Bethlehem set". A man rose from behind a couple of bedding cows.

The glorious figure, ascended a hundred feet into the air!

His robe, his beard, his sandals, and the goodness exuding from his heart, caused the soldiers to drop to their knees!

"Silent Night, Holy Night" as "Gruber" had written it, was sung in German by the Texans barricaded up in the Alamo Mission. The Mexican soldiers standing within feet of San Antonio's peripheral wall, joined in!

Davy Crockett's fiddle and John McGregor's bagpipes added much to the fleeting harmonious spirit. But then, 'Stephen Austin' (the Cerian) dressed as "Jesus" descended onto the village's main plaza!

He landed in the midst of the Mexican troubadours. After a "third-trimester" pause, in a reverberating holler, the Cerian spoke.

"I have come as your savior, not as your conqueror!

It was my father's wish for me to offer to every one of you, an alternative to war!

For those, who may prefer an existence crafted by god, which entitles you to an eternal life, and you are willing to lay down your weapons and follow me to the bright star just beyond the "Saspamco Mountain", then you, "Disciples", will be handed a five pound sack of gold!

Following your "initiation", you may travel the Earth in peace and doing good deeds for your awaiting brothers and sisters!"

Magically, the blue-white star began drifting toward the west but not before settling into a pause at treetop level. "It" was waiting to lead the "Christian Soldiers" who chose to follow the toga draped Cerian!

With two completed spins on top of Santa Anna's staff's dining table and a light spray of "green gas", Stephen Austin rose about forty feet into the air and flew over to the Commander's position as if he were leading a battalion of infantrymen out of the city's gates.

Eighteen hundred weaponless soldiers marched out into the "Medina" desert on that sunless day!

The officers slept at their tables while the "nonbelievers" scattered back to their tents. A light snow fell on all below.

Santa Anna's religious deserters spoke of the wonderous things they had seen. One by one, they straggled back to their units' campsites sporting a branded forehead cross and carrying a five pound bag full of gold trinkets(miniature statues of African animals).

One commonality shared by Stephen Austin's disciples was, every soldier stated, 'they had returned to Santa Anna's basecamp only to resign from the Mexican army and to invite their comrades to join them!'

"The Abode of Saints" was where they were going.

By the time Santa Anna's staff officers gained their wits about them, it was discovered, only a fifth of their command was still in the vicinity!

Some three thousand Mexican troopers had, without wearing boots, begun their pilgrimage to the western mouth of the Sonora Caverns, a.k.a., "The Abode of Saints".

After seven days and seven nights of rounding up wagonloads of lost and frostbitten soldiers, General Santa Anna managed to haul back to San Antonio all but eight hundred of his men. The "not found" were either dead or in the Sonora Cavern, it was assumed.

"Time" had provided the Texans with a host of opportunities; but, the biggest break of all, was making contact with the two operatives President Jackson had sent.

They (Sir Francis and Lord Alvarez) showed the Alamo's defenders an escape passage leading from the Parson's "outhouse" into the upper tip of the "Valley of Ice".

The Americans, within the Spanish mission, knew three days would not be enough time for Sam Houston's roughriders to get there before Santa Anna's return.

Already, his artillerymen were limbering up their field cannons. At best, they had twelve hours!

* * * * *

Milly Francis could hear the sounds of metal lanterns clanging against the cavern's sides. Voices, Latin singing ones, rose up and down in octaves as the cross-branded crusaders paraded toward "Devil's Pit".

Realizing, if she played her cards right, the "neo-zealots" could be of good use in breaking through to the cavern's eastern side. Boulders the size of well houses, blocked the passageway all through the "Sponge Rooms".

Because of certain overheard hints pertaining to the forehead crossed soldiers' reasons for entering the cavern, Milly concentrated on what was being said by the man using the most stoic vernacular.

The word "chalice" was heard several times. Consequently, the Red Stick set up a greeting table at the juncture of Devil's Pit and the Sponge Rooms.

Melting snow had raised the Rio Grande to a roaring level. The downward pointing stalactites glistened like slippery spears as droplets of water tapped onto the cavern's floor.

Two dozen candles flickered behind Milly's throne. Men began filing into the Devil's Pit.

When the soldiers were all in and seated on whatever they could find, Milly Francis stood. She was dressed as an Egyptian priestess.

"I am honored to be in your presence, Gentlemen!

As Jesus's holy disciples, you have been awarded the privilege of retrieving the "Holy Grail"!

Until now, no one has been worthy enough to place their mortal hands upon it; but, with god's grace, he has delivered you "immortals" to this place!

Instead of a prayer, it is customary to go around the body of 'anointed ones' and hear them tell their stories of how they achieved their "air-thin" standing with the holy spirit!

Listen to what they have to share; fore, it will make each of you aware of the trust the lord has put in you!

Who would like to speak first?"

"I shall testify for these pilgrims!

A while ago, I was their "First Sergeant"!

Today, I am "one" of many brothers on a mission to retrieve the relic known as the, "Holy Grail". We will return it to "Pope Gregory XVI" in Rome!

We got a boat ready and everything we need just waiting for us at the Brownsville Port!" pontificated the blood-washed first sergeant.

"Is that what my "big brother" told you?" playfully asked Milly.

"Your majesty, did you say, "big brother"? asked the smut faced sergeant.

"Of course, I did. Who else on god's green earth, would have brought you here?" jested Francis.

"Mam, please excuse my bluntness; but, who are you?"

"My name is, "Salome". I am the oldest of Jesus's three sisters.

Tell me how my brother selected such fine men as yourselves?" asked the venal woman.

"It's sort of hard to explain. One minute, we were singing carols with the Americans when a bright light appeared over what looked like, a manger scene!

We 'all' saw three camels, with riders, trotting toward the barn atop "Saspamco Mountain"!

When "your" flying brother got close to the "General" and his staff officers, he sprayed a green mist on them and then, 'SWOOSH', he flew off that damn hill like a bat out of hell! Exclaimed the 'mouse to the cobra'.

"I'll bet he flew around quite a bit since it was so windy that day, didn't he?"

"Well, yes. There were times when he would go away for a while but the "fire star" always brought him back, when we needed directions.

We must of walked twenty miles or more, we had no boots and it was snowing!" said the Mexican sergeant.

"I don't suppose you got a close look at Jesus's face, did you?

The poor boy got his eye scratched by one of my cats and I was wondering if he was still wearing an eyepatch?" innocently questioned "Salome".

"He wore no patch when I got a chance to see his face, mam." Answered the sergeant.

"Did my brother give you any specifics about what to do once you passed through the "Abode of Saints" entranceway?

Did he provide you with instructions as to where to locate the "Grail"?" pushed Milly.

"He gave us a map!

Jesus said, 'it was in a wooden box hidden in the furthest western tunnel in the "Crystal Palace"'!

"Were Jesus's eyes the same color as mine, Sergeant?" asked the Indian.

"Holy-Sister, I can't rightly say, because of the lantern light; but, from here, your eyes seem darker than his. I believe 'his' were emerald green!

If you don't mind, please point us in the direction toward the Devil's Pit. I believe you mentioned some debris standing in our way in the Sponge Rooms?"

"I can certainly see why my brother chose you valiant men!

Before we get started, gentlemen, make sure to extinguish all cigars and pipes. We are entering a long stretch that was drilled through a mountain of coal.

Unless you god-blessed folks, wish to hurry up your journeys to heaven, I suggest, you create "zero" sparks with your lanterns!

Strike not a single match nor fire a gun; because, if you do, we're all going to be blown to kingdom come!

Stay as close to the right side of the wall as you can; there is a steep drop off to the left." Excitedly whispered Milly.

* * * * *

Big Warrior and Tiger Tail were quite swift in disassembling Paddy Welch's balloon and having it moved into "Cascade Caverns". It was their staging ground.

Hundreds of Red Sticks stood silent as Paddy made his way up to the speaker's platform constructed for the occasion.

"It is good to look among your faces. Realizing you are anxious to sink your spears into those who hoodooed our land from us, let us take a few moments to reflect upon the great ones of our past!

Two brothers, "Tenskwatawa" and "Tecumseh" lived and died so that on a day such as this one, thousands of warriors would smite the white devils who traded whiskey for our lands!

We have come to join the great people of Mexico. Together, along with the rest of South America, we shall invade America!

Starting tomorrow morning, Santa Anna's soldiers will attack San Antonio; afterwards, they, the victorious Mexicans, from here to Oklahoma, will burn every village to the ground!

Within the hour, we are to follow the "Cascade" passageways as far east as we are able to. We must make quick time to Halo Lake where Big Warrior's battalion will enter the "Sonora Cavern" and come out through the parson's outhouse!

The Alamo mission's inhabitants are to be burned!

Tiger Tail's men will continue west through the Sonora passageways until they exit under the Rio Grande. Along the way, they are to extinguish the lives of all living things!

This is it, my good people; it is time to take back what is rightfully ours!"

Those Red Sticks holding javelins, began tapping them on the cavern's floor. Those taps and the sounds of fists beating against bone breast plates, from a distance, sounded just like "Tag's" rattling tail.

Throughout the quiet confusion of preparing for their departures, men began painting in the traced outline of their hands' shadows on the caverns' walls.

Long trails of peyote smoke hung slightly beneath the Cascade's ceiling while the men finished up their final testaments.

Weapons were checked for the user's safety. Lanterns were stored into each brave's backpack before they were permitted to tie onto the guide rope.

No one spoke, they carried their own opinions of what living meant to them!

Like shadows, the natives dissipated through the bored hole into the side of "Cascade Mountain".

Tiger Tail was the last man to speak with Welch before his launching. Just as the Shawnee was about to slip the anchor rope loose, he looked up at the Niburian and in a loud but warm voice, asked a fairly normal question.

"So, where are you headed for this time, old friend?"

"The Willard!" yelled the rising pilot.

"What's that?" loudly asked Tiger Tail.

"I'm going to kill Jackson!" hollered Welch.

* * * * *

On the morning of February the 23rd, San Antonio was jostled into battle by the sounds of military marching music and exploding mortar balls. Santa Anna's cavalrymen battered their way through the town's gate like a shark charging into a school of blues!

For spite, Santa Anna set up his headquarters on the exact spot where "Jesus" landed. His first command was for his standard-bearers to climb to the top of the bell tower of "San Fernando Church" and unfurl the scarlet flag of "No Quarter"!

In response to the visual message, Travis and his Texans unleashed a barrage of cannon fire while Crockett and McGregor sang a song they called, "Bloody Waterloo"!

The Tennessee sharpshooters prohibited any Mexican from exposing so much as a square inch of his body if within range of the snipers!

Blue coated bodies littered San Antonio's hard packed streets!

San Fernando's bell tower was gone!

Forced to flee the city's plaza and while in retreat, Santa Anna's artillerymen were ordered to batter the mission for twelve days and nights.

The idea was, 'to wear out the defenders inside, giving them no time to rest or sleep'.

Santa Anna reasoned, 'a weary opponent would be an easy one to defeat'. However, his thinking was far too myopic; because, within the din of battle, sleep deprivation weakened both sides!

Unable to distinguish clear targets, the Mexicans allowed courier after courier to escape from the Alamo.

On March the 2nd, racing through the enemy lines, the last group to reinforce the Alamo, arrived!

These were the relief force from 'Gonzales', the only town to answer Travis' pleas to send help!

The total number of Alamo defenders stood at between 180 and 190.

* * * * *

At 0400hrs. (March 6), Santa Anna advanced his men to within 200 yards of the Alamo's walls. Just as dawn was breaking, the Mexican bloodcurdling bugle call, "Deguello" reinforced the meaning of the once waving scarlet flag above "San Fernando"!

It was "Captain Juan Seguin's" Tejanos (native-born Mexicans fighting in the Texan army) who first heard the chilling music; but, other ears also heard it!

* * * * *

To Big Warrior, it was a signal that they were defeating the "whites"!

Illinois Johnson who was in hiding, found the bugle notes the sweetest sound he had ever heard!

Nearly a thousand Red Sticks waited in line to climb up a wooden ladder through the "papal outhouse". They were to restage in the Alamo's rose garden!

"Captain Carey's" artillerymen in order to save powder and shot, forced a local whore to do a little 'naked-struttin' so as, to catch the attention of each warrior as he climbed up the ladder.

When the brave's head came through the 'toilet's' hole, it was garroted by the man standing on the holed bench while another Texan pulled the headless Indian away!

This lasted all morning until a mortar ball made a direct hit onto the crapper's roof!

Two Anglos were killed. The strumpet was dying but even worse, the Red Sticks began pouring out of their scorched tunnel exit like singed ants!

Even Jackson's "Orleans unit", the "Greys", couldn't shoot them fast enough!

With the north wall and now, the chapel breached, Big Warrior's "Toluca Battalion" rushed toward the backs of those firing at the waves of attacking Mexicans!

Fighting was done with knives, pistols, clubbed rifles, lances, javelins, knees and fists. Not one single Indian survived nor did anyone defending the mission!

Santa Anna had lost fifteen hundred soldiers Additionally, five hundred of his men were wounded.

In three groups, twelve "death-angels" walked through the battlefield putting rounds of lead through the brains of the "not yet dead"!

As many of the Mexican bodies, as possible, were given the 'rites of the church' and buried. There were so many, there was not sufficient room in the cemetery!

Those not "winning" a private grave site were laid in a mass grave and blessed.

As for the Texans, Santa Anna ordered all the bodies of the Texans to be contemptuously stacked like cord wood (three heaps of them).. The mountains of dead Americans were doused with fuel oil.

Wood and dry branches from the neighboring forests were used to cover the "Texicans" before they were set on fire.

When the tremors ceased in the eastern half of the Sonora Caverns, Illinois Johnson continued through the Valley of Ice. Both he and his sparrow hawk ate bat breasts while sitting at the brink of a drop-off into a place where water ran underneath it.

For Illinois, he knew, he had narrowly escaped death. If only one of the Red Sticks had so much as glanced up and seen him crouched behind a rock ledge, they would have pushed him up through the 'beheading hole'!

'Had that happened', Johnson thought, 'he would have helped fuel one of the three bonfires blazing on San Antonio's plaza'. He prayed.

* * * * *

To the west, some twenty miles away from Johnson's position, Milly who also felt the ground shake above her, was making a beeline toward the "Abode of Saint's'" entranceway.

The 'forehead crossed crusaders' were busily doing god's work by opening up the passageway to the cavern's east side, where the "Grail" was!

Paddy had once again tricked her; therefore, Milly had no choice but to find out where he was and kill him!

After that was done, she would reunite with Santa Anna and poison him!

That was her plan.

* * * * *

By the smells of cordite permeating through the eastern section of the cavern, Tiger Tail suspected that trouble lurked ahead.

Instead of slinking along the sides of the cavern, the warrior ordered his men to "fire up" their lanterns, to unsheathe their lances, charge through the tunnels and fight as if the enemy were only feet away!

Archers were to shoot a fan of string attached arrows into the darkness ahead of them!

Every one hundred yards, the bowmen were to repeat the "blind-shooting" over and over until they either exited the labyrinth or died in it.

No matter the consequences, the Red Sticks were to do it both swiftly and with vengeance. They started to make good time.

* * * * *

Lord Horatio Alvarez called out the "messaged" letters to Sir Francis. Stephen Austin was blinking to them their final orders.

"Enter the town of San Antonio as if you were the same two surveyors representing "The Alpine Ore Mining Company". Remember, you are the same men who gained the legal papers from "Governor Porfirio Diaz"!

To disarm their suspicions of you, tell Santa Anna that a company of "Sam Houston's" army is camped along the "Buffalo Bayou"!

Further, explain to the general, if he would like to make a surprise attack, the place to do it would be through the eastern tunnel of the Sonora's and out the Halo Lake exit.

Houston's ninety some soldiers will never expect an enemy attacking from that direction....!

Once the Mexicans have inserted themselves, detonate your charges and let the waters of the Halo cleanse their souls."

* * * * *

"El Gallo Rojo's" patrons stopped doing what they doing (some even laid down their playing cards) when two very frazzled men stumbled into the saloon. Both dropped to the floor.

While Sir George vomited, Lord Alvarez crawled around kissing the boots of the attending soldiers. The Europeans pretended to be frightened out of their wits!

Someone from behind the bar blew on a seaman's whistle which signaled to everyone in the "Red Rooster", "to clear out!"

Not only was medical help on the way, so was Santa Anna!

"When might I be able to speak with those poor bastards, Doctor Hernandez?" caringly questioned General Santa Anna.

"General, I have ordered them to be taken to the medical tent. They should remain sedated for the next few hours; I believe you'll be able to talk with them then.

I'm not exactly positive of this, Antonio, but I believe I deciphered some kind of message the "Scottish one," was trying to pass on to you, Sir!

He wrote it with his finger on the floor beneath him; before, the orderlies scratched it out with their boots." Casually stated the army surgeon.

"Ricardo, what do you think he was attempting to say?"

"What I read was, 'SA, wife below. Welch betrayal'. That's all there was. Do you make any sense of it, General?"

"I'm afraid I do, Doc. I'll meet you at the "tent" within the hour!" said Santa Anna.

Because the Mexican doctor's administered sedatives were effective, it took a while for Sir Francis and Lord Horatio to get back into sync.

A man in a top hat introducing himself as "Timothy", awkwardly stood at the opening of the army's medical tent.

From the Europeans' perspective; that is, from supine and well strapped down positions, they saw an impeccably dressed older gentleman who looked to be, in his late sixties.

"Timothy" removed his hat and gloves as two of his assistants rushed over with a small table for 'his' winter trio to set upon. He seated himself on a high stool before he said his first word.

"In a few moments, Gentlemen, I shall invite my employer, "General Santa Anna" to join us. I am an extremely mean person which is why, I was summonsed here!

You see, my job is to extract the 'truth', plain and simple!

Either you cooperatively answer each of the questions with an authentic answer; or, I shall snip off the other's penis.

If you two behave during our "guest's" visit, one of you, will walk away as a free man while the other, dies from my pistol!

If need be, "a coin toss" will be the determinant." Silkily said Timothy.

Having taken a hot bath and dressed for the special occasion, Santa Anna sashed into the medical tent and with a slight balancing difficulty, sat on a stool identical to the one 'Timothy' was seated upon. His hair was still wet and he was drunk.

"Welcome, General!

As your Majesty can plainly see, the Europeans have been prepared for your questions. I have had a nice chat with these men; they have agreed to provide you with any and all the information you require!

It is my opinion, Sir, these fellows are potentially two very dangerous characters!

Not only am I sure they are the "nefarious types", I'd wager ten dollars, they were sent here to do you harm!" preached the high hatted truth-seeker.

"Thank you, Timothy, I too, have a nose for rooting out spies and assassins!

I have not become a, "legend within my own lifetime" by being incognizant of my surrounding dangers!

Let's see what they have to say before we jump too hastily into a sour opinion of these chaps; after all, I haven't asked them a single question yet!

Therefore, allow me to trouble you two 'Englanders', with my first and only question: 'Tell me exactly why you are here and please do not leave out any of the historic tidbits?'."

As if rehearsed, Sir Francis George of the Walkers cleared his throat and asked to speak; but, he was interrupted (actually over amplified) by Lord Horatio!

Like two fish clamped onto a cleaning board, they helplessly wiggled and gasped at the other!

Finally, Santa Anna appointed Sir Francis to speak first.

"Your "Highness", we returned to San Antonio to deliver a message to you!

One week ago, while we were finishing up our surveying analysis, a man by the name of, "Paddy Welch" approached us.

He wanted us to report back to our employers that the Sonora Cavern was a 'dead end'!

The man offered us 'ten thousand dollars apiece' to 'doctor' the cavern's drawings to indicate there was "no connection" to the western side (running beneath the Rio Grande River)!

Quite honestly, General Santa Anna, we were going to take the cash but because of the way he and those Red Sticks were treating the "woman", who sent you the note, Nelson and I agreed, we wanted nothing to do with the apparent rascal!" Calmly addressed Sir Francis.

"And your name, Sir?" asked Santa Anna.

"George."

"So, 'George', what did the note 'say'?"

"Sir, Mister Alvarez and I came here with good intentions!

But, your man here, "Timothy" told us, before you entered the tent, "after this interview's conclusion, a coin would be tossed to determine whether 'I' or 'Nelson' would be shot in the head with his pistol!

Therefore, under those 'rules', I'll neither tell you what she 'scribbled', where the passageway to rescue her is located, nor, will you ever get the opportunity to see the very intricate detail that "I" and my partner, put into the cavern's map!" Recklessly exclaimed the Scot.

"Timothy can be awfully encouraging, George!

Mister Alvarez, what say you, about this recent rhetorical exchange between your partner and me?

Are you an equal match on George's 'recalcitrance scale', Nelson?" mockingly jibed Santa Anna.

"If I had had the opportunity to address your question first, you would have learned far less than what my constituent told you!

Factually, and I'll tell you now, if you don't have Timothy taken outside and shot before the next minute passes, George and I will swallow a poison capsule hidden in our rear molars!

In forty five seconds, if Timothy over there, isn't dead, you, 'General', will have lost one wife and several million dollars' worth of gold!

Considering that you may not have the 'intestinal fortitude' that "Ole Bonaparte" had, I figure you'll let your 'leashed imbecile' do his thing!

Although, if it turns out that way, you'll both go to bed tonight dumber than when you awakened!" whispered Nelson.

Timothy was escorted out to the plaza and shot in the head by Santa Anna personally!

When he returned, he sat back down on the stool; although, when he again spoke, both Culpers knew, this time, Antonio was lethally serious!

"George, how long will it take for a battalion of men to enter the Sonora Cavern and reach the place in which, you last saw my bride?"

"Sir, if we enter the cave through the tunnel leading from the "parson's outhouse", we could make it to the "Crystal Palace" within a day!" Said George.

"And, Nelson, you mentioned some 'gold'?" sneered the Mexican dictator.

"Yes, I did." Quipped Lord Horatio.

"Well….tell me about the El Dorado gold!

Does it really exist and does the cavern actually run under the Rio Grande?" again questioned Santa Anna.

"General Santa Anna, until my sidekick and I are unshackled, there will be no more cooperation from us!

I'll also tell you another thing, we're not going to drag your men back down into that damn hole for free!

Look, I've 'seen' what you are wanting to see!

And, if your amazement is anything close to what mine was, you will in hindsight, wish you had treated your "teachers" a bit more kindly!

You see, Antonio, the map we've drawn not only depicts, quite accurately I might add, the cavern's precise layout; it also catalogues the cashes of certain types of treasures!" smoothly chatted Nelson.

"What are you trying to say?

Not only are you requesting your freedom, you are now wanting a piece of the action; don't I have that about right, Gentlemen?" questioned Santa Anna.

"We look at it this way, General, your granting us our freedom of which we appreciate, earned 'you' the Alamo's secret passage into the cavern, the location of your wife's suspected holding cell, the east to west exits; plus, you were given firsthand acknowledgement of the treasures existing below us!

If that isn't a fair swap, I just don't know what would be!

All we're asking for, is ten thousand dollars-worth of gold nuggets placed in two saddlebags with two good horses so that we can get to the ship that will distance us from this continent forever, I hope!

Nelson and I, shall retire to some island where virginity is taboo while you and your "saved princess", will become the most powerful duo the modern world has ever seen!" Bartered Sir Francis George of the Walkers.

"Very well, Gentlemen, I'll accept your offer!

However, I must insist on one caveat added to our agreement. While, I send a thousand of my men down the padre's shit-hole, I insist on the benefit of your company!" Chortled Antonio Santa Anna.

After looking at one another in visual search of the other's thoughts, Lord Horatio Alvarez of the Nils stepped forward with his hand extended in readiness of signing the deal. But, he stopped as if, "flash frozen"!

Through a rock hard chin, Nelson offered 'their' own addendum.

"We'll stay until a man of your choosing reports back to you with proof that our mapping is accurate and the tunnel abounds with winding passages filled with precious things!

At your nod of 'satisfaction', George and I will leave along with our penance in tow amid what I would anticipate as, "a jubilant celebration"!

That's why, we insist on exchanging our 'wares' upon the execution of the agreement!" Said Lord Horatio Nelson.

"Guard! Get me "Captain Smitherman"!" yelled Santa Anna.

"Present, General! Barked the steel eyed officer.

"Captain, this is important!

I want two saddled horses tied up at the "El Gallo Rojo's" hitching post!

Put five thousand dollars-worth of doubloons into each man's saddlebag. When that is done, line these men up in front of the Alamo's wall and shoot them when you can no longer see me sitting at my desk!

Make our "business partners" as comfortable as possible. Be sure they have a bench to sit on and plenty of food and drink.

Likewise, I want a fresh primed and ready firing squad rotated out every thirty minutes!

Our "partners" are to be shot under two circumstances: "upon my disappearance from my office window' OR 'their backs come off that wall by more than five inches!"

Captain Smitherman, are my directions clear to you, sir?"

"Yes, Sir!" snapped back the captain.

"One more thing, Captain, would you kindly request that "Colonel Candelaria" visit me as promptly as possible?" pleasantly asked the Mexican dictator.

Sir Francis and Lord Alvarez were escorted to the mission's west wall. Considering that both Culpers were attached by a six foot leg chain, Captain Smitherman saw to it, they were issued ergonomically pleasing accouterments within the cordoned off area.

One bench, one bucket of water, one wooden spoon were what they got!

Just ten paces in front of the convicted men, the newer officers practiced their commands during their 'firing squad' drills.

Since it was a 'dryfire' exercise, everyone in the remaining battalion, those not in "Candelaria's cave trooper unit", got an opportunity to experience the emotion "one would experience" during a real execution!

After a brief while, Nelson and George ignored the ferocious commands and went about playing their game of 'cloud animation'.

* * * * *

'Illinois Johnson' and his sparrow hawk had made it past the 'Valley of Ice' and were within earshot of the men who were attempting to open the 'Sponge Rooms' passageway.

Peeks of lantern light made Illinois believe they were a half day away from breaking through.

Johnson knew by the rock breakers' conversations, General Santa Anna's wife had been there. She had left them with a map to the Crystal palace!

The hawk seemed to smile when her master (Illinois Johnson) spoke of the 'word' mentioned by the "chiselers" on the cave's other side. They said, "Grail"!

Illinois figured, 'he would reverse his course and hide in one of the Valley of Ice's many crannies and await their passing beneath him'.

Once he exited from the "Abode of Saints" and took possession of his property's deed, he would return, close them off in The Butterfly, feed them on a regular basis, and then butcher one of them at a time, when the need for sustenance panged!

Without warning, an arrow trailed by a hemp cord, wisped over Illinois's shoulder!

He heard 'Tiger Tail's' voice through a span of darkness.

Including his blunderbuss, Illinois Johnson had four firearms on his person. He withdrew two pistols from their holsters and shot both of them into the Red Sticks' pitch black hole.

With his derringer, Johnson stuck its barrel into the only opening to the grail searchers' side, and pulled the trigger!

Yelling the word, "Attack" with an undistinguishable accent, silenced the men on the other side. The only sounds Illinois could hear were those of men scrambling to better protecting places.

One could have heard a pin drop had it not been for the white noise caused by the Rio Grande's flow, above them. Johnson and his "nisus" escaped to the 'Valley of Ice's' upper flanging tunnels.

Tantrums of speculative gunfire was returned. The ricocheting bullets developed an odd sort of whining tune.

Flocks of bats more curious than frightened, took flight. The flying mammals bothered the crusaders more than they did the Indians.

After hours of nulled assaults, someone from one end of the tunnel's blockage recognized an opposer's voice. The two sides began talking.

Soon, the conversations led to the conglomerate's conclusion, "Paddy Welch had hoodooed them!"

With some ingenious bolder moving, the previously blinded enemies, united!

Following a flurry of familial refreshment, it became clear, at the end of Crystal Palace was a priceless treasure!

All of the warriors swore, "once it was found, every bit of the cavern's spoils would be divided evenly among them and only them"!

None other than, "The Cave-Born Brotherhood" had the "Rights" to it!

*　*　*　*

Lord Horatio Alvarez of the Nils was the first to see Stephen Austin's balloon hiding in front of the sun. Santa Anna was still sitting in his chair but was watching his "prisoners" very closely.

Captain Smitherman's rotating firing squads had ceased their impotent rifle snapping. Colonel Candelaria and eight hundred of his bribed 'cavemen' were a half day into the General's wife's rescue.

* * * * *

Each soldier was issued a brown leather bag in which they could fill with the souvenirs collected from the 'Queen's' retrieval. That's what their payoff was to be.

Lanterns, pistols, and short pikes were what the boys were handed prior to their descension through the earth's crust. They were told to expect an adventure into a universe of golden stalactites and stalagmites!

* * * * *

In an attempt to prevent Santa Anna from reading his lips, Lord Alvarez lowered his head into its shadow and softly told Sir Francis of Stephen Austin's arrival.

He also warned Sir Francis George of the dictator's attempts at lipreading through the lens of his telescope!

"Our Cerian buddy, certainly isn't going to pull his 'manger' trick again!

I think, we're going to have to figure something out. Do you have any ideas?" side mouthed Sir Francis.

"Don't look up; Austin just messaged: "Attack in five minutes"!

We are to remain with our backs flat against the wall and cover our faces with our hands!" Said the slant-mouthed Irishman.

Houston's rockets, surgically, destroyed things of value to Santa Anna!

The Mexican emperor jumped up from his office desk and ran out to the plaza where Captain Smitherman's execution squads had been ordered to be!

In a scream resembling that of a newly castrated bull, Antonio Santa Anna demanded that his dawdling firing squad, "load up"!

Pandemonium spread like the fury of a firestorm when it was realized, Sam Houston's Texians had surrounded San Antonio!

Every hilltop up to a mile away, had an 'Orleans's Grey' aiming a field howitzer at the stronghold's integral (block and mortar) appendages!

After the first few minutes of the Texian's attack, Santa Anna withdrew his two belted pistols, cocked them both, and started running toward his chained together captives.

When he got closer to the men with their backs tightly pressed against the Alamo's wall, Stephen Austin's 'lord like' voice, overbore the battleground's din!

The cannons became silent. Santa stopped dead in his tracks. He then, looked toward the heavens!

"Drop your weapons, Antonio!

With your left hand, reach for the "key" in your right breast pocket; then, you are to unlock those men chained to that bench!

One false move and I'll put a bullet clean through your head!" said Austin from the basket of his hot air balloon.

Suddenly, Santa Anna lurched backwards and fired his two sidearms at the man's face peering down at him!

The first silver ball and therefore the quicker to reach it's intended target, slipped effortlessly through the Cerian's left ear while the later one, entered his gold filled mouth!

The downwardly speeding balloon careened into the town's freshly repaired front gate!

Austin's body flopped out onto the plaza's sunbaked surface.

At 4:40 pm "all hell" broke loose!

Hundreds of Sam Houston's roughriders stormed into San Antonio and began brutalizing the panic-stricken Mexicans!

Those escaping in mass, became a sport for the 'greys'; 10 got you $20.

Santa Anna and his generals shouted different and conflicting orders!

Even if their commands had been unanimously clear as a bell, nothing would have stopped the Texas Indian fighters.

They attacked from all sides. They shot, stabbed or bludgeoned every Mexican not holding their "weaponless" hands up high into the air!

Six hundred and thirty dead soldiers had to be gathered and stacked; but, the wooden kindling had to be constructed beforehand.

Santa Anna along with three hundred of his fellow 'surrenderers' did exactly that, for the astonishingly victorious Texans!

Sir Francis and Lord Horatio reassembled the downed aircraft while the Mexican prisoners were finishing up with their body-stacking.

Upon liftoff, thirteen separate piles of burning soldiers presented to the ascending Culpers, a panoramic view of mans' worst side.

*   *   *   *

Sam Houston's ankle had absorbed the impact of a rifle butt; nevertheless, he and Santa Anna worked through the night on treaties ensuring the Texans' of the "rights to their land in exchange for his and his men's lives"!

By dawn, the Mexican government had transferred its entire "holdings" north of the Rio Grande, to Texas!

The soldiers got to keep their boots and hats along with their pants and shirts. They lost everything else.

Ten wagons hauling three hundred defeated soldiers (each having had a swath of yellow paint mop painted on their backs) were escorted across the Rio Grande.

While Houston's escorts offloaded their prisoners in Mexico, "General Jose de Urrea" and his six thousand man army watched with disgust!

There before all of the soldiers' eyes was their country's "dictator" chained to the "yellow backed" survivors of an entire division!

*   *   *   *

Below, and just about the same time as Sam Houston's prisoner "drop off" was taking place, Tiger Tail's Red Sticks and the 'forehead crossed crusaders' made contact with Colonel Candelaria's 'queen rescuers' at the juncture of 'The Butterfly' and the 'Valley of Ice'.

Bullets, arrows, lances and diabolical threats were exchanged through total darkness!

With the practical use of an oarsman's megaphone, Lord Horatio Alvarez began calling for help as if the frantic appeals were coming from Milly Francis's (the Queen's) lips!

Despite Sir Francis's pleas to do otherwise, the Nil quickened his pace toward the dead ending depths of the "Crystal Palace".

His mimicry was spot on, the fuse to a hundred pounds of dynamite was lit; ergo, Halo Lake would soon flush the Sonora Cavern clean of its eighteenth century debris!

Nelson's charade worked. The amalgamated enemy stopped fighting and listened to the "echo chambers'" words.

"Antonio, there is so much gold! Release me from this cage, my love!"

* * * * *

Soon after mending some badly broken fences, Tiger Tail and Colonel Candelaria resumed a dialogue which quickly pieced together Paddy Welch's scheme.

The conclusion drawn was this, like the, "Rule of the Sea" admits, "the first to surface the treasure belongs to thee!"

Therefore, and by the use of the same "rule", the two thousand people (those brothers capsuled within the Sonora Cavern) were the rightful owners of its contents!

Individual wealth would be measured by personal toting power; i.e., 'what a man emerged with, was his cut'!

* * * * *

"Darling, please hurry! I am cold and hungry! Come see the diamonds, Antonio!

We can go to "Madagascar" now, just as we planned!" Hysterically pleaded Lord Horatio Alvarez of the Nils (pretending to be Santa Anna's wife).

Sir Francis ran as fast as he could toward the "Butterfly"!

From the sounds of the Nil's falsetto appeal, the Walker realized he had about two minutes before everyone in the cavern was left optionless!

He made one last attempt to convince the "Irishman" to leave the cavern!

"Colonel Candelaria, Sir, you won't believe what I am looking at down here!

Why, I bet there aren't enough zeros to account for all the fantastical jewelry surrounding me!

We're gonna need a metal saw!

Welch has got three locks on the Queen's 'cage' and we gotta get her out of there!" cleverly said the 'Scot' in an attempt to disguise his real message.

"But, I want "Antonio" to release me!" yelled "Milly". Rebutted Lord Horatio Alvarez.

"Your Highness, as you know, his "Majesty" has a very short fuse. I'm afraid I'll have to insist that you come back with us!

Once Colonel Candelaria gets here, you'll wish you had been more cooperative!

Come on now, dearie, let's just have a seat and be patient for you'll be back with your husband in no time flat!" signaled Sir Francis George of the Walkers.

* * * * *

A sparrow hawk out of the cavern's blackness, flew into Sir George's shoulder at close to twenty miles an hour!

Her talons immediately clamped into the 'Scot's' shoulder ensuring a steady base for the carotid's severance!

From behind the arm flinging 'Sir Francis', Illinois Johnson's called the fowl off of the Culper!

He then pronounced, "Under the powers divested to the one holding a blunderbuss, I now request that you rescue that damsel in distress!".

"And…what "damsel" might that be, Sir?" stupidly asked the Walker.

* * * * *

The solid coal floor shook like a busted wheel. With a deep rumble the initial wave of Halo Lake's glacial waters sped through the cavern!

When the second, third and final sets of charges blew, voracious currents intermittently smashed into the end of the Crystal Palace!

When it filled, the water returned. It came in search of others to drown.

* * * * *

It was three o'clock in the afternoon.

John Mason stood up from his desk, walked toward his coat rack, put on his deerskin jacket, finished his 'jaunt's' preparation and snatched up his cane and top hat.

He cracked his coachwhip above the horses' rumps and began his usual half mile haul to the bridge crossing over to "Arlington".

Including the 'double walked' (walking back and forth) pontoon bridge John's daily mail run fell slightly less than a mile's travel; however, in one particular grove of trees where the path meanders through them, "Little John" would (coming and going) light a pipe stuffed with opium dusted hemp.

As John was approaching the northern Virginia side of the low water bridge, he noticed a naked Indian woman standing at the top of the steps leading to the mail box!

Finding it hard to compose himself, given the numbers of cubic feet of smoke inhaled, 'Little John' tried his darndest to be debonair.

"Greetings, Madam!

How may I be of service to you?" Gallantly asked John.

"Would you like some "Creek" pussy?" asked Milly.

Stunned by the audacious question and almost reeling backwards into the Potomac River, "John Mason" boldly walked up to her.

His eyes for the most part, stayed locked tight onto hers. Milly's hands became mischievous titillates; John responded.

"Miss, we can't do this out here!"

"All you have to do is stand still, silly man!" said the busying stranger.

When the time came and John Mason's scream reached a first soprano's high "C", Milly worked herself around the short man's body and cut his throat!

* * * * *

Fully expecting their (except for the Sabbath) daily chat with Little John Mason, "Raleigh Ferguson" (Arlington's postmaster) came trotting down "Mosquito Road" only to run into the crime scene!

'A naked Indian woman had been raped and the "moral trespasser" was killed in self-defense!' Raleigh surmised.

One hour after the postmaster's feet landed upon the "Mosquito Road's" sandy surface, Raleigh's and Mason's bodies were weighted and sunk into the ocean bound river!

Milly jumped onto the mail cart's front seat, popped the buggy whip just over the horse's head and drove the colorful box carriage toward the Capitol.

On her way back from discarding the carcasses, Francis double-measured the pontoon's width with the carriage's axel length.

Milly swore she would lure Paddy out to the bridge and kill him!

"That sonofabitch has pulled his last con job; he may think he is safely hiding within the bowels of the mansion on "Mason Island". Even if it is, the "Niburian Headquarters", I'll draw the bastard out!" Milly said to the very boring horse pulling the mail cart.

* * * * *

President Andrew Jackson watched the sun drop down, he imagined, 'into a deep fishing hole on the Shenandoah River'. He had been thinking of 'Rachel and drinking'.

Hannah had walked down to the market to get away from him!

"I believe in a strong presidency. Washington is a snake pit; it possesses no moral compass of any sort!

My critics claim, I am a dictator. Why? ….Because I vetoed every piece of legislation which stunk of aristocratic pocket padding, that's why!

Shit! If I hadn't stepped in when I did, every poor working chap in these goddamned United States would have ended up getting his salary paid through the "National Bank" after every little federal "prick" got their cut from it!

'Schadenfreude' best describes the utmost joy I receive when I read of "Adams's" and/or "Clay's" misfortunes. They were the ones who killed Rachael with their venal gossip!

Once I leave this hell-hole, I'll never return; the Nibs can have it!" said Andy to the 'face' staring back at him, in the mirror.

At 1600hrs., "Freddy" from upstairs, brought him five different newspapers, a bag of "presidential post", two Virginia ham sandwiches and a jug of scotch.

Jackson was becoming concerned; 'Cocoa should have returned to the "Willard" an hour ago'. Andy fretfully thought.

* * * * *

"Martin Van Buren" had successfully won Jackson's populists' party's vote; therefore, it was a "shoe-in", he would win the presidency!

The two politicians liked one another and Andy was pleased that most of his passionately fought for legislations, would not be gutted.

The "slavery issue" was their only bone-of-contention; i.e., Van Buren considered the "negro" to be an 'inferior' being and felt that the eradication of the Indians was simply an evolutionary function called, "survival of the fittest"!

He was free to feel that way, Jackson felt; but, 'if the economic engines of the "South" ,that is, the slaves, were all of a sudden forbidden by federal law, to be "owned", then America would be ripped in half!'

The Indians living on the westside of the Mississippi were now well tuned into 'whitey's' "bait and switch" tactics; they had had time to build a disciplined army which was now under Niburian Command!

It would not be like the 'good ole days', Andy reflected.

* * * * *

South Carolina reacted to the "universal tariff" placed on "some" of their commercial ports. Transported negroes were taxed even though they were bought within the country, which made the plantation owners down there, downright furious!

"Those hot tempered ignoramuses", Jackson said out loud, "are too damn muleheaded to work something out; they'd just as soon fight!"

Freddy's bell rang.

Milly Francis had "Cocoa"!

Andy read the note.

"I am Milly Francis. You hanged my father.

Tomorrow at sunrise, I shall do the same to your nigger wife.

To spare her life, you are to kill Paddy Welch in a dual.

You will be at the "Mason Island Bridge" at five o'clock."

Andrew Jackson felt faint. He sat down on the edge of his and Hannah's bed. He tucked his head between his knees and screamed a terrifying cry of despair.

Even the people "upstairs", the supposed "Cerian communications depot", had been compromised.

He would have to be very careful about what he said and who he said it to. It appeared the "Niburians" had won; Washington was theirs!

* * * * *

A large tree-lined boulevard ran north-south down the center of "Mason Island". It led to a handsome "Georgian Revival" style mansion.

To the south of the Niburian Headquarters were formal gardens and a smattering of smaller buildings including, slave quarters, kitchens, workshops, and an icehouse.

Beneath that façade were soldiers' barracks, a submarine port, and a fleet of aerial attack aircraft. Another building held the munitions.

Paddy Welch sharply looked at the clock in the corner of his bunker's living room. It was 'four' and once again, no mail, no newspapers nor his twelve bottles of "Vin Mariani"!

Three days without mail was beyond coincidence; he rang for his aide.

""Colonel Barbarossa", I need you to find out a few things for me. I would like the latest update on the number of fatalities in the "Santa Anna fiasco"!

Secondly, message down to "Calhoun's people" and see what efforts have been made to recover Milly's body and finally, Colonel, see if there have been any claims of "treasure discoveries" within the local gossip hubs surrounding San Antonio!

Send a letter to, "General Jose de Urrea". Tell him, to move his brigade to "Matamoros" and sit tight; he'll attack Houston's army in June!

The Apaches will be ready by then, as well!

In the meantime, have 'Urrea' post a "hundred dollar reward" for proof of Milly's death!

Before I can feel safe to go outside, I'm going to need to know that she's no longer a danger to me!

I'd like to feel the sun on my face again. Do you know what I mean, Colonel?"

"Clearly, Sir!

From what our people are saying, "there were no survivors of those who entered the Sonora Cavern!"

"That may be so; but, I'd still feel more at ease if "her" carcass was affirmatively identified!

Would you be kind enough to check on "John Mason" and see what this week's foul up is?

And get me the goddamned wine I ordered; I've only got one more bottle left!" said Paddy Welch.

Once his aide departed, Paddy began packing his backpack. He had a funny feeling in his bones; it was like he could smell Milly's presence.

As the cork to his last bottle of 'Vin Mariani' was being pulled, Paddy Welch unbolted his quarter's front door once the proper 'knocking signal' was heard.

It was Colonel Barbarossa. He was holding a purple hat box.

A note marked, "Private" was addressed to: "The father of my children". The square officer's cap box weighed about twenty pounds.

When Paddy took it from the colonel's hands he felt something bang into the box's side, closest to his stomach!

He put it on the dining table before asking "Barbarossa" a few questions.

"Where did you find this box, Colonel?"

"It was in front of your door along with your case of Vin Mariani and a mail pouch full of newspapers!" answered the aide.

"Put the island under full alert, Colonel!

I want all men, "up-top" and every square inch of this plantation scoured and I mean, gone over with a fine toothed comb!

Ah, Colonel, since all of this was left in front of my door, why did you return so soon after our last meeting?" politely asked Paddy.

"Admiral, I returned to give you some good news!

Intelligence informed us that a drowned "sparrow hawk" was found at the mouth of the "Abode of Saints". That means, we got "Illinois Johnson", Sir!" proudly expounded Colonel Maxwell Barbarossa.

"That will be all for now, Max.

Let me know if anything out of the ordinary happens!

For caution's sake, and this will be an all-nighter, personally check in with me every thirty minutes!

Let's do it eyeball to eyeball if that's alright with you, Sir?" humbly asked Welch.

"Of course, Sir; I'll see you in thirty minutes!

The time, is eighteen hundred hours, I'll be back before you know it!

Maybe we'll have a drink of that 'peter-straitening' wine of yours while you tell me more about "Nibiru"." Softly stated the aide.

Following a comforting smile given to his departing assistant, Paddy double checked the Sonora Cavern's map. He was looking for every conceivable place Milly might be hiding.

* * * * *

There were only slits for windows. His blunderbuss and four pistols were primed and ready. By the hair raising on the back of his neck, Paddy Welch knew 'Milly' was soon to show!

Welch thought about the purple hat box, the note, the mail bag, and the newspapers.

He sat behind the dining table staring at Milly Francis's deliverances.

After an elimination series of coin flips, 'the note', won the blue ribbon!

It was to be read first!

Welch lit a cigar, placed his wine glass about four inches away from his blunderbuss's trigger housing, and opened Milly's message.

"As you peruse the newspapers, you will discover an important event occurring tomorrow morning at five o'clock on the "Mason Island Bridge"!

You and Andrew Jackson will, at the stroke of six, commence with a dual!

If you kill the President (this time!), I shall hand over to you, "The Grail"! Consequently, Hannah's neck will snap like a matchstick! (collateral damage)

For some reason you are unable to kill "Andy", I will most certainly provoke the nearby marines into a full blown attack against this island!

Three of "your" rockets are aimed at the "President's House" right now!

When the "security boys" figure out where the bombs came from, they're going to sink your little hideaway into the Potomac River!

Now, for my share (if you are victorious): I wish to gut you like a pig!"

* * * * *

Paddy jumped up from his chair tipping over his goblet of cocaine infused wine. With a pistol in his "favored hand", Welch ran through his three rooms peeking through each of their window slits in hopes of catching Colonel Barbarossa's attention!

He saw nothing (out there) but darkness. It was 2200hrs..

In a state of terrific panic, the Niburian ran to his bunker's only exit; he found, it had been padlocked!

He pulled a bottle of Vin Mariani from the mysteriously discovered wooden case. He opened it.

Uneasily, Paddy positioned himself in a strategically favorable corner. He blotted out the inchwide windows with strips of bedding.

The chemical adhesion of a "stimulant" and a "depressant" manifested itself into a temper tantrum!

In less than a minute, Paddy unloaded (shot) every single firearm he had at the purple box, the satchel of mail, and the bundle of newspapers!

Not even a sliver of lead touched the case of Vin Mariani.

A blunderbuss's disrespecting spread of metal pieces is practically indescribable. Needless to say, the destruction was great!

Yet, it was beneficial in one respect, "Tag" had been scattered; parts of the rattler laid on the floor.

Now feeling the super invigoration from his drink, Paddy Welch reached into the bullet perforated mail pouch. He wanted to read what the papers 'said' about a dual; but, that's when Tag's lover, "Vickie" struck Welch's shooting hand!

In shock and dizzied by the collision of toxins, the Nib stumbled over to the fireplace!

With savage blows, Paddy attempted to pummel the "rattle-snipped" snake with a coal iron; but, he never hit her!

He then noticed that "Tag's" tail rattles had also been amputated!

The serpent's venom had accelerated the "sleepiness" affects!

Breathing became a conscious thing!

The clock in the living room "bonged", relatively speaking, two times!

*　*　*　*　*

Jackson stared out across the "District of Columbia's" predawn landscape. 'Bad weather was coming, probably rain', Andrew thought.

It would be the last time he would breathe Washington's air and he was elated about that!

Now that "Warren Davis" was dead, the 'Rat Pack' had to deal with its own "tribe" of cannibals!

"Calhoun, George Poindexter and Van Buren", Andy predicted, would gobble one another up like obese piranha!

"Alright, 'monkeys', so you think you boys want to rule this country, do ya? Here it is!

You bought the damn thing with your souls and for that, the three of you, will burn in this manmade hell!" said Jackson (again) to his dressing mirror.

He had lost some weight. His military uniform made him feel younger. Andy hadn't had a drink in three hours so he flipped a coin to see if his luck had changed; but, it had not. 'He'd try again in thirty more minutes.' He thought.

Jackson practiced "dryfiring" his dueling pistol until he was interrupted by "Freddy's" knock on the door. His boots had been 'spit shined' to perfection!

After two more coin tosses, Andy got to toast himself in the mirror!

Andy then pulled up a chair in front of 'it' and spoke to his 'image'(reflection) as if it were his alter ego!

'Why, hello there, Andrew!'

'Looks like you're getting all dressed up for a Sunday-go-to-meeting kind of killing!'

'I know this is going to be a special one; how many does this make it, Andy, seven or eight?'

'Just in your duals alone, you've shot your share, son!'

'You're going up against a Niburian, aren't you?' asked the "mirror's likeness" of Jackson.

The president nodded.

'I know why, you're going out there.' "said" the president's reflection.

"How's that?" asked Jackson out loud.

'Thanatos!' charged the reflection.

"Only 'you' would know this; but, I love war!

It allows me to control the world's destiny; it's like, I become a god!

The smells, the sounds, the thrill of seeing men die for a cause gives me reason to believe "someone" very powerful "pushes me" to keep doing it!

It is a calling; I'm positive of it!" proclaimed Andrew Jackson to his empty suite.

*　*　*　*　*

Andy whistled while he finished rolling up various things into his duffle bag. Jackson then stepped into his black and gray zigzag-striped jump suite, put on his gloves and facemask, secured his rappelling rope to one of the hotel's support beams and made a three bounce slide down to the Willard's lobby's roof!

After hiding behind the hotel's stable for thirty minutes and when he was sure of the watchman's absence, the President hopped onto the naked back of a 'rental' horse and rode east.

Once Andy and his stolen quarter horse 'clip-clopped' out from under a "Pennsylvania Road's" gas light, Jackson gripped the filly's mane and kicked her ribs into a run unlike anything a typical Washingtonian would never have made her do!

Jackson covered the two and a half miles to the "Mason Bridge" in five minutes!

*　*　*　*　*

Crouched within a clump of rhododendron bushes just off "Mosquito Road", Jackson glassed the bridge spanning toward the island. He estimated the distance to the island was, 400 yards.

Despite the lazy ground fog, Jackson figured, 'he would be able to make out the structure that was setting halfway across the pontoon bridge at first light'!

There was no wind nor river sounds.

Brass colored prongs of sunlight elongating from the plantation's trees masked the "Dragon Fly's" gigantic masts.

Captain Jeramiah Yellott walked down the Dragon Fly's gangplank when he saw Jackson approaching the Mason Bridge.

Prince Hall and Hannah stood beside the field gallows that supported Milly's upside down body. Hannah had tricked Milly.

The mail cart blocked the bridge.